Newhuman Mars:

In The Shadow of Omen

by
Steven Burgauer

iUniverse, Inc.
New York   Bloomington

NEWHUMAN MARS
In The Shadow of Omen

iUniverse books may be ordered through booksellers or by contacting:

iUniverse
1663 Liberty Drive
Bloomington, IN 47403
www.iuniverse.com
1-800-Authors (1-800-288-4677)

ISBN: 978-1-4401-7909-9 (sc)
ISBN: 978-1-4401-7910-5 (ebook)

Printed in the United States of America

iUniverse rev. date:09/18/2009

To Kate Rose, my doorway into the future

ONE

Asteroid

Mars: 2433

Carina's eyes fluttered.

The dream was coming hard and fast now, just like the first time.

She strained her eyes, tried to peer through the haze into the real world. But everything was a blur, like in a cloud. Then, for a brief moment, the cloud parted and she could make out fuzzy details and washed-out colors.

. . . the fast-approaching asteroid was now visible to the naked eye. It was a big thing, big and ugly. All such rocks were. Big and ugly and dangerous, not smooth at all, tumbling end over end.

. . . the big rock was visible, now, to the naked eye. Before that, the reclusive men in the Mars Observatory had been tracking the big chunk of rock across the blackened sky by radar. A Ph.D. candidate back on Earth had been the first to pick up the tiny moon on his scope. He had charted its movement against a backdrop of a thousand other similar blips.

Physics was funny that way. No one could say with precision exactly what combination of forces was responsible for kicking the occasional asteroid out of the Belt.

But, whenever in a great while it happened, the jagged boulder bore close scrutiny. This one was on a collision course with the Red Planet. That was all but certain now. But the jury was still out as to exactly where on the surface it would fall. That would remain a mystery until just minutes before impact.

Even in her sleep, Carina knew the truth. The mathematics of real-time multi-body motion were daunting. Even if all the nonlinear equations could be solved, even if a scientist could work it out to the third decimal point, there was precious little anyone could do to alter the outcome. The last transport for Earth pulled out nearly a month ago. The next one wasn't expected for at least twenty more weeks. All the colonists could do now was wait. And pray.

Carina's eyes fluttered once again. The clouds blocking her view parted once more, ever so slightly. The nightmare was getting worse.

. . . the rocky projectile was 1100 meters thick at its widest point. Should the big rock strike anywhere within five kloms of the tiny scientific outpost, the results would be devastating.

The residents wouldn't stand a chance. Everyone living there would perish in a firestorm of hot gravel and white energy. To a person, they would all suffer a most horrific end. Indeed, it would be hard to imagine a more unpleasant way to die — the sudden decompression of the research facility, the flying shards of razor-sharp glass, the outrushing cocoon of earth-normal air, the bone-crushing cold as it swept in and enveloped its helpless victims.

. . . the big chunk of rock was clearly visible now, barreling down on the colonists like a flame-orange snowball, spewing hot, deadly gas. When it struck, events would unfold in rapid succession. The children would scream as their limbs were torn from their sockets as if from a rag doll. The parents would convulse, as their fragile bodies strained not to explode in the face of a precipitous drop in pressure. Then would come blissful unconsciousness, which would blot out the pain . . .

"Mayday! Mayday!"

The terrified words crackled through the comm, snapping her awake. Carina had had this nightmare before, almost every night since she first read about the terrible asteroid collision of 2227. For the longest moment she just lay there in bed, unable to decide whether the cry for help was genuine, or whether she was still asleep dreaming.

"Mayday! Mayday!"

The comm crackled again. This time, the panicked voice sounded close — and hauntingly familiar.

"We're coming in fast, and we're off course. Our landing thrusters are at half, and we're nine, no, make that eleven kloms south-southeast of the Colony One landing pad. Ship is filled with passengers, and we may need medical assistance.

"Mayday! Mayday! This is Councilman Samuel Matthews of the passenger transport *Tikkidiw*. If anyone can read me, please respond!"

Carina shook off the sleep, wiped the crud from her puffy, bloodshot eyes. She stumbled into the next room. On the table was the comm. It was blinking urgently, waiting impatiently to be answered.

Carina fumbled blindly for it in the dark. In her haste, her hand brushed up against the unit, sending it crashing to the floor.

"Damn!"

Carina cursed her clumsiness. The comm-unit was in pieces and she hadn't even told them yet that she was on her way.

Carina was about to swear for a second time, when a lump suddenly rose up in her throat. That voice, that hauntingly familiar voice speaking to her from across the kloms, that had been her *father's* voice. It was *his* Mayday she had heard. *He* was the one who was in trouble.

Carina choked back a guilty tear. She couldn't help herself. Their relationship had become strained these past two years, and she was at least partially to blame. Their philosophical differences were significant. They had led to disaffection, even alienation. She wasn't proud of that.

But Carina's regrets would have to wait. If the ship had indeed nosed-in, as her father said, there would almost certainly be casualties. *She might be the only one near enough to lend a hand.*

Carina sprang into action. She slipped a pair of coveralls on over her nightie, bounded out the door of the hut to fire up the landrover. It was parked just outside. Nothing could slow her departure, not the painful reminder of the empty crib she passed on the way out the door, nor the mournful whimpering of her faithful dog Sandy.

Carina seemed to forget about the nasty gash on her right hand as she grabbed for the door of the rover. Her palm and fingers were still wrapped in gauze, a vivid reminder of yesterday's fall.

But the oversight was short-lived. As soon as she moved to jerk open the cab door with her injured hand, pain began to claw its way up her arm.

The sudden pain stopped her cold, and she immediately switched hands. She winced audibly then dragged herself cautiously up into the cab, one step at a time. Her dog Sandy bounded in behind her.

A two-way radio sat on the dashboard. Carina reached for it with her good hand, adjusted the tuner to the appropriate frequency. Inda Desai lived just over the next hill. Rather than going out into the black night alone, it only made good sense for her to first try and raise him on the horn, insist he come along. Ever since BC pulled up stakes and left, Inda Desai was the closest thing they had to a medic in these parts. In fact, Inda was the one who had patched up her hand the previous day after her fall.

For several long minutes, Carina tried to raise her neighbor Inda on the radio.

But, when all she got for her trouble was the awful buzz of static, she slid Sandy onto the seat next to her and slammed the rover's heavy metal door shut. It peeved her no end to think that Inda wasn't home to answer her call, that he might be spending the night, not with Carina, but with some other woman, perhaps that bimbooker Saron.

Her cheeks were red with rage. In a fit of anger, Carina took hold of the ignition key as if it were a knife. She twisted the key into the ignition coil with an angry curse and a look of vengeance. In her mind, the steering column was Inda Desai's abdomen, the steering wheel his head.

Over and over she twisted it. By now, a crooked smile had begun to blossom on her otherwise pretty face. She kept at it until the big machine groaned with a convulsive start. Only then did she quit grinding the key symbolically into Inda's gut.

Carina paused a moment to listen for the reassuring whine of the magneto. Then she reached down with her good hand and jammed the gearshift into drive. It was all she could do to contain herself.

The landrover lurched forward. Whether the woman liked it or not, time was of the essence. She had no choice, now, but to take off across the Martian steppe alone.

*   *   *

When the spacecraft shuddered unexpectedly on its final approach into Colony One, Fornax knew they were in trouble.

And, when the helm went dead as he banked to set the ship down, he prayed that he and Sam and the rest of the ship's company would survive the impact.

This malfunction was no accident like the Council claimed last week's explosion was. No, this was another act of sabotage aimed at bringing their commercial flights to a halt.

The issue was quite simple. Certain disgruntled residents from Newton had begun to sabotage the Colony One mining operation. They were irritated how quickly the Colony One settlers had achieved material success.

But it was more than that. Some settlers were enraged that Sam and Fornax were bringing even *more* asteroiders here to Mars to work. Fornax and his speedy ship were the chief link between the two planets. That made him and his vessel the number one and two targets of the Newtons' wrath.

To understand what was at stake here, one had to grasp a basic dichotomy of human nature, a dichotomy as ancient as the conflict between Athens and Sparta, between capitalism and socialism, between the Renaissance and the Middle Ages. On the one hand, there was man's need, his quest really, for order and for authority. On the other hand, there was his thirst for freedom, for creativity, for progress. It was the classic struggle. Statism versus democracy. Dictatorship versus anarchy. Mediocrity versus genius.

Colony One was an unruly, wide-open, bustling affair reminiscent of the American West or the Brazilian Outback. Newton was fashioned more along the lines of a utopian Plymouth Rock or an Oneida community from upstate New York. Just imagine Wyatt Earp trying to explain himself to Saint Thomas More, the sixteenth-century philosopher who popularized the idea of a perfect society. Or imagine the gun-toting residents of Dodge City strolling down the golden streets of Shrangri-La. That's how Fornax Nehrengel felt as he struggled to safely land his ship.

More and more lately, Fornax found himself torn between the two extremes of chaos and order. On the one hand, he was in love with Carina — at least as in love as he had ever permitted himself to be — and yet, on the other hand, he was convinced she was crazy. Not crazy as in carefree, wild, delightful. But crazy as in nuts, weird, wacko. As if the settling of Mars wasn't a difficult enough proposition to pledge oneself to, this newhuman obsession of hers was outlandish. *Carina Matthews actually believed she was the Eve of a new race, the mother of a new species!*

The spacecraft shuddered again, jerking Fornax back to the here and now. He grabbed the tiller firmly with both hands, braced himself against the nav-console with his legs. Gunter, the advance man from the mining company, looked on with wide eyes. Gunter was a fearless man, or nearly so. Behind him, other passengers turned white. Their terrified screams ricocheted off the bulkheads.

Fornax Nehrengel pulled back on the stick with all his might. In this way, he did what he could to slow their rapid, almost free-fall descent.

Unfortunately, his efforts seemed wasted, as they had no effect whatsoever on their trajectory. They had already passed through the shadow of Omen and across the Great Sea, and were now actually closer to Newton than to Colony One.

With any luck at all, Sam's Mayday had been picked up by someone on the ground and help was already on its way. If Fornax wasn't able to set the ship down gently, it was a foregone conclusion that there would be casualties. And yet, despite their dire circumstances, Fornax couldn't help but shake his head at Sam and grin. No sooner had the old fellow clicked off the comm and strapped himself in for landing, than he started to lecture Fornax on the history of the term "Mayday."

"From the French *m'aider*," Sam explained in his usual professorial tone. "It means literally, 'come help me.'"

As the ground rushed up to meet them, Fornax's last thoughts were of her — the soft curves lining her face, the round laughing eyes, the well-defined bosom, the tough uncompromising demeanor. Carina was the would-be mother of a new race, and although they had shared a bed together just that once, he couldn't imagine life on Mars without her.

TWO

The Belt

On any other morning, Samuel Matthews would have found it pleasurable to linger here on the veranda of his palatial home, drink his daily glass of orange juice, and survey all that was his.

But not this morning. On this morning, his wealth brought him little solace.

Sam had made his money in the currency markets during the Great War. That was some twenty-five years ago, even before he and his baby daughter Carina emigrated here to Zealand from Canada.

But, after the mean streets of Calgary and the tragic loss of his wife to the genetic butchers of Alberta, all Sam wanted from his new land was lots and lots of space. So much space that, if he wanted to, he could shut out the entire world for a spell and crawl inside his little cocoon. So much space that, if he wanted to, he could avoid — for a short while anyway — the harsh realities of being alone.

Sam's property up on the cape of North Island had the dimensions of a medieval manor. An enormous white mansion. Sumptuous gardens. Meticulously kept grounds. A swimming pool. Two garages. A wonderful stable. Red and orange tulips by the hundreds.

Any arriving visitor — of which there were ordinarily few — had to pass first through a massive wrought-iron gate. The gate itself was part of a shrub-lined fence that enclosed the entire estate. Then, after passing through the gate, a visitor would proceed along a narrow, meandering driveway. It snaked its way up from the main gate, across an expansive lawn, and to the front door.

Inside the mansion, Sam had a Library rivaling the best in Auckland, plus a great sitting room crammed full with museum-quality pieces even the Louvre would have envied. A thousand-year-old suit of armor. A mummy case dating to the Middle Kingdom. An ornamental Chinese fishbowl said to be from the Ming dynasty. An erotic bronze sculpture of a naked woman consumed by passion.

Yet, in spite of all these trappings, Sam's untidy appearance made a mockery of his wealth. The man was always simply, if ordinarily dressed, and his light brown hair (which was never combed anyway) seemed as unruly as he was unconventional. Sam had already gone gray at the temples. Yet, somehow, he still projected an air of youthful rebelliousness.

Ordinarily, it would have given Sam great pleasure to stand here on his front porch, sip his morning glass of orange juice and down his daily vitamin.

But today was different. Today was another one of those days when he and Fornax would be making the multi-million-klom jump out to Mars. Suffice it to say, after the crash a fortnight ago, Sam was more than a little apprehensive about the prospect.

Every other week now for the past eighteen months, he and Fornax had made the trip, transporting dozens of refugees to a new life on the Red Planet. But not just refugees. They also ferried engineers and technicians bent on surveying the planet's commercial possibilities.

Most of this latter group stayed for a few weeks, then returned home on the next flight. In a sense, this is what caused the problem. Sam valued his privacy above almost all else. As a consequence, these developers were sworn to secrecy on two counts: First, as to the true identities of Sam and Fornax. But, most especially, as to the location of Sam's estate up here on the cape.

Unfortunately, people being what they are, it figured to be only a matter of time before Sam's veil of secrecy was breached. Just last month, he hired a security firm to maintain order and keep gawkers from crashing the gates. Only, it hadn't been enough. Now there was no way for him to reverse the damage that had already been done.

The amazing thing was, despite the irreversible loss of his coveted anonymity, what had him so terribly vexed this bright and sunny morning was something totally different. What was *really* troubling him was the deal he and Fornax had just cut to transport a top-level ASARCO executive to Mars.

The deal was straightforward. This trip, instead of remaining on Mars for a few days' rest and relaxation after unloading their complement of passengers and equipment, the two of them would be going on to the Belt. Fornax had developed a business plan detailing how a mining company might profitably harvest an asteroid and put it to good use. Today they were scheduled to take a team out to the Belt for a preliminary evaluation. The idea was to have the mining company assay a few hundred rock samples and bring them home. With the results in hand, Fornax hoped to convince the company to set up a permanent factory on Mars, a factory that could ease the growing unemployment problem brought on by the continuing influx of colonists.

Although the asteroid mining concept sounded brilliant enough when Fornax explained it, his idea was actually nothing more than a variation on the technique that had been used for years to mine the surface of the moon. There, ore was launched by railgun to smelters orbiting high above the Earth's surface. In the proposed version, giant motors would be assembled on Mars, then used to drag an asteroid closer to Earth, and to those same giant orbiting smelters.

But which company to choose? Of the dozen or so outfits capable of building motors that large, Sam had chosen ASARCO — and with good reason. As part of his inheritance from his grandfather, Sam had fallen heir to a big chunk of ASARCO stock. Thus, when it came time to find a partner for this project, the choice was easy. He and Fornax boarded a suborb for South Africa to make the presentation. Amazingly, the Board of Directors jumped at the idea. Preparations were made, and today was the day the company's assay team was scheduled to make the trip.

There was, however, one fly in the ointment. News of the project had somehow leaked out, and now hundreds of people were picketing outside Sam's fence sporting signs and shouting ugly obscenities. So much for privacy. So much for anonymity.

The conundrum, though somewhat nonsensical, was deeply rooted. Centuries ago, there had been an accident, an accident now universally referred to as the "Silver Cannonball Incident." On that occasion, one of the ore balls launched by railgun from the moon failed to be snared in orbit as it should have been. It crashed to Earth instead, killed a peasant farmer asleep in his field outside Kingston, Jamaica.

While one death hardly seems sufficient to have caused an uproar, this one did. As with the moral dilemma of genetic engineering in an earlier era, and anything nuclear in an even earlier time, unreasonable fears now surrounded anything that had to do with space mining. Thus, the Greenies parading outside Sam's gate.

Sam stared at the rabblerousers from across his cup of juice. After enduring a lifetime of upheaval, he didn't much care for controversy — and certainly not for one taking place outside on his own front lawn. The unhappy look on Sam's haggard face reflected his current misgivings.

The *Tikkidiw* was a large craft. Except for the enormity of Sam's estate, there would be no hiding it. To be perfectly candid, Sam had no idea how so many would-be settlers found their way to his doorstep each week. But dozens upon dozens did, each paying Fornax the requisite fee, each undergoing the bio-screening Carina had insisted upon, and each patiently waiting his turn to get onboard the specially-built ship.

The *Tikkidiw* began as an experiment. Only later was it redesigned to carry a full complement of passengers into space. Among the first changes Fornax made was to convert the ship's cavernous cargo bay into a giant passenger compartment. Its large size notwithstanding, space was still at a premium. Each Pilgrim was limited to a single luggage bin one cubic meter in size. Plenty of room for clothes and some small personal effects. But precious little room for much of anything else. Certainly not furniture, appliances, or most tools. These luxuries, if they came at all, would have to come later. — And for a price.

Fornax also made a number of modifications to the propulsion system. While these enhancements had the effect of reducing somewhat the ship's top speed, they also greatly increased the number of trips he could make between rechargings of the ship's durbinium battery.

Equally important was the machine shop Fornax set up near Colony One on Mars. It was completely outfitted with power tools and spare parts to repair the Drive, plus a supply of tungsten-aluminum sheets to patch the occasional ding in the ship's hull. These tough, alloy polymer sheets might come in especially handy today. They were traveling to an area known to be dense with micro-meteorites, thus raising the possibility for the skin to end up peppered with hundreds of tiny holes.

The three-man team from the African Smelting and Refining Company was headed by a big, obnoxious fellow by the name of Oskar Schaeffer. Schaeffer's advance man, a fellow Euro by the name of Gunter, had been on Mars for several weeks already, scouting out a site for a motor factory (should they decide to build one), plus honing a few of his mountain climbing skills on some of the smaller Martian peaks. If all went well, he intended to have a go at the tallest peak, Olympus Mons, in about three weeks' time.

Gunter had been onboard the *Tikkidiw* the day of the crash. But thanks to Fornax's expert piloting, the mishap had proved more harrowing than dangerous. Though the came in hard, it escaped serious damage. The passengers, though badly shaken by the episode, were none the worse for the wear. Like so many of the others onboard the *Tikkidiw* that day, Gunter had escaped with little more than a nasty bruise. Beyond that, the incident had led to a fortuitous meeting between him and Carina, a meeting that was soon to upset her father even more than he already was.

Without need for further provocation, Oskar Schaeffer was the sort of man Sam abhorred. Plump, like an overstuffed turkey, and self-important to the point of exhaustion. And when, a month ago, after a dozen replies of "you'll have to talk to so and so," Sam and Fornax finally ended up at Oskar Schaeffer's desk in Johannesburg, Sam nearly called off the meeting solely on the basis of the fat man's pompous attitude.

That day, it was everything Fornax could do to settle his partner down. He pulled Sam aside, tried to talk sense to him. If Oskar Schaeffer had any redeeming qualities whatsoever, it was that he was greedy. Greedy and willing to risk plenty of ASARCO's money to find out whether or not this asteroid mining scheme of Fornax's could be made to work. This much Sam conceded, and a deal was soon struck. But nothing could change Sam's poor opinion of Oskar Schaeffer.

The plan, now, was to rendezvous with Gunter after dropping off the current batch of settlers at the Colony One clearing house. Then the five of them would make the jump out to the Belt. It would be a hazardous jump, one that required hours of computer time and lots of careful advance planning.

But, with the Fornax Drive at their command, and with Fornax himself at the helm, what used to take months — what *still* took months for everyone else in the solar system — would take them only minutes. Even though Sam and Fornax had done their level-best to keep it all a secret, a time would come when they could no longer hide the truth from the public. If and when that time came, there was sure to be trouble.

When Fornax set the ship down at Colony One to drop off the settlers and pick up Gunter, Carina was there in the landing bay with him. Sam took one look at his daughter and sized up the situation immediately. To say that he was annoyed, would have been to put it politely.

It wasn't so much that Sam was surprised to see his daughter — Carina was, after all, constantly screening incoming immigrants for suitable candidates to join her fledgling newhuman settlement — it was more her damnable habit of sticking her nose in where it didn't belong.

Sam had seen this before. But, given that Gunter had been there on Mars only two weeks, how could Carina already have taken such an interest in a man she hardly knew? *Stupid question for a father to ask.*

Gunter was a man unlike any Carina had ever met. As soon as she learned his reasons for being on Mars, she wouldn't let him out of her sight, not even for a moment.

Gunter was a climber, here for sport. Everything about the man turned her on — the piercing blue eyes, the unruly mop of wavy blond hair, the slow Aussie drawl. Carina decided at once that she had to have him. Only, thus far, he had put her off quite deliberately.

In her own impertinent way, Carina chalked up the rejection to her being the daughter of Councilman Samuel Matthews. Perhaps Gunter figured it would be bad for business. Or maybe he was afraid of her. She often had that affect on men. Or maybe he was just timid. He certainly couldn't be pulling to the left, not a big, strong guy like him.

But, whatever the reason Gunter had for putting her off, Carina hadn't given up on him, not yet. In fact, she was clinging to the man like a vine to the wall when Oskar Schaeffer, Fornax Nehrengel, and her father got ready to reboard the *Tikkidiw* for the next leg of their journey.

She stood on the gangway and addressed her father in a scolding, petulant manner. Her face was painted with an accusing stare and she pointed a finger at him.

"I understand from Gunter that the lot of you plan on going out to the Belt."

Carina waited impatiently for her father to answer. It occurred to her that he didn't look as well as he had, that he was a bit paler, a bit more stooped over than the last time she had seen him — and that was only two weeks ago.

"That's correct, Carina," the elder Matthews replied, a rattle of a cough clogging his throat. "We're taking Oskar and your new friend Gunter here, plus their chief geologist, out to the Belt to see whether or not the mineral deposits are rich enough to be commercially mined."

Carina's body language made her father uncomfortable. It seemed incongruous to him that she should be hanging so tightly onto Gunter's arm. Especially with Fornax standing right there next to her.

"I can't believe my ears!" Carina exclaimed, anxiety coloring her voice. "If you're successful out there, that would mean there'd be *miners* coming to Mars!"

Judging by the inflection in her voice, the way she enunciated the word "miners," it was as if she'd just said something profane.

"Actually, the miners would be staying on Earth, just where they've always been — it's the *engine* makers that would be coming to Mars."

Sam smiled and leaned easily against the bulkhead. Fornax sat next to him, at the nav-console, busily inputting coordinates.

"I really don't see the difference," the feisty young woman intoned. "How are engine makers better than miners?"

Even as she spoke, Carina stole a glance in Gunter's direction. To his credit, the man appeared nonplussed by what she was saying — or how she was saying it.

"Daughter, to be quite frank, this is actually none of your concern," Sam said, peeved by Carina's meddling. "This is a project Fornax and I have been working on for a good long time. And I'll not stand for your interference."

"It's every bit my concern!" she bellowed, not backing down. "I was the first one here — I should have my say!"

This statement was undeniably true. Therein lay the rub. Not only had Carina been the first one here, she had also been the one primarily responsible for provoking the current friction between Newton and Colony One.

And, if that alone weren't trouble enough to keep a man awake at night, her obstinance had led to a falling out between her and her father. The only thing that could be said in Carina's defense was that their difference in opinion was already in full bloom well before that frightful day some twenty-four months ago when she first defected from the planet of her birth to settle here on Mars.

But, to truly understand why this tough young woman considered Mars hers to do with as she pleased, why she thought that so much was at stake in its settlement, why she was so unyielding in her position. To do all these things required turning back the clock a full two years to those earliest of days when she unexpectedly found herself stranded alone on a red planet two-thirds the size of Earth.

It was only then, with the closest living thing more than a hundred million kloms away, that Carina's story really began.

PART I

THREE

Abandoned

Two Years Earlier: 2431

Carina touched herself. With her fingers. Below the waist.

It wasn't the first time. Loneliness was legion. Hours melting into days. Days collapsing into weeks.

What does a young, hot-blooded woman do when she is lonely? Men have a purpose, after all, maybe even two. But what to do when there isn't one around?

The options are pathetically few. A candlestick? An Autoclit? Two fingers, long and searching?

But how many times? How often? Once a day? Twice? How long had he been gone anyway?

As the hours dragged into days, and the days into more days, Carina began to come apart at the seams. All the way apart. Like a torn sweater. Like a fissure in the earth. Like a deep wound from a sharp blade. Apart.

The overcast days rolled by in endless procession. An endless procession of gloom.

It had been more than two weeks since BC left her stranded here alone on Mars, and she couldn't take it any longer. Frustrated at being without a man, any man, her dejection had turned first to anger, then to hysteria.

This very morning Carina had woken up before dawn screaming. Her beleaguered mind was churning as she replayed the same scene over and over again in her head. She had been acting out in her dreams the story she read in the Library only yesterday about the horrifying asteroid calamity some two hundred years before. When the rocky projectile struck the tiny scientific outpost nearly head-on, it had the force of a hundred neutron bombs. Everyone perished.

Carina sat upright in bed now. The woman shivered as she struggled to erase the stark images from her subconscious. The bone-crushing cold rushing in to envelop its victims. The agony of the sudden decompression. The inexplicable feeling of resignation as the oxygen and nitrogen cocoon was lost.

Though the physical damage to the facility was eventually repaired, the psychological damage never was. The manned exploration program never fully recovered from the shock and, in time, man's adventure in space ground to a halt. In fact, if it hadn't been for Fornax Nehrengel and his amazing machine, it might have ended altogether.

Carina Matthews moved, now, from her bed to the galley. She sat in the messhall picking at her breakfast. All things considered, it was not a bad place to be this time of day. From here she had an unobstructed view of the Martian landscape through any one of four lumina-glass windows cut into the bulkhead. What she saw, took her breath away.

The sunrise revealed an austere, rust-colored planet of rugged beauty, a planet boasting an unimaginable variety of landforms. Canyons. Craters. Volcanoes. Ice fields. Flat plains. Together, they combined to make Mars a world of great visual drama.

She swept the horizon with her eyes. Many of the geologic processes known so well to Earth had also once been active here on Mars. These forces had sculpted her terrain in a fashion unparalleled in the solar system.

To begin with, ancient tectonic movement had disfigured the fourth planet, leaving behind two remarkably different hemispheres. To the south lay heavily cratered highlands. To the north, smoother plains dominated the landscape. By dint of some incredible combination of geological forces, the northern steppe ended up a full three kloms *lower* in average elevation than the southern plateau. Immense canyonlands and giant extinct volcanoes were among the spectacular feature that straddled the demarcation line between the two hemispheres.

When the terraformers first established their colony here in 2097, they built it just north of the huge bluffs in a low-lying area of ancient lava flows spotted with silent volcanic cones. They chose this location principally because landing an interplanetary transport here was far easier than among the massive cliffs which girdled the planet further to the south. Apart from that, this was also one of the more promising sites in which to search for Martian fossils, a goal that had been uppermost in the minds of early explorers from the very beginning. Yet, in a way that Carina was only now beginning to understand, this choice of a low-elevation spot would ultimately prove to be her undoing.

Carina returned to her breakfast. Despite her current dilemma, she had to count herself lucky. If a woman had to be stranded alone anywhere in the galaxy, the abandoned Mars Base was as good a place as any. It had several virtues: plenty of dried provisions stored underground in the basement, a well-stocked Library to help keep her mind occupied, an ultramodern gene depository filled with frozen plants and animals.

Carina recalled the first time she entered the facility. It was several weeks ago. The five of them had been outside — on the planet's surface — she, Fornax, BC, her father, and her uncle. They had entered through the outer airlock. It was a high-compression airlock, not unlike the sort they had used in Luna City for years. Inside the chamber they were greeted by the tepid glow of a ceiling lamp and the sound of an eerie mechanical voice. It droned out a set of prerecorded instructions. *Depress the flashing green button on the far wall to pressurize the chamber.* This they did. Then there was the reassuring rush of fresh air as the atmosphere in the chamber was made earth-normal. The inner door swung open, beckoning them all to enter and remove their pressure suits.

The main room was in the shape of a hexagon twenty-five meters across. Sprouting from this central hub, like so many legs on an insect, were corridors. The corridors branched out to the rest of the complex, including the sleeping quarters beyond. Each of the sleeping wings were actually huge cargo bays flown in from Earth, soft-landed here on Mars, then fitted together in a modular fashion around the central messhall. Seen from the air, the corridors looked somewhat like spokes on a giant wagon-wheel. Huge compression bolts punctuated the junctions of the connecting pieces. If the necessity ever arose, and the Base had to be relocated, the modular units could be separated from the main node, placed on pallets or skids behind the landrover, and dragged to another spot, where they could later be reassembled.

In the center of the main room were several tables, some flanked by benches, others by chairs. This arrangement accommodated the room's dual function, as both an eating area and a community meeting hall. Closets and shelves lined one wall from floor to ceiling. These pantries were filled to overflowing with an extensive assortment of sundries: items which, while essential to the smooth operation of the colony, had been far too bulky to take back to Earth with them when the settlement was abandoned half a century ago. Taking inventory, Carina & Company found the shelves stocked not only with mundane necessities like toilet paper, cleaning detergents, medical supplies, kitchen utensils, and cooking spices, but also with an abundance of trivial diversions such as playing cards, poker chips, chess pieces, dominoes, and electronic video games.

Across the room, a second set of cabinets housed all manner of electronic equipment. Together with a bank of keyboards, a pair of vid monitors, and four data-entry ports, this was the command center for the entire facility. From here the colonists could control dozens of instruments to monitor and adjust a wide variety of environmental elements, including temperature, air pressure, solid waste treatment, food preparation, and perimeter security. Clearly, this area was the "brains" of the entire complex.

Carina finished her breakfast. She moved to the window. Storm clouds were gathering in the distance. She could feel the low rumbles of thunder reverberating against the glass. The storm was two, maybe three kloms away. It wouldn't be long now.

Carina thought again of her new home, of her earliest days on the planet. There was much more to the Mars Base than just the community room she presently stood in. Radiating out from the central hub or else drilled into the bedrock below, were the sleeping quarters where she and Fornax first made love, plus the gene-store, the equipment garage, the food lockers, and the Library. Who could have guessed that, in the long run, it was this last room — the Library — which would prove to be the most valuable resource of all? Certainly not the people who left it behind.

To the contrary. When the terraformers gave up on Mars fifty-four years ago, they had no idea they were bequeathing her this wonderful archive, this incredible pool of information. Yet, ever since BC disappeared, seemingly forever, Carina had spent untold hours thumbing through the hundreds of threadbare printbooks and scanning the thousands of vids and microfiche for interesting subjects to bone up on.

A Library was like that — beauty and pleasure wrapped in leather. It was the only thing that kept her half-sane and, in the process of reading everything in sight, she learned about a thousand things, from Anasazi farming techniques to setting up a herb garden inside a greenhouse to the proper installation of a solar collector at high altitude to what the terraformers originally had intended in terms of "fixing" Mars for human habitation.

From her readings, Carina soon discovered that when the first wave of colonists set out from Earth to remake the Red Planet, they had much more in mind than just the lichen they blanketed the surface with. They had in mind an entire ecosystem, complete with ferns and flowers and pine trees and farm animals. And although they were forced to throw in the towel on this effort before the job was done, they left behind the means for someone else to complete their work. This the early colonists did in the form of a climate-controlled storeroom filled with more than six dozen varieties of seeds, all meticulously preserved — every cereal, every fruit, every vegetable, every domesticated plant of consequence. Then there were a dozen or more varieties of tree, including representatives from the pine, cypress, maple, oak, and willow families.

But there was more! Beyond the walls of this first room, there was a *second* room, a gene-store stocked with fertilized embryos — several dozen species of farm animals, laboratory-bred and cryogenically frozen. The stockpile included everything from 'roo to camelid, from hog to bio-stallion, from squid to salmon-carp. The place was simply amazing. If not for her current predicament, Carina would undoubtedly have been thrilled by the possibilities the gene-store had to offer for her vision of a new Eden.

* * *

Carina stood again at the window. The storm was drawing nearer. Dark clouds. Heavy thunder.

She shivered involuntarily. Choked back the fear. This one could be bad. The last one certainly was.

As the overcast and rain-filled days flowed endlessly from one into the next, there was nothing Carina could do to lift herself out of the deep depression she had sunk into. Faced with the prospect of never getting off this planet alive, of never again seeing another human being, of never again having sex with a man, Carina began to psychologically unwind.

When he left, BC told her he would be back within the hour.

But what had it been now? A week? A month? In her present agitated state, she had lost all track of time.

What could possibly be keeping him? How could he do this to her? Where had he gone? Why hadn't he returned? Was he hurt? *By God, was he dead?*

This last thought was almost too much to bear. She owed everything to BC — indeed her very life.

But still, what did she really know about the man? BC was a spy of some sort, a military man, working for Commonwealth Intelligence. But what sort of a man was he really?

Take a young boy, one who has been orphaned at an early age. Put that boy in a military academy before he has had a chance to make money or to be out in the business world. Line the corridors of his academic halls with humaniform busts of victorious generals, perhaps the captured flags of conquered nations. Tell him day after day that his most valuable possession — perhaps his only one — is his pride and his personal honor. Let him see his classmates bilged for telling a casual lie or sneaking out after taps. Tell him that he will never be rich, but that if he is courageous enough, he may one day stand a chance of having his name inscribed on the walls of some Memorial Holo. Entrust him with state secrets. Feed him on tales of heroism. Indoctrinate him. Teach him how to fight. Do all these things faithfully and diligently and you will produce a man who is trained to respond to danger within the limits of a certain code. Such a man will exhibit a certain pattern of behavior. Once visions of "honor" and "duty" have pushed aside thoughts of economic success in his mind, you can depend on such a man to be utterly fearless in the face of personal danger, no matter how debilitating the sick feeling in the pit of his stomach. BC was such a man.

But what if she had lost him? What if he were dead?

A cold sweat broke out on Carina's forehead, and before long she found herself doing laps around the perimeter of the community room.

Round and round she went, arms pumping furiously, her feverish mind in overdrive. The woman was desperate — desperate to burn off her anguish with exercise. Desperate to wear herself out sufficiently that she might sleep tonight. Desperate not to be woken up again by the nightmarish dreams that had been haunting her sleep.

Round and round she went, racing along the interior walls of the messhall, almost at a run. The storm was closer now, nearly upon her.

Where was BC? When was he coming home?

Carina's eyes were puffy, as if she hadn't slept in days. Her long hair was grimy, as if it hadn't been washed in a week. The woman was finally there, at her wits' end.

Carina stumbled through another lap. There were tears in her eyes. She began to think that perhaps there was no way out of this, that the only way out of this was to take her own life, that she should do it while she still had the strength.

But no sooner had Carina begun to contemplate the least painful way for committing suicide, than a massive thunderclap exploded outside.

Carina screamed. The magnitude of the crash was audible, even through the station's heavily-insulated walls.

Terrified as much by the sound of her own voice as by the thunder, Carina raised her hands to cover her ears.

But before she could, a second, even louder clap of thunder erupted. At almost the same instant, the sky went white with lightning.

Carina dropped to the floor, eyes filling with tears. At first, she was too terrified to move. Then a sixth sense urged her to take cover. She quickly scurried under a table for protection.

Carina dabbed at the tears with her sleeve. She tried to get comfortable. Once a storm like this got going, it could last for hours. The last one, two days ago, turned out to be a deluge unlike any the world had seen since the time of Noah.

The rain pelted the windows like tiny BB's. The sound was unnerving, and it wasn't long before she was sobbing hysterically. What she couldn't understand was how a formerly dry planet could suddenly have rain. The answer was rather complex:

Without an atmosphere, without water vapor, neither clouds nor wind nor rain could exist on Mars. And so it had remained for untold millennia.

But the terraformers changed all that. The lichen they brought with them from Earth, the lichen they planted with so much care here on Mars, took hold to such an extent, it permanently altered the face of the planet.

As the lichen spread across the surface, it thickened the atmosphere and warmed the continents. Even the lichen's tenacious, ground-hugging roots helped speed the thickening process. They fractured and broke down the surface rocks, releasing the gases bound up within them into the air. And, as was true of all green plants, the water vapor given off as the lichen grew, acted as a greenhouse gas which, while not as potent as carbon-dioxide in this role, also helped to trap the sun's warmth near the surface.

Though the formula for warming the planet worked well enough, it was painfully slow. But before long, the planet-molders fell on a way to do the lichen one better — CFC's. Long experience on Earth had shown that chlorofluorocarbons were notoriously efficient greenhouse gases, albeit with one drawback — they interfered with the development of a protective ozone layer. Finding the risk acceptable, the terraformers began pumping tons upon tons of CFC's into the frigid atmosphere, thereby taking yet another crucial step towards warming the planet.

Seeded with these gases, the maturing atmosphere began to have an impact on the planetary heat cycles, moderating somewhat the prevailing temperature extremes. That moderation spurred even more lichen growth, which moderated the temperature extremes even further.

The tempering process was textbook Chaos at work. Once the critical stage was reached, the self-reinforcing cycle took but a geologic instant to run its course. As the lichen blanketed the planet, its color darkening the surface, more and more of the sun's warmth was captured, stirring the witch's brew of weather still further. By the time Carina and her friends arrived on Mars, the newly-warmed planet already had rudimentary atmospheric mixing, plus a burgeoning weather system. With heat had come humidity. And with lightning had come thunder. And with nightfall had come rain — tons upon tons of cold, wet rain.

Tearing out of the highlands to the south, the howling squall blasted the Base, now, with hurricane-force winds. The torrential rains which accompanied the stormfront arrived in sheets, depositing hundreds of thousands of liters of water just beyond the walls of her steel and concrete cocoon. It was an explosive tempest. It triggered a chain reaction all across the region.

The flood began simply enough — with a series of nearly undetectable water channels. But from there, it exploded outward in an almost geometric fashion. Frothy streams fed small rivers. Ponds grew to fill in every depression. Small lakes formed. Small rivers overflowed their puny banks. Bigger lakes formed. Water swept urgently across giant waterfalls, dumping into even larger rivers. And even greater lakes. These were emptied by larger waterfalls still.

Night after night it rained. Day after day. Before long, the low-lying basin where she lived began to fill up with water — black, churning, dangerous water. Eventually, as one horrendous storm system after another ripped across the face of the planet, the valley in which the Mars Base had been built became inundated by the massive runoff. *An ocean had begun to form right outside her front door!*

With the shores of the burgeoning sea literally swelling up to her front stoop, with the awesome, nonstop downpour threatening to swamp the entire complex, with Carina herself likely to be drowned in the process, once again the question arose —

To be or not to be? Once more, she contemplated whether or not to take her own life. Only this time, the context was different than before. This time, it was more a matter of doing it her way, of doing it first, before the rising floodwaters could finish her.

While such thoughts might have seemed unreasonable, even premature, to a disinterested bystander, considering what Carina was up against, considering what she had already been through, it would have been easy for her to have ended it all right there. The only question was how.

A sharp blade to the wrist? A knotted rope over a ceiling joist? An overdose of dangerous pills? What about a megadose of radiation, or a single headshot from a blaster?

It didn't dawn on her until this very moment that taking one's life took planning. That committing suicide wasn't easy. That there can never be a woman so lost as one lost in the vast and intricate corridors of her own lonely mind, where none may reach and none may save. That there can never be a woman so helpless as one overcome by indecision. At that realization, the tears again began to flow.

Time was running out, and soon she would have to make up her mind. The choices were stark. Should she abandon the colony for higher ground and an uncertain future, or stay with the proverbial ship and die onboard?

Outside, the thunder again began to roll. It seemed inconceivable that she should be forced to die this way, that she should be denied the opportunity of passing on her special newhuman genes to an undeserving world. *By God, there must be another way!*

Carina wiped the tears from her dirty face, decided she wasn't ready to give up just yet.

Perhaps suicide wasn't the answer. Perhaps there was a way to survive this ordeal after all.

But simple survival wasn't enough, not for a woman like Carina. No, her life had to have meaning.

But what was worth living for? There could be only one answer. If she lived through this, Carina had to commit herself to building a place where only newhumans could live, an Eden reserved exclusively for the newest branch on the primate tree — *her* branch!

Hail pelted the roof and walls. Too frightened to move, Carina sat huddled beneath the table in the messhall. Numbed into silence by the ferocity of the storm, Carina shivered. A tidal wave of emotion swept over her. She touched herself. With her fingers. Below the waist. Her heart pounded. Her thighs quivered. Her nipples stiffened.

It had long been her hypothesis that newhumans would be sexually hyperactive, that for them sex would be a tonic, a form of highly sophisticated tactile entertainment, an activity they would indulge in to pacify their heightened imaginations. It wouldn't be a perversion — not even in the oldhuman sense of the word — but rather an unquenchable thirst for physical pleasure. Orgasm floods the brain with chemicals the soul finds addictive. Sex was the ultimate narcotic and Carina its most enthusiastic junkie.

Exactly what had triggered her sudden carnal urgings was not immediately clear. A smell, perhaps. A taste. The stress of her situation. The fierceness of the storm. Her unanswered longing for BC.

Whatever it was, the urgent wash of desire was overwhelming and she found she had no choice but to answer it, to deal with it right there, right then, this very moment.

Carina crawled out from under the table, where she had been hiding. Her joints ached from the long hours of confinement.

Carina was desperate for relief. She loosened her bra, gently flexed her torso to restart her circulation.

She dropped her panties to the floor. Outside, the thunder rumbled. The storm was at the height of its fury.

Her hands were not bashful as they roamed freely across her firm, flat stomach and onto her small, but attractive bottom. The smooth and tender massage brought forth a sigh from deep within her chest. She could wait no longer.

Carina sat astride a chair in the center of the room. She leaned back, adjusting the position of her hips until they were just right. With one hand, she spread her legs open wide. With the other, she began to rub her naked breasts.

Then, moaning sensually, she started to stroke herself ever so slowly. There was no use rushing the self-administered therapy: she had nowhere to go — and no one to go there with.

Despite her leisurely pace, the ambidextrous remedy produced the desired effect in a surprisingly short time. Fingers deep and long, fingers wet and deep.

When, in a great gasp of ecstasy, relief finally pulsated through her being, Carina slipped from her chair, curled up on the floor, and fell instantly asleep.

Another day of loneliness had come to an end.

FOUR

Expulsion

The sound of the buzzer snapped Carina from a deep sleep. She had been curled up on the floor of the messhall. Now she rolled over and opened her eyes.

Still groggy, she wasn't sure at first what the low-pitched staccato signal meant. Was it a fire alarm? The klaxon warning her of an air leak somewhere? The enviro . . . ?

Then she remembered. *A signal sounded inside the community room whenever the outer airlock was opened.*

Carina flew to the airlock still half-naked. There could only be one explanation — *It had to be none other than BC returning at long last to save her.*

In her excitement it never occurred to her to first peek through the glass in the door to see who was there. If she had, she might never have popped the hatch.

Carina spun the locking-wheel to unlatch the inner door, flung it wide, ready to leap into her lover's arms.

But he wasn't there! No one was there! The chamber was empty! In fact, when the ponderous inner door swung clear, Carina was greeted by nothing more than a splash of cold, rust-colored water at her feet. Somehow, the power of the storm must have short-circuited the outer door's locking mechanism, allowing it to swing free. By opening the inner door without thinking, she had just sealed her fate.

For an instant, Carina stood there frozen, watching the terrible drama unfold. Wave after wave of brackish sea water crashed through the opening. And yet she did nothing. It had not yet dawned on her that as more and more brine seeped into the normally watertight facility, every electrical component in the place — every piece of equipment she depended on to stay alive — would spark once or twice, then burn out. Sea water was highly corrosive. The interior of the complex had not been designed to sustain such harsh treatment.

Cold water swirled up around her toes. She looked down at her legs and feet as if they belonged to someone else. The woman was still half-naked from before, but didn't remember why.

Suddenly, the cold against her skin snapped Carina out of her stupor. The adrenaline kicked in. *She had to undo her grievous error!*

Spurred to action, Carina began pulling frantically on the handle of the inner door. *She had to stop the flow of water!*

In the background — blotting out her every thought — the mechanical, prerecorded voice droned on and on about how important it was to shut the airlock doors, how it must be done right away to prevent a serious loss of pressure.

Carina kept tugging at the door, trying to shut it. She found it helped if she screamed. So she screamed. The walls screamed back.

Carina pulled at the door with all her might, a Herculean effort. *But the damn thing wouldn't budge!*

Suddenly sensing the inevitability of it all, Carina started to panic. Phlegm came into her mouth. Her knees felt weak. With every heartbeat, her apprehension rose.

This mustn't be allowed to happen, she thought desperately, her hand still on the door.

Carina moved to the opposite end of the pressure chamber. Her breath was labored. Each step brought a new splash of cold water against her legs. She reached for the outer door and tugged. But it too wouldn't budge.

Carina wasn't smart about such things. She didn't understand. Was the problem caused by an electrical short, or was it purely mechanical? If it was a short, how could she fix it? If it was mechanical, could she jimmy the damn thing with a crowbar? Or did it just take more strength than she had?

Either way the result was the same. The insulated metal doors that would ordinarily protect the interior of the climate-controlled Mars Base from the ravages of the Martian tundra were now stuck partway open — *and there wasn't a damn thing she could do about it!*

Understanding came slowly, like exhaustion on a hot summer's day. Her future was literally dissolving right before her very eyes. Carina suddenly realized that, like it or not, she was about to be ejected into the wilderness. Could any prospect be more terrifying?

It wasn't so much that the outside air was unbreathable. To the contrary. Like the cold and thin air one might expect to find in a remote Andean village, the Martian atmosphere was tolerable once you got used to it.

No, it was more a question of shelter. Once Carina left the Mars Base, she had nowhere else to go, no other place to live.

Carina had a serious problem. She wasn't handy with a saw or a screwdriver or a hammer or any of a dozen other common tools. She knew even less about bricks and mortar and plumbing and wallboard.

Moreover, how could she go about constructing a place to live in without lumber or cinder blocks or masonry or copper pipe or porcelain or any of a thousand other materials common to Earth, but unavailable to her here on Mars? How would BC have approached the problem? How would her father? How had the Brazilian Outbackers managed it? The Amerinds? The Vikings?

Wielding their axes and their shovels and their knives with the expertise of the natural woodsmen that they were, the pioneers of the past who conquered Earth's untamed stretches not only had the good sense to site their wilderness cabins where game was plentiful and where giant oaks towered overhead, they also had the presence of mind not to set off into the wilds alone. Circumstances being what they were, Carina enjoyed neither luxury. The nearest tree was 90 million kloms away; the nearest person no closer.

Carina moved out of the airlock and into the community room. She grabbed her clothes and moved towards the Library, sealing off behind her the corridors that led from the messhall out to the rest of the complex. She had to figure out a way to build herself a new home. Maybe the Library would provide her with some answers. Wood was obviously out of the question. *But even on the desolate Martian prairie surely there were other materials besides lumber a pioneer like herself might use.*

Carina entered the Library. Concrete was foremost on her mind. How to make it. How to use it.

She made her way to the encyclo and dialed up the entry: **CONCRETE**. A quick study revealed that making concrete required mixing four elements together in the right proportions — clay, limestone, sand, and gravel. *But where to find them?* That was the question.

Carina thought about it. The last two were simple enough — sand and gravel were everywhere she looked. As for clay, that shouldn't present much of a problem either. The Martian soil was not unlike Earth's in this regard. Knowing this, an early explorer had marked a map of the area with clay deposits he had found. Perhaps that fellow intended to exploit these clay deposits in much the same way as Carina presently had in mind.

But finding the fourth element, limestone, was apt to be a bit more problematic. Limestone was an artifact of earlier life. By most indications, Mars had always been a dead planet. No life, no limestone. No limestone, no concrete. It was just that simple.

Carina frowned and turned off the machine. If not wood or concrete, then what?

She wandered down the hall thinking. She stopped at the first window and looked out. That's when it hit her. Mars did have one resource, and in great abundance — *lichen!*

Going all the way back to when the original Mars Colony was established here in 2097, the terraformers had been sowing a genetically-altered variety of terran lichen, one hearty enough to withstand Mars's bruising cold, yet capable of spreading fast enough to cover the planet quickly. The bio-engineers had tinkered with the tiny green plant's genetic code to make it serve both functions more efficiently, a task that proved to be quite difficult, given that the plant didn't conform to the usual arrangement.

A lichen was, after all, actually a dual organism — an alga plus a fungus — and the two lived in a truly symbiotic association, each requiring the other to survive. The photosynthetic alga provided both it and the fungus with glucose, while the fungus converted the output into a sugar alcohol which the dual organism could then safely store as food. The alga also provided the symbionts with vitamins, as well as fixing airborne nitrogen. In return, the fungus provided the alga with physical protection and with moisture, not to mention providing the tough, weather-resistant spores by which the mutualistic plant reproduced.

On Earth, lichens survived in a wide range of habitats, including dry deserts, moist woods, mountaintops, beneath the soil, and even in the sea. The Arctic varieties were among the hardiest. They were also the ones most amenable to genetic manipulation. Which made them ideal candidates for the job.

In fact, the strains selected by the terraformers for implantation on Mars were so successful, by the time Carina arrived on the scene more than three hundred years later, the atmosphere had been fully oxygenated and the entirety of the planet — save the giant extinct volcanoes like Omen — had been blanketed by the stuff. It was human ingenuity at its best! Now all she had to do was figure out a way to harness the plant and make it work for her.

A possibility suggested itself in short order. Just as primitive tribes once fashioned huts from bricks of grass and mud, perhaps she might do the same, only using blocks of lichen-sod. Of course, there would be a bit more to it than that — finding a way to heat and cool the place, for starters. But, once she hit upon the idea of building a hut from clumps of lichen-sod, she again turned to the encyclo. A Boolean word-search brought up several entries under the heading: **LICHEN — uses.**

The first entry told her how her own Amerind ancestors (on her mother's side) had once used wicks of lichen soaked in animal fat to fuel their stone cavelamps. Two entries further down, it related how the Norsemen had carved a life out of Iceland, a place not unlike Mars in the sheer enormity of the challenge it presented. There, too, the settlers had had to climb a steep wall of adversity. But what the entry *didn't* tell her, what she still had to learn, was how? How to meet the challenge on her own?

Carina had a sick feeling in the pit of her stomach. She felt the walls of the Library closing in around her. The woman wasn't any closer to solving her problem now, than when she first started. In fact, she was worse off. The waters were still rising inexorably around her, and she had lost precious time engaged in study. Lichen or not, *she still faced the same horrible dilemma as before.*

Panic once again threatened to seize her. And why not? Here she was, unable to communicate with her home world, unable to remain where she was, unable to survive for long on her own outside.

Carina didn't know which way to turn. Only yesterday she had told herself that death wasn't an option. Now, all of a sudden, she wasn't so sure anymore. Now, all of a sudden, everything in her life seemed to be going wrong — and all at once!

Her mind again reeling from a lack of sleep, Carina started pacing the hallways. She attempted to convince herself that everything would turn out okay, that her father was still alive, that BC hadn't been killed, that someone — anyone — would come looking for her before it was too late.

A lesser person would surely have cracked before now, taking the easy way out. Yet, somehow, she managed to hang on just this side of sanity. If only there was someone for her to talk to. If only she wasn't so damned alone, she might be able to cope. If only . . .

The more Carina thought about it, the more appealing the idea became. She needed someone to talk to. Anyone.

Her pace quickened. Finally, as she wandered aimlessly through the empty corridors of the abandoned colony, she made up her mind. All she need do was go down to the gene-store, select something from the cryogenic freezers, and cook herself up a companion. A puppy, perhaps. Someone to talk to. A friend. Then everything would be okay.

She turned her head, now, in that direction. It wasn't long before she found herself framing the entranceway to the gene-store.

"A puppy." She said, outloud. The words had a nice ring to them.

There was a wild look in her eyes. She cackled and rubbed her hands together, like a witch at her cauldron.

Carina crossed the threshold. She was driven as much by loneliness, now, as by scientific curiosity.

The mammoth chamber was filled with bin after bin of carefully preserved seeds, plus case after case of frozen animal embryos. Like the first time she stood in this doorway looking around the climate-controlled room, Carina tried to digest what the original settlers must have had in mind when they left behind this awesome legacy.

Clearly, the terraformers' original plans were of a truly global nature. They intended to sow the newly-oxygenated planet with all the species of flora and fauna they had so painstakingly preserved here in the gene-store. That they weren't able to do so was more a question of bad economics than poor planning. Clearly, they meant to give birth to a new Eden in this primeval wilderness. It had undoubtedly been their goal to achieve a balanced food chain with sufficient green plants to support grazing animals, plus enough predators (mainly man) to keep the number of grazers in check. Carina's present plans were much more modest.

Not that it hadn't occurred to her to consummate the planet-molders' original goals. But there was one problem. One very big problem.

Whereas several hundred colonists might have been able to keep all those many animals in check, *one* colonist certainly could not. Carina was afraid of being overwhelmed by sheer numbers, and with good reason. A couple of harmless dogs could quickly swell into a pack of hungry wolves. A few meandering cows could grow into a crushing stampede. A pair of cute bunny rabbits could multiply into a pestilence capable of raping the countryside.

While it was certainly true that in time Mars would develop its own delicate balance of hunter and hunted, meat-eater and grazer, tyrant and weakling, ecological equilibrium would just have to wait for someone else. Homesick and desperate for companionship, all Carina wanted was someone to talk to before she cracked.

"Defrosting" a puppy and incubating it in a warm bath of Acceleron, proved far easier than she could possibly have imagined. Within the hour, she was bottle-feeding a precious little collie, suitably named Sandy. His presence did more to mollify her depression than any wonder drug could have. Though she still paced restlessly around the complex talking to herself, at least now she had company.

Acceleron was one of those fortuitous curiosities of human invention. Much like the episode of Charles Goodyear, the man who slapped a piece of sulphur-treated rubber against his brother-in-law's Franklin Stove, inadvertently discovering vulcanization in the process, Acceleron was also discovered by accident. It was one of several modern drugs developed from ethnobotanical leads; that is, drugs developed by scientists analyzing the chemical constituents of a plant used by traditional peoples either for medicinal purposes or to produce unusual biological effects. Drugs as disparate as aspirin, codeine, quinine, and scopolamine were all novel therapeutic agents discovered by observing the gathering habits of medicine men in the back reaches of Africa before the Great Fire or healers in the outback of Brazil before the Influx. In fact, some very important drugs were unearthed in just this manner. In the late 1700s, for instance, a British physician reported that ingesting dried leaves from the purple foxglove plant eased dropsy, an accumulation of fluid now known to be caused by the heart's failure to pump adequately. The physician credited an unexpected source for his information. He was told that this use of foxglove — a member of the genus *Digitalis* — had long been kept secret by an old woman in Shropshire, a woman who was known to sometimes make cures after the more regular practitioners had failed. Digitalis has been helping cardiac patients ever since.

The story of Acceleron is no less remarkable. Late in the twentieth century, a team led by Dr. Elvin-Lewis obtained samples of a tree sap the Jivaro Indians of Peru applied to their skin to hasten the healing of wounds. The active ingredient in the sap, a compound called taspine, was subsequently tested by zoologists and found to be useful for the same purpose in mammals. After a great deal more testing and refinement, it was eventually approved for use with humans. Dubbed *Acceleron* by its promoters, in its purest form the wonder drug could promote rapid healing. In the presence of an amino-acid wash, it could hasten embryonic growth. Its only known drawback was that the more serious the wound, the more painful the accelerated healing. For Carina and her father and for other members of the Matthews clan, this had always been a bit of a conundrum. Every single one of them was allergic to the standard painkillers of the day, thus making Acceleron not quite the blessing for them as it was for the rest of mankind. In fact, this was one of several genetic defects the Matthews family suffered from, and for which modern science had not yet offered a cure.

Carina stroked the fur on her new friend's head. She scratched him behind the ears. Dogs liked that. She was still troubled, though, and about one thing in particular:

Dating all the way back to high school and her earliest course in biogenetics, it had always bothered her how much of a complete lottery evolution had been, how chaotic and unpredictable its outcome. Evolution had not been survival of the fittest, as some had so eloquently put it, it had been survival of the *luckiest*. And, if God were to rewind the tape of life back into His giant video machine and let it play out again now, He would undoubtedly get a whole new set of survivors. Perhaps humans wouldn't even be among them!

From the outset, humans had been inquisitive territorial beasts, beasts who objected to being caged. And yet, the post-industrial world presented them with cages at every turn, cages that withered mankind's spirit and sapped his very strength.

Not only had the physical frontiers like the American West and the Brazilian Outback been closed, the intellectual frontiers had been closed for the most part as well, as millions of naysayers around the globe waylaid innovative thinkers in their webs of bureaucratic hurdles and stifling, politically-correct dogmas.

Those who were the most ambitious and the best educated saw most clearly how the borders of exploration had been slammed shut in their faces. And, not wanting to introduce children into a world no longer able to cope with nonconforming overachievers, they began to postpone parenthood — or avoid it altogether — always being sure to abort any accidental indiscretions along the way.

Without any new lands to conquer, without any migratory havens to escape to, without any isolated places for the geniuses of the world to take refuge in, the defining human characteristic atrophied. The species had reached an impasse, a cul-de-sac, a virtual *plateau* in its intellectual development.

Carina looked at her new friend. She spoke aloud, as if Sandy could answer.

"Can you point to even a single sign that, as a species, we are getting smarter? Was Albert Einstein a better scientist than Isaac Newton? Than Archimedes? Was Durbin? Has any playwright in recent years topped William Shakespeare or Euripedes? We have learned a lot these past 3000 years, yet much of the ancient wisdom still seems sound today. Which makes me think we haven't been making all that much progress. We still don't know how to resolve the inherent conflict between individual goals and global interests. And we are so bad at making important decisions that, whenever we can, we leave to chance — or to someone else — what we are unsure about. I ask you, Sandy: Does that sound like progress to you?"

Sandy flashed her a knowing smile, but did not answer. He was only a dog, after all, with cares no more distant than his next dish of water. Still and all, it seemed incongruous to her that Mother Nature would allow herself to be boxed in this way, that the human race should end with a whimper instead of a bang, that Carina herself should have to die such a meaningless death.

The woman hadn't slept in hours, and once again she began her frenetic pacing. It took another hour, but finally, exhausted, she collapsed into a chair to rest. Sandy made himself comfortable in her lap. As she sat there petting him, it hit her — *she* was the solution to mankind's dilemma.

It was a wonder Carina hadn't thought of it before, because the answer was so perfectly clear to her now. The only route out of the evolutionary cul-de-sac man had so blindly fallen into, was a genetic megajump *around* the impasse, a huge leap *over* the blockade, a giant step onto an untested new path, a path marked out by the stretch of signature genes she had inadvertently stumbled across in her research back on Earth. Newhumans were evolving in response to the insurmountable obstacles oldhumans had created for themselves — that was plain enough from her data — but for her to die without first sharing this insight with the rest of the world would be a shame of Biblical proportions.

Believing, now, that more was at stake here than simply her own death, and being far too stubborn to give in to the Martian gods of rain without first putting up a proper fight, Carina came to a decision. She would take the landrover and make a run for it. She would try and find a dry cave somewhere, a place where she could hole up until she could build herself a proper home.

Carina gathered Sandy in her arms now, headed for the equipment garage where the all-terrain vehicle was parked. A determined look creased her otherwise pretty face. She was making a mental list of what supplies she needed to take with her.

As she packed, it occurred to her that a future generation of settlers might truly appreciate having the nutrition only a living sea could provide. And, since defrosting Sandy had been so easy, she decided it only made good sense to seed the ocean with all the species of fish and crustaceans the gene-store had to offer. That, plus the several varieties of seaweed and kelp on deposit there. Perhaps some of the animals would survive. At the very least, the kelp would help oxygenate the murky water.

Playing God made Carina feel good. In her heart, she knew she had done the right thing. Even so, something was lacking. It was only then, as she stood shivering at the water's edge contemplating the many plants and animals she had just sent on their way, that Carina realized her job wasn't done. Without trees there could be no wood. Without wood there could be no fishing boats. Or paper. Or any of a thousand other things a healthy future would require.

No, her job wasn't done. Before abandoning the colony for good in the landrover, Carina would have to return one last time to the gene-store and perform her magic.

So, with her hormones running wild and Sandy lapping at her feet, Carina retraced her steps up the long hallway to the climate-controlled room. If Death were to take her now, she could at least die comforted by the fact that the next generation of colonists might sit under the shade of one of her pines, or eat from the fruit of one of her trees, and wonder how it all came to be.

Playing God made her feel good. The plants she selected had to be hardy, the sort that could survive both wet and dry, hot and cold, storm and sun. Pine trees were self-pollinating, with the male cones above and the female cones below. They grew fast, produced plenty of oxygen, and could survive the harsh Martian winters. Mountain yuccas were tough, grew in all kinds of habitats, and bore a fruit which was edible. Woodland ferns were a superb groundcover, especially as a second-generation plant in places where the lichen had started building the soil. Prairie grass would keep the fragile land from eroding, as well as provide excellent grazing should there ever be herds of livestock. The list went on, with animals too. Llama. Cow. Mountain goat. Horse. Nearly an entire ecosystem. It took hours, and then she was done.

Her work complete, Carina slung the last box of dried provisions into the all-terrain vehicle. On her last pass through the messhall she had watched as the spray from yet another wave crashed through the open doorway of the airlock and into the room. To conserve power, she had long ago silenced the mechanical voice that had been chanting out meaningless instructions to close the door. Now it didn't matter. Now, nothing mattered.

Would the terraformers approve? She wondered.

Did those first peoples have any idea the enormous climactic changes they would be setting in motion when they planted that first swatch of lichen so many years ago?

Carina climbed up the short ladder into the landrover, propped Sandy on the seat beside her, and fired up the motor.

She reached down to engage the magneto, ground the gears to get started.

Then she drove off into the storm without so much as a clue where she was headed.

FIVE

SOD

Two Months Later

For the better part of a millennium it had been a tenet of modern science that no two snowflakes were exactly alike. Whether or not this proposition was true could not be resolved beyond a shadow of a doubt. Yet, for some inexplicable reason, this question nagged at the man as he dragged himself doggedly forward through the bleak mixture of sleet and snow, his load tailing behind him.

In a previous life, BC's enemies had been nefarious spies and paid assassins; now they were the newly-awakened Martian gods of nature.

Nevertheless, as only a man of his constitution could, BC was determined to wrestle these frightful gods to the mat. And what a mat it was. That he should even have been involved in such an enterprise was testimony to how bad things had become between father and daughter these past months. Let it only be said that stubborn was an adjective which could have been applied with equal force to either Matthews, though most would agree that Carina deserved it more.

Ever since her signature gene discovery, it had been Carina's hope to establish an isolated colony on Earth somewhere, a reserve set aside exclusively for a clan of newhumans. Over time, it graduated from a hope to a dream to an obsession, an obsession that could be given voice here on Mars in a way it never could back home. For BC, it was only after several heated exchanges that he began to have an inkling what she was truly after — and why.

Which still didn't mean he agreed with her. To the contrary. BC found himself powerless to counter her arguments point by well-reasoned point. Even so, the man had learned that life with Carina Matthews could be fascinating.

Had it been any other way, they would have parted company long ago. As it was, each time he stopped, now, to catch his breath between setting lichen-blocks into place for their new home, he found himself going over her newhuman hypothesis one more time in his head:

Just as some Bible Literalists vehemently denied the possibility of evolution out-of-hand, others still clung in quiet desperation to the myth of an immutable unchanging Man, a Man created in God's image once and forever.

But Carina subscribed to neither philosophy. To her mind, these were nothing more than deeply ingrained human conceits. Thus, it was with confidence that she set out three years ago, in 2428, to prove that the present human model was not a finished product as so many before her had contended, but rather just the latest in a long string of experimental designs.

The first step in building her case was to make a comparison of her own gene-map against the template assembled nearly four centuries earlier by the Human Genome Project. Then, widening the scope of her research with a much broader sample, it wasn't long before she had gathered enough evidence to confirm her suspicions — *a remarkable genetic variation was working its way through the population from its apparent point of origin somewhere on the continent of Asia.*

Though it was impossible to pinpoint exactly where the mutation first got its start, her evidence suggested it could have been as far south as Afghanistan or as far north as the East Siberian Sea above the Arctic Circle.

But discovering the precise point of origin wasn't as important to Carina as understanding the discovery itself. Here was an amazing thing, an altered stretch of human DNA, a stretch she took the bold step of labeling as "signature genes." From that moment forward, Carina became convinced that the presence of these signature genes corresponded with the budding of the latest branch on the hominid family tree, a branch she dubbed *Neo-sapiens*. Literally translated from the Latin, the term meant "new thinker." She took the liberty of translating it somewhat differently — newhuman.

Although the outward differences between the two species were subtle and few, in time she learned of several physical characteristics which — along with the altered stretch of DNA — distinguished the new species from the old.

Their teeth, for instance. Newhumans had one less set of molars; two up and three down instead of the customary three up and three down; thirty teeth in all, rather than the customary thirty-two. Apparently, more-advanced humans required less grinding power. As with so many of her discoveries, the unpredictable nature of evolution often surprised her,

Then there was the appendix. From electronic body scans and from autopsies she learned that instead of the normal three-inch-long appendix, newhumans had a tiny half-inch-long vermiform pouch. And, instead of it being open on the end, it was closed. This too might have been expected, especially in light of the first discovery. The appendix was, after all, nothing more than a pouch for storing excess chemicals, a relic leftover from the days when digestion was more difficult.

Finally, there was the clitoris. This was a genuine surprise. In newhuman women such as herself, the small erectile organ was greatly enlarged.

On the face of it, this development should not have been entirely unpredictable either — sexual stimulation was, after all, of greater importance to intelligent animals than to less intelligent animals, and therefore more important to newhumans than to oldhumans.

But the curious thing was, rather than her enlarged organ being a source of pleasure, it was in fact a constant source of irritation. No matter how hard she tried, satiation always seemed just out of reach. That, no doubt, is how she ended up with two suitors to begin with, and why neither man — nor any other she had encountered thus far in her short life — had been able to satisfy her thoroughly.

(For the record, Carina hadn't yet examined the newhuman male appendage in sufficient numbers to draw any firm conclusions regarding *its* size. But she was constantly on the lookout for additional hard data.)

As for the enlarged clitoris, it was all a question of testosterone. For centuries already, it had been known that the topical application of the male hormone to a woman's clitoris enlarged the organ and intensified her libido. Perhaps, newhuman women had a little more "man" in them than their oldhuman mothers did.

Knowing what Carina did about the processes of natural selection, it was her fear, nay her obsession, that unless a sufficient number of these newhumans were physically separated from the rest of humanity, the new species would falter. Only in isolation would *Neo-sapiens* have a chance to flower and prosper. This had been the flashpoint with her father.

Samuel Matthews wanted to see Mars opened for settlement to whomever wished to make the journey; Carina Matthews wanted to apply a litmus test, excluding all but those who could pass it, which is to say, the entire oldhuman race. "The Great Unwashed," as she had come to call them.

So convinced was the woman that her thinking on this was correct, she did something rather shocking at the conclusion of that long and lonely night two months ago. That night, on her desperate escape to nowhere, she foolishly rolled the landrover down a steep embankment.

That wasn't the shocking part. Nor was the part where she was later rescued by Fornax. No, the shocking part was how she repaid the man who saved her life. With open arms and open legs. *And why not?* He was an Afghan, after all, and thus in all likelihood a signature-gene-carrying newhuman. *So what if the thought of motherhood revolted her?* Fornax was the perfect gene-donor for what she had to do.

Make no mistake about it. By the time Carina drove off into the storm that night, she had persuaded herself that she had a duty, a duty to produce a newhuman baby, a duty she bore as part of her obligation to propagate the *Neo-sapiens* line.

Therefore, she had no real choice in the matter. She had to seduce Fornax in the hopes of impregnating herself with his newhuman seed.

Which meant she had no choice in something else as well. She had to deceive BC. She had to keep him from learning that the child growing inside her belly belonged, not to him, but to Fornax. If BC were to find out the truth, everything she had worked so hard for, would suddenly fall apart.

Make no mistake about something else. Carina was determined to have her utopia, and there was nothing Sam or Fornax or anyone else in the colony could do or say to convince her otherwise. Six weeks ago it had all come to a head.

Convinced that she had to have things her way, convinced that there had to be two separate colonies, the fight had ended with Carina leaving Colony One. Only, like that first night, she had nowhere else to go.

Like everything Carina did, once she made up her mind to leave, that's all there was to it, no matter how irrational it was. Neither the man who raised her, nor the man who loved her, nor anyone else, could stop her from heading out into the wilderness on her own. It seemed that only BC, the obedient soldier, cared enough to keep a watch over her. For him, this turned out to be both a pleasurable job — and a thankless one. Pleasurable in that she never ceased to amaze in bed; thankless in that she was stubborn and never ceased to confound the rest of the time.

Two months ago, when Fornax and Inda and the other Afghan refugees landed on Mars, they found the Mars Base deserted and a set of caterpillar tracks leading away from it into the hills. They also found one end of the Base submerged under the rising waters of what would soon be called the Great Sea.

They followed the tracks Carina's landrover left behind in the mud and soon found her out cold at the bottom of a ravine. Not knowing how to drive the big machine properly, she accidentally rolled the landrover down a steep embankment, knocking herself out.

After rescuing her, the first thing Fornax & Company did was try and salvage what they could from the partially flooded facility. This meant disconnecting certain key portions of the modular complex and hauling them upland by crane to a plateau high enough to be out of reach of the rising waters.

Safely out of harm's way, the relocated cargo bays formed the nucleus of what was soon to be called Colony One. The new site would have been the perfect core around which to build the newhuman settlement Carina envisioned. But she was determined to get as far away from Colony One — and her father — as possible. In characteristic fashion, she left the details up to someone else to figure out — in this case, BC.

BC was a smart, good-looking man. Making use of a Quonset hut the early explorers once bivouacked in, he established them (dog included) in a satisfactory spot a few kloms south of Colony One.

Unfortunately, this would turn out to be only a temporary home. Despite its newly breathable atmosphere, Mars still presented a wilderness as forbidding and hostile as any Earth had ever seen.

The Quonset hut quickly proved inadequate for long-term habitation. At night, the temperatures still got frightfully cold. During the day, should a stormfront blow in, the winds were formidable enough to topple their half-track. Besides, with the constant rain of gamma rays down onto the surface, living under an insulated dome was a necessity.

And forget about going outside unprotected. A single-density bodysuit, plus a wide-brimmed hat, were the absolute minimum. With a baby on the way, a baby BC believed to be his own, he quickly recognized that something more substantial than a Quonset hut was called for.

BC knew enough from his survival training to appreciate what their minimum requirements would be if they were going to survive on their own in the wilds this far afield from the reassuring confines of Colony One. It would have to be in a heavy and sturdy structure, one that couldn't be easily blown over by the wind, one that was simple to heat, as well as impervious to the elements. All in all, a pretty tall order.

It was Carina who first put him onto the idea of using blocks of lichen-sod to build with. The idea had come to her on that long and terrible night when — with the waves lapping at her doorstep — Carina nearly gave up hope. Despite her despair, she hadn't used what she thought were her last hours frivolously. In fact, she spent most of that last day in the Library reading. She learned, for instance, that in the absence of adequate timber, the Vikings once built sod-houses in Iceland. As a necessary precaution against the icy winter winds, the earthen walls were between one and two meters thick and the main rooms extended up to thirty-five meters in length. Like the long houses of SKANDIA on which they were based, the sod-houses of Iceland were heated by hearths running down the length of their earthen floors. Later, when the Norsemen ventured to the New World, establishing a small community in Vinland prior to that fatal encounter with savages they called Skraelings (probably Algonquin Indians), they lived in houses made of turf and stones, and roofed with sod-covered driftwood.

Similarly, when it came to heating primitive homes in lands short of wood, her research turned up an Old World practice which offered a promising possibility for Mars as well. It seemed the Irish had found an innovative use for their abundant peat. By cutting away the top six inches or so of living bog — the "scraw," as they called it — then using a turf spade to remove the sods of peat, Irish farmers piled the peat-blocks into cairns ten sods high, then left them to dry over the warm summer months. Although a typical bog was almost entirely water, when the peat was cut into sods and exposed to the wind and sun, it contracted, becoming an ideal fuel for cooking and heating, a methodology that might be worth mimicking here on planet number four.

That's why BC stood here now, contemplating the physics of a snowflake. Because, after an incredible bout of lovemaking one night, Carina convinced him that it could be done, that it was possible for him to build them a hut made from blocks of lichen-sod. That, like the Amerinds before him, and the Vikings before *them*, he would be the latest pioneer to improvise in a land without wood. It went without saying that he would have to do essentially all the physical work himself. But BC knew he could count on his friend Fornax to tap the resources of Colony One and supply him with much of the materials and equipment he would need. Plus, there were others — neighbors — who might help in a pinch.

But that still left the first question unanswered. *Was every snowflake unique or not?*

BC stared at a pair of them in his gloved hand as they fell from the sky. Didn't the one on the left look just like the one on the right? Weren't they both the same as the pair he looked at twenty minutes ago?

BC shook his head, let the snowflakes fall to the ground. He was tired. There was no getting around that. But he couldn't rest any longer. He had to get back to work.

Engaged as he was now in the hard labor of carving out blocks of lichen-sod from the surrounding hillsides, BC found himself getting weary. The chunks of Martian turf were heavy. They reminded him of blocks of peat he'd seen stacked in the English countryside as a boy, the same sort of cairns Carina had learned about from the encyclo.

The job began with him laying out a rudimentary foundation of stone. Then he arranged the lichen-blocks, one atop the next, in an interlocking stepwise fashion around the base, just as a youngster might, with a set of giant Lego building-blocks.

Continuing in this manner around the base of the structure, BC worked along the perimeter until he had enclosed an enormous rectangular building thirty meters long and twenty meters wide. Except for a front and back entryway, and a couple of small window-openings on each of the four sides, the lichen-block walls would be unbroken and stand more than three meters tall. Their thickness would make the walls first-rate insulators against the fury of a cruel Martian winter. With a little care, the lichen would continue to grow. This would seal off any narrow fissures between the blocks.

It was early on, when he was trying to wrestle one of the first lichen-blocks into place, that a distressingly familiar voice intruded upon his thoughts.

"Here, let me help you with that," the man said, with forced politeness.

The speaker extended his hand to assist BC. He was a lanky, good-looking Afghan named Inda Desai. Inda had been among the first contingent of newhumans to arrive here from Earth. Young and outspoken, Inda regarded himself as one of Newton's staunchest supporters, a True Believer, if ever there was one.

BC didn't care for the man, not one little bit. Call it spy's intuition. *Beware of fanatics. You never know when they're going to turn on you.* It came from a life of being an agent for Commonwealth Intelligence.

"I don't need your help," BC replied sternly.

"Oh, but I think you do," Inda remarked good-naturedly. "We're to be neighbors."

"I have no objection to that. Only I'd like to handle this myself, if you don't mind."

BC's tone was severe. Though he didn't say it in so many words, completing this job himself, without any help, was a matter of some pride, a personal test of his manhood. BC was a loner by nature. While he might come to regret his decision later on, for the moment he wanted nothing more than to be left alone.

"If ever there was a place where no man is an island, surely this would be that place," Inda retorted coolly. He was disappointed by BC's go-it-alone attitude.

BC looked the man straight in the eye. "I am not an island — I am a continent."

"Suit yourself," Inda said, shrugging his shoulders. "But if my bed were being warmed by a woman as wild and lovely as the one you're putting it to, I'd want to be on good terms with my neighbors. If that were my woman, I'd want to be living next door to someone I could count on, someone who might be trusted to keep a watch over her should I ever be away from her bedside for a while."

As the handsome Afghan spoke, his eyes drifted in the direction of the Quonset hut. Carina stood in the doorway waving to him in what could only be described as a flirtatious manner.

BC angrily motioned her back indoors. He could take Inda apart in nothing flat, splinter his bones, and not even break a sweat. He could kill him four different ways and not even leave a mark. *But why get agitated?*

"Well, neighbor, Carina's my concern, not yours. Besides, I don't need anyone to keep watch over her. I'm not going anywhere."

"Not today, perhaps. But you never know when things might change."

Sarcasm crept into BC's voice. "Well, neighbor, as anyone can plainly see, I'm not an Afghan myself, I'm white. I don't consider myself bound by your Code, nor do I consider myself a Newton. I'm just a man, a white man at that. And all I'm trying to do here is scratch out an existence for the two of us — she and me — so you had better keep your distance, if you know what is good for you."

"Mars is for Newtons, you white son-of-a-bitch. If you're not one of us, if you're not *for* us, I can only assume you're against us. We don't want your kind coming here, white boy — and we certainly won't tolerate Fornax bringing any more of your kind here to set up housekeeping with our women!"

"That's right neighborly of you," BC replied, leaning against his power-shovel. "You speak for the whole planet then?"

"You know I do." There was a haughty, even derisive edge to Inda's answer.

BC was resolute. "If you have a beef with Fornax, that's between you and him. But unless you have a beef with me personally, I suggest you step aside and leave me be. And I mean now!"

Inda was arrogant, but not stupid. No use picking a fight he couldn't win. Maybe later, with the help of Lotha.

Inda briefly narrowed his eyes, then turned on his heels and walked away.

BC watched him go. For the moment, there was far too much work that needed doing for him to grant their conversation more than a passing thought.

Even so, it bothered him that there should be this much resistance to newcomers this early on. If Fornax had his way, a flood of immigrants would soon be wading ashore to join the other footprints in the sand of this beachhead in the Martian wilderness. What would happen then? What would happen when the number of outsiders counted in the hundreds rather than the dozens, when they counted in the thousands rather than the hundreds? What then? Wasn't it like the snowflakes — all different yet all the same?

BC tried to put Inda out of his mind. He turned back to the job at hand — moving lichen-blocks. It was hard work, even with the help of a power-shovel. BC was no slouch. He was in superb health and exceptional physical condition, a fact the insatiable Carina never tired of pointing out to him when they were making love and she was on top the way she liked to be. Even so, he was nearly not up to the enormity of the task he was presently engaged in.

For openers, building this sort of hut with little more than his ingenuity and his own two bare hands was incredibly exhausting. And, if that weren't enough to give a man pause, BC had to combat the Martian equivalent of altitude sickness, as well as the severity of the elements.

Between the howling winds, freezing cold rain, and thin Martian air, BC found himself constantly panting for oxygen. It was a dangerous combination.

At sea level, the Martian atmosphere was equivalent to 4000 meters elevation back on Earth, the height of a good-sized mountain in the Peruvian Andes.

And, much like Earth, the higher up one went, the lower the air pressure became. To compensate for the loss of pressure, your body responds by breathing faster and ordering the heart to pump harder. This causes the blood to become more alkaline. It also allows the chemicals that regulate the porosity of your blood vessels to get out of balance. Fluids leak through the blood-vessel walls and into the internal organs, causing them to swell. This swelling causes edema, and the edema will be most intense in the lungs and brain. In severe cases, the damage can be permanent and death may follow.

All this BC knew by rote. He had been a medic in the army before joining the Agency. So, as one hour dragged into the next, he took precautions, resting often and drinking lots of fluids.

The man's daily work schedule went something like this: Allowing for breaks to stop and catch his breath, it would take him upwards of twenty-five minutes to slice out each lichen-block from the Martian landscape.

To make the blocks easier for him to manage, each block measured a uniform one meter in width, height, and depth. Even with the help of the landrover and a skid Fornax lent him, it would take anywhere from a quarter of an hour to as much as two hours to lug each heavy block into place.

Until the job was finished three weeks later, BC kept up this punishing pace for ten solid hours a day. Most nights, when he returned home to the Quonset hut, he fell instantly to sleep from sheer exhaustion, his protective single-density flightsuit drenched in sweat.

Under any other circumstances, with BC coming home tired every night, Carina might have been upset that he was no longer regularly servicing her needs. In fact, now that she was pregnant, her libido was even more elevated than before.

But Carina had her ways of dealing with such things. In any case, while BC was outside completing work on their sod-hut, she was inside, busily conducting nesting activities of her own.

As soon as Carina realized she was pregnant, she tested the fetus for the presence of signature genes, just to be sure. The amniotic fluid tested positive, as she knew it would. She naturally assumed the father was Fornax. Oh, she had had sex with other men, yes, including BC. But it never occurred to her that any of them could be the baby's father. Only Fornax was a newhuman. Or so she thought.

In any case, let it only be said that Carina was using BC in the worst possible way. To secure his help and guarantee his loyalty, she callously deceived him into believing the child was his. Otherwise, he might not have agreed to put forth the superhuman effort he was making to keep her alive and happy. For her, it was a genetic imperative, nothing more.

But to say that Carina was ambivalent about the prospect of motherhood would have been a gross understatement. Sex was one thing, motherhood quite another. In the twenty-fifth century — as in every century since the dawn of mankind — contraception was woman's work. A man's job was to spray his sperm into every vagina he could; a woman's job was to block any unwanted spray. And, except for abstinence — that most unlikely of all sexual fantasies — preventing a pregnancy in this day and age meant either ingesting a monthly sterility pill or else accepting an implant. For Carina the decision was simple: she couldn't stomach the thought of something foreign being placed beneath her skin. The only option open to her was the monthly pill.

For a sexually-active woman, the monthly birth-control pill was a blessing. It functioned like a heat-guided missile, zeroing in on and destroying any foreign microbes as they entered the body. Thus, it simultaneously insulated a woman against both disease and the occasional spray of unwelcome sperm. In the civilized world, the introduction of the monthly birth-control pill sounded the death knoll for sexually transmitted disease and, to a lesser degree, fatherhood.

But on Mars, things were somewhat different. Renewing a prescription at the local pharmacy was simply not an option. Which meant contraception had to be done the old-fashioned way, with an abortion pill. Carina was so whetted to the idea of bringing a newhuman into the world, downing an abortion pill was the farthest thing from her mind following her brief liaison with Fornax.

But what she didn't know, what she couldn't possibly have known, what she never knew until the very moment the baby was actually born, was that she had been wrong all along. *Carina was already pregnant with BC's child even before she and Fornax spent the night together!*

To complicate matters further, Fornax had drawn his own erroneous conclusions as to whose child she was carrying. Though he never once breathed a word to BC about the night he spent with Carina, Fornax assumed the child was his from the start. Thus, it was with more than mere friendship in mind that he had been doing everything in his power to make sure Carina and BC were successful establishing themselves in their new surroundings. Fornax would slip out of Colony One once or twice a week to resupply them — even over Sam's objections not to.

While BC was busy putting the finishing touches on their hut, Carina found herself knitting, something she never would have dreamed possible just two months ago. The cultivation of multicolored cotton had been an integral part of Andean culture for more than a thousand years. Bringing the hardy, mountain plant here to Mars as part of the gene-store repository had been another one of those brilliant decisions the terraformers had made before setting out to colonize the planet. The *algodón nativo* was naturally resistant to insects. It thrived on the eastern slopes of the Andes, a thousand meters above sea level. Carina was only just now beginning to learn how to cure the fibers and spin them into yarn. Sometimes, she even amazed herself.

Once BC finished putting up the sod walls, what he did next was something torn from the pages of The Swiss Family Robinson. Using metal timbers Fornax scavenged for him from the old Mars Base, BC erected a roof for the sod-house, a roof which extended like a canopy some two meters beyond the outside edge of the walls all the way around the house. And, like he had done earlier with the walls, he covered the roof with a thick layer of sod.

The overhang offered several advantages. It prevented even the stiffest of rains from pitting the earthen walls. Plus, it offered the two of them protection of another sort. With no protective ozone layer in the sky overhead, gamma ray radiation was a constant concern, and shielding one's head from it, a daily struggle. The overhang provided them with at least a partial shield. As an added benefit, it also afforded them a pleasant veranda all the way around the exterior of the homestead.

Using downspouts and pipe (also courtesy of Fornax), BC pieced together a rain recovery system. The system provided them with a continuous supply of fresh, running water. The excess was directed to an overflow basin that ultimately emptied back into the Great Sea.

Insulated wall-tiles were laid over the earthen floor. Glass door-panels filled the window openings. Carpet lined the walls, like tapestries hung in a medieval castle, to cut down on drafts. A suntracking solar panel array adorned the roof, supplying the hut with a renewable source of heat and power.

Between what Fornax brought with him on his weekly visits, and what BC himself could scavenge from the inflatable Quonset hut they had been temporarily living in, he outfitted the place with two stoves, three toilet fixtures, a table, four chairs, bedding, clothing, medicine, a supply of dried goods, and a long list of sundries he thought they might need in their new home. The stripped-down Quonset hut would double as a storage shed once they moved out. Finally, to afford the two of them with a measure of privacy once the baby was born, and to isolate the cooking and eating areas from the rest of the house, BC erected four non-sod interior walls, plastering them with a wattle and clay daub covering.

These last jobs, including construction of the roof and inside walls, took a little over a month to complete.

But, finally, it was done. For the first time in many weeks, BC could rest. He had completed a monumental task.

Now, having briefly wrestled the Martian gods of nature to a draw, their experiment in wilderness living was about to begin in earnest.

The two of them were now honest-to-goodness pioneers on an actual prairie, the first untamed prairie any man had tried to conquer in more than three hundred years!

SIX

Summer

Three Months Later

It has often been the case in human affairs that greed unintentionally gives birth to good. This paradox was probably best articulated by the 18th-century philosopher Adam Smith, who hypothesized in his *Wealth of Nations* that an "invisible hand" would operate in such a way as to inadvertently lead the profit-maximizing activities of greedy capitalists to enrich the entire populace. That such a force was at work in the early stages of settling Mars was indisputable. That Fornax Nehrengel was the fuse that lit the runaway explosion of newcomers was undeniable. After mankind's first push into space had failed so miserably, he was the one making humankind's *second* thrust to the stars possible.

It could only be said in retrospect that despite some noteworthy successes at the outset, Man's initial attempt at colonization had been a total bust, accomplishing nothing more than making the moon a convenient dumping ground for the world's nuclear wastes. But, offering promise for the future course of space travel, Fornax identified a means for harnessing this otherwise useless radioactive sludge in a battery, a battery so advanced that crossing the solar system became a trip measured in hours rather than months or years. In no time at all, Fornax's ship, the *Tikkidiw*, became like a *Mayflower* to hordes of courageous people.

Whereas Carina's notion of what role migration might play in human affairs was rather narrow and elitist, Fornax's vision was immense. To be perfectly honest, he had no "vision" at all, at least not in the sense of "grandiose idea" or "master plan." But he could see the commercial possibilities clearly enough. His philosophy was simple: "Keep one hand playing in the dirt," he said, "and the other pushing towards the stars." In fact, with Sam's help, Fornax had a sure-fire way of making money — lots and lots of it.

Even at the exorbitant price they were asking for each empty seat to Mars onboard the *Tikkidiw*, and even without the benefit of advertisement, the partnership of Fornax Nehrengel and Dr. Samuel Matthews had no trouble whatsoever filling the available berths with paying passengers. Each month, on nothing more than word of mouth, a steady stream of eager immigrants found their way, first to Sam's doorstep, then on to Mars. It was exceedingly dangerous work, however; and understandably so. Political refugees numbered among those they transported to this Brave New World. This was unavoidable. As a consequence, it wasn't long before both Sam and Fornax were on the most-wanted lists of half a dozen nations. This included the worst secret police of them all — Johannesburg.

Within a month of Carina's defection from Colony One, three other newhuman huts had begun to take shape in her neighborhood, each new homesteader having passed her signature-gene litmus test with flying colors. First, there was Lotha, a big bestial man who suffered from some sort of bone deformity that gave him an eerie, almost monster-like look. Then there was Nandu, Lotha's frail younger brother, who might have been of the limp-wrist persuasion. Finally, there was Inda, long-haired and slender. Circulating among them were several unattached women, including the voluptuous and seductive Saron.

To Carina's mind, the Afghans were a perplexing lot, bound together as they were by a strict Code of Honor. It was a three-part code, actually — the first element being hospitality, what the Afghans called "milmastia" in their native tongue. This was the obligation to protect — with one's life if necessary — the person and property of one's guest. And, should that guest choose to take refuge with you, it was your *milmastia* obligation to take up his cause as well.

The second element of their Code — the element that got them into constant trouble — was the "badal," the obligation to avenge the spilling of blood. A *badal* was not simply a matter of trading a death for a death, but rather the more singular tooth for a tooth. Once initiated, these revenge-quarrels could last for generations.

Finally, there was the obligation to be merciful. Except for adulteresses, one did not kill women, nor small children, nor poets, nor Hindus, nor priests, nor men who had taken sanctuary in a mosque. And, except where a blood feud was involved — and here only blood money could discharge the debt — mercy was to be granted at the intercession of a woman, or a priest, or one's opponent in battle if he begged for it.

Taken together, the Code provided a moral framework that bound the community into a single, cohesive unit. At the same time, the rigidness of the Code was a sort of tinder which could ignite smoldering tensions into an inferno of revenge and war. Thus, from the start, there was a natural friction between Carina's outpost — Newhuman Town (later shortened to Newton) — and Colony One, the much larger settlement that had sprung up around the old Mars Base to service the refugees, and later, the asteroid movers.

The points of friction were several. Sheer numbers, for one. Relatively few of the newcomers could vault Carina's genetic hurdle.

Wealth, for another. Wealthier newhumans had little reason to abandon Earth for life on Mars. Thus, the ones who *were* willing to emigrate were, for the most part, rather poor.

Attitude, for a third. Many were desperate and disillusioned after a life of persecution back home.

Yet, despite these difficulties, those who *did* come, were here to stay.

A decision was made, after a fashion, to set aside a centrally-located tract of land where a community house might be built. As envisioned by Inda Desai, the self-appointed project leader, this Commons hut would double as a town meeting hall for the Newtons, and as a saloon for everyone else. Of greater importance, the Commons would serve as a place where the tradition-bound men could gather to take refuge from their women — and from their responsibilities.

Whereas it was self-evident to Inda that a retreat of some sort should be built, by the time he hadconvinced enough of his neighbors that the project should be undertaken, the warmth of the brief Martian summer had evaporated, giving way to much damper, cooler weather.

Even so, Inda was confident that, by acting in concert, it wouldn't take the team he had assembled more than a week or so to complete work on the building. In an unexpected display of solidarity, even BC, Sam, and Fornax agreed to pitch in and help. In spite of this air of camaraderie, it wasn't long before the underlying rift separating the two camps revealed itself.

Like all the huts on the planet, the Commons was to be built from blocks of lichen-sod. Only, it was to be much larger, larger than anything any of them had ever built before. In fact, more than a few eyebrows were raised when Inda paced off the corners of the giant building and everyone saw just how immense a structure he had in mind. Not Fornax, though. He had seen Inda's plans ahead of time and had procured a dozen roughhewn timbers on his last trip home, timbers long enough to span the considerable distance separating the outside walls, yet sturdy enough to safely support the heavy, sod-laden roof. When the building was complete, it would vaguely resemble a messhall out of a California gold-mining camp circa 1850, or a loggers' dormitory from the

Brazilian Outback circa 2080. Rustic might have been an appropriate adjective to describe it, or perhaps crude. Still, as the old saying goes, wherever you hang your hat is your home.

Using Inda's thumbnail sketch as a guide, the twelve-man team he assembled set to work at dawn, proceeding with the job slowly and methodically so as not to tire themselves out prematurely. Much as BC had done earlier in the season to build his own sod-hut, the team cut lichen-blocks from the surrounding hillsides. By working in teams of two to four men each, the job went that much quicker.

While the men worked, the women spun yarn. An old Peruvian woman, with chalk-covered hands, showed them all how. To shield her eyes from the worst effects of the sun, the old woman sat under the shade of an oversized umbrella. Her skin was leathery, her voice hoarse. She pulled and plied chocolate-colored fibers from a cone of raw cotton held in place by a large stone. Then she gathered the fibers onto a weighted spindle. The chalk on her hands allowed the fibers to pass smoothly through her fingers.

Though it would take the woman upwards of a month to finish the job, in due time she would have spun enough yarn to make a poncho of the type worn by the men of her mountain community for more than 3500 years. Like her mother before her, and her grandmother before that, the elderly weaver provided her family with clothes, blankets, saddlebags, and fishing nets, all woven from naturally pigmented Andean cotton in shades of rust, beige, mauve, and chocolate.

The *algodón nativo*, as the mountain cotton plant was called, survived at elevations where other varieties of domestic cotton failed. On Earth, it had value as a textile fiber. But it also played an important role in traditional medicine. This was a field of study Carina had recently taken an increasingly more active interest in.

As it turned out, cottonseed was rich in antibiotics, a little-known fact that might have accounted for its wide-spread use in folk remedies. Even so, its primary use was as a fiber, and producing a textile from this mountain cotton was arduous and time-consuming labor.

Several days before it could be ginned, freshly-picked cotton had to be laid out in the sun to cure. While the paler shades of mauve and beige gave up their seeds easily, the seeds of the more fragile rust and chocolate-colored fibers were more firmly embedded and therefore more difficult to gin by hand.

But, once cleaned of their seeds, the locks of cotton were stretched, flattened, then gathered into bundles, some weighing as much as a pound. These bundles were then beaten flat with sticks, folded and beaten again, this time until the fibers became smooth and homogenous. With that step completed, the flattened bundles were then rolled into cones.

Compared to what came before, the spinning process was relatively simple. The cone of cotton was tied to a stationary post or else held in place beneath a heavy stone. Then, holding a weighted spindle in a horizontal or slightly inclined position, fibers were drawn from the stationary cone onto the spindle. To make a finished garment, both cotton and camelid furs were woven together on a traditional backstrap loom anchored to a wall or post.

For several hours this went on, with both men and women working in relative silence, each diligently doing the jobs they'd come here to do. It was not until late in the morning, during the men's first real break of the day, when the women arrived with food and drink, that tempers began to flare. As was so often his habit, Inda was the one to ignite the fireworks. This was a shame because he had been the one who had taken the initiative to spearhead the project.

Sam, the oldest of the group, had kicked back to close his eyes. Fornax, a constant bundle of energy, was cracking his knuckles and checking over their handiwork. BC, strong and good-looking, was scratching at the unshaven stubble on his chin. Inda gestured towards Carina as she approached the worksite in the company of two others. She wasn't yet far enough along in her pregnancy to show much. But the red glow of motherhood was painted like a flag across her face.

"She sure looks good, all knocked up like that," Inda smirked, lighting a fire under the other three men.

Fornax was the first to react. His dark eyes flashed with anger and he reached across to strike Inda with an open hand. BC intercepted the slap before it struck skin, coveting the honors for himself. For a long moment the two men struggled with one another, then Inda laughed a deep belly laugh.

"What is it with you two?" he chuckled. "Can't you see she doesn't belong to either one of you?"

Surprisingly, Inda's remark had a calming effect. Sam opened his eyes.

"You're mistaken," Fornax said, unclenching his fist and signaling for his friend to do the same. "The woman's totally devoted to BC."

"Oh, I don't doubt it," Inda declared haughtily. "But don't forget. This piece of Brit-shit isn't one of us. You are."

"What the hell difference should that make? BC's got just as much right to be here as you do." Fornax glanced across the work area to Sam, hoping the old guy would step in and help. But Sam answered him with a shrug of the shoulders and an irritated frown.

"It makes all the difference in the world," Inda said, suddenly keeping his voice low so the women couldn't hear. He gestured towards BC. "The woman carrying this man's seed is obsessed with making this land a sanctuary, a sanctuary for a new race of people, my people. You've heard her. All she ever talks about is newhuman this and newhuman that. I happen to agree with her. But it doesn't help our cause if she's inconsistent."

"Inconsistent? How?"

By this time, Saron had arrived with a flask of water. BC took the flask from her, then passed it around to the three men seated nearest him. Inda waited until she left, then started again.

"By sleeping with an oldhuman, she defeats the very goal she set out to pursue," Inda barked, drawing Carina's attention. Her look told him to shut up.

"Maybe she likes me," BC said, obviously uncomfortable.

"No doubt," Inda replied, a juvenile smirk smeared across his face. "And what about you, Fornax?"

"What *about* me?"

"You're one of us, damn it! And yet you bring more of . . . of . . . *them*." There was contempt in Inda's voice. From a few feet away, the hulking Lotha grunted his agreement.

Now a new voice was heard, a mature voice made wise by age. For the first time since the heated exchange began, Sam spoke up. "Them. Us. Do you even know what you are talking about? Land's sakes, you fool, can't you see it's all one and the same?"

"That's where you're wrong, old man," Inda carped. "It *isn't* all one and the same. We newhumans just want to be left to ourselves. Only, you and your business partner here are making that all but impossible."

Sam shook his head, grumbled, and climbed down from the half-finished sod-wall where he had been sitting. "Well then, I guess my presence is no longer welcome here. I've seen your kind before, Inda, and they always wind up the same way — skinned and boiled alive in a porridge of their own making. Mark my words, young man. As closed as your mind is, it can only end one way for you — and that is badly."

Obviously upset, Sam shook his head in disgust. He brushed the red dirt from his coveralls, laid his gloves on the sod-wall. "Not only am I tired of your mouth, young man — I'm tired period. Good day to you, sir."

With that, Sam tipped his wide-brimmed hat to BC, and to Fornax, and walked away. Neither man dared stop him, and they stared glumly after as he left. Even Carina said nothing as her father brushed past. Inda just smirked. *Sooner or later he would convince them all that he was right* — no matter what it took!

*   *   *

From the outset, the building of this Brave New World was work, followed by more work, followed by even more work. And, while it was true that the colonists would eventually prevail in taming a small corner of this vast wilderness, it would not come easily, nor be without setbacks. Before that first summer ended, lichen-sod homes had to be chipped out of the hillsides to house the new residents, and, once the provisions they brought with them from Earth were depleted, the struggle to survive began in earnest.

Knowing that to feed themselves the Newtons would have to either trade with the Earth they had just forsaken or else fend for themselves and raise their own crops, most of them opted to give farming a chance.

Initially, with most of the early settlers being from Afghanistan, they had an advantage, of sorts. They had come from a land where centuries of nonstop warfare had leached the soil of its few precious nutrients. Plus, they were held together by the teachings of their Code of Honor. Having somehow managed to scratch out an existence from the miserable soil and poor growing conditions of their homeland, these immigrants were stubbornly convinced that if grains could be raised in Afghanistan, they could be raised anywhere, including Mars.

Yet, as these would-be farmers soon discovered, raising crops on Mars took a bit more than simply dropping seeds in a furrow and praying to Allah that they take root.

In the first place, the settlers had to experiment with Earth-bred grains to determine which ones would actually grow in the thin Martian soil. Some, like corn, would take root but never mature. Others, like wheat, would wither, never producing a ripened grain. The crops indigenous to North America fared poorly, whereas others, like barley and squash, did well. Experimentation and ingenuity were the key.

In the second place, hundreds of man-hours had to be expended before a new field could even be opened for cultivation — removing boulders, big and small; stripping lichen from elsewhere in great quantities and plowing it under as mulch; harvesting cow or llama dung as fertilizer, then spreading it over the areas to be sown.

Lastly, the soil was itself a big question mark. Even use of the word "soil" to describe what covered the ground bordered on the absurd. As compared with the rich loam covering great hunks of the third planet, what covered the surface of the fourth was more of a pebbled sediment nearly devoid of organic content. In some spots, its consistency was more akin to sand; in others, more like clay.

But neither the ruddy sand nor the red clay held moisture well, and crops planted in the sandy areas, especially, were liable to having their roots exposed in the face of a harsh wind or persistent rain. The soil was fragile, like the cryptobiotic soils of central Utah, and the alternatives few. One promising solution was to employ a technique used on Earth with great success for thousands of years, that of contouring their fields.

The technique was simple. A two-foot-wide strip of lichen was left untouched, a strip that ran down the entire length of the field. Next to it, the homesteaders planted a three-foot-wide strip of squash and barley. Then, by alternating strips of lichen with parallel strips of crop, the farmers proceeded in this fashion across the entire width of the plot. This arrangement was not only successful in arresting the worst effects of wind erosion, it also prevented even the most punishing of rains from washing out an entire crop.

A second technique, which worked with equal success, was one based on the Anasazi approach to farming practiced on the high mesas of Colorado and Arizona. By stacking pebbles around the base of each stalk, the settlers fashioned a protective mound that simultaneously prevented the plant from washing out in a heavy rain or losing the thin veneer of topsoil from which it drew its nutrients. As the Anasazi discovered, certain hardy plants like the wild strawberry and the mountain yucca took hold easily and provided variety to their diet.

As with so many things in their life, sowing and harvesting was done almost exclusively by hand. The same held true for transforming their harvest into usable foodstuffs like bread and soup. In fact, about the only aspect of farming on Mars that was more pleasant than farming back on Earth, was the weeds — or more accurately — the *lack* of weeds.

If a weed could be loosely defined as any opportunistic green plant not expressly put in the ground by a human being, the 3000-year-long history of agriculture could be thought of as one long battle to exterminate these pesky, unwanted intruders. The remedies man designed over the centuries for eradicating these undesirable pests were affectionately known to farmers as herbicides, and they varied in strength from the merely toxic all the way up to the wildly carcinogenic. Thankfully, Martian life was still too new — still too young — to have spawned any herbs requiring such genocidal treatment.

There was something else quite un-earthlike about Mars. It had no insects, at least not yet. The terraformers had been very selective in this regard.

Nor were there any lethal diseases. Mars had been a completely sterile body before terraforming began, and, in the meantime, Fornax had been particularly careful about who he had let come aboard his ship. While it was true that everyone who could afford a ticket was ultimately sold one, no one was permitted to leave Sam's estate and get onboard the *Tikkidiw* until they had been subjected to three separate bio-screens. These rigorous toxicological tests were capable of ferreting out any of a thousand possible contagions, from viruses to bacterium to fungii.

Now, make no mistake about it. No one believed Mars would remain sterile forever. It was a mathematic certainty that distinctly Martian diseases would eventually arise. Bacteria and their ilk were, after all, far and away the most successful class of organisms on Earth, and had been since the inception of life.

No, no one believed that Mars would remain forever sterile. But, with only one medical facility on the planet and only one part-time nurse on call, great care had to be taken to prevent the outbreak of something serious. Here on Mars, in a tiny community, the results could be devastating. Just witness the Black Death of the 1300s back on Earth, or the fast-mutating AIDS epidemic of the twenty-first century, or even the arrival of Nile Disease in 2341. All were caused by relatively simple microbes which ran amok, and for which no ready cures were available. All wreaked terrible havoc upon the fragile human race.

Still and all, there was some hope that Mars might remain disease-free for a long time. The constant rain of gamma-ray radiation from the sun acted like a cauterizing oven, baking nearly every unprotected microbe into harmless dust. The downside to this was the risk which arose from the capacity of this energetic form of x-ray to produce genetic mutations. Unlike Earth, Mars had no everpresent ozone layer to screen out the harmful rays. Therefore, the residents had to wear single-density bodysuits at all times, plus lined, wide-brimmed hats when they were outside. Of course, this made for a certain uniformity in their dress — sort of like an entire planet of Pennsylvania Dutch — but it did protect them from the threat of deadly skin cancers.

Of the one or two exceptions to the "no insect" rule were those considered absolutely necessary for plant pollination. Take the mountain yucca, for example. Its pollen was too moist to be carried by the wind. It required an insect of the order *Lepidoptera* — the yucca moth — to do its dirty work.

When the yucca moth moved from plant to plant, laying its eggs, it also obliged its host by transporting its pollen. Though many yucca plants were stemless, the ones adapted for life on Mars had a woody trunk eleven meters tall. Sword-shaped leaves grew in clusters at the tip of the stem, and bell-shaped flowers grew in the center of each leaf cluster. The flowers were whitish-green in color. At night, when the flowers opened, they emitted a strong odor. It was this odor which attracted the yucca moth on which its life-cycle depended. Once pollinated, the yucca bore a tasty fruit that contained hundreds of small black seeds.

At one time, long ago, Amerinds used the yucca plant for food and for clothing, even weaving nets from yucca fiber. As versatile as the plant was, the necessity of introducing moths into the Martian ecosystem had its drawbacks. Unchecked, their larvae were capable of transforming millions of tons of plant matter into animal matter. Thus, the long-eared bat had to be introduced as well. At night, when the moths were active, these capable winged-hunters would take their turn at the top of the food chain, protecting the colonists' fledgling crops from destruction at the hands of the moths. As on Earth, each member of the ecosystem had its role to play.

Espousers of philosophy, down through the ages, have theorized that the collective life of communism would naturally follow in the hollow footsteps of capitalism's demise. In practice, though, it was the other way around. It was the indigent pioneer societies which began in a communal state, graduating only later to the maturity of capitalism. Mars was a prefect example of this progression, and the ownership of farm animals a case in point.

At the outset, steers and horses were in such short supply, the early settlers of Newton had no choice but to share these highly-prized chattel whenever there was work to be done, such as tilling the fields or dragging away the unending stream of boulders. While, in some distant future, the thousands of square kloms of open grazing land might lend itself to a healthy stock of both animals, in the present, this forced sharing of resources was a source of constant friction.

And, to complicate matters further, it quickly became apparent that both the bovines and the equines were ill-suited for life on Mars. The temperature extremes were too violent, and neither animal found lichen to their liking. Fortunately, it wasn't long before the colonists learned of a sturdy ruminant that appeared to *relish* the taste of lichen, so much so, that in short order the most prized pack animal by far was neither cow nor horse, but camelid — the llama.

Prior to the arrival of Euros in the New World a thousand years ago, the llama and its cousin, the alpaca, were indigenous only to South America. Having originally sprung from the same lineage that produced the modern camel (hence the term, *camelid*), the evolution of the llama was obliged to follow a different path when tectonic forces broke up Gondwanaland and South America was separated from Africa. Although both creatures were suited for survival in marginal conditions, the llama evolved away from its camel-ish cousins, adapting to the cold of the Andes, where it grazed on the relatively-thin mountain vegetation. Domesticated by the Incas, they soon became so popular with the Euros that by the end of the twenty-first century, llama herds in SKANDIA, Zealand, and Canada numbered in the hundreds of thousands.

By the time Newhuman Town was established here on Mars, it was a foregone conclusion that the llama would eventually have to be introduced as well. And it was a fortuitous decision, because the llama was well-suited to cope with the Martian climate and vegetation. All that was required to make the llama fit in was a tiny adjustment in its genetic code, one that would allow its naturally-thick fur to shield it from overexposure to gamma-ray radiation.

Other than that, the llama was a perfect choice for Mars. Not only was the animal capable of carrying heavy loads for long periods with practically no water and little food, it was hearty and sure-footed. Plus, the animal was long-lived and fecund. Alpacas, for instance, gestated for just under a year and could live for anywhere from fifteen to twenty-five earth-years. Under normal circumstances, a herd of seven could grow by four or five a year, more once the offspring started reproducing.

In time, the llama would become a stable (if somewhat chewy) supply of meat, an inexhaustible source of wool, a reliable mode of transportation, and a highly-valued producer of organic fuel. In fact, between the llamas and a coterie of other farm animals, the settlers were soon on their way to solving two of their most pressing agricultural needs — a lack of credible farm implements and a shortage of fertilizer.

The horse became the engines that moved the plows. The cows, a prodigious source of badly-need mulch for enriching the nutrient-poor soil. And the llamas — their compact feces dried and pressed — a supply of combustible fuel to heat the settlers' dank and drab huts. Unlike other cultures that had used animal spoor in this fashion, the Newtons were a bit smarter about it. By burning the excrement in an outdoor furnace, heated water could then be circulated around the inside of the hut giving off radiant heat in a practice reminiscent of what the Euros had done in their homes for centuries.

Yet, in spite of all these innovations, during the fledgling early days of the settlement, life was still unmechanized and brutally hard. Each day was an unending river of work flowing seamlessly into the next. For the time being, only the tempo of the weather ruled their existence, determining the success or failure of their crops, and even of their lives.

And, it was only following the harvest, when the farmers were driven indoors to endure the worst of the Martian winter, that work could take a holiday, and only then because leaving one's hut at that season was suicidal.

SEVEN

Winter

Late One Afternoon, Two Months Later

As BC made his way back up the boulder-laden path, he solemnly hummed the traditional BeHolden Day hymn. The words he cherished came to him easily. "Oh, beautiful, for spacious skies, for amber waves of grain . . . "

Although, by Earth's calendar, it was nowhere near the fourth Thursday of November, the approach of winter here on Mars reminded him of the one holiday he had always loved, the one holiday that was so distinctly American, the one holiday he had looked forward to even as a little boy in the orphanage.

BeHolden Day could count as its antecedents the American tradition of Thanksgiving, plus a host of English harvest festivals dating back a millennium. Because of its universality, the tradition quickly spread to a thousand other cultures around the globe. Whereas in the smaller towns and simpler families it was still a genteel and civilized affair faintly reminiscent of its twentieth-century cousin, in the larger cities the holiday had degenerated over the years into an ugly caricature of its former self. Sure, the oversized turkey was still there, along with all the trimmings. But, nowadays, it was an orgy of engorgement, an orgy marked by excessive eating and immoderate drinking. In some circles, these bouts of overconsumption were followed by ancient-Rome-like rounds of forced regurgitation, a spectacle that was even a matter of some pride. The would-be throwers-up would line the streets with buckets in their hands and compete for distance or else volume. And, if that weren't enough to mar the solemnity of this once holy celebration, by nightfall, widespread brawling would erupt in pubs throughout the land.

Now, as BC climbed ever higher along the rocky path back towards the top of the cliff where his very pregnant companion waited dinner for him, he could only hope that on Mars, BeHolden Day would once again become the dignified occasion it had been on Earth so many generations ago.

Pausing, now, in his tracks to scrape a chunk of red ochre clay from his boots, BC thought back on everything he had accomplished these past seven months. The work had been physically punishing. The blocks of lichen-sod. The assembly of the hut. The thin air. The wet conditions.

Since first agreeing to follow Carina into the wilderness more than half a year ago, BC had been tested in ways he never dreamed possible. But now, at long last, with winter close at hand, the hard work was finally behind him.

BC moved further along the trail. Ahead of him was a huge boulder he had taken advantage of before. The big, flat stone was like an old friend, and he leaned against it, deliberately cocking his wide-brimmed hat a notch further back on his head. Many times he had stopped here a moment to rest his weary body and enjoy the view from halfway up the cliff.

Now, through tired eyes, he contemplated the glow of the setting sun, its feeble rays glancing eerily off the churning ocean surf far below him. Across the way, a handful of tiny pines struggled to gain a foothold in the red sand and gravel. Every once in a while, the silence would be broken by the bark of a dog or the incoherent bleat of a young farm animal — a sheep, perhaps, or maybe a newborn llama. The air was thick with the pungent smell of mountain yucca, and every once in a while he had to brush away one of the many moths that would swirl around his head when he stood still.

The faraway roar of crashing surf lulled BC to the edge of consciousness. He slipped ever closer to sleep, unaware that someone was approaching him from higher up on the trail.

Suddenly, the sound of a boot striking against flat rock jerked him awake. BC spun around and, with instincts oiled to respond, clenched his fist, ready to strike. He was greeted by the turn of a familiar face.

"Honestly, Sam, you scared the hell out of me!" he exclaimed, settling back onto his boulder.

"Nice to see you, too," Sam answered, smiling. The rambunctious tenor in his voice made the man seem younger than his days. Actually, BC had no idea how old Samuel Matthews really was, though from what he'd been able to gather, the old coot had to be in the neighborhood of sixty.

Sam was tall and fit and, regardless of his age, his eyes still gleamed with a certain youthful mischievousness. His hair, uncombed as always, was graying at the temples, and it seemed to BC as if his lean body was a bit rounder than before. At least Sam was smiling, something he hadn't been doing the last time they saw each other. But smile or no smile, something told BC that the man's health was deteriorating, an unusual condition for a fellow so far from the century mark, when such problems were commonplace.

The two men shook hands warmly, then Sam spoke. It was as if they had resumed a day-long conversation after a brief interruption. Sam gestured with a flair towards the open expanse of ocean which lay before them.

"Did you know that the English word for water has an interesting etymology?"

"Sam, you should know by now that I couldn't give a hoot about your silly word histories."

"You're an uncultured rascal."

"And you're a pompous ass."

Sam laughed. So did BC. He was happy to see the old fellow again. Ever since father and daughter had their falling out over the establishment of Newhuman Town, relations between the two had been strained. Sam's visits to see Carina had been sporadic — and for the most part unwanted. This was his first since that day he left the Commons jobsite on account of Inda's insolence.

Sam wasn't prone to losing his temper. But when the Commons was raised without further need of his help, it took him quite a while to work up the courage to come by again. When the Commons was finished, it was a masterful job. The rub was, since Inda had been the one to spearhead the project, his position in the community had risen appreciably. This irritated Sam no end.

He continued, now, with his word history. "The word water comes from the Germanic 'wasser.'" Sam rolled the w on his tongue, making it sound like a v. "But that's not the end of it — wasser itself has an antecedent. It derives from the Hittite word 'watar,' spelled w-a-t-a-r. Going back yet *another* step in time, we find that watar is rooted in the term 'yotor' from an even *earlier* proto-language."

BC scratched his head in confusion, offered Sam a seat next to him on the big boulder. "Where in the blazes are you going with this, old friend?" BC asked, his face wrapped in a frown. As was so often the case with Sam's daughter, sometimes BC couldn't make heads nor tails of the older man's train of thought.

"I was just wondering what the Martian word for water will be in, say, five hundred years. Word histories fascinate me no end, you see. Consider the English word 'milk'. As a noun, it means that stuff you get from a woman's breast or from a cow's udder. As a verb, it means 'to suckle'. The English didn't invent the word, however. It came from a people they conquered, or perhaps from one that conquered them."

"Have you no sense, man? What a ridiculous notion! I've never heard of it, not in the history of the world! Who could have ever conquered the English, for heaven's sake?"

Sam smiled. The boy was smart; but not educated. BC had spent his earliest years confined to an orphanage in the Hawaii Free State. Even so, BC's best memories were of England, where he grew into a man. Indeed, he now thought of himself more as a Brit than anything else. Nonetheless, he obviously knew precious little of English history and found Sam's suggestion that Britain had once been overrun, an insult bordering on the ridiculous.

BC focused his cold, blue eyes on Sam and repeated his question. "Tell me the truth, Sam. The British are one damn, tough race of people — who could ever have conquered them?"

"Numerous peoples, my good friend. But don't take it so personally, the list is long."

"How long?"

"Well, let's see. To name a few: the Romans, the Vikings, the Normans, the . . . "

"Okay, already."

"In all fairness, I should point out that the Normans were nothing more than Viking descendants themselves," Sam elaborated in his usual professorial style. "But back to the point I was trying to make earlier."

"Which was?"

Sam continued, rolling his tongue with each foreign word he uttered. "In German, milch is milk. In Latin, mulg-ére means 'to milk.' In Hungarian, mell means 'breast.' In Arabic, mlj means 'to suck the breast.' In Old Egyptian, mnd means 'woman's breast.' Now, if you trace all these etymologies back to their common ancestor, you'll come to an extremely ancient root MALIQ'A, whose meaning can be roughly translated as 'to swallow,' or in some translations, as the noun 'throat.' Even in the New World, the Amerinds who migrated east along the coast from Eurasia, brought the word-idea of milk along with them. The Halkomelem tribe of Canada had mə̆lqw meaning 'throat.' Oregon's Tfaltiks had milq, 'to swallow.' The Mohave, malyaqé for 'throat.' The Akwa'ala in Baja, California, had milqi, meaning 'neck.' In Panama, the Cuni had murki, 'swallow.' In Equador, mirko, 'to drink' . . . "

"Whoa, slow down there, Tex," BC jibed, squaring his hat back down on the center of his head. "No wonder your daughter is such a nutball. With you in her gene pool, how could she miss? Now seriously, Sam — what the hell point are you trying to make?"

Sam smiled and nodded his head knowingly. "Don't you see how alike all these words are? The chances that such word-resemblances arose independently are vanishingly small."

EIGHT

Rift Valley

"Has my daughter finally become a mother?" Sam asked as the two men scrambled up the steep trail towards the collection of sod-huts known as Newton. In the thin Martian air, only minutes passed before Sam was panting to catch his breath.

"In more ways than you can possibly imagine," BC said, waiting patiently beside the fatherly old fellow until Sam was ready to move on again. "But if by that question you mean to ask whether or not she's developed any irksome habits, I would have to answer in the affirmative."

"I didn't know her mother long enough, God rest her soul. But I believe every woman alive has the capacity — nay, the tendency — for nagging. I think it's those two oversized X chromosomes. Unfortunately, it's only the truly enlightened ones who can overcome this terrible, inbred curse. And it's a shame, really, because as a race, women are a genuine delight to be with when they're young."

An audible sigh escaped Sam's lips as he privately debated the accuracy of his assertion. Satisfied that he hadn't overstated the case, Sam started up the trail again, this time ahead of the younger man. He sidestepped a pile of llama spoor, then, around the next bend, the llama itself. "Confounded animals," he swore. The beast spit at him, as if with contempt.

"Well, maybe it'll get better once the baby is born," BC said, with hopeful conviction.

As he spoke, BC crossed his fingers and held them up in the dim light for Sam to see. Silently Sam returned the gesture. Then, with nothing more to add, the two climbed the rest of the way up to BC's hut without exchanging another word.

It was clear from the get-go that a wide gulf still separated father from daughter. Sam had sworn years ago, when Carina was still just a baby, that he would never let anything come between him and his little girl.

And yet, despite his best intentions, something most definitely had. Now, here he was, faced with this ponderous philosophical chasm that was keeping the two of them apart, and — as a father — he felt it was his responsibility to try and bridge the gap. In fact, patching things up with Carina had been the sole reason for his visit here this evening. Sam was determined to work things out with his daughter, no matter what it took. Still, as he stood there in the cold, his knuckles poised against her door, how he wished he could have turned back the hands of time, back to a day when he could still make her understand how foreign her newhuman ideas were to him, how repugnant they were to his own beliefs about mankind and humanity, how he found her obsession with having a separate newhuman colony ethically, if not morally wrong.

"May I come in?" Sam asked, when Carina answered his knock.

"If you wish," she replied coolly, scolding BC with a frown for bringing her father by uninvited.

"I won't stay long," Sam promised, recoiling as he spied his daughter's dour expression. Staring past her into the musty room, Sam could see her dog Sandy scampering across the floor. The dog was unaccustomed to having strangers in the house.

"Suit yourself," Carina snapped, turning her back on her father and retreating into the dingy sod-hut. Sam followed her with his eyes.

Although BC could be justifiably proud of the accommodations he'd been able to scratch out of the wilderness for him and Carina, spartan would be a generous term to describe their circumstances. As Sam thought of his own, quite expansive home back in Zealand, and his own rather substantial material wealth, he recoiled ever so slightly at seeing the place these two called home. It had never occurred to Sam that his daughter could be happy in such pedestrian surroundings.

Sam stole a quick glance at Carina's pregnant belly and opened with what he hoped was an innocuous comment. "Honey, I happen to know a very good OB in Auckland. When the time comes, I'd be happy to . . . "

"When the time comes, I plan on having the baby right here. BC will deliver it."

"You can't be serious," Sam bellowed, turning to BC with anger in his eyes. "Are you crazy, young fella? I don't mean to run down your medical abilities, BC, but you're not a doctor, now are you?"

"No apologies necessary. Carina and I have been over this a hundred times already. She knows very well that I'm only a medic. But that daughter of yours can be very insistent. She even has me practicing C-sections on a humaniform doll over in the Colony One Hospital, just in case the little bugger is breech and can't be turned."

As BC delivered Sam his explanation, his brow crinkled with doubt. He had been unable to change Carina's mind on this child-delivery thing, and that irritated him no end. BC was used to getting his way. He'd made a life of working alone, of vanquishing dangerous adversaries. But never once had he had to deal with anything like this. Oh, he'd killed men with knives, with guns, ropes, his bare hands, even poison. But never once had he had to cut into someone he loved, not for any purpose, not even for the delivery of his own child — *it just wasn't in his nature!*

Like every Commonwealth field agent, BC had undergone the requisite medic training. Nevertheless, his practical experience was limited to setting the occasional broken bone and stitching up the occasional knife wound. And, except for that one time when he had been forced to cut open a fellow officer's belly to extract a delayed-fuse bullet, BC had never performed anything more complicated than emergency field-surgery.

He explained all this to Carina in some detail a month ago. When, for the umpteenth time, he balked at doing the C-section, she reacted in a way that still shocked him.

First, she slapped him hard across the face, insisting he was capable of pulling this surgery off if only he would try. Then she locked him out of the hut without a coat, leaving him there to freeze in the cold until he relented. All the while, she stood on the other side of the door screaming at him that she would rather die here on Mars giving birth to his son than be transferred earthside for the delivery. With blue lips and chattering teeth, BC gave in, in under an hour.

But then came the hard part, learning how the surgery was actually done. Though the ordeal was somewhat traumatic, the large and diverse medical Library left behind by the first batch of settlers proved invaluable to his efforts.

When Colony One was disassembled and moved to its present location, the medical portion of the original Library was incorporated into the new hospital. It included not only dozens of medical texts, but also holographic videos detailing each and every step of countless medical procedures.

The reason for this archive was simple enough — the first settlers had to be completely self-sufficient. There would be no returning home in a medical emergency. Nor would there be any medical bots to depend on for assistance.

No, if the settlers were to survive, they had to have the means for handling such things on their own, right there on Mars. The 3-D holographic videos gave them that means. By allowing a viewer to see an operation from every angle, to even be a "participant" in the surgery if he so choose, to practice it over and over again until he got it right, the colonists were never more than a view-screen away from solving even the rarest of calamities.

And so it began. With medical text in one hand and laser scalpel in the other, with one eye on the 3-D video and the other on Carina, BC began rehearsing. Time after time he practiced the Caesarean procedure on a sophisticated humaniform medic-doll. Time after time, until he got it right. Injecting the anesthetic. Cutting the doll open. Suturing it shut. Injecting the anesthetic. Slicing it open. Sewing it shut. Checking the vitals. Applying the Acceleron to speed the healing. Over and over he practiced, his anxiety growing with each repetition.

Now, as Sam stood in the doorway of BC's hut, questioning the young man's ability to handle this surgery, it all came rushing back. BC couldn't help but wonder all over again whether he was up to the task.

"Land's sakes!" Sam boomed, his eyes darting nervously from one to the other. "You're both out of your minds! Here you are camping out on the prairie like a bunch of pioneers from the seventeenth century, when just down the road a couple of kloms is civilization. Damnit, daughter, I don't understand what you're trying to prove!"

Disrespect filled Carina's voice when she answered. "What I'm trying to prove, Daddy Dear, is simply this: In order for an entirely new species of human to develop, it is absolutely essential it be physically segregated from the old species. The circumstances here on Mars are precisely analogous to the situation eons ago in Africa, when several precursor races of primates populated the continent."

"Honey, we've been through this before," Sam interrupted testily. "Isolation is not a necessary condition for speciation. Being the most able fish in the pond doesn't matter one wit if the pond should suddenly dry up. Why must . . . "

"Now listen! You asked me what I was trying to prove here, so why don't you just shut up and allow me to explain."

Chastised, Sam fell silent. Carina continued. "About eight million years ago, a tectonic crisis arose which sunk the Rift Valley and gave birth to the line of peaks that now form the western rim of that canyon. The breach and the barrier disturbed the existing circulation of air. It divided the extensive region into two distinctly different biological zones.

"The west remained humid. The east became ever less so. The west kept its forests and woodlands. The east evolved into an open savanna. By force of circumstance, the common ancestor of man and chimpanzee found itself divided. Now, under the influence of altered selective pressures, the two groups diverged.

"The western descendants of these common ancestors adapted to an arboreal life in the humid milieu, giving rise to the genus *Pan*, the chimpanzee.

Meanwhile, the eastern descendants of that common ancestor invented a completely *new* way of life, adapting to a more difficult existence out in the open. This second group of creatures gave rise to the *Hominidae*."

"The Homin-*what*?" Sam spluttered. He had completely forgotten how technical his daughter could be once she got going. Sometimes he lost sight of the fact that Carina had been one of the youngest women to ever be granted a Ph.D. in biogenetics from the university in Auckland.

"Hom-ah-ni-day," she repeated, mouthing the syllables as if reading from a dictionary. "Our particular branch of the primate tree was cut off from the rest of the tree by virtue of its geographic isolation. The subsequent genetic divergence was driven by the need to adapt to the drier, more barren habitat of the savanna."

Sam's voice rose an octave in impatience. "And on the basis of all this mumbo-jumbo I'm somehow supposed to understand why you left Colony One to be on your own?"

"If only you'd just let me finish!" Carina growled, her demeanor that of a spoiled child. "Later on, when the whole Earth cooled and eastern Africa became even drier some three million years ago, a *further* adaptation became necessary. Less vegetation meant developing the ability to scavenge for other sources of food. It was at this point that some of our truly remarkable innovations arose. Upright posture. The opposable thumb. A larger brain capable of making use of a more opportunistic diet. With the need for catching meat came greater mobility, and for the first time in history, hominids began to spread out from their humble origins in Africa. These early creatures were the *Homo erectus*. Later, they were replaced by a second wave of strictly modern humans about a hundred and fifty thousand years ago. This wave eventually gave way to the races we see today."

Carina continued. "What's important to understand here, Dad, is that this succession of beings has been — and continues to be — an ongoing process. Now comes the newhuman to replace the old. If you think about it, the Rift Valley Theory of Evolution is merely a variant on the situation found so often on islands, a situation Darwin himself observed in formulating his remarkable theory of natural selection. And, if you think about it, it is precisely that thinking which led me to my decision regarding newhumans here on Mars. All I want to do is separate old from new. Is that so hard to understand."

"Yes, it is," Sam replied, fidgeting uneasily. "When I asked what you were trying to prove, that was a rhetorical question — I never expected an answer, and certainly not a lecture. But since you've chosen to deliver me one, let me tell you why I find your reasoning so hard to fathom. Carina, no man is an island. Humans thrive on interchange. Civilizations atrophy without it. In the past, every time a small group of human beings have settled on an island, where they were isolated from the mainstream, the outposts have withered, sometimes disappearing altogether. The Norse settled Greenland, and later, Newfoundland. The mutineers, Pitcairn Island. The Polynesians, Easter Island. It always ended the same way — with stagnation. Land's sakes, child, look what happened here on Mars the first time around."

"Yeah, but that was different, and you know it."

As always, Carina did her level best to derail her father. She edged closer to the radiator running along the base of one wall, and warmed herself. The ultimate source of heat for the hut was a stove that burned llama-spoor as fuel. The heat was carried, not by radiating warm air, as had been the case with one-room log-cabins in the American West, but rather by circulating warmed water through baseboard pipes.

Sam wasn't put off that easy. "This segregationist idea of yours is nothing more than the same sort of racism that killed your mother."

"That isn't fair, Dad, and you know it. Anyway, we've argued this one before."

Carina disappeared into the next room for an instant, to get a cup of piping hot cocoa from off the stove. She made no move to share it with either BC or her father. All she said was, "Racism? Perhaps. Genocide? Absolutely not."

"If not racism, if not genocide, then what? Utopia? Is that what you're after, Carina? Utopia?"

"And why not?"

"Let me tell you a little something about utopia," the father said. He was offended that his daughter hadn't offered him something warm to drink. "To begin with, the word itself means 'no place' in Greek. That alone should tell you something. Plato's *Republic*, written way back in the fourth-century BC, is generally regarded as the earliest and greatest work in the genre, although the Garden of Eden story, as described by the Hebrews in the Torah, might also be considered as one. The term itself was first coined by Saint Thomas More in the 1500s when he published a philosophical piece by the same name. In it, he depicted a perfect society sited on an imaginary island. All the social, political, and economic evils afflicting humankind had been eradicated, and the State functioned only for the good and happiness of its citizens."

"What's so wrong with that?" Carina asked, never failing to surprise her father with her naiveté.

"Really, Daughter, you can't be serious," Sam chided, looking at the ever-silent BC. "From about the nineteenth century on, numerous attempts were made to actually establish utopian communities. Most were experiments in some form of utopian socialism, though a few regarded technological progress and large-scale economic organization as being of utmost importance. The founders of these communities — while they differed considerably in their specific views — all uniformly believed that their ideal societies could be created without much difficulty, starting with nothing more than the formation of a small cooperative community made up of loyal followers. Utopian thinkers set up experimental settlements in Europe and in the United States. Perhaps the most famous was Robert Owen's cooperative in New Harmony, Indiana. Like I said, most of these enterprises did not survive long, although one of the most enduring was the Oneida Community of New York, which lasted more than three decades before folding. The utopian socialists were later eclipsed by more militant radical movements — Marxism in the twentieth century; Rontanians in the twenty-third. No matter what you think, Mars is no Shangri-La."

"But it could be."

"And do all the other colonists share your enthusiasm for this newhuman stuff?" Sam questioned pointedly.

"I'd like to think so. But even if they don't, I can tell you this much — every individual living here in Newton has submitted to a blood test and a gene-print and, without exception, every single one of them is carrying a pair of signature genes."

"Including BC?"

"There's no need to test him — he's with me!"

"I see. And what if someone refused the test? What then? Or what if someone took the test, expecting to pass, and flunked instead? What then?"

"It hasn't happened so far," came the meek reply.

"But what if it does, Carina? What then?"

"I'd have to ask them to live elsewhere."

"Who died and made you God?" Sam snapped. "What if they *refused* to leave?"

"Then I'd have to use stronger language."

Her tone was cocky, and it irked Sam. Carina downed the last of her cocoa, then reached down to pat Sandy. He stood between her feet, wagging his tail.

"All I can say, Dad, is since it hasn't come up yet, it's useless for me to waste my time worrying about it. Will there be anything else?"

Now her tone told him that he was being dismissed. This angered Sam further.

Obviously livid, Sam turned to BC. Up until now, the younger man had judiciously stayed out of the argument.

"And just how do you fit in with all this?" Sam asked. "I'm amazed, son — how can you stand to live with this woman? You're not even one of the chosen people!"

"Don't I know it," BC grumbled, disquieted by the ease with which Sam had brought it all into such sharp focus. "But believe me when I tell you, Sam

— I've got my reasons. Ask me again sometime, and I'll try to lay it all out for you."

Sam shook his head. He had heard enough. In his pocket was the bottle of expensive perfume he brought along, intending to give Carina as a peace offering. Now he changed his mind.

"Well, I'm out of here," Sam said. "I have someone else to see yet today."

"And who would that be?" Carina asked, a tinge of jealousy creeping into her voice.

"That would be Saron," Sam replied, knowing how just the mention of the woman's name would get a rise out of his daughter.

"She's nothing but a whore! A bimbooker!"

"That may be. But bimbooker or not, Saron would never have failed to offer me a warm drink on a cold day like today, something you did not."

Sam turned to BC. "Walk me out, son, and I'll tell you a little something about the word 'bimbooker'. It has an interesting etymology, you know."

"Here we go again," BC sighed as he took Sam's arm and led him across the room to the door of the hut.

"Be patient. Be patient, and perhaps you'll learn something. I have much to teach, my boy."

NINE

Saron

Never in his entire life had Sam been more anxious for a long rest than he was right now. For months already, he and Fornax had been shuttling back and forth between Earth and Mars, delivering shipload after shipload of people to the Red Planet, people desperate to escape their miserable lot back home, people eager for a new lease on life. It was honest work, but tiring. And there was a downside. He and Fornax were now being hounded by people wanting to put a stop to their operation.

Sam was tired of being constantly on the move, and it wasn't long before he found himself physically and mentally exhausted by the effort. Clearly, the man needed a rest, and despite his daughter's hardhearted attitude, he intended to use the occasion of the upcoming birth of his grandchild as an excuse to sit out a few months and winter-over on Mars. Besides, he was most anxious to learn more about the progress of the two settlements since this bold experiment in colonization first began.

While hundreds of people from many walks of life had already emigrated to Mars — a few joining up with Carina as residents of Newton, the great majority joining up with the opportunists of Colony One — Sam was especially eager to see how the first batch of Afghans had fared since their arrival on Mars nearly eight months ago. Not only had the Afghans been the first ones here, Sam himself had been the one responsible for convincing them to come.

As Sam quickly learned, the formation of families in Newton had, for the most part, followed the ancient Afghan traditions. Though times had certainly changed from the days when Afghan women were mere chattels of their men, and though women no longer wore the all-enveloping "chadhuri" garments so typical of their nomadic roots, Sam found it disconcerting to see that there was still a setting apart of the women from the men in their meals and upbringing.

He had already gotten a taste of this setting-apart that day when the villagers came together to raise the Commons.

In all fairness, though, things had improved markedly for the females since the old days. Back then, it was not uncommon for an Afghan nomad to tattoo his women with the same mark he put on his sheep. And to think that in this day and age Zealander women still accused their Aussie husbands of being chauvinists. Hah! If they only knew!

Of special interest to Sam was a young Afghan woman named Saron. Despite Carina's disparaging remarks about Saron and her profession, Saron remained one of the few unattached females on the planet, much to Sam's good fortune. He had been without a woman himself a good many years now, and was uncommonly lonely for companionship. Even if that meant paying for the privilege, Sam was simply happy to have someone to be with, no matter what the price. Saron was that someone. Her given name was Surasundari, "darling of the Gods" in her native tongue. A bimbooker by trade, Saron was doing a land-office business from her bed. Somehow, despite their differences in age, despite their obviously different outlooks on life, the two of them got along. She and he enjoyed a special relationship.

Sam had explained the meaning of the word to BC on the way out the door that day. "You see, my friend: the word bimbooker has a fascinating history well worth recounting."

"Must we?" BC groaned.

"To begin with, much of its meaning becomes immediately clear if only you pronounce it correctly. The word isn't *bim*-booker, it's bimbo-*hooker*. One who gives pleasure. A female vendor of pleasurable escapes, generally of a sexual nature, but frequently including narcotics and other diversions. The term is actually a compound word first used by Vander Logsdon in his heavily censored novel *Pleasure and Pain* circa 2200, a book in which the author linked the words 'bimbo' and 'hooker' together into a single derogatory term he used to describe the novel's heroine."

"Well, excuse me for being a dumb-ass Brit. But I've never heard the word 'bimbo' before. What the hell is a bimbo?"

Sam enjoyed having his ego stroked, and he was only too happy to oblige with a further explanation.

"A bimbo is a woman of loose morals. A floozy. In the nineteenth century, a punch made with cognac or possibly with rum, was referred to as a 'bimbo,' probably from the Italian 'bombo,' which was a child's word for drink. Another derivation has it coming from the Italian word for silly — 'bambo'. Like the progression that occurred with the word 'tart,' from a small fruit pie to a prostitute — both being delectable, I should imagine — the idea of a potent alcoholic punch may have come to be naturally applied to a saucy, loose woman.

Another possibility is that this particular drink made a woman silly or looser sexually."

"You don't know for sure?"

"Are you pulling my leg? Etymology is not an exact science."

"Then why study it at all?"

"Some learning is for learning's sake. Besides, it's history, and we all need to know from whence we came. Take you, for example. I know you were raised in an orphanage. Haven't you ever wondered who your parents were, or why they gave you up for adoption?"

"Life has never afforded me the time to think about such things. Anyway, at this age, I guess it's a little late to be worrying who my father was."

"It's never too late, my boy, never. But I would be happy to step in, in a pinch."

"I'll keep that in mind."

"Don't mention it. Now back to bimbo. In its first known use, bimbo meant just another pretty face — someone without any brains — and it could be applied equally well to members of either sex. In fact, initially, it was used to describe a fellow who was unimportant or undistinguished. Later, it underwent a gender shift."

"What the hell's a gender shift?"

"It's common in our language. What once applied to a boy is later applied to a girl. Or vice versa. Brothel, for example, originally meant 'worthless fellow'. Then it came to mean 'scoundrel'; then later, 'prostitute'; then later still, 'house of prostitutes'. A 'harlot' was originally a 'vagabond' or 'knave', both male terms.

"The use of the word bimbo to describe a sexually promiscuous woman or tramp caught on in the popular literature with the Depression-era detective novels which perpetuated the stereotype of the beautiful but dumb blonde who was taken out for a night's entertainment in exchange for granting sexual favors. By the end of the twentieth century, the term had become more generic, meaning simply an attractive woman viewed by others solely as a sex object. The more modern meaning is, of course, in the context of bio-bimbo, a genetically altered woman built to service more than one man at a time."

By this time, BC was frustrated with Sam's explanation and politely excused himself to return to the hut. Sam understood — he was lonely and liked to talk. This wasn't the first time he had bored someone to tears. Anyway, he had a full day ahead of him. So he meandered down the hill towards Saron's place.

Though Sam never quite understood why this fine woman felt compelled to sell her body in order to make a living, he made no moral judgment. To the contrary. No matter what labels her detractors tried to pin on her, Sam was overjoyed to find a few hours solace in the woman's arms each week. In fact, whenever the loneliness of winter started to get him down, he would seek Saron out.

Sometimes, Sam would have to wait his turn. Saron had a large and diverse business, one not limited strictly to just the Afghan men or even to just the men of Newton. Colony One'ers came to her all the time, and for one very good reason — unattached women were in terribly short supply. Like any commodity in short supply, price was high and selection limited. Which allowed this enterprising young girl to charge nearly any price she wanted for the service she provided. It also gave her the privilege of being very discriminating in who she serviced, something Saron took quite seriously.

But with Sam, everything was different. Although their first liaison cost him the bottle of perfume he originally intended to give Carina, what began as a professional relationship soon evolved into a thriving friendship. Sam was a whiz with money, and he helped her invest her profits in the stock market back home. In front of paying customers, Saron referred to him as uncle or grand-uncle; he to her as niece. From most men, payment for her services was either in cash or, more often, in terms of barter. But when Sam was particularly down or lonely, like today, she would offer to do him for free. It went without saying that he was sworn to secrecy about these freebies under threat of having more than just his privileges cut off.

"Uncle, you're early," Saron said, when she came to the door. It was snowing outside, but the woman was dressed like it was summer, in a nightie and cotton slippers.

"I can wait outside, if need be." Sam was hesitant, almost bashful.

Saron licked her lips with the tip of her tongue. The way she licked those lips, it was a lewd act, probably illegal in half the galaxy. She invited him in, took his parka, hung it behind the door. His face looked long and drawn.

"Just couldn't stand to be away from ole Saron, eh?" she teased, trying to lift his spirits.

Sam broached a tentative smile. He looked at Saron. The courtesan was a dark-haired beauty, perhaps twenty-two years of age. She was endowed with a lithe, cat-like frame and a worldclass bosom, the sort of woman that no matter how many times a day she consummated the act, each coupling was a new adventure. Her current profession notwithstanding, Saron had attended college in Sydney before being drawn into the Resistance as an Afghan freedom-fighter, and later as a colonist to the Red Planet. In the short time he'd known her, Sam had always found the woman to have as ready an ear as a body. Tonight, there was little doubt as to what she had on her mind. She kicked off her slippers, approached him clad in nothing more than a scant, silk nightie.

"I only came to talk," Sam said, meekly resisting her advances. But even as he untwined her arms from around his neck, he couldn't help but notice how wonderful she smelled. There was always something irresistible about a woman fresh from the shower.

"Saron knows what will make you forget all about talking." She cooed wantonly, undid the ties that bound the left half of her nightie to the right. As she did so, her golden orbs started to work themselves free of the sheer material.

Sam protested, held up his palms as if he meant to push her away. "Honestly, I really did only come to talk. And since I'm paying for the hour, I really ought to be able to use it any way I please."

"Suit yourself!" she snapped with mock anger. She twisted the ties of her nightie back together. But her breasts visibly protested their confinement. "What's happened?" she said. "Why are you so sad?"

"It's my daughter," Sam said, sinking down into his favorite chair. No matter how rustic or simple a home, as long as there was a chair he could call his own, Sam always felt welcome.

"Her again?" Saron groaned, knowing how much Carina could infuriate him. "The way you let that girl under your skin, you'd think she was your wife, not your daughter."

"You would have liked her," Sam mumbled, his eyes glowing with the smoke of a distant fire.

"Who?"

"My wife. Nasha. She was an Amerind. A beautiful woman. Like yourself." His short sentences were punctuated with emotion. "Sometimes you remind me of her. The way you carry yourself. That gorgeous dark hair. That same clean and wonderful smell. Like you just stepped out of a shower."

Saron's feelings seemed bruised by the revelation. "Is that why you keep coming back to me? Because I remind you of *her*?"

"Maybe a little, I suppose. But don't draw the wrong conclusion. I cherish each and every moment we spend together."

"So tell me, dear Uncle Sam. Besides being obviously very pregnant, what in the world is the matter with Carina now?"

"The girl has this crazy notion about starting a new race of humans, a race separate, yet superior, to the existing one."

"Yes, I've heard her lecture," Saron noted, coming over to sit down next to him. Taking Sam's hand in hers, she gave him her full attention.

"What do you make of it?" he asked. Unlike some men Saron knew, Sam was genuinely interested in her opinion. She appreciated this about him.

"Your daughter is right," Saron replied without hesitation.

Sam wasn't expecting this. But before he could react, she added, "And she is wrong."

"How so?"

Saron explained. "She is correct in the sense that, over long periods of time, separation does lead to the formation of new species. The example of the Rift Valley Carina is so fond of talking about is a good case in point. But as right as Carina is on the separation issue, she is wrong on no less than three other points."

"You have given this some thought, I take it."

"Plenty. In the first place, speciation cannot occur in as short a time as she envisions. It takes a thousand generations, not one or two. Secondly, by using just one set of genes as the sole criterion on which to base her conclusion — these so-called signature genes — she is being too narrow in her approach. As Carina herself has written elsewhere, Explosive Diversity is what leads to radical new lines, not slow change."

"You've read her book?"

"I've been to college, you know."

"I didn't mean to imply that you were uneducated."

"No, of course not. Now, where was I? Oh, yes. Point number three. Newton's too close."

"Come again?"

"Newton's too close. There's nothing to prevent the two gene-pools from mixing. Old and new can still have contact. The only correct modern analogue to the African Rift Valley scenario is for the newhumans to settle on a completely different planet. As it stands presently, there's just too much opportunity for the inhabitants of the two colonies to have sexual intercourse. There's no way for Carina to ever get the clean gene-pool she so desperately wants. For this to work, she and her followers will have to leave the Red Planet altogether."

"Land's sakes, girl, don't tell my daughter that — she just might!"

"To the contrary. Carina wants everyone *else* to leave. And, while we're on the subject, I think some of her band might just be crazy enough to try and make that happen. I've heard talk in the Commons of sabotaging the mining operations ASARCO is setting up here."

Sam was stunned. "That can't be more than just idle chatter, can it?"

"I think it's more than just idle chatter. I hear it more and more often lately. Especially from Inda and that big beast Lotha."

"It figures with those two," Sam said thoughtfully. "Now don't get me wrong, Saron. But in your line of work I know you're privy to a great many things. Promise me you'll tell me right away if you learn of anything concrete. Anything that sounds particularly alarming, anything at all. As a Councilman, it's important I be apprised of any such developments."

"Your wish is my command. Now, are we done solving the problems of the world?"

The devilish twinkle in Saron's eye said it all. For a second time tonight, she undid the clasps of her nightie, permitted her breasts to fall free of their restraint. She took his hands, placed them over her nipples.

"It's time for me to be done," she said, eager for the game. "And it's time for you to do the doing."

"Your wish is my command," he echoed, planting his hands on her hips and letting her nipples dance against his chest. They were hard, hard like river stones.

His lips moved from her mouth, to her neck, to her chest. It seemed to him that no matter how many times her breasts entertained his hands, and his mouth, they never lost their firmness.

Making love was like riding a bicycle. Easy to learn. Hard to forget. In the many long years since Nasha was taken from him, Sam had had precious few women. It wasn't that his enthusiasm for the sport had diminished, only that as a single father opportunities had been few and far between. With age he had lost some of the vigor he once enjoyed as a younger man. It took him longer, now, than he would have liked, to reach the point of climax.

The delay didn't seem to bother Saron in the slightest. To the contrary. She rode him that night with great vigor for nearly half an hour. In the middle somewhere, they switched positions, and with him on top now, she coaxed him to fruition, stroking his genitals with her hands even as she reached the point of collapse herself.

Despite the gathering tempest outside, Saron's body was all the warmth a man needed. It was as if the entire galaxy were a frozen tundra and she the sole source of energy powering the stars and the planets.

Afterwards, when they were done and fell apart, their energies spent, he lay there staring out her window contemplating the frozen land only inches from his face. The first cold winds of winter were just now taking aim at the prairie on the other side of Saron's heavy wooden door. Sam shivered at the thought of what was to come. Rain. Sleet. Snow. Wind. Ice. Drifts two-stories high. Cold that could crack the hardiest soul. Inland, away from the Great Sea, it would be worse. But even here, near its shores, the severity of the weather could be daunting.

This surprised Sam in an unusual way. He carried with him many fond memories of his youth. As a boy he had summered at a Boy Scout camp in Wisconsin, not far from two of America's greatest freshwater lakes — Michigan and Superior. Sam knew from experience how, in the summertime, a large body of water like Lake Michigan tended to absorb the heat of the season slowly, and how, in the winter, it shed the accumulated warmth begrudgingly as well. The overall effect of this gigantic heatsink was to moderate the temperature extremes along Michigan's shore all year-round. It only made good sense that the Great Sea of Mars should act likewise for the two colonies, allowing the stored heat of summer to dull the edge of the ensuing Martian winter.

But for all the sense that explanation made, it didn't seem to be working out that way. As far as Sam could tell, precious little moderation was taking place. In fact, the intensity of the Martian winter still made his memories of a Calgary January seem tame by comparison. This itself was remarkable, considering how, at the time, Calgary's weather seemed brutal next to the mild Missouri winters of his childhood.

Sam had grown up in the rural nowhere that was Missouri in the late twenty-fourth century, a place where people still had no reason to lock their doors at night, where tall corn and echoes of Mark Twain filled the summer landscape, and where a thin blanket of snow was about all one could expect from a winter storm. When, at age eighteen, Sam emigrated to Canada at his grandfather's behest, he was flabbergasted by the sorts of squalls that repeatedly came tearing out of the Rockies, riding the so-called Siberian Express. And yet, Mars was still in a class by herself. Indeed, winter on planet number four was far worse than any Siberian nightmare Sam could have ever imagined. And twice as long! Even the hardiest of Afghans found it astonishingly cold.

Living on the Martian tundra was harsh at best. And surviving the long winter, a questionable enterprise. During the summer, the primary focus had been on animal husbandry and raising enough grain to keep the livestock alive through the winter. Now the primary focus was on staying warm.

In most cases, a farming unit consisted of a cluster of houses and outbuildings loosely encircled by a fence or crude stone wall. Typically, the main dwelling was a long, rectangular structure built either of sod or wattle and daub interwoven with branches and twigs then covered with clay. At one end were the living quarters and at the other, llama and cattle stalls. The arrangement was crude. But, by living in close proximity to the animals, the colonists gained a welcome source of heat during the cold winter months.

For those settlers not fortunate enough to have a hot-water radiator system as BC and Carina had, an open hearth, raised above the earthen floor in the center of the living quarters, supplied heat as well as some light. Elevated platforms along the side walls accommodated both seating and sleeping near the fire. Most houses lacked a chimney, having only a hole cut in the roof to let out the smoke. Thus, in this one long room, the farm family cooked, ate, entertained their friends, churned their butter, worked their looms, fashioned keen edges for their blades, treated their sick, had sex with their mates, and slept until morning.

The short days and bitter nights meant months of confinement in a small, damp hut. Confinement with a set of bored and cranky children starved for exercise, sun, and fresh air. Confinement with a wife that, on occasion, the husband might have wished had been ejected from the *Tikkidiw* without benefit of a parachute before the ship fired its thrusters to land on Mars. Let's face it — no matter what any love-struck poet may once have written in some book, it was a sobering fact of life that even the most happily married of men could only take so much "wife-ing." Oh, most women meant well enough, it was just that the vast majority of them didn't know when to shut up. Indeed, some men would argue their wives didn't know *how* to shut up. In those instances, the wives would have been wise to remember that if their husbands had wanted mothers for wives, they could have stayed at home with the one they were born to.

In contrast with the hard labor of summer, when every man, woman and child ended the day too exhausted to make trouble, the boredom of winter made for rebellion and drunken excess; the confinement, a sure recipe for domestic violence. While, on the one hand, the Afghan Code of Honor provided the sinew that bound the people together, its rigidness encouraged social pressures to build up beyond a healthy level. Sometimes, these emotions could explode with zealous fury, and knowing this, Inda Desai had had the foresight to try and remedy matters ahead of time. He was a natural born leader. By bringing the men together as a cohesive unit to build themselves a place they could call their own, a "Men Only" Commons, he hoped to defuse these passions before they could spin out of control. Sam could see the sense of it now, where he couldn't earlier.

The Commons was meant to be a place of refuge during the long Martian winter, a place where the men could escape both their wives and the weather, a place where they could do manly things like brawling, when necessary — and even once in a while when *not* necessary — plus drink and carouse until morning. Naturally, having an outlet saved a score of marriages and probably prevented a couple of murders as well.

To a newcomer, the Commons would be hard to describe. It was a strange mixture of British pub, American pool hall, Italian brothel, and Aussie saloon. The lighting was poor, and the smell could knock a man back ten feet. Try a locker room following a rugby game. Your team has won. All the players have showered and hung up their sweaty socks to dry. Beer is everywhere. So is tobacco. That was the Commons. And despite the "Men Only" policy, one woman was always welcome there — Saron, darling of the Gods. During the long winter and into the spring, it was the one place where she could profitably ply her trade. And, judging by the number of customers lined up outside her door each day, she must have been good at what she did. No matter how grumpy a man was upon entering the premises, he always emerged with a smile.

In no time at all, Saron had become the self-appointed proprietor of the Commons. Without any discussion, and with no one putting up much of a fight, Saron simply took over operation of the building, livening the atmosphere with her candles and homemade perfumes and serving up a strangely intoxicating brew of her own design.

Flocking there even from Colony One, every man on the planet knew Saron's bosom was winter's only warmth, and her special ale the only thing worth drinking. It began with barley she raised in a greenhouse the men built for her just behind the Commons. After the barley sprouted, she converted it into malt, mixed in hops and other spices, and brought the whole thing to a boil in a brewkettle. Then, after being taken outside and fast-chilled in a Martian snowbank, she placed the drum of beer in a fermenter, where she pitched in the yeast. This part was fun, and Sam helped her do it on more than one occasion.

Now came the magic of chemistry as the tiny cellular creatures went to work, eating the simple sugars already in solution and excreting the carbon-dioxide and alcohol which gave the beer its potency. This step took three days at seventy degrees Fahrenheit. But the process was still not complete, as ten days of aging at forty degrees was yet to come, as well as the final filtration and carbonation. Only then would the beer be ready to rent to her customers — and for a good price to boot.

Considering all that was involved in its manufacture, it should have come as no great surprise that as demand for Saronale grew, so too did the number of colonists she came to employ in this, the second oldest profession on the planet. Saron, enterprising young woman that she was, was quickly on her way to cornering both markets.

And at each step of the way, Sam saw to it that she expanded her portfolio of stockholdings back home.

TEN

Baby

The signs that she was about to give birth were unmistakable. Nothing was in proportion, all setbacks were unmitigated disasters, bright green was drab, blue was magenta, and pictures of the seashore made her cry. Strange enzymes, with unpronounceable names, had been running amok in her body for weeks now and she was simultaneously too hot and too cold, with ankles stiff and swollen, bladder constantly full, and sleep impossible. There was a titanic rush of energy accompanied by a bout of dementia. In other words, everything was just as it should be.

A short while afterwards, and despite one false start, her labor began in earnest. For several hours it proceeded as the medical text said it should, with the contractions becoming ever more frequent and more pronounced. But then, all of a sudden, for no apparent reason, the intensity of her labor mysteriously leveled off. Within a quarter of an hour, it had ceased altogether.

Women know their bodies in a way men never can, and Carina was mentally prepared for this possibility. By contrast, BC found it unnerving. The problem wasn't that he was at a loss what to do — he had, after all, spent the better part of the past three weeks honing his skills for just this contingency — it was more that having to confront the sudden reality of doing a Caesarean section on a woman he loved, was a terror of the nth degree.

For a moment, the virile, good-looking man was gripped by a fear unlike any he had ever known. Beads of anxious sweat pooled up in his palms. The sickening taste of dry fear clogged his throat. His pulse quickened. The blood vessels in his head throbbed, pulsing with each beat of his racing heart. Then, just on this side of hyperventilation, BC shook it off, his iron will reasserting command.

Focusing his mind, now, on the job before him, the former Commonwealth agent began to recount the steps he had to take. Step One — Perform A Holoscan. Step Two — Get Her To The Colony One Hospital. Step Three — Do The Procedure.

Though it seemed obvious the baby was breech, BC couldn't be absolutely certain until he did an f-photon holoscan. It was the twenty-fifth century's equivalent of an MRI, but at a hundredth the size and without the million-dollar price tag.

He reached into his medi-bag, now, for the inexpensive, handheld instrument no larger than a standard-sized comm, then pressed it flat against her abdomen. Thirty seconds later, BC had his answer. *Instead of being head-down, the infant was presenting butt-first.*

BC's first thought was that maybe he could turn the baby. This was often the optimal solution if the birth canal wasn't too narrow.

Moving into the center of the room, BC projected the 3-D holoscan where they could both see the image. Then, using the straight-edge function, he measured off the dimensions of the baby's skull. He did the same with the width of Carina's pelvic cavity, measuring the narrowest point, and compared the two. It was just as he expected. Even if he could reach up inside her to physically turn the baby, the child's skull was simply too large to pass through Carina's narrow hips and out her vagina.

Which brought him to Step Two — Get Her To The Colony One Hospital and Prep Her For Surgery.

The road from Newton to Colony One was little more than a rutted path, the ride in the half-track bumpy and uncomfortable. Her water had broken and she was already partially dilated.

With one hand on the wheel and the other on the shortwave, BC tried repeatedly to raise the resident nurse on the radio. There was no answer.

BC cursed her absence. But it couldn't be helped. The nurse probably had to answer an emergency elsewhere.

BC didn't waste any time. As soon as the two of them arrived at the doors of the hospital, he helped Carina into a wheelchair and rolled her upstairs. Once there, he set straight to work.

He began by steaming all the utensils he would need for the operation. This would kill whatever bacteria might be lurking about. Into the pot went the scalpels, the staples, the needles, and the forceps. While they cooked, he positioned two overhead lamps and an operating table where he wanted them, then boosted Carina up onto the table beneath the lights. Tired from her earlier unsuccessful labor, she lay back on the shiny, white table exhausted. The skin of her swollen belly was drawn taut, its elastic fabric seemingly stretched to the limit.

BC gently scrubbed the area where he would have to cut. As he did, he could feel the impatient baby kicking at him from inside Carina's womb. The sponge tickled her skin. She giggled at the touch.

Her laughter put him at ease, and as BC reached for a tube of poly, he returned her brave grin with one of his own.

Bioelastic materials were particularly good as tissue replacements because, depending on the polymer chain, they could be made in a wide range of consistencies, from gelatinous to rubbery to rigid.

But of even greater importance, elastic sheets of poly were simply ignored by the immune system. Thus, they were perfect for sealing an incision shut, leaving behind nothing but the tiniest of skin discolorations, where a cut had been made.

The bell on the steamer rang, signaling that his instruments were fully sterilized. From the cabinet next to the door, BC took out a laser cutting-knife plus a syringe-full of Acceleron. He slipped on his sterile gloves and lined up his tools on the worktable in the precise order he had rehearsed when practicing this routine with the holographic video.

He rolled his worktable up next to the one Carina was already laying on. Images of the humaniform doll BC had trained on flashed through his head.

Drawing a deep breath to flush the adrenaline from his system, BC tapped into some deep reservoir of internal strength for the confidence he would need to see his way through this ordeal. Up to this point, the two of them had exchanged barely a word.

"Are you ready?" he asked, maintaining his calm.

She rocked her head in the affirmative, flashing him her best I-know-you-can-do-it smile. "It's time," she said. "My water has broken. This baby we made needs to be born."

Signaling his agreement with a tight smile, BC started down the list of carefully memorized steps to put her under. In many respects, administering the anesthetic was even more dangerous than the actual cutting. Too strong a dose would lower her metabolism, inviting coma or death. Too small a dose, and her body would wake screaming as her brain felt the pain of his incisions.

Knowing this, BC took his time. There was no use rushing a procedure as crucial as this one.

The drugs quickly took effect, and as they did, he carefully monitored her reaction. He gave her swollen tummy several tentative needle pricks to be sure she was out. Only then did he pick up the laser scalpel from the worktable.

He marveled at the tool. What a wonderful magic, modern technology. No pain, no blood, no infection.

With slow and deliberate precision, BC made the first cut. Her soft, pink flesh peeled away at the touch of the laser beam.

But then, unexpectedly, blood spurted everywhere.

Aghast, BC lurched backward, banging into the worktable and sending his sterilized tools clattering to the floor. Something was desperately wrong! *There wasn't supposed to* be *any blood!*

The way the tool was supposed to work was that the high-energy ray of the laser scalpel was supposed to cauterize the wound as he went. *Only the damn thing seemed to be malfunctioning!*

BC wiped the blood from his face with the sleeve of his gown. Phlegm filled his throat. He fought back the urge to vomit. *Think, man, think!* What could have gone wrong? What damnit?! There *had* to be an explanation!

BC racked his brain for an answer, struggled to remember his lessons. This had come up once before. He had seen this in one of his practice sessions! Too much blood? *Increase the knife's cauterization rate.*

BC reached for the calibrated dial. He urged it to the left. The splishy sound from the blood-removal tube rose. This meant the machine was functioning properly, clearing the excess fluid from the site of the incision.

"Yes!" came the staccato cheer.

BC exhaled. An audible sigh of relief escaped his lips. He had figured it out. Problem solved. Time to move ahead.

Yet, even as he prepared to resume the operation, adhering to the carefully rehearsed script he had drilled into his head these past weeks, his doubts grew.

A real doctor would never have attempted such a procedure on his own, not without a bot at his side, not without having first mastered the procedure by assisting an experienced surgeon dozens of times before.

A real doctor would have had at least one, if not two or three nurses at his side, to hand him the scalpels and the pads and the sponges and the needles, to wipe his forehead if he needed it, even scratch his balls if he had an itch.

A real doctor would have had a trained anesthesiologist to constantly monitor the patient's heartbeat and pulse and respiration at every moment of the operation, a person trained to respond instantly if the patient faded or if the newborn met with complications.

A real doctor did not reside on Mars. Nor even did a full-time nurse. It was all up to one badly shaken medic, Bartholomew Collins, better known in these parts as BC.

The man shut out his emotions. He blocked out his fears. He did what was expected of him, cutting deeper into the woman he loved with the laser scalpel.

The skin and underlying muscle separated far more easily than he expected, and he instantly felt the hard, distended shape of the womb. He massaged the big muscular organ with his hands, felt yet another surge of panic welling up inside of him — *The baby wasn't moving!*

During the course of Carina's pregnancy, BC had spent countless, joy-filled hours watching her tummy bump up and down as the baby — *his* baby — kicked and swam and did backflips inside her.

Countless times he placed his palm on her abdomen and felt the tremors of movement within. A pregnant woman lives with that motion inside her all the time. Before long, it becomes *part* of her.

But for a man, that motion is a constant source of wonder and amazement. To a woman, life begins when she feels that first kick upside her ribs. To a man, life begins when the kid takes that first, wonderful crap all over his brand new white shirt. But now, all of a sudden, *he felt nothing!*

"My God, what have I done?" BC exclaimed, as if the walls could answer. "What the fuck have I done?"

Believing that he had somehow killed his own child, BC's lips fell silent. He calculated the possibilities: *If the baby was dead, could Carina be far behind?*

BC scolded himself. *How stupid could he be?* Why the hell had he let her talk him into trying this stunt to begin with? Why hadn't he taken her back to Earth for this thing, like Sam suggested? How could he have been so foolish?

BC shook his head. He put his anger aside and pressed on. Precious minutes had been lost — *he had to move fast now!*

BC stole a glance at the monitor to check her vitals. They were strong. That was good.

Moving with alacrity, now, he sliced through the muscled wall of the uterus. He reached into the cavity of the womb with his hand, thinking that perhaps the baby wasn't dead after all, that perhaps the anesthetic had knocked the baby out along with its mother.

Hopeful once more, BC gently pulled the infant from its womb. He couldn't help but notice the presence of a tiny prick dangling from between the legs of the newcomer as he tugged the child free.

"A boy!" he gasped, his eyes brimming with tears. "A son!"

While BC would have been equally delighted with a daughter, he was not unlike most men, who wished their firstborn to be a boy.

But then again, what did it matter, so long as the child was born healthy and alive?

Hardly able to suppress his excitement, BC placed the boy under the comforting warmth of the heating lamp until he could finish up with Carina.

Then he charged ahead on automatic pilot. When it was over, a minute or two later, and he was caressing the pruned face of his new son and doing his best to choke back a few anxious tears, he couldn't remember cutting the cord, or setting the boy's breathing into motion with a sharp spank, or filling the incision in Carina's belly with poly before stapling it shut, or monitoring her blood pressure, or conducting the APGAR test, or watching for signs of shock or of hemorrhaging, or performing all the tasks of a full surgical team, with near perfect precision and almost textbook timing.

All he could remember thinking was that perhaps this was what fatherhood was all about.

When Carina came to, she squeezed his hand and choked out a hoarse, "Thanks."

He shushed her off to sleep before she even had a chance to ask to see the baby. At the time, he thought nothing of it — there would be plenty of time for bonding in the morning.

*   *   *

The night was short and miserable. Carina kept complaining that she was in a great deal of pain.

Seeing her suffer, BC was wracked with guilt. He imagined that he had done something wrong after all, that her pain was somehow his fault, the result of a surgical blunder, that when it was all said and done he had been a fool for not taking her to a hospital back on Earth to have this done.

BC re-counted the sponges, the scalpels, the needles, the staples, thinking that perhaps he had slipped up and left one behind inside her. He did it twice, then twice more. Each time the count was perfect.

He replayed the delivery in his mind, step by step, thinking that perhaps he had forgotten to stitch something closed.

Yet, each time he thought back through it, he always came to the same conclusion: he had done everything right — there had been no mistakes — he hadn't overlooked a thing.

Still, there she was, in pain, and there wasn't a damn thing he could do about it. Like her father and her uncle, Carina was allergic to all the major classes of painkillers. Which left her no choice but to stick it out cold turkey.

That's why, up until now, at 4 a.m. in the morning, she hadn't even asked to hold the boy. Finally, as the sun peeked above the horizon, she propped herself up in bed with great effort and coughed out a feeble, "May I see my baby?"

"I thought you would never ask," BC replied, happy to finally have something to divert both their attentions away from her discomfort. For hours now, he had been shuttling back and forth from mother to baby, and he was exhausted.

"The kid's gorgeous," he bubbled, doing his best to forget the long night as he went into the adjoining room and rolled the crib up next to Carina's bed. "Looks just like me," he announced proudly.

Despite her delirium, Carina found his comment rather curious. Months ago already, she had the amniotic fluid tested for signature genes. There was no doubt about it. The baby was definitely newhuman. BC couldn't be the father, at least not based on what he had told her about *his* ancestry. No, the father had to be Fornax. And if that were true, there was certainly no way the baby could have resembled BC. Fornax was swarthy, with deep dark eyes and a mop of jet-black hair. BC was an Anglo-Saxon-type, with blue eyes, fair skin, and flaxen-colored hair. There would be no confusing the two men in a bar or anywhere else for that matter.

"Isn't he beautiful?" BC beamed, presenting her with a fair-skinned, blue-eyed, ten-pound baby boy. "What shall we name him?" he asked, proud as a father could be. "Have you given any thought to Sam, Jr.?"

Carina's face went white when she saw the child. "Oh, my God! I . . . he's . . . "

BC instantly knew the truth. Sam had been right about the baby all along, only with an awful twist, a twist the elder Matthews could never have anticipated. She *had* had intercourse with Fornax. Worse yet, she *had* expected the baby to be his! Worse still yet, she had used BC in the most horrible way imaginable — coaxing him into building them a place to live, playing with his emotions, turning him into her personal slave, forcing him to do this operation. And, through it all, *she believed she was carrying the seed of another man!*

BC exploded.

"You didn't think I was the father, did you?" he screamed in an accusatory tone.

"Whatever do you mean?" Carina said, feigning innocence. Even at this late date, she was still toying with him.

"Don't play games with me, you conniving woman!" he ordered, a fierce look coming into his face. "After all I've done for you, I deserve some straight answers!"

"I s'pose," Carina said, reaching reluctantly for the child. She put it to her breast in an amateurish fashion. If not for the tension between the two adults, it might have been a heartwarming scene.

Carina made a half-hearted attempt to explain herself. "You were gone, remember? You said you would be right back. But you never *did* come back. I thought you were dead."

A tear came conveniently to her eye. "Fornax arrived that day. With my father and the others. You weren't with them. It was anybody's guess what had happened to you. I swear, BC, it only happened that once."

BC stared at her hard but did not reply.

"I swear. It only happened that once."

"Why should I believe you?"

"Why should I lie? I've been faithful to you ever since."

"Sam tried to warn me."

"Warn you? The nerve of the man. He's my father, for God's sake!"

"And I'm your lover. Yet you kept the truth from me," BC exclaimed as he paced nervously back and forth across the tiled floor of the recovery room. "You thought this kid was Fornax's, and yet you led me to believe it was mine. Why?"

"I don't love him," she said, hoping to soften his anger.

"But you don't love me either, do you?" he asked, posing the question that had vexed him from the beginning.

"Do I have to answer that?" she asked, burping the baby over one shoulder. Her milk had just barely begun to come in.

"You already have," he concluded crestfallen. "You already have."

"Love doesn't come easily to me," she stated matter-of-factly.

"Easily? Let's face it, Carina — you love only one thing."

"Oh, and what's that?"

"Yourself."

"I have a mission, BC, you know that. My importance to mankind supercedes even my own personal happiness."

"Oh, how very noble of you," he declared disdainfully. "You aren't going to start with that Lucy crap again, are you?"

"It's not crap!" she said, finishing with the baby and lowering him gently back into the crib. "You know as well as I do, Lucy is little more than a shorthand name for an idea. Four hundred and fifty years ago, on a hillside in Ethiopia, anthropologists uncovered the skeletal remains of a female hominid forty thousand years old . . . "

"Yes, yes, yes. You've told me this damn story before. They were so excited by their find, the team worked throughout the night, digging the fossil out. To keep their minds focused on the job at hand, they played their favorite song over and over again on their portable audio-machine — 'Lucy In The Sky With Diamonds'. By morning, the precious fossil had acquired the nickname Lucy."

Carina smiled. "And here, all this time, I thought you weren't paying attention. After the remarkably well-preserved bones were dug up and studied, it was concluded that she constituted the oldest skeleton of a distinctly modern human ever found. Lucy was declared to be the first of her kind — the mother of a new race — and all *Homo sapiens* are thought to be her descendants."

"And now along comes you. Only *you* think you're the mother of the *newest* primate line, the newhuman line."

"Exactly."

"You're daffy."

"Don't you think it's a little conceited for us to assume that primate evolution conveniently ceased with our species?"

"Don't you think it's a little conceited for you to assume that you're the *matriarch* of that new race?"

"Not at all," she declared, thinking she had made her case.

"Well, that's all well and good," he said, moving closer to the crib. "But my patience isn't infinite. In fact, I don't even think I belong here."

"I've known that from the beginning," she replied icily.

"That's a shame. Because I did not."

All of a sudden, BC made up his mind. He reached into the crib, wrapped the baby snugly in a blanket, and walked out the door. She barely raised a protest as he left.

Though BC wasn't exactly sure where he was headed, or how he would manage to get there, he was certain of two very important things. First: Carina had been so ambivalent about motherhood, the child would never be safe with her. Like a spider that eats its young or a Rontanian who commits infanticide, it was anybody's guess how she would have treated the boy.

Second: BC himself had grown up in an orphanage without benefit of having ever known his mother. If that upbringing was good enough for him, it would be good enough for his son. At least the boy would have a father, something BC never had.

Sam wouldn't stop him — he was wintering-over with Saron. And Fornax? Fornax owed him one. Maybe more than one. Even if BC had to break the man's arm, he would convince Fornax to take him and the boy back to Earth. And Carina? May he never see her again as long as he lived!

*   *   *

Carina had watched BC walk out of her life, yet she had been powerless to stop him. No sooner had she put the baby back in the crib after attempting to breast-feed him, than her abdomen was wracked by a set of contractions rivaling labor pain in their intensity. This was part of nature's "get-back-into-shape" program: breast-feeding stimulated the production of certain hormones which helped flatten the mother's tummy. But, between those contractions and the lingering pain of surgery, she found herself in agony, too weak to speak, too weak to stop him.

Not that it mattered, really. Carina didn't actually believe BC had what it took to leave her. In fact, as she lay there early that morning waiting for him to return, it wasn't his leaving that troubled her as much as it was something else.

For the life of her, Carina couldn't understand what had gone wrong with the signature gene test she performed on the baby's amniotic fluid. As far as she could figure it, there were only three possibilities.

Either, the test itself was unreliable, something she seriously doubted. Or, she had somehow contaminated the sample, perhaps with a drop of her own blood — also highly unlikely. Or, horror of all horrors, BC was himself a newhuman.

And, if it were the latter, then only two possibilities made any sense. Either, the gene had spread faster and further than she initially thought. Or, BC's ancestry was a lot more complicated than he knew or let on. Either way, she would get some answers when he returned.

Only he never did.

ELEVEN

Spring

Sunlight streamed in through the window above her head. Animated, Carina sat up, yawned lazily, and peered out at the world beyond her door. A smile came to her face. Something was different today, new and different. The transformation had been so glacial, she had hardly noticed it. The seasons had changed. Suddenly, winter was gone, and what had arrived to take its place was something novel and unique.

Thanks to mankind's tampering, winter on the Red Planet was no longer the year-round phenomenon it had been for a thousand million sunrises. Nor was the planet even actually red anymore. With the terraforming of Mars now essentially complete, something vaguely resembling spring followed winter.

But it was an emasculated spring, watered-down and dilute. Mars lacked the enormous variety of life-forms that earthlings took so much for granted. Thus, the cacophony of noises which marked the onset of a terran spring were absent here on Mars. There were no chirping robins, no buzzing bees, no belching frogs, no biting flies. And yet, even without all these things, the advent of spring on the fourth planet was special in its own right.

With the long dormancy of winter finally at an end, there were buds upon the trees, and rivers of mud upon the ground. Once again, fields of alpine flowers dotted the meadows. Once again, the rhythm of the agrarian way of life ruled each day. Once again, the bleating sounds of farm animals filled the air. The cud-chewers mooed, the egg-layers cackled, the newborn sheep squealed, the two-toed ruminants spit. The farmer next door — having just slipped on a turd of wet llama dung — cursed.

But the most enduring sound of the season, by far, the one which could bring tears to a settler's eyes, was the roar of children's laughter. Somehow, they too had survived the ugly confinement of the dreadful season just ended, and the renewed opportunity to run wild in the vernal fields satisfied what could only be described as a singularly human hunger.

Yet, spring was more than merely the end of winter. It also marked the rebirth of the human spirit. Just as the thick, spring sap rose up from the roots of the trees into their trunks, so too did it rise up into the trunks of the settlers. This was true not only in a strictly literal sense, but in a looser spiritual sense as well.

In the literal sense, there was a marked resurgence of animal lust as the men and their women rediscovered the passion stolen from them by the frigid months. Spiritual aspirations soared again too, as the farmers of Newton observed the time-honored ritual of annual renewal. Fields were carefully cultivated, homes meticulously tidied, cows tenderly calved, and a new crop of babies energetically planted.

Above all else, the thawing of a frozen world meant being out-of-doors again. When, after enduring months of seemingly endless blizzard, the first scents of spring made themselves known, it was a welcome and uplifting scene. Escaping their long winter's incarceration, the men returned to their fields, and before long, the fallow, sleeping lands sprang forth with new color.

Nothing could compare, of course, with the intense variety of color to be found in a prairie field Earthside. But still and all, the meadows of present-day Mars were more electric than the bland, lichen-green of earlier years. Now, the flowers the settlers brought with them from Earth diluted the monotonous lichen-pastures with hues and smells and tastes which couldn't help but trigger hungry cravings for terran springs left behind. This was the season when homesickness for old Earth ran strongest. But it was also the season when hopes for this bravest of new worlds ran highest.

The cold winds became steadily less threatening. The irregular snows warmed to rain. The dark winter clouds scattered. The daylight hours lengthened. The children giggled. Even Saron's business declined, as thoughts turned again to hearth and home, and faithful husbands lingered in their doorway a moment, to ponder both moons in their various phases.

Somewhere in the distance, a gentle rain began to fall, and before long the thin Martian soil had become a muddy, ruddy pool, and the llama wool, a dusty, musty stench. *It was spring on Mars, and it was nothing if not exquisite!*

Seeing the colors, hearing the sounds, smelling the scents of the explosive onset of the new season, Carina was energized. She threw off her bedcovers, dressed quickly, and bounded out the door — there was someone she just had to see!

*   *   *

"You don't like me much, do you?" Saron questioned, leaving Carina stalled on the doorstep of the Commons. The two women had gotten past the pleasantries okay, but not much further. Saron had no intention of asking the other woman in, this despite Saron's well-established reputation for being congenial and easy-going. Upon seeing Carina on her doorstep, her disposition this morning could only be described as surly.

"I'm not your biggest fan, if that's what you mean," Carina admitted, peering past Saron into the interior of the darkened bar. Carina had never actually set foot inside the Commons, of course. But, from her vantage point at the doorway, she could see that the place was presently dark and empty.

"We do what we have to, to survive," Saron declared, twirling a lock of bountiful hair around the tip of her index finger. "Not all of us were spoon-fed like yourself. Some of us had to fight for every morsel. But then you wouldn't know about that, now would you?"

"Look, I didn't come here to fight. In fact, I'll leave if you ask me to. What goes on between you and my father is none of my business. I came here because I'm told you have a functioning datacomm in the back room, and I'd like to use it."

As Carina spoke, she advanced towards the door as if she meant to brush past the other woman and enter the premises uninvited.

"Not so fast," Saron said, holding her ground and blocking Carina's way with her arm. "What if I do have a datacomm? What's it to you?"

Carina scowled, and for an extended instant she appeared to be calculating the odds of getting past Saron unharmed. The mathematics must not have worked out, because in the next instant her tone softened. "May I please come in? I promise I won't stay long."

"Let's understand each other, shall we? My place, my rules. So long as we're clear on that, then by all means, do come in." Saron stepped aside to let Carina pass.

Inside, the place was dark. Cigar smoke hung in the air, and it still reeked of cannabis and Saronale from last night's crowd. Carina turned up her nose, then began asking questions. "Is it true? Do you have a datacomm hidden here somewhere?"

"Yes, as a matter of fact, I do. But, like everything else around here, I earned it the hard way, either on my back, legs in the air, or else on my knees with mouth full. Either way, why should I share the fruits of my labor with the likes of you? When was the last time you had to earn anything the hard way?"

Carina didn't answer.

"I thought as much. Follow me."

Saron led her guest across the peanut-shell-covered floor of the saloon, past the entrance to the herbal garden where Saron raised her barley, and on towards a small room in the back. There was a heavy, wooden door. It was bolted shut.

Saron took her time opening it. She removed a long, silver chain from around her neck. A skeleton key dangled from a ring at one end of the chain. With key in hand, she stood poised beside the door, refusing to unlock it until she first had some answers.

"What exactly is it that you want?" Saron asked, massaging the key between her fingers.

"I had hoped to use your terminal to conduct a bit of research," Carina explained, impatient at the sudden delay.

"Research? Into what?"

"Contraceptives."

"Oh, I get it now — you want to avoid any more unfortunate accidents. And, let me guess — because I bim for a living, you figured I would know all about such things. Is that it?"

Carina nodded, but did not answer.

"You figured right." Saron said, unbolting the door and reaching inside for the wall switch. With a gracious sweep of the hand, she bid Carina enter the tiny room.

Carina was awestruck. It was a bit like entering another world. On one side of the door were sod walls and spoor-burning furnaces. On the other side, technology to rival the best on Earth.

Half of Newton was still without electricity. But certainly not this tiny corner of Saron's place. Solar collectors on the roof generated whatever power was necessary to run the datacomm, printers, and other equipment. From what Carina could tell, Saron used the room as an office of sorts, to manage her various enterprises.

The bimbooker was justifiably proud of what she had been able to assemble here in this little corner of Mars. She proceeded to answer Carina's question.

"Most of what I know about contraceptives, I learned from my mother back in Afghanistan. This was before she was butchered by the Overlord and his men. She was a smart woman, my mother, and she began teaching me about the ways of the world when I first started menstruating. The rest I learned right here, from that."

Saron pointed towards a small, corner desk. On top of it sat a state-of-the-art datacomm plus a printer. Both were protected from the elements by a thin sheet of poly. A length of double-density coaxial cable connected the high-tech machine to a mini-receiving dish on the roof of the Commons. With this setup, Saron had the ability to call up virtually any file in the Colony One database, even tap the encyclopedic free-net back home. Carina was amazed, and she gasped in admiration. She had a good idea what a top-of-the-line unit like this one cost new.

"How in blazes did you get your hands on a sweet setup like this?" she quizzed, unable to hide the astonished envy in her voice.

"Just a gift from an admiring customer," Saron replied, enjoying her guest's reaction. Carina had always been so aloof, so difficult to impress, it felt good to be able to turn the tables on her, if only for a while. "Legs in the air, remember? Anyway, he's helped me invest my money wisely. It has allowed me to buy a great many things."

"What customer?" Carina snorted, believing the benefactor to be her father. She had never been one to hide her disapproval of his relationship with this woman. "Who gave you this?"

"You think he overpaid?" Saron taunted, shamelessly strutting her stuff.

"No . . . of course not," Carina stammered as the other woman pranced by. Saron had purposely pulled her blouse taut around her breasts to accentuate their youthful upward swell. Dancing in place to some distant samba, she left nothing to the imagination.

Suddenly feeling inadequate, Carina decided that no man — not even her father — could ever pay enough for a woman of Saron's obvious talents. Still fumbling for words, she said, "I only wanted to know who . . . "

"It wouldn't be proper etiquette for a woman in my position to reveal her sources, now would it?" Saron was still toying unmercifully with her opposite. But Carina was beginning to catch on.

"Hooker-client privilege?" Carina said, regaining her footing.

"Something like that."

"But the question remains. May I access your terminal to conduct my research or not?"

"That depends."

"On what?"

"On what you propose to do with what you learn. Knowledge is power, my dear. To my mind, you've already got a bit too much of both. In fact, you might be a bit too educated for your own good."

If Carina was insulted by this latest remark, she let it slide. She was aching to get started with this, her newest project, and refused to be put off any longer.

"Listen to me, Saron. I want the women of Newton to have complete control over their reproductive lives. I don't want them to be pawns of their men, as they have been on Earth since at least the fall of the Roman Empire."

"Normally, I would stand up and cheer. Only, after what you have just been through with BC and that baby of yours, this sounds more like sour grapes to me. For heaven's sake, woman, do I look like a pawn to you?"

"Not in the least," Carina replied. "That's why I came to you — I knew you would understand."

That answer seemed to placate Saron. "It's true, you know. Women in antiquity did have more control over their reproductive lives than most people have been led to believe. Even in my country, where women have had practically no rights for centuries, they've been known to chew these little beauties as a natural contraceptive."

From a shelf beside the door, Saron took a shallow dish and held it out to Carina. The dish held a dozen or more yellow, pebble-sized granules.

"Dried seeds?"

Saron nodded.

"Is this just some Afghan folktale, or do these things really work?" Carina was suspicious. She took one of the seeds, studied it closely.

"Do I look pregnant to you?"

"No, of course not."

"Then don't be so damn quick to turn up your nose. You might find that ole Saron can teach Little Miss Spoon-Fed a thing or two. Now, have a seat," Saron instructed. She pulled the poly cover off the terminal and slid a bench up in front of the desk. "Go ahead — satisfy your curiosity."

With that, Saron spun and walked away, leaving a stunned Carina sitting in muted silence before the keyboard. It took her a moment to recover, but only a moment.

Carina put her hands on the keyboard. She knew she might never get another chance like this for a long while.

It was time to get to work!

TWELVE

Silphium

One of the more curious dilemmas accompanying the evolution of Man has been that once the survival of the species was assured, the overwhelming drive to fornicate has always kept Him at the brink of self-destruction.

Back on the savanna, on the eastern rim of the Rift Valley, where man first evolved, conditions were so tough and infant mortality so high, if the species had any chance of enduring, it had to engage in procreation literally at every turn. Not knowing when the male would return home from the hunt — or for how long — the female had to be receptive to his advances literally on a moment's notice. The male himself had to be ready and willing to copulate whenever she showed even the slightest interest. If the species were to survive the marginal conditions of the arid savanna, both sexes had to constantly be in heat, a circumstance that made great sense in the species' infancy.

But, in transporting that need into the twentieth century and beyond, where mere survival was no longer an issue, that heat, that drive, that unquenchable passion, meant a burgeoning population of nearly uncontrollable dimension. In modern times, the issue was no longer *promoting* birth, it was preventing it. And while there was always a certain segment of society who was advocating abstinence as a means of population control, for a species as whetted to having sex and making babies as this one was, abstinence was a rather silly prescription to give for birth control. Indeed, with Man's sex drive as deeply ingrained as any trait Mother Nature had ever devised, there were only three sensible means for controlling the number of new mouths to feed — contraception, abortion, or infanticide. Each had its role to play. From the relative comfort of Saron's back room, Carina examined each of them in turn.

Contrary to what modern historians had been telling people for five hundred years, Carina soon learned that since ancient times women had been practicing birth control with little or no interference from religious or political authorities. The knowledge of which plants to rely on — and the loss of that knowledge by the time of the Renaissance — was a story that emerged with greater and greater clarity the more Carina delved into it. That Carina should even have been concerned with such matters was as much a consequence of BC's defection as anything else. Carina missed him — that much was true — but not for the reasons one might expect. So far as Carina was concerned, a man served at most two functions — one sexual, and the other protective.

Since men were, for the most part, larger and stronger than women, keeping a big strong man around the house served to prevent other, unattached males from making unwanted advances. But there were other ways to chase away unwelcome suitors, and that was to be properly armed with a weapon. At one time or another in her life, she had tried them all — guard dogs, alarm systems, robotic sentries, guns, knives. Each had their advantages, of course, but nothing beat a good, old-fashioned blaster. After BC left, her neighbor Inda Desai lent her one, though where he had gotten it was still an open question. Thus, it was the other function, the sexual one, which she was in dire need of satisfying.

Carina masturbated constantly. But no arrangement of fingers, no cylindrical object, no elongated piece of exotic fruit, no mechanical contrivance, could take the place of the real thing. Unfortunately, here in Newton, eligible and worthy males were few and far between. The "few" were attracted more to the likes of Saron than they were to the likes of Carina. She found that the only way to keep her mind off her vagina was to work. And this she now did with vigor.

Saron's wonderful machine opened up a whole new world of inquiry for Carina. At the same time, Saron's homegrown folktales of chewing certain dried seeds as a method of birth control, put Carina onto the idea of incorporating herbal contraceptives into their Martian society. Somehow, this solution was eminently appealing. All she needed was this machine and a couple of hours, and soon she would learn all there was to know about birth control.

Sitting, now, before Saron's datacomm terminal, Carina encoded the keywords initiating her subject-search and began highlighting the text she would print out later. This is what she found:

In the seventh century B.C., Greek colonists founded the coastal city of Cyrene in what is today the Mediterranean Kingdom of Israel, a kingdom which, until recently, stretched across North Africa from the Straits of Gibraltar to the Straits of Hormuz. According to newly-unearthed texts, shortly after arriving on the North African coast, the Greeks discovered a plant that made some of them wealthy and all of them famous. They called these plants, with their deeply divided leaves and yellow flowers, silphion; later Latinized to silphium.

The pungent sap from its roots and stem made a good cough syrup, gave food a rich, distinctive flavor. But of far greater significance to the early Greeks was its application as a contraceptive, and as an abortifacient.

(This one Carina had to look up before going on. The online dictionary told her an abortifacient was anything that produced an abortion.)

Because of its many uses, demand for the silphion plant grew quickly. By the fifth century B.C., silphion prices were so high in Athens, the Athenians experimented with growing it elsewhere. Fortunately for the Cyrenian economy, attempts to cultivate the plant in Syria and in Greece failed, leaving them as sole exporters of the plant. Known commonly as the giant fennel, silphium soon became the city's distinctive symbol. In fact, one series of Cyrenian coins actually displayed a seated woman touching the plant with one hand and her genitals with the other.

Because the plant grew only on a narrow stretch of land along the dry mountainsides facing the Mediterranean, and because attempts to cultivate it elsewhere failed, the supply of silphium could not keep up with demand. By the first century A.D. it was scarce from overharvesting, and, by the third or fourth century A.D., it was extinct. Luckily for the Ancients, silphium was not the planet's only naturally-occurring birth-control pill.

Besides silphium, the seeds of Queen Anne's Lace — the wild carrot — was also effective as a contraceptive. Hippocrates, among others, declared that, when taken orally, such seeds prevented, as well as terminated, pregnancy. Recent studies have reinforced the strength of this assertion. The seeds have been shown to inhibit both fetal and ovarian growth. They have also proven effective as a postcoital antifertility agent. To reduce fertility, women living in rural areas of Indiastan have chewed dry seeds of Queen Anne's Lace for at least the past 2500 years.

(Just as Saron said, Carina reflected pensively. Maybe she should make peace with the woman, or at the very least thank her for her hospitality. Maybe, if Carina was nice, Saron could be persuaded to set aside a small corner of her greenhouse to grow these plants domestically, instead of having to import the seeds from Earth.)

Another plant used in Classical times as a contraceptive and perhaps also as an abortifacient (there, that word again!), was pennyroyal. This pulegone-containing plant grew wild in the region and would have been generally available to women of the time, although — because of its toxicity — it would have to have been taken in precise amounts in a tea. But the list didn't end there

— willow, date palm, and pomegranate all contained compounds that reduced fertility and terminated pregnancies.

As might be reasonably expected, long before either the Greeks or the Romans were practicing birth control, the ancient Egyptians were, and with much the same compounds. According to the Ebers Papyrus, a medical document written about 1500 B.C. but containing ideas dating from a much earlier time, unspecified amounts of acacia gum, dates, plus another unidentified plant, were to be mixed with plant-fiber and honey to form a pessary or vaginal suppository. Interestingly enough, modern researchers have found acacia to be spermatocidal and, when compounded, it produces the lactic acid anhydride, one of the very same active ingredients used in today's contraceptive jellies.

Unlike the debates that erupted in more recent times, beginning with Pope Pius IX's outlawing of abortion among Catholics in 1869, neither Greek nor Roman nor Hebrew law protected the fetus until it had formed recognizable features. Up to that point, a woman could abort her child without fear of reprisal from religious or legal authorities. Indeed, both Plato and Aristotle advocated population control to ensure stability in the ideal city-state, suggesting that abortion be induced before sense and life outside the womb had begun. And, whereas the Hebrews directed their people to be fruitful and multiply, the Babylonian Talmud records that a man was commanded concerning the duty of propagation, but a woman was not. In other words, men were encouraged to spread their seed, but women — being the ones who had to suffer the pains of pregnancy, childbirth, and child-rearing — were excused by God from the commandment to be fruitful. Moreover, Hebrew law did not even regard a woman as being pregnant until forty days *following* conception.

The story was much the same with the Greeks. Although the Hippocratic Oath formulated in the fifth century B.C. forbade initiates from administering an abortive suppository, the terms of the Oath did not amount to a blanket condemnation of abortion. To the contrary, most ancient physicians were left free to employ oral contraceptives, oral abortifacients, and surgical or even manipulative procedures to end pregnancies. It was not until the Oath was *misread* in the first century A.D. by the Roman physician Scribonius Largus that the misinterpretation against abortion got added. Regrettably, Scribonius' misreading of Hippocrates survived into the modern era and the error became particularly important in the nineteenth century, when so many states in the Americas and elsewhere passed anti-abortion statutes based at least in part on Scribonius' misreading of a medical doctor's sacred obligations.

How many ancient peoples actually practiced birth control, and to what degree, is of course, open to question. Nevertheless, historical demographic studies suggest that premodern societies did in fact regulate family size by one means or another. For instance, it is known that between A.D. 1 and A.D. 500, the population within the bounds of the Roman Empire declined. During that same period, the overall population of Europe is estimated to have declined from about 33 million to about 28 million. By the year 1000 the population was only 39 million, a net growth of under six million over the course of ten centuries! How to account for this tiny increase? Disease, of course. War. Maybe famine. But part of the answer lies elsewhere, with infanticide.

(This surprised Carina, and for a second she paused to consider the implications. Then she pressed on.)

To begin with, in those days, in fact all the way through the Middle Ages, infanticide was not illegal. Because of this, and because it seems to have been widely practiced, many scholars have hypothesized that infanticide is the only possible explanation that can account for both the low overall population and small family-size typical of both ancient and medieval times. And, of course, in the twenty-*third* century, it was Ali Salaam Rontana who seized on this population-leveling solution to advance his own brand of terrorism and further his genocidal aims.

Although Rontana's precise origins remain clouded in obscurity, a little more than two centuries ago a lunatic appeared on the world stage leading an army of Moslem bandits operating out of a mountain hideaway in Persia. Like every psychopath the world has ever known, Ali Salaam Rontana had a manifesto, a manifesto which directed his followers to silence their rivals' voices by exterminating their rivals' genes. Rontana's maniacal cry was nothing more than the latest version of the age-old master-race excuse for slaughtering one's neighbor, and he neatly packaged it all in a book entitled *Deicide, Infanticide & Ecocide*, or D.I.E., for short. Although it was pure unadulterated lunacy, in a seemingly flawless, perfectly logical way, Rontana led the readers of his book through the compelling case for murdering children in order to spare the environment.

(Though Carina had heard this story before, from her father, it was all so sick and twisted, she had no choice but to read it through again, just to be sure. Like every holocaust in history, unless you actually experienced the bloody thing firsthand, you tended not to believe it ever happened. Or, if it did happen, that the stories being told about it were exaggerated lies. Nothing focuses the mind quite like reality.)

First, there was the exploitation of infants as a food source. Cannibalism, to be precise. To Rontana, maniac that he was, this was the ultimate in recycling and should be carried out for the common good.

Second, there was the competition for resources. By starving or murdering — but not actually eating — the infant, the killer increased the quantity of resources available to himself and his kin.

The competition between males for access to breeding-age females was reason number three on Rontana's list sanctioning infanticide. It was told how, on a hunting trip to Africa as a child, Rontana witnessed a telling event, an event that formed the basis for much of his thinking. He observed that when a new male took over an existing lion pride, the first thing the new male did was to kill off all the cubs. Chimpanzees did much the same thing.

At the time, Rontana could make no sense of this behavior. Only later, as he wrote his manifesto, did the answer dawn on him: The male had evolved with but one purpose in life — to disseminate his genes as widely as possible. By killing the cubs, he would bring the females back into heat, allowing them to be impregnated with *his* genes and preventing the females from wasting their time nurturing another male's offspring. If good enough for lions and chimps, why not people? By murdering another man's offspring and breeding with his mate, the killer gains the opportunity to utilize that female to produce more of his seed. This "murder and rape" approach was always Rontana's number one personal favorite.

Number four — "compassionate" infanticide. Where it has been practiced, it has typically been committed by a mother with regret. The usual case is following the birth of a newborn, when the mother sadly realizes her thriving four-year-old will die because she doesn't have the resources to raise both children at once.

Then there was reason number five. This one is pure social pathology. Beyond the sheer joy of killing, there is no gain of any kind for the killer.

*　　*　　*

As Carina concluded her review of the relevant literature, she found herself drowning in questions.

If herbal birth-control agents had been so effective, why had they faded from common usage? If silphium and other similar plants were being described in the medical texts of the Middle Ages, why, by the onset of the Renaissance, were physicians no longer writing about them? If the knowledge was still being passed down through generations of women, why were physicians no longer aware of it? How did civilization lose what was once so well known? A little further study gave Carina her answers:

The disenfranchisement of women and the loss of herbal remedies began with the rise of the guilds in the Middle Ages. As the guilds began to require that one be a university graduate in order to practice medicine, the compounding and dispensing of drugs fell out of the realm of physicians and into the domain of pharmacists. At the same time, gynecology became more and more the province of midwives, a group who had learned the uses of herbal birth-control agents in the field. It wasn't long before they were the only ones who truly knew how to identify the necessary plants, make the extracts, and properly administer the doses. Because these women often gave of their knowledge freely, this had a dampening effect on the fees men could charge and generally interfered with their ability to dominate the medical profession. When the backlash came, it was vicious. These female reservoirs of herbal knowledge were dubbed witches, and nine million of them were burned at the stake, often with the Church's assent. Small wonder the knowledge vanished except from isolated rural pockets!

With the learning chain broken and the arrogant medical guilds becoming increasingly distrustful of folk medicine, physicians of the Renaissance no longer had the occupational or professional means of acquiring the midwives' knowledge. Thus, it was lost. To make matters worse, as time passed, church doctrine, canon law, and legislative statute all worked together to restrict a woman's right to regulate her own reproduction.

By now, Carina had read enough. She was angry. Infanticide. Abortion. Contraception. All very complex matters, and all of them under the control of men.

It was perfectly clear what had to be done. After a thousand years, the process of denial had to be reversed. Women had to be re-empowered. It had to begin somewhere, so why not here, on Mars? It had to begin with someone, so why not with her? If Saron could only be persuaded, Carina would cup a handful of pennyroyal seeds in one palm and a handful of Queen Anne's Lace seeds in the other, then scratch out a narrow furrow in the soil of a tiny spot Saron might lend her in the back corner of her greenhouse.

If only Carina could accomplish this much, she would be able to advance the cause of women's rights immeasurably. *History was about to change!*

THIRTEEN

Storm

As the days steadily lengthened in anticipation of summer, the inauguration of planting got underway in earnest. Raising crops on the Martian steppe was an uncertain enterprise, one made even more precarious by the unpredictable rainfall and erratic temperatures. Too little precipitation and the feeble seedlings would bake to a crisp in the hot afternoon sun. Too much, and they would drown in a deluge of crimson mud.

And, to complicate matters, hard downpours of devastating proportion were still not all that uncommon. Just this morning, Carina had been rocketed out of bed by a clap of thunder rumbling like a freight train in the distance. It scared her, just like in the old days. Back then, she would sometimes sit huddled under a table for hours, terrified by the fury, the sheer destructive power of a passing storm. *How could she forget?* It seemed like only yesterday that the rising waters of the Great Sea had compelled her to abandon the original Mars Base and run for her life. Even now, as she sat bolt upright in her bed, rubbing the sleep from her eyes, she remembered.

But, like the temper tantrums of a young child, the intensity of the weather systems seemed to mellow with age, becoming less and less violent as the atmosphere gradually matured. Oh, there were still the occasional violent outbursts. But, for the most part, the squalls were now short-lived and certainly nothing to match the explosive, wall-shaking events of that first spring. Indeed, with storms seemingly less potent nowadays, it made little sense to run for cover every time a dark cloud appeared on the horizon. That's why this morning, when Carina climbed out of bed, the threat of an impending thunderstorm didn't cause her to vary her schedule in the slightest.

She set the dog free to run in the yard, ate breakfast, then started down a long laundry list of chores she had planned for the day. There were floors to mop, windows to clean, and sausage to make. The storm would arrive on its own schedule — by nightfall, no doubt — but that still left her most of the day. Plenty of time for her to get all her work done.

In much the same way that early travelers could read the skies and make weather forecasts based on nothing more than a few rule-of-thumb sayings, Carina could smell a storm brewing on the horizon. Her neighbor, Inda, had told her as much when he stopped by her hut this morning on the way out to his field. What had he said? *Red sky at night, sailor's delight; red sky at morning, sailor take warning.* The storm was coming, he said, and they both agreed. The air was heavy, the moth-bats nervous, the smell of yucca strong. It would be hours, yes, but the storm *was* coming. For a farmer like Inda Desai, the delay was a blessing. H e had crops to get in. The chance to get seeds in the ground before the rain started was reason enough to set out early for the farthest point of his field.

Carina thanked him for stopping by and watched as he headed over the next rise. Inda had been courting her for several weeks now, but with little success. Even with BC gone for some time now, she had found it difficult to get started with another man. It wasn't that she could live without sex — as always, that was a constant and overriding concern with her — it was more that she couldn't bring herself to make the sort of long-term commitment a man like Inda was looking for. The man was most definitely on the prowl for a wife, only Carina was hardly the marrying kind.

Inda had a complex, almost brooding, double personality. On the one hand, he was a capable, natural-born leader. On the other, a short-tempered, misguided rebel. On the one hand, he had a modern, cutting-edge intellect. On the other, he was still bound by traditions reaching back a thousand years.

Yet, despite the dichotomy, Carina couldn't help but hold the man in some regard. Few men on the planet possessed the personal charisma, the chutzpah, yes, even the sheer guts needed to draw a bunch of disparate, unrelated persons together to complete a project as big and time-consuming as the Commons — yet somehow he had managed it.

Joining hands to build the Commons was an instance of communal cooperation found time and again in rural societies, but rarely anyplace else. *Why should this be?* she wondered. And how best to rationalize such forms of voluntary mutual aid, especially in terms of the biogenetics she had used to frame her entire philosophy?

These were the questions that occupied her mind, even as her body carried out the more mundane tasks of soaping down windows and doing floors.

From a strictly "selfish-gene" point of view, helping someone who wasn't related to you — either a direct ancestor or a lineal descendant — made no sense to her. By its very nature, the calculus of natural selection was cruel. It put a premium, not on the reproductive success of an entire species, but on the reproductive success of each separate individual. It tended to favor those organisms that helped their close relatives, because, in doing so, they increased their own representation in the gene pool. Thus the conundrum. *How could the same mechanism that put a premium on self-preservation also shape behavior that was altruistic?* Or, to put it another way, behavior that benefited an unrelated someone at the expense, perhaps, of one's *own* progeny?

The man who runs into a burning building to save a neighbor's child. The woman who jumps onto a railroad track ahead of a speeding train to rescue a dog. The Boy Scout who climbs out onto a frozen pond to save a drowning stranger. *What sense was there in such behavior?*

As near as Carina could figure it, the question itself turned on one's definition of "kin." Was kinship limited strictly to one's own progeny? Or did it extend further, perhaps to the members of one's community, or even further, to the citizens of one's nation?

If it was *your* kid in the building, instead of the neighbor's, it might make sense. Or if it was *your* dog on the railroad tracks, a mother might reason it was worth risking her life to protect her own child's well-being. But a stray? A stranger from an unknown village? Why, for God's sake?

Within a family, a good turn was always its own reward. But a good turn to an unrelated fellow-being? Such an act had to somehow be returned in order for it to pay off.

Viewed in this light, reciprocal aid was essentially an economic exchange. I help you at a cost to me of 4. But, because it was your life I saved, the benefit you collect is 100. Even if you pay me back 10, you are still ahead 90. And if you *don't* pay me back, the kudos I will receive for being a hero are worth at least the 4 that I spent. Reciprocal aid is an economic exchange: *the uncoerced trading of altruistic acts in which total benefits always exceed total cost.*

The problem in the real world is that such economic exchanges are vulnerable to abuse. Two parties might strike a mutually profitable bargain, but each could gain still more by withholding his contribution to the deal. Only where the parties are related, that is, where kinship is a consideration, would the temptation to cheat (hopefully) be powerful enough to resist.

Deciding, then, who your kin are, is a matter of no small importance. And kin recognition would be as much an issue for intelligent beings like *Homo sapiens* as it would for lower animals like an insect or an amphibian. Indeed, along with the rise of civilization, humans developed quite elaborate means for identifying their kin. The use of surnames, for instance. The cataloguing of detailed genealogical records. The application of nonvisual markers like club or church membership. The wearing of distinctive clothing or facial hair. One's street address. The possibilities were as endless as man's imagination.

But, as inventive as humans were in this regard, kin recognition strategies elsewhere in the animal kingdom were equally creative; although, for lower animals, the cues were understandably different.

For mammals and other creatures heavily dependent on sight, kin were commonly differentiated by means of visual references — fur color, for instance, or plumage.

For organisms that had to attract mates across a distance in the dark — such as the bullfrog — auditory signals were often employed.

And, for a multitude of plants and animals that were incapable of expending the considerable energy required to compress air in an effort to generate a sound, chemical odors were, of course, invaluable as distinguishing markers.

For the most highly-evolved animal species of all, the *Neo-sapiens*, there were several signposts marking the way — the presence of signature genes; the number and size of their molars; the length of the appendix; even the size of the clitoris. Hidden characteristics all, it was nearly impossible for one newhuman to correctly identify another. Which is one reason why Carina was prompted to require bio-screens for new residents. It had all boiled down to nothing more than being certain who her kin were.

Properly understood, then, kin recognition was driven by the interplay of two diametrically-opposing forces. On the one hand, close inbreeding could allow the accumulation of deleterious characteristics. On the other hand, mating with an individual who had materially different genes could *also* produce detrimental effects, breaking up gene combinations that had proven themselves capable of generating favorable traits.

Thus, optimal breeding patterns required that organisms pay considerable heed to both tugs, preferring to mate with those to whom they were neither too closely, nor too distantly, related. As it applied to the circumstances newhumans faced here on Mars, it seemed intuitive to Carina that a liaison between her and Inda would be in the best interest of the colony, if not the species. But there was a problem:

Nowhere in the discussion of optimal breeding patterns was there any mention of love, nor even of cohabitation. Surely a man of Inda's intelligence could understand that. While the two might have had an obligation to produce a newhuman baby together, surely the man was mature enough to understand that she could accomplish this without making him her husband, or she his wife. It was something Carina would have to take up with him in the days ahead. If he agreed to her terms, she would stop taking her pennyroyal until she caught.

There was a rumble of thunder in the distance. Carina had forgotten about the storm. But she could smell it, now, getting closer.

When the air was heavy, like now before a rain, the sharp odor of mountain yucca clung like ivy to the lichen-walls of the hut. Outside, beneath the eaves, a constant rustle, the sound of bat wings as the animals moved and jostled for position in their tiny hutches. Now, as the first raindrops began to splatter against the roof, Carina set aside her squeegee. Any further effort cleaning windows would be wasted.

The rain was light, barely a mist. No emergency yet. Her dog Sandy was in the yard, running wild, chasing butterflies and moths across the contoured fields between her property and the next. No need to call him in yet. The heavy stuff, should it come, was still hours away.

Carina moved into the back room. She was about to try her hand at making llama sausage. This was messy business. But served up any other way, llama was simply too gamey, chewy, and stringy to be palatable.

Carina looked at the recipe. She had already completed the first step. Take between four and five pounds of llama rump, cut it into small pieces, then grind approximately one-third of it finely. The next step was to thoroughly mix the cut-up meat with the ground-up meat, work six chopped cloves of garlic into the mix, as well as one teaspoon each of cinnamon, pepper, and salt. This, she did.

Next, the mixture went into a bowl, where she added a quarter grated nutmeg, one-half teaspoon marjoram, one-half cup corn flour, and one-and-a-half cups water. Now came the hard part: kneading the meat and spices together until doughy, then spooning the odd-colored mixture into a fresh sausage casing until plump. Saron had told her, for best results, to use a cleaned and boiled bovine intestines as a casing, which Carina did.

The next step was to coil the filled casing into a circle, place it in an even larger bowl, sprinkle the entire ensemble liberally with salt and cover the whole thing with boiling hot water. The instructions said to let the bowl stand for twenty minutes, then place the sausage on a greased baking pan. It also said to prick the skin in several places to prevent the casing from bursting.

So far, so good, Carina thought, admiring her handiwork. She had never made sausage before, and this seemed to be going well!

The final step was to pour melted lard over the sausage, which she did, and shove the whole thing into the oven, where it would bake at high temperature until brown, probably about twenty minutes.

Carina closed the oven door and set the temperature to high. A crack of thunder, closer than before, made her look up. In all this time she hadn't once bothered to stop and step outside to check up on her dog. Now she suddenly regretted her decision. While she had been hard at work making sausage, the weather had taken a turn for the worse.

Carina looked out the window, then stepped to the door. The sky was black. Bolts of lightning sliced through the air like electricity. It would only be a matter of minutes before all hell broke loose, *but Sandy was nowhere in sight!*

With panic-stricken eyes, Carina scanned the horizon. She couldn't see far. But there was no sign of her little dog.

The pace of the rain accelerated. First, a drizzle. Then, a downpour. Then, a torrent.

The air temperature plunged. The sky suddenly went white with lightning. The thunder was first a drumroll, then more like exploding sticks of dynamite. The wind tore at her face. The sod walls of the hut shuddered with each violent downdraft.

Carina broke out in a cold sweat. Sandy was still out there frolicking someplace, *and it was her fault!*

The guilt was more than she could bear. Carina bolted from the house, ignoring any possible risk to herself. No commonsense notion to stay put could hold her back. *But then who could blame her?* With BC gone and she and her father barely on speaking terms, Sandy was all the kin she had.

Carina didn't get far. Indeed, she hadn't gone more than a dozen paces when a brutal crosswind slapped her to the ground, knocking the air from her lungs. She rolled to one side in pain, her already soaking-wet body saturated now with a thin veneer of red mud.

Undeterred, Carina staggered to her feet. She lurched in the direction where she had last seen the dog running. Her feet were unsteady, and she stumbled first this way, then that, shouting out the animal's name as she went. Had she known that Inda had already scooped up the pet and deposited him safely with Saron at the Commons before making his own way home, she never would have ventured forth in the first place and would have certainly returned home now herself. But it was not to be.

Unable, now, to make out a thing through the blinding rain, Carina had no way of knowing which way she had come — or even how far. Yet, instead of doing the smart thing and turning back, she pressed irrationally forward. Two years ago, in the midst of her most desperate hour, she had conjured that dog up from nothing, and now — no matter what it cost her — she wasn't about to lose him!

Pushing on, now, despite her disorientation, only moments passed before she tripped and fell against the stone fence BC had built to mark off one border of their property from Inda's next door. She tried to break her fall, but — with arms flailing wildly — succeeded only in scraping one hand badly as she slammed it against a jagged rock on the way down.

Pain shot up her arm, and she cried out in agony. But it was no use. *Success seemed further out of reach, now, than ever before.*

Blood ran from her palm, where the flap of skin hung loosely. The pounding rain sharpened the sting of pain. She needed medical attention, as well as a set of warm, dry clothes.

Carina knew she could feel her way along the stone fence back towards her own house or else forward toward Inda's place. She opted to go forward. Inda had a medic kit he could use to bandage her hand. Plus, he might be willing to help her find Sandy before the little dog perished in the storm.

Carina half-walked, half-crawled the next hundred meters on her knees. With one hand on the stone fence to help keep her on course, and the other tucked under her armpit to help keep out the elements, she made her way slowly along the ground toward Inda Desai's hut. She was shivering feverishly.

As the fury of the storm grew, the downrushing cold air caused the temperature to plummet. Summer became winter in a split second. What was once freezing cold rain swiftly became sleet, driving the feeling from her fingers.

It seemed, now, as if her hands and face were being cut to ribbons by the maelstrom. The frozen ice-rain slashed at her skin with incredible force. The ice-cold slivers of rain were like shards of broken glass thrust down upon her by some infuriated god. Blood ran from her arms. Tears flowed from her eyes. She cried out in pain.

Exhausted by the ordeal, Carina collapsed to the wet ground and curled up against the fence to curse her misfortune. She had long ago quit nursing her wounds. It had gone beyond that now.

Believing that death was close at hand, Carina labored to come to grips with her existence, to make a final peace with her world. If only they had listened. If only they could all just understand . . .

But apparently it wasn't her time, not yet anyway. Even as she drifted down towards the brink of unconsciousness and eternal sleep, a strong, dark-skinned hand reached out through the storm and locked onto hers. The muscular arm jerked her suddenly to her feet, and a moment later, she found herself slung across Inda's shoulder like a rolled carpet.

Carina pounded her fists against his broad, straight back, fighting against him much as a drowning swimmer might his would-be rescuer. But, by this time, her strength was waning. Once again, she began to shiver uncontrollably. The tornado-like wind whipped her long dark hair against her ashen face, and before long, Carina's arms hung limp.

Undeterred by the dead weight of his soggy load, Inda made his way doggedly across the uneven ground and up to his hut atop the next rise. By the time he arrived at the threshold of his spartan home, her breathing was labored and she was sinking fast.

With her condition deteriorating, the man sprang into action to try and arrest the precipitous fall in her body temperature. He set her next to the fire, tore off her soaking wet clothes, wrapped her cold, limp body in a blanket. It was one of those the old Amerind lady had made for him on her handloom. Then he threw on a second blanket. And a third. He kept adding layers until he could add no more.

She looked sort of amusing, like a mummy with a blue face. But there was nothing amusing about her condition. Hypothermia could be deadly.

Several long minutes passed. Her eyes fluttered, and she groaned. Color filled her cheeks. Then she threw up. Phlegm filled her throat and she spit it out. Then she began to scream incoherently at the top of her lungs. Her voice was hoarse. She had to find Sandy. She had to escape from the Mars Base before it flooded. She had to get her baby back from BC. She had to pass on her signature genes before it was too late.

Inda waited patiently. She went on and on, sometimes sobbing, sometimes gagging, always crying. Her moans were muffled by the confining layers of blankets.

Inda tried to calm her. He figured she was suffering from shock and exposure. He rinsed her mouth out with water. She spit it back in his face.

Then things took an unexpected turn. Suddenly, and without warning, her quivering lips found his.

Had the whole thing ended right there, it might have been excused on the grounds that the dangerously cold weather had made her experience so frightening, a thank-you kiss or even a perfunctory grope was an acceptable means for unbundling the sexual tension between them, while at the same time rewarding the rescuer for his heroism.

Only it *didn't* end right there — it went all the way.

Like so many of the weird, inexplicable things Carina had done in her life, this was an impetuous act. If she thought about it at all, she would have argued that there were but two viable reasons for a man and a woman to be together — lust or convenience.

Lust was easy enough to understand: If he got turned on whenever he thought of her, and she wanted it every time he walked by, well that was lust. For couples living out on the frontier as they were, sexual relations were bound to be as open, frank, and necessary as downing a bowl of hot soup on a cold winter's day. Living on the edge, as it were, pioneers would be slow to adopt simpleminded puritan rituals like abstinence or false modesty.

As for convenience, this was an equally compelling reason for two people to be as one. Humans were, after all, social creatures. Going through life without a companion, without a partner, often meant having no life at all. Even a bad pairing might be preferable to no pairing. And, contrary to what every fairy tale writer since Grimm had said, being in love was not a necessary condition for making a couple work, nor was fidelity even a stipulation. Not to put too fine a point on it, but what most young couples called love was in fact lust, only with their clothes still on. So-called "true" love took a lifetime of nurturing before it could be coaxed into bloom. What Carina had here was opportunity, and she found herself powerless not to act on the impulse.

At first Inda resisted, convinced she was still suffering from shock. "What about BC?" he asked.

Carina's answer was simple. She didn't love him, never had. They had exchanged no vow of fidelity.

Inda stalled her advance, even after she reached up to kiss him for a second time. "But do you love *me?*"

Carina was hungry. Hungry to have him inside her, hungry to have his ponderous manhood penetrate her, hungry to have something beside her own fingers stimulate her clitoris. She said what he wanted to hear. Then, consumed by passion, she flung off the layers of blankets he had wrapped her in and threw Inda to the floor.

A woman in heat always gets her way. They don't call it forcible rape when a woman is on top. But what Carina did came close enough. She laid Inda down and forced him to have sex with her. He was helpless to object, even if he meant to. All Inda could think was that it was about time his courting efforts paid off, that it was about time she did him like a good wife should.

When it was over, and she had stumbled back to her hut that night after the storm, after the sex, after the passion, she wondered why.

Why couldn't she keep her pants on? Why was her appetite for sex so ravenous? Why did she need it over and over again? Why was every relationship she entered into so shallow?

Carina brushed her teeth and collapsed into bed exhausted. She had opened the window to flush out the smell of burnt sausage from the hut, and could now hear the wind in the trees. The storm had passed and all was quiet.

Dreams overtook her right away. *Who could have guessed that by morning she would be infatuated with yet another man?*

FOURTEEN

The Belt (Redux)

In the midst of her recurring nightmare about the asteroid collision of 2227, Carina had been awakened by the sound of her father's desperate cry for help over the comm.

"Mayday! Mayday! We're coming in fast, and we're off course. Our landing thrusters are at half, and we're nine, no, make that eleven kloms south-southeast of the Colony One landing pad. Ship is filled with passengers, and we may need medical assistance. Mayday! Mayday! This is Councilman Samuel Matthews of the passenger transport *Tikkidiw*. If anyone can read me, please respond!"

Catapulted into action by the ship's urgent distress call, Carina Matthews burst out the door and into the landrover. Her hand was still bandaged from yesterday's jarring fall against the stone fence. Her first thought was to try and raise Inda on the two-way radio. But when he didn't answer, she knew she had to act. Fearing the worst, she fired up the landrover and rushed out in the direction where her father said the ship was coming down.

Although Carina was first on the scene, there was actually very little she could do to help. Fortunately, the Colony One nurse had heard the Mayday as well. While she had come from further away, her rocketsled brought her to the crash site only minutes behind Carina.

As it happened, the whole thing turned out to be not much of a crash at all. At the very last possible instant before impact, Fornax had regained enough rudder control to put the ship down gently and without killing a soul. A couple broken bones, yes; a couple bruised noggins, yes; but no deaths.

As the shipload of immigrants streamed from the hull, some kissing the ground happy to be alive, others crying aloud in joy, one stood out from the crowd — a big, athletic hunk of a man with rugged good looks.

Carina went to him immediately, fawning all over the new arrival. She spoke to the man. But he practically ignored her. All she could get out of him was that his name was Gunter, and that he was fine.

With a "Hell's bell's, little lady" he told her to look after the others. But Carina already knew she had to have him. Only later, after trying for several days without success to bed the man, did she learn he was a miner — a mineralogist, to be precise — here to scout out a site for a motor factory (should ASARCO decide to build one), then to join the rest of his team in two weeks' time for a special mission out to the Belt. If all went well, he was then to be given a fortnight's leave to climb Olympus Mons.

They were standing, now, the five of them, in the arrival lounge of the Colony One immigration hall — Sam and Fornax and Carina and Gunter and Oskar Schaeffer. Swirling just beneath the surface-calm, like a shark waiting to strike, was an undeniable tension.

To begin with, Sam didn't care much for this Oskar Schaeffer character. He found the man from ASARCO to be an arrogant son-of-a-bitch, with the slobbish looks to match. Under any other circumstances, Sam would never have chosen to do business with the man.

But this asteroid mining venture was so costly, he and Fornax really had no choice — Herr Schaeffer had the financial backing they needed to successfully bring this thing off. If the ore assays they were about to collect proved satisfactory, ASARCO had agreed to begin assembling motors on Mars, motors that would then be used to tugboat asteroids out of the Belt and on to smelters orbiting high above the Earth's surface. And, as icing on the cake, ASARCO had agreed to foot the bill to retrofit the *Tikkidiw*. The changes would make it easier to carry passengers and allow room for more of their belongings, something Fornax had wanted to do for some time.

But, to be perfectly frank, Oskar Schaeffer wasn't the only burr beneath Sam's skin this bright and shiny morning. There was also the small matter of his daughter. Carina had this annoying habit of sticking her nose in where it didn't belong. This problem dated back many years, of course, and you would think by now that Sam would be used to it. But, when she showed up at the landing pad with Gunter in tow, Sam knew to expect problems. The way she hung on him, it was obvious she was infatuated with the man. Like BC before him, and several others before *him*, Gunter was a classic Euro — piercing blue eyes, big broad shoulders, unruly mop of wavy blond hair. Sam had seen this before. But it still amazed him. His daughter seemed to melt just listening to the man's slow Aussie drawl.

And yet there was still a third reason for the smoldering tension polluting the air — *Sam had never even met his grandson!* As if Carina's insistence on having a separate newhuman colony wasn't enough to drive a wedge between father and daughter, there was still the small matter of the grandson he had never met. To this day, Sam didn't know who to be the most angry at — his daughter for not telling BC the truth, BC for absconding to Earth with his grandson, or Fornax for helping them both escape. Of the three, Fornax had the least to answer for — he probably figured that with BC out of the way, he was improving his own chances with Carina. So far, anyway, it seemed the joke was on him. The effort had been wasted. Carina still wasn't giving him the time of day.

She barked at her father, now, in a rather scolding tone. "I understand from Gunter that the lot of you plan on going out to the Belt."

As Carina stood there, impatiently waiting for her father to answer, it seemed to her that he didn't look as well as he had. Maybe a bit paler, maybe a bit more stooped over than the last time they'd seen each other, just two weeks ago.

"That's correct, Carina. We're taking Oskar and your new friend Gunter here, plus their chief geologist, out to the Belt to see whether or not the mineral deposits are rich enough to be commercially mined."

"I can't believe my ears!" Carina exclaimed, anxiety filling her voice. "If you're successful out there, that would mean there would be *miners* coming to Mars!" The inflection in her voice made it sound as if the word were somehow profane.

"Actually, the miners would be staying on Earth, just where they've always been. It's the engine makers that would be coming to Mars."

Sam smiled and leaned easily against the bulkhead. Fornax sat next to him, at the nav-console, busily inputting coordinates. With the potential for striking any of a million micrometeorites peppering the Belt, this jump had a certain dangerous quality to it.

"I really don't see the difference. How are engine makers better than miners?"

Even as she spoke, the feisty young woman stole a glance in Gunter's direction. So far, anyway, the man hadn't flinched.

Sam was peeved by Carina's meddling. He especially didn't like the way she had taken to Gunter. "Daughter, to be quite frank, this is actually none of your concern. This is a project Fornax and I have been working on for a good long time. I'll not stand for your interference."

"It's every bit my concern!" she bellowed, refusing to back down. "I was the first one here — I should have my say!"

Samuel Matthews, father to Carina, sighed. What his daughter said was unquestionably true — as far as it went. Yes, she had been the first one here. But no, she didn't deserve to have her say. After two years of colonization, Carina was now just one of many — several hundred, to be precise.

"If you don't settle down, young lady, you may very well be the first one asked to leave!" Sam sputtered, applying his finest father-knows-best tone.

"As far as I'm concerned, it would be in all your best interests if I came along." Carina folded her arms across her chest. She had no intention of yielding.

Sam glanced around the room looking to the others for moral support. He found himself outmaneuvered. Fornax gave him a look of "How much trouble can she possibly get into?" to which Sam silently answered "Plenty!"

Sam really didn't want his daughter to come along, but clearly there was nothing he could do to stop her. He threw up his hands in defeat and shouldered in next to Oskar and Gunter aboard the *Tikkidiw*. It was time to make the jump out to the Belt.

Fornax was still at the computer, programming in the correct jump-coordinates. Carina moved in behind him, peering over his shoulders as if she meant to check his math perhaps verify that he was keypunching the right numbers.

Fornax looked up at her and smiled. It had been some time since she stood this close to him. He had nearly forgotten how attractive she really was. Auburn hair. Round laughing eyes. Proud, firm breasts. Tight, thin rump. A pretty package at half the price.

Unfortunately, she was more interested in making eyes at the muscle-bound Gunter than she was in repaying Fornax's longing gaze. This had been the story of his relationship with her from the very start. Carina never failed to be infatuated with everyone else but him.

"So this must be your daughter," Oskar Schaeffer remarked gruffly as Fornax calibrated his machine, checking and rechecking the coordinates for the jump. Plotting this course was a bit trickier than plotting a jump from the moon to the Earth, say, or from the Earth to Mars. The Belt was, after all, not a single body like the moon was, but rather, hundreds of thousands of *separate* bodies, not all of whose orbits were known with definition. The orbits of the known bodies were etched on the bubble-chip BC had smuggled out for him from the Minor Planet Center for Astrophysics in Cambridge. Considering all the favors Fornax had done for BC these past two years (including risking Sam's fury over absconding with his grandson), it seemed like a fair trade.

Nowadays, it was common knowledge that most of the main Belt asteroids traveled in the space between the orbits of Mars and Jupiter. But, for eons, no one even knew asteroids existed. Not until 1596, when the German astronomer Johannes Kepler began to suspect that the 560 million-klom-stretch of space separating Jupiter from Mars was simply too vast to be unoccupied, did the search begin for a missing planet. A fellow Euro, Johann Bode, had devised a formula that confirmed the mathematical likelihood of such a body. He observed that the formula, 0.4AU + (0.3AU X N), correctly predicted a planet's distance from the sun, where AU was expressed in astronomical units and N was an exponentially increasing variable which doubled for each planet out: 0 for Mercury, 1 for Venus, 2 for Earth, 4 for Mars, and so on. A snag arose, however, when Bode inserted the value 8 for the next known planet, Jupiter. Instead of producing Jupiter's observed distance from the sun, 5.2AU, the formula indicated that an undiscovered planet should orbit at 2.8AU. But, instead of finding a planet at 2.8AU distance from the sun as expected, astronomers began discovering asteroids!

(For the record, an N value of 16 yielded the actual distance of Jupiter, while an N value of 32 resulted in the correct position for Saturn, 10AU. With N equal to 64, the value was 19.6AU, the location of Uranus, but further out the formula faltered — both Neptune and Pluto were found to be in orbits closer to the sun than Bode's Law permitted. This, of course, fueled the somewhat later debate as to whether Pluto was actually a planet, or just a dried-up dead comet, and whether there was still a Planet X to be found out there somewhere in the hinterlands.)

Although the great majority of these "starlike" objects — hence the name *asteroid* — were found to travel in the open space between the orbits of Mars and Jupiter, the movement of two groups were closely aligned with the movement of Jupiter itself — one group orbiting just ahead of the giant planet, the other just behind, both lodged in Jovian Lagrange points.

Estimates placed the total number of asteroids at about one million. The vast majority of them were far too small to be seen from Earth without the aid of a telescope, as they ranged in size from as little as a speck, up to as much as eight hundred kloms across. More than 5000 of them had a diameter in excess of fifteen kloms! All evidence suggested that these irregularly-shaped chunks of rock were the remnants of one or more planetesimals that collided and broke apart under the tidal forces of Jupiter as the solar system was forming long ago. And, like all of the rocky planets — Mars and Earth included — the asteroids were laden with valuable ore.

Nearest the sun and accounting for roughly fifteen percent of the Belt's population were the S-type or silicaceous asteroids. These consisted of an olivine shell enclosing a core of nickel-iron alloy.

Dominating the Belt's middle region and separated from the inner ring by a Kirkwood gap, were the M-type asteroids. These were metallic chunks of nickel and iron that had emerged eons ago from repeated collisions among the S-type bodies.

Finally, inhabiting the Belt's outer reaches and making up three-quarters of the Belt's population, were the C-type asteroids, the carbonaceous or carbon-rich asteroids.

Fornax & Company had come hunting for one of the M-types. The only drawback to this venture was that this class of asteroid was the most difficult to reach and the fewest in number, barely ten percent of the total.

The M-types were hardest to reach, because — being in the middle of the Belt — there were the gravitational disturbances of the Kirkwood gaps to contend with. Named for the American mathematician Daniel Kirkwood, who first linked unoccupied orbits in the main Belt to Jupiter's gravity and orbital frequency, these were the zones where a ship traveling at Fornax Drive speeds was most likely to be thrown off course. Simply put, any asteroid circling the sun at a rate that was a simple fraction of Jupiter's orbital period of twelve earth-years — say an asteroid with a four-year orbit (3:1 resonance) or one with a six-year orbit (2:1 resonance) — would get a gravitational boost every time it lapped the gas giant, eventually being kicked out of that particular orbit. Over the course of millions of years of repeated tugs, asteroids in eight different orbits had been kicked clear, leaving behind the several Kirkwood gaps.

Despite the inherent risks, the hunt was apt to be worth the while. Fornax estimated that a single nickel-iron asteroid just one klom in diameter could fetch a price of some five trillion credits in markets back home on Earth. His plan was to employ an electromagnetic mass driver that would use the asteroid itself as fuel, propelling the big rock through the vacuum of space by ejecting pieces of it forward, *into* its orbital path, as retro-thrust; that is to say, counter to the asteroid's current direction of travel. Only by *slowing* orbital speed, could a satellite be brought down from orbit. Although this method of propulsion would consume about fifteen percent of the asteroid's mass in transit, enough raw material would remain intact to fund several terrestrial fortunes, his own included.

This and more went through Sam's mind as he watched Fornax fiddle with the knobs, making his final adjustments before the jump. He had nearly forgotten that a question had been put to him just before he drifted off. Oskar had said, "So this must be your daughter," a question Sam had not yet answered.

"Yes," he said, at long last. "This is my daughter, Carina."

"I've read some of your work," Schaeffer remarked. Though his voice seemed laced with contempt, the revelation that he had read some of Carina's work surprised her as well as her father. "Yes, indeed. You see, in my business, every time we set up a new quarry or open up a new mine anywhere on the planet, we have to file a dozen or more highly detailed reports, including a very expensive fossil-impact study. This two-hundred-plus-page report owes it life in large measure to you, young lady."

Carina's eyes narrowed. But she refused to be goaded into a retort.

Schaeffer continued. "Perhaps you have forgotten, little one. But you once wrote a paper in which you advocated banning the issuance of any new mine permits until a planet-wide fossil survey had been completed. The purpose of the survey was to pinpoint the most likely sites for major new fossil finds. Sadly, much of this malarkey was eventually adopted by the member countries. Believe me when I tell you, it has cost us a pretty penny to comply with the regulations. Thanks goodness your father doesn't share your narrow, elitist view of the world."

"Oh, is that so?" Carina exclaimed, shooting an angry glance in Sam's direction. "And to what view, pray tell, does my father hold?"

"Now, now, little girl," Oskar Schaeffer declared, his manner patronizing. "Not everyone can share your grand vision."

Carina's face reddened. "Well, I'll have you know, I've conducted plenty of valuable research myself. And I plan on doing loads more. In fact, in a couple of weeks, your man Gunter here is going to take me to the top of Olympus Mons, so I can look for fossils."

"He's gonna *whaaat?!*" Sam and Fornax exclaimed in unison.

At the sound of their incredulous outcry, the brawny Gunter lowered his big, blue eyes and shifted uneasily in place.

"Gunter and I are going to climb Olympus Mons," Carina repeated firmly. Then, looking Oskar Schaeffer squarely in the eye, she said, "You see, Mister Smart Guy, I wrote the book on Explosive Diversity, and I want to ascertain whether or not life ever got a start here on the Red Planet."

"Explosive what?" Schaeffer asked, doing his best to feign an interest he didn't actually have.

"Explosive Diversity. The theory that evolution is not a smooth, slowly-occurring process as everyone has maintained for centuries, but rather, a sudden, violent one, where environmental stresses like ice ages and volcanic eruptions produce explosions of genetic change in a geologic instant."

"That's preposterous!" Oskar said, shaking his head as if Carina were out of hers.

"No, listen to her," Fornax interrupted, hoping to garner some Brownie points with her in the process.

"Okay," Schaeffer relented. "But just for a moment — we have important work to do here."

Even as he gave up the floor to allow Carina to speak, Oskar Schaeffer already had his mind made up. This woman, this pesky little woman, was bound to be an obstacle to his plans before long. Clearly, if ASARCO was to have a prosperous future here on Mars, her newhuman settlement would have to be shuttered, and she herself deported. Everything hinged on finding the right Newton for the job, someone who was a natural-born leader, yet dissatisfied with the status quo. Someone who could be paid to instigate trouble, yet someone idealistic enough to believe he was doing it for a noble cause.

Surely, in a small community like Newton, the right someone could be found.

PART II

FIFTEEN

Act Of God

With a nod of a pretty head, and the wink of an appreciative eye, Carina acknowledged Fornax's effort in letting her speak.

In a sense, this whole discussion was quite ironic. Two-and-a-half years ago her department head at the university, along with his Board of Inquiry, had interrogated her in much the same way, with minds as closed as the one she was currently facing in Oskar Schaeffer. Her opening gambit today was much the same as it had been with the Board back then. And just like that first time, it wasn't going particularly well.

"I'm not arguing that Darwinian-style evolution never occurred. I'm only suggesting that there have been instances of inexplicably huge jumps of change, as well as miniscule adaptations. Granted, the overwhelming percentage of these huge jumps proved to be poor biological designs — misfits, if you will, that left no progeny behind to be captured in the fossil record — but every once in a while, one of these huge leaps produced an organ or a limb or even a completely new creature that *was* successful."

"Oh, and by what variety of sorcery were these huge leaps of change produced? Or should we call them leaps of faith?" Oskar Schaeffer harrumphed derisively. Though his tone stopped just short of mockery, the man had a haughty, cavalier air to him that even Gunter found offensive.

"There are cataclysmic forces at work here — An asteroid collision with the Earth, perhaps. Maybe a radiation burst from the sun. A strange wobble in the Earth's axis. Perhaps none of these things. Perhaps something else altogether. But whatever the cause, the triggering event is so stressful to existing strands of DNA, an explosion of mutations result, yielding a torrent of new species. Of course, as I said before, the overwhelming majority of these new species are duds. But a few actually survive. And those that do, are truly masterpieces of innovation."

"Preposterous! Now I suppose you will tell me next that Man himself was an accident, not the work of God at all."

Even as Oskar Schaeffer blurted out his proposition, Sam cringed. He knew any talk of God would set his daughter off for sure. Carina didn't believe in God. Knowing this, Sam settled into his launch-chair for what was bound to be a protracted wait.

"Hah!" Carina retorted vehemently. "You see God's hand in all this? Then you are a bigger fool than I gave you credit for. Evolution is not survival of the fittest, it is survival of the luckiest!"

"And it's my bad luck to be stuck here with you. Let's get going already," Schaeffer whined, his bulk jiggling as he pressed Fornax to leave.

"No, let the lady finish." This time it was Gunter coming to her defense.

"Thank you," she replied, blowing him a kiss.

Sam rolled his eyes and turned his head, not believing his daughter's shenanigans.

"Our impression that life evolves toward greater and greater complexity is little more than a self-centered conceit, a conceit with us humans at the center of the story. Western culture, especially, has made it a central tenet of its belief system — our history inevitably culminates in human beings as life's highest expression. We have to discard those ideas. We have to toss out the deep social traditions which tell us that we humans are Earth's intended steward. It is hard to accept, I know. But we are here purely by accident."

"Sam, your daughter needs to see a doctor," Schaeffer muttered. "Or else a rabbi."

Carina didn't pause long enough to give her father a chance to respond. "There is a contingent aspect to the pattern of life's history here on our planet. Of all the millions of plausible outcomes that could have conceivably occurred, only one actually *did* occur. *Homo sapiens* did not appear on the planet because evolutionary theory predicts such an outcome. Rather, humans arose as no more than a single lucky outcome from thousands of linked events, any one of which could have occurred differently and then sent history careening off on an alternative pathway which might or might not have led to consciousness."

"All this talk about contingencies and luck — I just don't see it," Schaeffer muttered, his mind churning with intrigue. Like a boil that had to be lanced, Carina was a negative influence, one which had to be neutralized if ASARCO was to be able to run things here on Mars the way they had back home in Johannesburg for generations.

Carina continued. "In life, as in so many things, webs and chains of historical events are so intricate, so filled with random and chaotic elements, the standard models of linear prediction and straight-line replication, simply do not apply. History includes too much chaos, too many unique — and uniquely interacting — objects. There is such a great dependence on tiny and immeasurable differences in the initial conditions, they cannot help but lead to massively divergent outcomes. And the divergent results are all based on tiny disparities in the starting conditions, disparities we may not even be aware of. In the case of *Homo sapiens*, let me cite but four of the lucky accidents our lineage has had along the way:

"First — If our absolutely unimportant and, if I may say so myself, somewhat fragile lineage had not been among the few survivors of the Cambrian explosion of multicellular life half a billion years ago, then vertebrates would not have survived to inherit the Earth.

"Second — If a small and unlikely group of lobe-finned fish had not evolved fin bones with a central axis strong enough to support their weight on land, then vertebrates might never have moved onto land.

"Third — If a large extraterrestrial body had not struck the Earth sixty-five million years ago, then dinosaurs would still be dominant and mammals would still be the rat-sized pipsqueaks they had been for the previous 100 million years.

"Fourth — If a small line of primates had not happened to evolve upright posture on the drying African savanna just four million years ago, then our ancestry might have ended in a line of apes which, like the chimpanzee and gorilla, would have become ecologically marginal and doomed to extinction despite their remarkable behavioral complexity.

"So you see, Herr Schaeffer. No God here. No God anywhere — All luck."

Schaeffer shook his head. "But what about natural selection? What about the struggle for survival? Are you going to claim that's all luck too?"

"Oh, as a theory natural selection works well enough. But that struggle is strictly metaphorical. No matter how we dress it up in the textbooks, natural selection need not be viewed as overt combat, guns blazing. Reproductive success includes a variety of less lethal activities. Earlier and more frequent mating. Improved cooperation between partners in raising their offspring. More ingenious uses of the resources in their environmental niche. Again, no God here anywhere."

"Well, let's hope for all our sakes that there *is* a God," Fornax suddenly interrupted, his long fingers poised on the "GO" button. His calculations were now complete. All that remained was to power up the Drive. "I would hate to count strictly on good luck for the success of this jump. Get strapped in people — it's time to go asteroid hunting!"

The Fornax Drive was at once simple and complex. Simple in that it was nothing more than an atomic storage-cell of a sort. Complex in that, of all the tens of thousands of nuclear physicists in the world, only Fornax Nehrengel had worked out all the pieces of the puzzle making near-light-speed travel possible. The exact arrangement was still a closely-guarded secret. But, by inserting finely-machined strips of the strategic alloy durbinium into a modified energy-exchanger, and by linking a standard regulator to the energy-exchanger with an O-ring coupler of his own design, Fornax had been able to achieve something no one else had: a Battery capable not only of sopping up high-energy neutrons from spent fuel rods, but also of controlling the rate of neutron release with precision. This made his invention quite valuable.

As Fornax waited patiently for his passengers to get securely buckled into their launch-chairs, the ever-curious Oskar Schaeffer questioned him. "What I don't understand about your Drive is this. Why don't we feel the acceleration? I mean, if we're jumping to sixty or seventy percent of light speed in an instant, why don't we get smashed like pancakes by the g-forces?"

Fornax smiled. Knowledge was power. "Much as the corner baker doesn't reveal the recipe for his hottest-selling muffin, I have no intention of telling you how much nutmeg I add to the dough, so to speak. But I will tell you this much: In accelerating through conventional speeds, say from 100 kloms per hour up to say 10,000 kloms per hour, g-forces work in the conventional way. But when the physics were worked out years ago uniting gravity and quantum mechanics into a single Unified Grand Theory, it was hypothesized that there would be a phase shift at around five percent of light speed where the so-called g-forces would fall away. Just as the sound barrier proved to be purely psychological and not physical at all, so too is the fear of being smashed flat at high rates of acceleration. It's sort of a case of *outrunning* gravity so that it can't catch up to you."

Having said all he cared to, Fornax punched the POWER button to engage the Drive. With a whoosh, they were off, and within minutes they were there, in the midst of a snowstorm of particles, large and small.

At first, Fornax couldn't believe his eyes, none of them could. The view outside their window was stunning. Even in his wildest imagination, Fornax could never have anticipated such a beautiful sight. Out here, in the M-type partition of the Belt, the sun was some 500 million kloms away. Still, there was enough sunlight to turn the nickel-iron shards of rock into a literal garden of jewels. Like a kaleidoscope or a shattered icicle off the roof, the patterns of color, of reflection, of refraction, were astonishing. It took their breath away.

For minutes, they all sat there mesmerized by the spectacle until a big chunk of rock bounced off the hull sending a frightening echo reverberating through the bulkheads and giving each of them a start. The hollow sound of rock against metal served to remind them all how dangerous this little escapade of theirs could truly be. One tiny tear in the fabric of the *Tikkidiw*'s outerskin, and they would all instantly be dead.

"Let's get to it," Fornax ordered, opening the cargo bay doors remotely and ejecting the giant net out into the ether.

Like fishermen transported out of another time, they had brought with them a net made of a tough, beryllium-copper alloy mesh for trawling the "waters" of the Belt. Any rock measuring above a tenth of a meter in diameter would be snagged. When the net was full, they would haul it in like so many pounds of lifeless tuna. The contents would have to be taken back to Earth, of course, and studied before a final decision could be made whether or not to proceed with the EMD project. This determination would take several weeks. But, if the results were positive, ASARCO would then move quickly to protect its claim.

SIXTEEN

Omen

Three Weeks Later

Kneeling at the edge of the ancient sea in the shadow of Olympus Mons, Carina scratched at the sedimentary rock with her sharply pointed tool. In an earlier epoch, when Mars's climate was more benign, this lake had been alive with stromatolite-like microorganisms. Carina was determined to be the first scientist to find definitive fossil proof of their existence. The thing was, prior to the asteroid collision that destroyed the colony two hundred years ago, there had been reports of such fossils. But those reports had turned out to be false, and the specimens were later shown to have been discovered in Utah, not Mars. Carina had it in her head to set the record straight once and for all.

No less important to her research here in the valley was next week's climb to the summit. Ever since running into Gunter five weeks ago when the *Tikkidiw* nearly crashed, she had been working out with the man for several hours each day. She was now arguably in the best physical shape of her twenty-nine-year-old life. It hadn't hurt, of course, that the man was a hunk and stayed after her day and night. But it also hadn't hurt that her father had been totally against the idea of her making this climb in the first place. That alone would have been enough to convince her to go, and now she was definitely committed to scaling the mountain along with Gunter and his crew. In fact, she expected him to join her here at any moment.

Though they only had two weeks for the ascent, Carina figured that would be long enough for her to make a cursory examination of the terrain and prepare a report for the governing Council. She wanted to convince them that a larger expedition should be mounted next season.

But, it was an uphill argument. Such ventures were expensive, and there was little taste among the members of the Council to finance it. Once again, that which seemed intuitive to her, others found outlandish or just plain silly. Even the idea of a separate colony had done nothing more than make her an outcast, leaving her estranged from her father and from the only two other men who ever really loved her.

Going back to her earliest days on the planet, when Carina first realized that the terraformers had succeeded in making Mars livable, she had been on a campaign to reserve this vast, undeveloped prairie as a homeland for newhumans, a venture (to use her father's words) so "narrow-minded as to be ludicrous." Sam's idea of what Mars ought to be like was more along the lines of the Oklahoma land-rush days of 1889 — a chaotic free-for-all based on nothing more than a grab-all-that-you-can-as-fast-as-you-can mentality. Carina's idea was for a much more controlled, much more rational approach to colonization — just the right number of the right sort of people living in precisely the right spot.

Not that it mattered so much at first. Mars was, after all, a rather big place. But, in no time at all, two very distinct spheres of influence had grown up, each vying for attention, each vying for resources. All of a sudden it was the free-wheeling frontier sort of settlement Sam had championed versus the ivory-towered, Camelotish settlement Carina had envisioned. The irrefutable dichotomy between Colony One and Newton was that the ivory-towerers of Newton were basically eggheads — people who, though industrious, were easily bored by the mundane intricacies of trade and finance and commerce — while the frontiersmen of Colony One were little more than uneducated, money-grubbing slobs. From the standpoint of who could better scratch out a living from the lichen-prairie, it was no match — the slobs handily outearned the snobs, a circumstance that peeved Carina no end. All along she had harbored the conceit that her newhuman colony would prosper in an almost geometric fashion. But, with each passing day, it was becoming more and more clear that this has been nothing but a pipe dream. Much as her father had tried to warn her, utopian-style experiments often failed.

In the beginning, terrans couldn't have cared less about the tug-of-war between the two settlements. Except for immigration-minded people like Carina, Mars held little in the way of commercial possibilities to offer Earth — the gravity well was too deep, the intervening distance too far, and the mineral deposits either too similar or else unknown.

The nearby asteroid Belt was a horse of a different color. To begin with, all but a few of these rocky planetoids lying between Jupiter and Mars had no gravity well to speak of. Moreover, assuming that one or more of them could be boosted nearer the Home Planet, it would be technologically feasible to mine them in high-earth-orbit much as the moon had been for years. To do this, however, required motors unlike any the world had ever seen, electromagnetic mass drivers of such dimension, an entirely new breed of factory had to be forged and hammered together out of bedrock. Thus, to resource-poor terrans, Mars was a platform, not for civilization or commerce, but for assembling the giant motors necessary to guide mineral-laden asteroids closer to Earth. And now that the ores Schaeffer and his crew had collected on their trip to the Belt assayed out so remarkably well, the motor-builders would be coming to Mars in great numbers.

Much to Carina's dismay, the sorts of people required for this kind of work (the "slobs" in her vernacular) were generally long on brawn and short on brains. Not exactly the types she envisioned filling her newhuman colony with. This, coupled with a curious, longstanding quirk of human nature, whereby the brainier types she was so enamored with were often attracted to the brawnier types she detested, provided fertile ground for trouble. Even she had succumbed to the temptation on occasion. And why not? These men were strong, virile specimens of manhood. Always ready to conjugate, never worried about the consequences. Even now, these ruffians were beginning to swarm in across the Martian landscape like so many dung beetles. This would just not do, not if she was to have her utopia.

To avoid this loathsome, detestable interaction between her snobs and their slobs, her utopia would have to be isolated even more from the centers of commerce that were quickly springing up to service the incoming asteroid movers. In fact, this is what was on her mind, now, as she ranged along over the old lakes and ancient riverbeds at the foot of Olympus Mons, scouring the countryside for any signs of earlier life in advance of her upcoming climb to the summit.

Scratching in the red, marbled clay with her tool, she didn't hear Gunter's approach until he was almost upon her. Suddenly, there he was, all tall and handsome.

"You're late!" she snorted. Though her remark was unquestionably framed as a complaint, there was no harshness to her voice.

"I could fabricate an excuse if it would make you feel better," he replied, not one to be easily outmaneuvered.

"Only if it's more amusing than the truth. Otherwise, just stick to the facts."

"Climbing's my business, little lady, not excusing my behavior. If you want some prim and proper gentleman to train you, then you had better look elsewhere."

"What makes you tick exactly?" she asked, her nose turned up in a pout beneath the wide brim of her hat. Like any sensible Newton, she wore the headgear to protect her skin against the worse effects of the sun.

"Please?"

"I mean, scaling this mountain looks like work — hard work — only you treat it as if it were a game."

Gunter grinned his big Aussie grin. "Hell's bells, little lady, how can anything fun be considered work? For the real climbers, getting to the top is only half the fun!"

"How so?"

"If we have the strength, we always have the option of rappelling down into the caldera."

"That sounds dangerous."

"It is!" he said, excitement filling his voice. "But the folks over at the Guinness Foundation proposed just such a stunt as one for the record books. Don't forget — climbing equipment is expensive, damn expensive. Their honorarium should help defray some of the costs."

"With you men it's always the same macho, dare-devil crap."

"And with you women it's always the same holier-than-thou crap. In case you've forgotten, Carina, may I remind you. We're the climbers. You're only along for the ride, our visiting guest-scientist."

"I'll be sure to bring my nail polish and handcream."

"Look, this trip isn't going to be a vacation. To the contrary, this climb is apt to be hard work for all of us. But most especially you. And it could be dangerous. That's why, unless you're in topnotch physical condition by departure date, I won't even consider bringing you along. Now, shut up, slip on this pack, get down on the ground, and show me thirty good pushups carrying this weight on your back."

Even as he spoke, Gunter handed her the heavy rucksack he had slung over his shoulder. Grumbling, she took it, slipped it on, and got down on all fours. As he counted off the reps, she thought about the trip ahead.

Gunter told her the ascent to the rim would take between ten and fourteen days. With several days of rest and loitering at the summit, he allowed an equal amount of time for the descent. The ascent team would consist of her, the four climbers, plus two Sherpas with experience in the Himalayas. These strongbacks would give the mission the added physical strength it would need to transport the life-support and other gear to the top. All the climbing and bivouac equipment they required for the trip would be delivered to the start point either by llama or else by electric dune buggy, a contraption Gunter called an "itty-bitty."

Because of the elements, they would have to wear protective dee-dees for the entire climb. These body-fitting double density spacesuits, while state-of-the-art, were uncomfortable as sin to wear. As was her way, Carina objected immediately.

"Why do I have to wear this damn thing?" Carina whined that day when the team assembled in Gunter's office to fit themselves for pressure-suits. Catching a glimpse of herself in the mirror, Carina was shocked to learn that her very attractive figure was completely camouflaged by the ungainly bulk of material. "It's ugly!"

"You have no choice," he boomed. "Wear it or stay home. Up on the mountain we face many hazards. Gamma-ray poisoning. Mountain sickness edema. Cold. Heat. This ain't no fashion show we're going to!"

Gunter went on to explain that most edema victims were fit, nonsmoking, middle-aged individuals who believed good health rendered them immune from altitude sickness. Nothing could be further from the truth. In fact, fitness had little or nothing to do with it. High-altitude pulmonary edema could strike anyone. The symptoms included a dry cough, blue lips, gurgling in the throat, and a pink frothy spittle. Left untreated, a victim would soon drown in his own fluid. High-altitude cerebral edema — fluid on the brain — was rare, but more deadly still. Here, the symptoms included severe headache, vomiting, confusion, slurring of speech, and lack of coordination. Coma and death could follow. Gunter's advice was to ascend gradually, drink lots of water, avoid tortan or other ale, and eat plenty of carbohydrates. Carina intended to follow his instructions to the letter.

*   *   *

One Week Later

Camping at the foot of Olympus Mons was not simply indescribable, it was fundamentally so. Indeed, standing at the foot of the giant, extinct volcano, Carina couldn't even see its summit because the rim was so far away, it was over the planet's horizon. Being a terran by birth, and a flatlander at that, her brain couldn't quite get the knack for relating to anything as utterly large as Olympus Mons. O.Mons, as the climbers called it. Only they pronounced it like a Jamaican might — Oh, monn. To her, that sounded suspiciously close to Omen.

Still, no matter how you pronounced it, there was no denying the fact that the mountain was huge — nearly five hundred kloms across at the base, and twenty-seven kloms high. And, atop this implausibly big mountain was an equally stupendous caldera. It was composed of nested craters eighty kloms across and three kloms deep. Or, as Gunter kept reminding her, larger than anything on Earth.

For almost its entire circumference, a circumference Carina had viewed with apprehension from the air several weeks ago when the *Tikkidiw* returned home from its trip to the Belt, Omen was encircled by a series of cliffs and scarps ranging in height from four to six kloms. And while it was true that she was adequately awed by the mountain from here at its base, Omen was most impressive when seen from the air. Only then could its entire bulk be judged on a planetary scale.

There are relatively few geologic formations on Earth as immense, as eye-riveting, as Omen. Almost none of them can compare with Omen for sheer size. Perhaps, El Capitan in Yosemite, or Ayers Rock in Australia. But even those formations would be like babies against their momma. True, they are big things which, when viewed from a distance, seem to stay the same size as you approach them; things that you eventually reach only after hours upon hours of walking; and yet, these blemishes on the terran landscape are puny by comparison.

That day, as the *Tikkidiw* approached, Omen just sat there waiting, waiting to jump out at her as the ship drew nearer. And when it eventually did start to grow, it grew so much that its summit moved quickly out of view. Just looking up at the mountain now, Carina couldn't escape the feeling that the entire planet was pear-shaped, swelling to a point directly in front of her. Indeed, Gunter told her that the Tharsis Bulge, which contained Omen plus several other massive volcanoes, had caused the Red Planet's spin-axis to shift over the eons, much like an off-balance top. With tectonic activity not as pronounced here on Mars as on Earth, and continental plates nearly absent, these giant volcanoes hadn't moved around much over time like they would have back home. Instead, while they were alive, these monsters stayed put and spewed out lava for more than a billion years, deforming the entire surface of the planet.

*   *   *

Somewhere Along the Road Between Newton and Colony One

The shadows of Mars were as effective a cloak for clandestine activity as any there ever had been on Earth. Thus, it was under the cover of darkness that very same night that the first and only meeting took place between Oskar Schaeffer of Johannesburg and Inda Desai of Newton. It would be difficult to predict in advance the actions of such men, or to understand what drove them, but in Inda Desai, Oskar Schaeffer had found the right mix of natural-born leader, dissatisfied subject, and idealistic buffoon to make his project a success.

"Let's see if I have this straight," Inda said, doing his utmost to keep his voice low. Given how angry Schaeffer had already made him, this was not an easy task. "You are almost singlehandedly responsible for bringing this crush of outsiders to our planet, and yet you want to hire me to help you put a *stop* to it? To help you undermine the entire operation? You can hardly blame me if your true agenda escapes me."

Oskar Schaeffer's face was severe. "I don't blame you, young man, if you don't understand. But your thinking is linear, not creative at all. If you learn nothing else today, learn this: It is only through extremism that we achieve moderation. Never forget that. It is not I who brings these outsiders to your planet, it is Samuel Matthews and Fornax Nehrengel. They want industry brought here so they can entice more newcomers with the promise of jobs. I want to harvest the asteroids, yes. And I want to build a motor factory, that is true. But I wanted it built at one of the moon's Lagrange points, not way out here. Sam and Fornax were the ones who insisted the factory be built here, on Mars." Though Schaeffer knew this last statement was a flat-out lie, it suited his purposes.

"So why are you telling me all this? What do you want from me?"

"Rabble-rous, my boy. Stir up dissent. Plan a demonstration. Burn something down. Get the workers to go on strike. Blow up the place if you have to. Do whatever it takes to convince Matthews and Nehrengel that the factory shouldn't be built here on Mars."

"And what would I get for my trouble?" Inda asked. There was a practical edge to his voice as he looked nervously over his shoulder for any sign of an eavesdropper.

"Well, to begin with, success is its own reward. — If you succeed in this, you and the other Newtons will have the planet to yourselves, just as you have wanted from the start. But beyond that, I will supply you with enough money and enough arms so that when Matthews *does* give up on this motor factory idea of his and goes back to his cushy little manor in Zealand, where he belongs, you will be left in charge. Think of it, boy — you could rule an entire world!"

"That *is* food for thought," Inda had to admit. "And I can't deny being a hungry man."

"I thought as much," Schaeffer replied, a satisfied smile on his face. "I've seen that lean and hungry look before, and it has always worked out the same."

SEVENTEEN

Belay

Three Days Later

When the four humans, six llama, and one hundred and fifty kilograms of suits and gear arrived at the northwest escarpment of Olympus Mons ahead of schedule, Gunter graciously offered them all a day off to rest in preparation for the big wall. Four point two vertical kloms of rock awaited them — a virtual smorgasbord of Martian basaltic rock types. The wall was a vast expanse of cracks, fissures, and columns, interrupted by several broad ledges. Just the right mix of challenge and security to give the climbers goose-bumps, and Carina an upset stomach. Their climbing style would be a blend of alpine tradition, plus some tactics developed since. And, like their forebears, Gunter's team would use ropes, carabiners, and belay devices to get them safely to the top.

Ever since she was a little girl watching climbers scale the alps of Zealand, Carina had always wondered how it was done, how the rope got "up" there. But, as Gunter demonstrated in one of their practice sessions, it was all quite simple — *the climbers carried it up there with them.*

It begins with the lead climber. He hauls with him a rope attached to his waist by a safety harness. The other end of the rope is fed out to him by a "belayer" below who is himself secured to the rock either by a "nut" — a piece of metal threaded with small rope and wedged into natural crevices in the rock — or by a "friend" — a multi-radius camming device capable of expanding to fill any available nook or cranny.

By design, these protection pieces, these nuts and friends, could be placed and removed quickly with just one hand. As he climbs, the lead climber sets the protection pieces in the rock, clipping his rope through attached snaplinks called "carabiners." These limit his potential for a fall to no more than twice the distance between the lead point and the last protection piece. After completing a "pitch" — a distance determined by a combination of the rope's length (usually fifty meters) and the availability of good belay spots — the leader secures a new belay, then takes up the rope while the second climber follows.

Climbing gear has always had a history of utilizing the latest in materials technology, and the equipment they were carrying was no exception. Materials constructed from polymerized buckyballs, forged micro-g alloys, and bioengineered polymers offered them the latest in strength-to-weight ratios. The carabiners, for example, were forged from exotic beryllium-copper alloys fired at ASARCO's microgravity foundry at L5. To hear Gunter talk about them, you would think they were his own flesh and blood.

Actually, a carabiner was nothing more than a D-shaped ring with a spring catch on one side. In spite of its technical simplicity, the carabiner's importance to a successful climb could not be understated — *it was the exclusive means a mountaineer had for fastening ropes.* Even her father said the word said something about its function. According to him, it was from the Austrian "karabiner," meaning a carbineer or soldier armed with a carbine, plus "haken," meaning a hook. Together, the term "karabinerhaken" came to describe a hook originally used to fasten a carbine to a bandoleer. Later shortened to just "karabiner," the idea of a tough, unbreakable fastener ring was adopted by the first mountaineers, many of whom were Austrians.

The ropes, too, were the best money could buy. Composed not of hemp but the latest in manmade fibers, even an experienced alpinist couldn't tell them apart from the ropes used by terran mountain climbers two hundred years ago. Human hands, even gloved ones, were, after all, still the same size they had always been.

From her several weeks of preparation for this adventure, Carina knew their efforts would be significantly eased by putting to good use several climbing tools that had been developed specifically for use on Mars, among them the Bolt Gun. This device fired a diamond-tipped projectile, or bolt, with such force, it was capable of penetrating virtually any type of rock. Attached to the bolt was a loop, a loop through which they could affix a variety of carabiners and ropes which were, in turn, affixed to the climbers' suits. Whenever possible, the team would climb the cliff surface itself. This was, of course, the preferred traditional way of climbing. The bolts and ropes would only serve to catch them if they fell. When there was nothing obvious or available to hold onto, they would use the Bolt Gun or artificial holds, and then grab for whatever they could. Or they could simply walk up the ropes themselves using Gunter's patented mechanical-ascender.

Whatever the climbers used, this would all begin tomorrow. Today was still today. Right now she had a little free time on her hands to jot down some notes for her report to the Council. She also had a hands-free microcorder she would use on the climb. Her observations began with a physical inspection of the landscape:

Unlike the green lowlands where Newton and Colony One were situated, Omen was still painted the sandstone-red the whole planet had been for all eternity before terraforming began. Since time immemorial, this colossal mountain had stood here resolute, waiting for mankind to arrive. So far, at least, the mountain seemed unimpressed.

Each morning it was hugged at the base by a patch of lowland fog. Then, as the day wore on and the ground warmed, the fog would lift, eventually reaching them on the side of the mountain by midday. Because the air up here, where they were, was so thin and cold, it couldn't keep the moisture suspended in it as a vapor for long. As soon as the fog-cloud began to rise, ice crystals would form. By late afternoon, even the thickest of clouds had dissipated and the troop of climbers would be inundated by a rain of ice.

Gunter had chosen late summer to make the assault figuring that at this season there would be a reasonable balance between tolerable temperatures and the risk of encountering one of Mars's trademark storms.

Just hearing the word "storm" still made Carina cringe. A thousand years might pass and she would still never forget that terrible night two years ago when she was traumatized by a ferocious weather system.

Or how about that night just a month ago when Inda reached out through a freezing cold downpour to rescue her from an almost certain death?

Then too, what about those dismal days she spent alone waiting for BC to return as the murky waters outside the Mars Base rose ever higher and higher?

The memories were painful, and Carina tried to push them aside. Her thoughts drifted back to the present and she resumed her study of the arching mountain ridge. It had a jagged shape, not one smoothed by wind or water erosion. Set against the backdrop of the deep purple sky, the colossal extinct volcano was foreboding. She prayed she would be able to manage the next leg of the ascent. Nightfall was fast approaching, and it was as the team made its final preparations for tomorrow's assault on the wall that Gunter stopped to talk with her at length for perhaps the first time since they left base camp. She put away her microcorder to give him her full attention.

"I don't understand what it is you're after, little lady," he began in his slow Aussie drawl.

"Life," Carina replied simply. Even after all this time, she still wasn't sure she liked the appellation "little lady."

"Life? Hell's bells, little lady, there's life all around us," Gunter said, checking the tension on each of the expedition's Bolt Guns. Gunter was a big man, with an unruly mop of wavy blond hair and a set of piercing blue eyes. He kind of reminded her of BC, and she found it difficult to concentrate whenever he was near.

"Not *this* life!" she snapped, as if the answer should have been obvious. "Past life. Fossil life."

"Rock hunter, eh?" he said, scrutinizing the last of the Bolt Guns before moving on to the ropes and carabiners.

"You might call me that," she granted modestly. "That's some of what I did back on Earth anyway."

"So Schaeffer said. But what kinda life you after, little lady? Hasn't Mars always been a dead planet? I mean before us humans got here?" His penetrating azure eyes looked right through her.

"No, Mars hasn't always been a dead planet," she answered, averting her gaze. Whenever the big, muscular man stared at her, it seemed like a come-on, like he was trying to bed her on the spot — only he wasn't. "Long ago, when Mars was warmer, liquid water collected on her surface, just as it did on Earth."

"Oh, yeah, you're talkin' about those dry riverbeds, aren't you?"

"Indeed I am, ya big lug. And where there was once liquid water, there was at least the *possibility* of life."

As Carina spoke, she put on the air of a professor, the sort of air which made her seem terribly aloof to a fellow as simple as this one. This, more than anything else probably accounted for her inability to bed the man so far. Still, when it came to satisfying her needs, she wasn't the sort to give up easily.

"Well, where did it go?" he asked, desperately trying to keep up with her. Out on the mountain, circumstances were reversed — he was the expert and she the novice. But here, in the classroom, he was the student and she the teacher. Still, he was a man and had no intention of allowing her to get the upper hand.

"Liquid water habitats survived on Mars for at least as long as it took for life to begin to evolve on Earth. Therefore, it only makes good sense that life probably had time to arise here as well. The cause for its *demise* is an altogether different matter. That had a lot to do with Omen here."

"Whatever do you mean, little lady?" Gunter asked, arching his head back to see whether he could see the summit through the clouds. He could not.

"Omen is a dead volcano, isn't it?"

"Let's hope so, or else Guinness is really going to have something to write about for his next edition."

"Yes, of course. But you see — there are no live volcanoes on the planet whatsoever."

"Ma'am?"

"In the presence of standing water — Mars had years ago — atmospheric carbon dioxide is eventually depleted. Without plate tectonics and volcanism to recycle the carbon, the atmosphere would be rapidly leeched of its $CO2$ and the greenhouse effect lost."

"Now I see what you mean," Gunter nodded. "And without the greenhouse effect, the planet got too damn cold. Just like it was before the terraformers went to work on it. But then how does the lichen manage it?"

Carina explained. "The lichen planted here is a genetically-engineered strain of an Earth-lichen that weathers the cold by converting the water in its vascular systems from liquid to gel without permitting cell-bursting ice crystals to form."

"If you say so, little lady, but what are *you* looking for?"

"Omen would have been one of the last warm spots on the planet. What I'm looking for is any evidence of fossil remains or fossil-bearing strata."

"Warm at twenty kloms up? Even volcanic, that sounds rather fanciful to me. And even if it were true, wouldn't any fossil remains be buried now under meters of old lava?"

Carina didn't answer.

"Well, little lady, all I got to say is this. I want your eyes on the ropes at all times when we're climbing, not on the ground. Is that clear?" he barked, tightening the last of the restraining straps that would hold their equipment in place should a storm kick up overnight.

"Yes, boss," she replied demurely. "Whatever you say."

"And while we're at it. Isn't it about time you hit the sack?"

"You wouldn't want to hit the sack with me, would you?" she asked, her genitals throbbing at the prospect.

"Little lady, these mummy bags we sleep in out here on the mountain are barely big enough to sleep one, much less two. We've got a tough climb ahead of us. So I suggest you get some rest and quit pestering me with silly questions."

"In a minute. There's still one more question I have to ask you. I've told you why I'm out here, why are you?"

"Pardon?"

"I mean, I know why I'm making this climb, why are you? And don't give me some macho crap like: Because it is there. I want a straight answer this time."

He laughed. "You are a handful, aren't you?"

"Depending on the size of your hands, maybe two handfuls," she said, batting her eyes at him through the face mask of her pressure-suit. There was no mistaking her intentions. Her body language said it all.

"The people supporting my climb want to build a rocketsled or perhaps a railgun up the side of either Omen or Arisa Mons so they can offer cheaper payload-to-orbit launch costs for those big asteroid moving motors we want to assemble here. More exports mean more money."

"It always comes down to that, doesn't it? Money."

"What's wrong with money? They say your father's swimming in the stuff."

"Drowning more like."

"Have it your way. But, in the meantime, just imagine the tourist trade. Once Disney and Tortan-Cola get their hooks in here, there will be no stopping it. No one will want to go back to Earth."

"How depressing," she sighed, now having yet another reason to cordon off her settlement from Colony One. "Why money moves the male of the species has always been a great mystery to me."

"You enjoy solving mysteries, don't you, little lady? I can tell that about you."

"Yes. And collecting fossils can solve a great many of them."

"My boss warned me that you had an obsession with this stuff. Give me a for-instance."

"Of what?"

"Of a mystery that fossils have solved."

"The disappearance of the dinosaurs, for one," Carina said, turning pensive. "We've learned from the fossil record that mass extinctions are as central to life's pathway as DNA itself. Beginning with the Alvarez data in the twentieth century, we've learned that the impact of an asteroid seven to ten kloms in diameter set off the last great extinction sixty-five million years ago, the one which wiped out the dinosaurs."

"Yes, I'm familiar with Alvarez. Geologists even discovered the so-called smoking gun, a crater of appropriate size and age located off the Yucatan peninsula. But that's ancient history — who can relate to something sixty-five million years back? Give me something more recent."

"It's true — humans have a devil of a time relating to geologic age. And why is that? Is it because human life is so short? Because we live on another time-scale entirely? An apple turns brown in a matter of minutes; a banana in a matter of days. A compost heap decays in a season. A woman is pregnant for a mere nine months. A lifetime lasts barely a century. Not one of these common, everyday experiences can prepare us to comprehend the meaning of sixty-five million years. Okay, you want something more recent? Try Greek mythology."

"Huh?" Gunter grunted as he crouched down to help Carina pound in the stakes for her one-man Igloo. Like all the tents they carried with them on this expedition, the Igloo was made from insulated, tear-resistant bio-canvas. Lightweight and breathable, it maintained a constant inside temperature of 58 degrees Fahrenheit — perfect for sleeping.

Carina explained. "Legends of giants and monsters have long been associated with fossil-rich areas. Take the Greek legend of the Cyclops. Paleontologists and folklorists alike agree that prehistoric discoveries of elephant skulls commonly found in Mediterranean caves undoubtedly account for the Cyclops Homer wrote of. The large nasal cavity would have led someone unfamiliar with elephant physiology to visualize the skull as being that of a giant one-eyed ogre."

"Are you suggesting that all of our boogeymen are nothing more than misunderstood fossil finds?"

"Perhaps not all, but at least some," she said, her eyes suddenly brightening. Carina had finally stumbled onto a subject that caught the man's attention. "If you're not happy with the Cyclops, consider the griffin. What kind of prehistoric remains might have inspired the folklore surrounding the griffin?"

"You're talking about that bird-like thing so many people are scared of, aren't you?" Even as he spoke, Gunter rammed the last tent pin into the ground. "Threatening beak, long ears, forehead horns?"

"Yes, that's the one. They were favorite subjects for casting in bronze by the ancient Greeks. Even the word itself is scary — from the Greek 'gryps' for hooked, as in beak, as well as from the Persian verb 'giriften,' to grip or seize. The Ancients described these animals as formidable predators the size of wolves, with strong beaks like those of an eagle. They were thought to be fearsome creatures likened to silent hounds with terrible hooked beaks.

"But for us, as modern, nonsuperstitious people, the question we have to ask ourselves is this: Were they real? Was there ever such a thing as a griffin, with four legs like a lion, talons like an eagle, even ears and wings by some accounts? Or, were they the product of someone's vivid imagination?"

Gunter objected. "We discover animals all the time that we didn't know existed. Some that we even thought were extinct. Why should the Greeks have been any different?"

"Fair enough. But maybe, just as with the case of the Cyclops, paleontology can offer another explanation. Remember, by the time of the Greeks, the Euros were beginning to trade extensively over the silk routes to Asia. Griffinology kept pace. In the arid regions where griffins were legend, there is little vegetation, making it possible to spot fossils on the surface."

Gunter was about to question that when she said, "Believe me, I've been there myself. Did a summer there between my sophomore and junior years."

Even as she spoke, her mind drifted back ten years to scenes of wind-scoured dunes and red sandstone cliffs. The Gobi Desert, where she did her practicum.

"The soft rock makes it easy to uncover partially embedded bones. The white-colored fossils stand out against the red sandstone. That's why this area is a literal treasure drove for fossils. In fact, the area is thick with *Protoceratops* skulls as well as fossilized dinosaur eggs. Also the bones of other dinosaurs like pterosaurs. It seems intuitive to me that ancient nomads traveling along their caravan routes would have observed fully articulated remains of dinosaurs about the size of a wolf and resembling a large, flightless, four-legged raptor. Pliny the Elder described them as such in his *Natural History* circa A.D. 77. To ancient observers, such fossil finds, combined with knowledge of contemporary animal behavior, may have suggested scenes of fierce animals defending their territory or their young."

"Tell me, little lady, how would any sensible man come to such a conclusion?"

Over the big man's shoulders, the sun could be seen slipping rapidly beneath the horizon. Unlike on Earth where, with its thicker atmosphere, dusk was often a long, drawn-out affair, here darkness arrived with startling speed.

"*Protoceratops* and other beaked quadrupeds are the most common remains found in these deserts, and they share many characteristics with the classical image of the ancient gryps. Of course, other dinosaur remains were undoubtedly found there as well, and they certainly contributed to the overall legend. These would have included such things as large isolated claws, pterosaurs with sharp beaks, crested skulls and ten-foot wingspans, plus a wide assortment of other bony, ridged, frilled, knobbed, or spiked skulls. The stiff, stylized wings and head knobs seen on some griffins in ancient art may have been an attempt to account for these odd features. Perhaps wings were added by some creative artist to complement the strange avian characteristics these fossils suggested — the presence of a beak, obvious nest building, and of course, egg-laying."

A stiff wind suddenly threw Carina to one side and she found herself in Gunter's arms.

She smiled. But he set her back on her feet and said, "I find a lot of truth in what you are saying, little lady. But maybe we had better pick this up again in the morning. Nightfall is upon us, and I don't want to be fumbling around out here in the dark. Good night and sleep tight."

With that, he turned and disappeared into the night.

EIGHTEEN

Mountaineering

Four Days Later

After the wild climb up the wall, this portion of the ascent seemed more like a stroll in the park. In fact, Carina found the current stretch of rock to be a monotonous terrain with a slope of only four to six degrees throughout.

With the exception of Gunter's fall two days back, climbing the wall had turned out to be a surprisingly routine enterprise, once she got the hang of it. One thing was for certain: no matter how hard the climbers tried to be careful, there was no escaping the everpresent element of danger.

When it happened, Gunter had been in the lead. He had unintentionally pulled a rock loose from the mountain with his gloved hand, and was careening downward before she could even react. The rope finally caught him, thank God — but before it did, he had fallen a good ten meters and smashed his face right-smack into the side of the cliff.

When he slipped, Carina screamed her bloody head off, thinking first that the man was dead, then, seconds afterward, that his body weight would pull all the bolts out of the rock, killing every single one of them in the process. The results were not nearly so dramatic.

To begin with — and this is what separated Gunter from lesser trek leaders — he had anticipated this hazard even before leaving base camp. Positioned in front of each of their faceplates was a shock-resistant face guard. This, no doubt, is what saved that noble chin of his from damage.

Looking back upon the accident now, Carina realized that making it up that wall had required every bit of the four weeks of training Gunter had given her. The entire crew's welfare greatly depended upon this man and his expertise.

The sport was made safe — if indeed rock climbing could be properly termed a sport — by a technique called the "hip belay." If a climber's partner belayed him properly, he could only fall as far as the slack in the rope separating the two climbers. If a climber was in the lead, as Gunter had been the day of the accident, or if one were mountaineering solo, he would have to be belayed by some sort of protective hardware.

In the old days it would be a piton, or metal spike, that had been pounded into the bedrock. Nowadays, climbers used protection that could be removed — bolts, chocks, and cams. With the hip belay, one depended on the climber above him not so much to be strong as to be alert. With proper technique, even a small climber like Carina could easily hold up her end. By the same token, bad technique or lack of attention could not be overcome by sheer strength.

So it was that, with carabiners dangling from a sling around her shoulder, the coarse rope paying out from her mentor above, and the mountain falling away from her in several thousand meters of what climbers like to call "exposure," the real climb had begun.

Reaching up, now, with fingers that trembled with effort, she found a little shelf of rock and gripped it hard, hard enough to dig tiny grooves into it with her gloves.

Then, finding another ledge with her foot, she raised herself up half a meter. She followed this tentative move with another. And then another.

Each time, the slack in her rope disappeared above her as Gunter took it in. Then she made another, slightly more confident move. Before long she was climbing the wall competently, if not skillfully. And, as she went along, the words Gunter drilled into her head over and over again during her training began to take on meaning:

While everything in your mind and in your body tells you to cling to the rock, to hug it, what you actually need to do is lean away from it. That drives the point of contact deeper into the rock and makes you stick. It is counterintuitive, little lady, but you have to force yourself to believe in it — and to do it.

Concentrating, now, with all her being, Carina made the moves precisely as he had taught her. Hardened by weeks of training, her muscles rippled beneath the skin of her suit. Her breath came faster, but not dangerously fast. Her heart beat quicker, but well within safe limits. She smiled at her own success and began to feel lightheaded, even giddy.

Climbing a vertical surface was a challenge. But in a pressure-suit, it became a challenge of the second order. While she was free to move her limbs almost without limitation, and while the gloves she wore had several hundred years of design history behind them, her dexterity was limited. She couldn't help but feeling trapped inside the suit.

The garment she wore was actually a modified dee-dee, a descendant of the earliest spacesuits the astronauts wore. Inside was a skintight pressure-suit made of a bodyheat-activated bio-fabric. Then a bulkier tear-proof thermal layer on top on that. Plus a tough yet flexible outer layer that was resistant to both micrometeors and solar radiation.

At this elevation, Mars's atmosphere was so thin, it offered no protection whatsoever when it came to weathering solar radiation storms. Of course, in an emergency, a person could survive more than a week in one of these suits. But it wouldn't be a pleasure cruise.

For this trek the standard dee-dee had been augmented with a larger air conversion system and a more efficient storage battery, though neither changed the one thing that had been true of spacesuits since the dawn of the space age. They still smelled awful after a couple days' wear, no matter how many times they were redesigned. This, despite the manufacturer's claim that 98 percent of the wastes would either be recycled or else "stabilized," whatever that meant.

In addition to the problems associated with movement in a one-third-g field, Carina found that living on a mountainside exerted some peculiar effects on her point of reference. Down was still down of course, at least in a physical sense. But everything else had changed. To bivouac on a cliff — or "bivy," as Gunter put it — was to experience climbing at its most intense. After a few days of vertical living, she found herself thinking about up and down in a totally different way than before. "Up" became "ahead." "Down" became "behind." The cliff became an endless expanse she had to somehow haul herself "across." Before long, her eyes were playing tricks on her. And it didn't matter that the local value of gravity was only 0.38g; she couldn't conquer her fear of heights. In this regard, Gunter wasn't much help. He constantly reminded his crew that once you were above a hundred meters or so, it didn't matter what planet you were on, a big fall would almost certainly kill you.

Yet, in spite of her fears — or perhaps because of them — after conquering the wall, Carina figured that she owed it to herself to stop a moment and take a closer look around. The view which greeted her was mind-bending. They were more than sixteen kloms above sea level. From this elevation, she could see a distance of nearly three hundred kloms without the slightest effort. From this height, Mars was unmistakably round. The sunset revealed some of the violence of its earliest history. Whereas much of Earth had been smoothed by water and wind — and later still, by Man — Mars remained a planet of austere and rugged beauty, a planet blessed with precipitous ravines, giant craters, craggy mountains, dangerous icefields, and enormous, flat plains.

Sweeping the horizon with her eyes, Carina recognized what she already knew to be true — many of the geological processes known so well to Earth had also once been at work here on the fourth planet. At times, the parallels between the Earth and Mars were so blatantly obvious, the more one had seen of Earth, the more one understood about the history of Mars.

Ancient tectonic movement had disfigured the planet, leaving behind two remarkably different hemispheres. To the south lay heavily cratered highlands. To the north, smoother plains dominated the landscape. Immense canyonlands and giant extinct volcanoes like Omen were among the spectacular features straddling the demarcation line between the northern steppe and the southern plateau.

But, in the three centuries since the terraformers arrived, things had changed. Whereas in the past the Martian mesa would have been the color of red sandstone, now it was the blue of ocean and the green of lichen as far as the eye could see. In two places, the green was punctuated by spots of brown and gray. These were Man's colors, the colors of buildings, part of humankind's fledgling attempt to wrest control of Mars from the throes of its premature death and mold it into a reasonable facsimile of Earth — Newton to the east, Colony One to the west.

*　　*　　*

By the time Gunter's team reached the "chute" just below the summit two days later, Carina was feeling a sublime blend of confidence and enthusiasm in her newly-acquired climbing skills. Though she hadn't seen a single fossil since the ascent began, nor even taken out much time to search for any, she had accomplished something equally remarkable: *Carina Matthews, Ph.D. had scaled the tallest mountain in the solar system!*

Leaning out from the rock, now, and stretching her hand to find a fingerhold, she kicked her foot up high enough to reach the next ledge, extending herself in a move she would never have thought possible only a month ago. As the slack in her rope disappeared above her, she came around one last outcropping and then she was there, on top of the world!

Mere words could not possibly begin to describe the feeling. Here she was, at twenty-seven thousand meters elevation, in as perfect a vacuum as any physicist back home could ever create in his laboratory. Despite the burgeoning atmosphere at sea level, the sky up here was jet-black with a faint whisper of haze on the horizon. The stars did not twinkle as they had down below. There was no air to carry the sound of her unabashed hurrah. *She had made it!* For all intents and purposes, the woman was in space!

But, as quickly as Carina swallowed her sense of exhilaration, she knew her fun was over. Sitting in a gap three hundred meters away was an official-looking jetchop. To conserve on batteries, the climbing team never turned on their two-way radios unless they had something important to say to one another, and certainly never just to listen and see if someone was trying to call *them*. No, it wasn't the Colony One jetchop that surprised her — after all, she never intended to rappel back down with the others anyway — it was that the pilot was holding a text message for her in his hand.

She approached the craft with trepidation. The message was from Saron. Carina's father had been to see her and hadn't looked well. She had recommended he go back to his estate in Zealand for a good long rest, only he refused. Later that same day he collapsed and was now laid up in the Colony One Hospital. For several days already, he'd been asking for his daughter. When Carina was done with her climb, it was vital she come to the hospital right away and see him before he got any worse.

Carina stared at the note. Her first impulse was that it served him right. Gallivanting around the galaxy with Fornax. Making trips out to the Belt. Engaging in sexual congress with a woman one-third his age. *What the hell was he thinking?* Didn't the man have any sense?

But then Carina changed her mind. Her father had done so much for her over the years, it didn't seem fair. How could they have grown so far apart? Not only had he helped save her life that time two years ago, he had also rescued her spirit on that occasion as well. *Damn it anyway!* It had never been her intention for the two of them to become estranged — *How could she have let this happen!*

Carina nodded to the pilot and climbed into the jetchop with her gear. As the helicopter-like craft rose above the caldera and headed out across the mountain, she thought back to those exciting first days before she and BC set off to try and scratch out a foothold in the wilderness.

If only she'd been able to hold her tongue, maybe things would have turned out differently.

NINETEEN

Diary

The barrier separating father from daughter was not built in a day. Still, it would be no exaggeration to say that the foundation for their troubles could be traced to a November evening three years ago. Carina had just missed celebrating BeHolden Day with her father on account of her busy schedule, and he was understandably upset. Yet, in spite of his anger, he had invited her to come join him for dinner anyway, up at his estate on the Cape. They were halfway through the meal when the argument erupted. Sam was trying to explain to her how her mother had died — and why — but Carina wasn't having any of it. Before the night was over, the disagreement had come down to a difference of opinion as to the proper use of genetic information.

Was such knowledge to be brought to bear for the purpose of tampering? To assemble better people, as it were? To "fix" nature's mistakes?

Or, should biogenetics be abandoned altogether and people left to fend for themselves with whatever genes God had chosen to give them?

In Sam's estimation, manipulation was the first step down the long road to genocide. Carina, of course, disagreed.

"What is the reason for persecution?" he had asked her in the heat of the discussion. At the time she had no answer for him, and the question had continued to vex her ever since. Even now, as she turned to the entry she made in her diary that afternoon, she found herself debating the correctness of her answer:

November 26, 2430, 2:00 p.m.: Madame Diary, once more we will try to answer father's question. I would hypothesize that the reason for persecution is as old as life itself. Over the eons, the phenomenal rise in animal intelligence was driven by the world's predators and their relentless hunting of less capable game. This must have been true not only in the obvious sense of a smarter animal being able to outwit a faster carnivore, but it also must have been true in a more subtle way as well. That is, smarter animals eventually graduated from correctly judging whether a jump over a ravine could be managed, to devising an alternate means *around* the ravine.

As smarter prey more successfully eluded their predators, hungrier predators had to get more cunning too. Anticipation and second-guessing became an integral part of their survival, and this vicious feedback must have driven the intelligence of the hunter — and the hunted — higher still. These interlocking cycles must have reinforced one another with each round until our species leaped from the jungle, mad as hell and ready to fight. Armed with their big brains, these hairless apes were exceedingly well-equipped to fend off any and all predators. Therefore, it should come as no surprise that Man is a hunter, pure and simple; a territorial beast compelled by instinct to defend, and whenever possible, expand his dominion. Ironically, once Mother Nature ran out of credible predators for Man, he became his own worst enemy. Evolution had simultaneously made him the most aggressive of all hunters and the most resilient of all prey.

When the human race was young and the Earth sparsely populated, the standard survival response to cruelty and persecution was to pick up stakes, leave one region, and settle in another, less oppressed land. Interestingly enough, as an unintended consequence of these periodic upheavals, waves of desperate immigrants often catapulted their adopted societies to greatness, unwittingly boosting the living standards of torturer and tortured alike.

Unfortunately, the reverse has also proved to be the case. Once the Earth got crowded, and there were no longer any places to hide, the world's most ferocious hunter began to hunt *himself* to extinction. As migration increasingly became an impossibility, and as the rallying cries of genocide swept across the globe, brutality and subjugation led, not to escape, but to extermination; not to new and more promising lands, but to gas chambers and other horrors. Rontana and his nightmarish atrocities were but one shadowy reflection of the general malaise, all of which was rooted in the closing of the frontiers.

As the migratory outlets slammed shut, living standards stagnated. Not everywhere, to be sure, and not all at once, but by the twenty-fourth century a new Dark Age had descended upon much of the world. Although some, like the Overlord, were grabbing for themselves a bigger slice of the economic pie, the pie itself — for perhaps the first time since the Middle Ages — was no longer growing. The future had become bleak.

Fruitful and multiplied well beyond the carrying capacity of their little planet, mankind was skidding headlong into a giant bend in the road. Only it wasn't a U-turn, it was a cul-de-sac. Pressed by the confines of a tiny world, overwhelmed by sheer numbers and drowning in an ocean of their own wastes, the oldhumans were consummating their own pitiful version of the lemmings march to the sea.

Yet, I am convinced there has to be a way out of this morass. The answer *has* to be migration. If newhumans are to have a legacy, if my signature genes are to have a future, I must get off this planet!

But how? That was the question she asked herself that day. How to get off the planet and where to go? By now, of course, the answer had presented itself — Mars. In the meantime, though, the problem had taken on a new dimension.

Was Mars to be a haven reserved solely for newhumans alone, or was it to be opened for settlement to all humanity?

This was the question on which the relationship with her father had foundered, the question on which *all* her relationships had foundered.

Now, as she entered the sterile corridors of the Colony One Hospital where her father was, Carina realized she had no choice — she had to face him, and she had to face him alone.

Carina peeked around the doorway and into her father's room. She quietly approached the bed. He was lying there quietly, with his eyes shut. She studied his face. His breathing was regular. But his skin was pale. As Saron's message warned, he didn't look healthy. Not that her father had ever been muscle-bound, but in Carina's memory anyway, there had always been a certain buoyant athleticism to the way he carried himself, a certain boyish bounce to his step. These were most definitely absent today.

He opened his eyes and looked at her. As if reading her mind, he said, "I'm sick, yes, but not quick sick enough to die, at least not yet. I'm afraid you'll have to wait a bit longer for your inheritance, my dear."

"You know very well that money doesn't interest me," she scoffed, disappointed by his rather crude opening line.

"Yes, of course, how could I forget?"

Carina looked around the room. She couldn't be sure, but it appeared to be the very same room she had given birth to her son in. The memory of what took place that night was still painful. She had held the boy just that once and had never seen him or BC since.

"Just exactly what are you supposed to be dying of?"

"Matthews Disease," he replied, as if every third grader had heard of it.

"And what in blazes is Matthews Disease?"

"Actually, I don't rightly know," Sam replied, shifting uncomfortably in his bed. Like Carina, he was allergic to all the standard painkillers of the day. He managed without them as best as he could. "All I do know is, my grandfather died young, as did his father. As for my own father, America died before he ever got a chance to die of natural causes."

"Why haven't you told me this before? Is this Matthews Disease genetic? That's my field, you know."

Sam looked at his daughter with sudden warmth. Carina was an attractive woman, always had been. But now, after having just completed the arduous trek to the summit of Omen, the woman was radiant. Glowing red cheeks, clean fresh hair, wonderful smell. Her presence in the room with him there made Sam feel young again, young and homesick for his own long dead wife in a way he could never have anticipated. He swallowed hard to avoid revealing his true emotions. Finally, he spoke:

"Well, I have no hard proof mind you. But yes, I would say it's genetic. My guess is, you have it too. I should expect my grandson has it as well. Of course, I wouldn't be able to say for sure — I've never even met the boy, now have I?" His tone was somewhere between rage and contempt.

"That's my fault."

"Yes, it most certainly is, Carina. And I'll never forgive you for that."

His rebuke was answered with silence.

"How can I make it up to you?" she asked finally, her voice muted.

Again there was a long silence.

"How?" she repeated.

"Bring him to me. It is my wish to know my grandson before God takes me."

"That won't be easy."

"Last wishes never are," he said, his voice cracking.

Sam sat slowly up in bed. Using all his strength, he swung his legs out over the side of the bed as if he meant to get up.

"I would have to find BC," she said. "And even if I do, I can't be certain he'll see me."

"Can you blame the man?" Sam retorted, tentatively touching his bare feet to the cold, tile floor.

"Where do I begin?" she asked, uncertain how to locate the father of the son.

"I would start with J, in London," Sam said, slipping his feet into the slippers at the side of his bed. Even as he spoke, he thought again of the man he once met at C.I. Headquarters. Like Oscar Schaeffer, J was a pompous, arrogant monstrosity of a man. Stout and gray-haired, he had a heavy British accent and a chiseled face. Plus lots of body hair — on his knuckles, his arms, even the back of his thick neck. Sam didn't like him one little bit.

"J? You mean BC's boss at Commonwealth Intelligence?" Carina was uncomfortable with the suggestion.

"That's where I would start, if I were you."

"Well, you're *not* me! Anyway, what you're talking about could be downright dangerous." Now her tone was combative.

"Hah! What do you know of danger?" Sam challenged contemptuously. "As a race, and as a civilization, we have been suffering a growing retreat into the delusions of a risk-free society. This has been going on since at least the second half of the twentieth century. And what has it gotten us? Land's sakes, girl, what's happened to the bold chance for dangerous adventure?"

Sam continued. "The answer is obvious and sad. Those who believe in a risk-free society are winning, perhaps already have won. Safety and security have become the watchwords of the day. Fear of failure permeates our very lives. Have we forgotten that without the opportunity to fail, there can be no meaningful victory? That the price of progress is risk? America, the land of my birth, was built by forward-thinking people who accepted the risks, not by cautious naysayers. By those who fought the wars, not by those who dodged the draft. By those who wanted to really prosper, not merely subsist."

Sam continued. "Had there been one of today's weak-kneed Enviro activists at the head of the wagon train, we might never have made it across the plains, much less over the Rockies. Our real limits have always been those we placed on ourselves. Face it, Carina — in a world that has survived one crisis after another, each worse than the previous, none has been more important, more distressing, more devastating, than our current crisis of will. Today, we fail, not out of an inability to do something, but out of an unwillingness to tackle it in the first place. We are simply unwilling to take the risk."

"Okay, already, I get your point, Dad. And, of course, you're right. But if I am to go back to the Earth that I've forsaken, it has to be for a more important reason than just locating BC — it has to be to solve the riddle of this genetic disease afflicting our family."

"What's to solve, Carina? What is, is."

By this time Sam had found his slippers and was up roaming anxiously around the room. It seemed as if he were waiting for someone else to arrive.

"There must have been someone earlier in our line who didn't die of the disease," she reasoned. "Someone who wasn't plagued by this abnormality."

"How do you propose to find this someone? As far as I know, I am the oldest living Matthews on the planet."

"But there must be records."

"I sincerely doubt it. When America was overrun, pretty much everything was destroyed. Except for a few isolated pockets of humanity, like N'Orleans or Sane Lou, ashes are about all that remains of the country I once called home." Even as Sam spoke, he lowered his eyes in reverence to the land of his birth.

"Perhaps. But I have been told that the Church of Latter-day Saints, when they were kicked out of Utah, established a bunker in SKANDIA somewhere, and another in a place called Missouri. I don't know where those places are. But perhaps one or the other bunker still exists. Supposedly, these people kept all kinds of genealogical records."

"Suit yourself, daughter. But it's all a big waste of time. I couldn't give a flying fig about any of it. Whether I live five more years or fifty, is of little concern to me now. All I'm interested in doing now is meeting my grandson before my days are up. Can't you understand that?" There was brave determination in the man's voice.

By this time Saron had arrived at the doorway. She edged past Carina and into the room. "This is no place for you, Sam. Now that you're back on your feet, I'm going to take you home. You'll be more comfortable there. From here on out, you're staying with me."

"How dare you decide what's best for my father!" Carina objected, playing the role of concerned daughter.

"As if you cared," Saron snapped, taking hold of Sam's arm and helping him pack his few things. "I'll have you know, Carina, I am the only one who knows what is best for your father. You get along now and get back to your tidy little utopia. Lord knows, we wouldn't want to dirty your pretty little hands with a dose of reality."

Carina's eyes narrowed. She didn't appreciate being spoken to this way. But one thing was undoubtedly true. Without need of further prodding, Saron had helped her make up her mind. *Carina had to go back to Earth and unravel the mystery of Matthews Disease.* Beyond that, she also had to find her father's grandson. Come to think of it, she didn't even know the boy's name!

Bold chance for dangerous adventure indeed! *I'll show them,* Carina thought. — *I'll show them both, just you wait and see!*

*   *   *

Inda sat alone in his hut. A wooden crate lay open before him on the floor. The lid rested beside it, next to his chair, where he dropped it in surprise.

This morning, when the crate showed up on the loading dock where he worked, Inda was certain it had been delivered to him from Earth by mistake. He hadn't ordered anything, that much was certain. And yet, the manifest had his name clearly marked on the electrostatic label. Fully paid for and cleared by customs.

A present? he thought. *But from whom?* His terran family was dead, his childhood sweetheart sold into slavery. Who could possibly be sending him a gift?

It was only now, after he had pried loose the lid from its moorings, that he began to figure it out. Oskar Schaeffer was his benefactor.

After their brief meeting nearly two weeks ago, Inda didn't know what to expect. *Food for thought* was all he'd said to the man, and that's how they left it. And yet, here it was, a crate filled with weapons and explosives.

At first, Inda didn't know what to think. While certainly not a pacifist by nature, he understood that violence was a negative-sum game. Rarely did the accumulated benefits exceed the accumulated costs.

But then again he was angry. Angry about how things were going here with the settlement. Angry that Carina had gone off for two weeks to climb that damn mountain. Angry that the woman who was supposed to be sleeping with him, was probably sleeping with that Euro.

Inda began to unpack the crate. Inside he found three weapons — a force gun with power load, a satchel of manual firebombs, and a cylinder of Tovex. The first two he was familiar with, the third he was not.

A force gun was more like a photon cannon than a gun, more like a bazooka than a rifle. Its barrel was short and its stock wide. At any range under two hundred meters, its awesome electronic shell would blow a fist-sized hole clean through a man.

A manual firebomb was circular at the top, like a conventional grenade, but its hull was covered with a sheet of heavy plastic. At the base was a handle twelve centimeters long, a handle which enabled the thrower to hurl the explosive further and with greater accuracy than an ordinary grenade. The trick was in the accuracy and the timing, for once the plastic shield was removed and the casing of steel-like adhesive exposed to the air, the bomb itself would adhere instantly to any surface it made contact with. The thrower had only fifteen seconds from the removal of the plastic covering until the explosion of the firebomb.

But the Tovex? Inda didn't have a clue. It was clearly some type of plastique, but there were no instructions inside on how to detonate the stuff or even how to properly store it. Inda supposed that Schaeffer would eventually dispatch someone to show him. But, until then, he would have to find a place to stash the crate where no one else was likely to look. *But where?*

PART III

TWENTY

Skandia

When Carina left Earth more than two years ago, she thought it would be for good. Only now, circumstances had changed. To unravel the mystery of the Matthews Disease meant tracing back her family's gene-map as far as she could. No easy task under any conditions. Everyone she spoke to told her that much of the original documentation had been destroyed along with America. Which made the task nearly impossible. There was one chance, however, and that was the vault in Trondheim, Norway. It might hold some clues.

Centuries earlier, when the first countrywide genealogy tables were compiled by the Church of Latter-day Saints, copies were made, then stored in a concrete-hardened bunker blasted into a hillside at the edge of this maritime community in central Norway. Later, when gene-prints came into vogue and DNA testing became commonplace, America's national identicard files were duplicated, with one copy being kept in St. Louis and a second in Trondheim.

On the trip in from Mars, Fornax told her of his own travels in SKANDIA, of the picturesque fjords and bucolic settings. But nothing in her experience could prepare Carina for the pristine air or for the sheer cliffs that lined the jagged bays or for the unadulterated landscape.

It was as if time itself had stopped here just below the Arctic Circle, as if there had been no human encroachment in a thousand years. It wasn't true, of course. But halfway up the western coast of the Norwegian province of SKANDIA, nothing had changed since the days when the Vikings first set sail in their long ships from the protected waters of their fjords to conquer much of Europe.

In a sense, a fjord was nothing more than a bay, a spot where a finger of ocean had punched a hole into the mountainous mainland.

But to call a fjord a bay was to miss the whole point. To call a fjord a bay was to rob it of its beauty, to somehow deny that a tree-lined cliff crashed from a rocky precipice above, ending in a churning sea below. It was to somehow pretend that the windswept landscape was a product of man's intervention, not nature's, or that trees like these and colors that bright could be painted by some blond-haired Michelangelo.

In this season — fall — the aspen and maple were an explosion of color — reds and oranges set against a blue-green backdrop of sturdy Norwegian pine. The crisp air spoke of a winter yet to come, a winter when mounds of wet, virgin snow would blanket the countryside, its unbroken surface peppered with tiny hoof and paw prints from mule deer and snowshoe rabbits. Now, though, with the hoary season still safely imprisoned several months in the future, Carina found herself awed by the autumn. Regrettably, she had to turn away from the wondrous scene before she had had her fill.

As Carina stood on the cusp of the steel-hardened concrete bunker, she was approached by an elfin man with a shock of black hair, a man who managed to be simultaneously distracted yet acutely alert.

"You must be the enigmatic Ms. Matthews that Fornax told me all about," he said, extending a bony hand in her direction. Carina found it a struggle to return his handshake. Her muscles hadn't yet adjusted to the leap from 0.38g back to earth-normal gravity.

"Carina," she replied coolly. "Or else Dr. Matthews. I find the designation *Ms.* to be demeaning in the extreme."

"Fornax told me that about you," the little man said in a congenial tone. "Said you like to go your own way. Trust me, I have no intention of insulting a good friend of Fornax's. Would the appellation *Froken* be more to your liking?"

"I guess that would depend on what the word means."

"Quite right, of course. My apologies — I had forgotten that you don't understand our language. Froken is SKANDIAN. Translated, it is roughly equivalent to Fraulein, or mademoiselle, or your missy."

Carina smiled. Missy sure beat little lady. "Yes, Froken would be perfectly okay with me. And you? You must be Viscount Nordman."

When the man nodded in the affirmative, Carina relaxed. The little man matched Fornax's description down to the last detail. Fornax had journeyed to SKANDIA on at least two previous occasions — indeed would have accompanied her now if she had let him. During one of those stays he met Viscount Nordman. Once Fornax got to know the man, he found the Viscount to be a trustworthy and knowledgeable fellow. For what Carina had to do, there was no better place to start than with this man.

"What is it that you seek, Froken? My old and dear friend Fornax said only that you were wanting to peruse certain genealogy records." When he spoke, the Viscount was barely tall enough to meet her gaze straight on.

"That's correct, Viscount. The Matthews family, *my* family, is carrying a defective gene, a gene I believe is responsible for shortening our life expectancy considerably."

"He's soft on you, I should think."

"Who?" There was surprise in her voice.

"Who do you think?"

"Could we please stay on the subject?" Carina said, blushing. "My reason for coming to see you is to learn when this genetic defect first arose on our genome, and then, if I can, to identify a close living relative that will allow me to extract a donor gene. With a template to work from, perhaps the next generation of Matthews can be spared this terrible tragedy."

"Froken, what you ask is certainly possible. We do have such records on deposit here. For four hundred years, a gene-print record was made of every live birth in the United States. The longstanding policy of the U.S. government was to maintain a duplicate copy of its entire citizenry. One set was stored right here in Trondheim."

"I am so relieved to know that," she sighed. "When can I start?"

"It's not quite that easy."

"Oh, but it is," she said with a determined look.

"Let me explain. The records are here. That part is unquestionably true. But we cannot read them all."

"I don't understand."

Viscount Nordman took her hand, and they walked. Behind them, on a ridge, a gull barked. Its mocking tone set the stage for his explanation.

They passed through a security gate and down a long corridor. Glass-enclosed offices lined the hallway. Inside each cubicle, people could be seen working at terminals. Beyond them, on the far wall, was computer hardware of every sort: big, sixteen-inch spools of magnetic tape, boxes of yellowed punch cards, racks of diskettes in three different sizes, cylinders filled with bubble-memory globes. VRT screens of every imaginable make and model filled the tables, along with various sized keyboards and printers. Row upon row of filing cabinets lined the impregnable concrete walls. The air was filled with the gentle hum of fan-cooled silicon chips completing their assigned tasks.

Pride filled the Viscount's voice as he imparted his story. Every once in a while, when Carina least expected it, an elfish grin would swallow his entire face.

"Although digital information is theoretically invulnerable to the ravages of time, the physical media on which such information is stored are far from eternal. Stray magnetic fields. Oxidation. Even material degradation. They can all easily erase or jumble such disks. In fact, the contents of most digital media evaporate long before comparable words written on high quality paper do."

"You mean to tell me that centuries of records have all decayed?" she exclaimed as they arrived at the Viscount's office. It was a plush hollow in this manmade cave of concrete and steel.

"No, Froken. The problem is actually of quite a different nature," he said, pulling up a chair to sit at his desk. "For the most part, the digital information is still there. We just can't read it."

"This just keeps getting better and better!" she said, her voice animated.

"To understand our predicament, you need to understand the nature of digital storage. Digital information can be saved on any medium capable of representing binary digits as a series of zeros and ones. We refer to these binary digits as 'bits'. Any meaningful, intended sequence of bits with no intervening spaces, punctuation or formatting, we refer to as a 'bit-stream'. Retrieving a bit-stream requires a hardware device, such as a disk drive, plus a software program which interprets the bit-stream after it has been retrieved."

"That seems simple enough. — What's the problem?"

"Retrieval is not as straightforward a task as it sounds. A given bit-stream can represent almost anything from a sequence of integers to an array of dots. For instance, a bit-stream could represent a sequence of alphabetic characters. It might consist of a series of fixed-length chunks, or bytes, each representing a code for a single character. In one early scheme, the eight bits 01110001 stood for the letter q. To extract the bytes from the bit-stream, thereby parsing the stream into its components, we first must know the length of the byte. In some cases we know this. In others, we don't. But even if a document can be parsed properly, we still face a recursive problem."

"What do you mean recursive?"

"It's the old story of which came first, the chicken or the egg? Since a byte can represent any number or any alphabetic, we need to know each document's particular coding scheme. But more than that, most files contain information which is meaningful solely to the software that created them. In many cases, the software has been irretrievably lost."

Carina peered at the little man from across the desk. "I don't see the problem. If you would just print out the document, you could extract its content in a visual manner. Why would you need to run the original software at all?"

"Froken, you're a smart girl. But content can be lost in subtle ways. Translating word-processing formats, for instance, often displaces or eliminates headings or captions or footnotes or special fonts. If we need to view a document as complex as a gene-map, and we need to view it as the author viewed it, with columns and italics and underlinings, we have little choice but to run the software that created it. Think of the many hundreds of formats that have been used over the years. Punch cards. Magnetic tape. Videotape. Magnetic disks, of several sizes. Optical disks. Laser fiche. Bubble globes. Bio-disks. The list boggles the mind!"

Carina shifted uneasily in her chair. "So what are you telling me?"

"Your answer lies in the written word, Froken. Maybe a story will help illustrate my point. In 1799, a French demolitions squad assigned to Egypt uncovered the Rosetta Stone. The parallel inscriptions of Greek script and Egyptian hieroglyphics etched into the stone made hieroglyphics and demotic Egyptian comprehensible, something they had not been up to that point. The reason they hadn't been deciphered sooner was that they suffered from much the same recursive problems true of bit-stream interpretation today. Besides still being legible after two dozen centuries, the Rosetta Stone owes its preservation to the visual impact of its content, an attribute absent from all digital media. Or, to consider another example, how about Shakespeare's first printed edition of sonnet 18 circa 1610? Now there's something which exemplifies the longevity of the printed page. — The words are still legible after eight centuries! Go ahead, take a look."

As he spoke, Viscount Nordman pointed to the original parchment hanging behind him on the wall. It was sealed in a transparent airtight container so it couldn't be harmed by the elements. Carina wandered over to look at it as he continued.

"Unlike Shakespeare's sonnet, most digital media are unreadable within a decade. The written word, you see, possesses the enviable quality of being readable with no machinery, no tools, and no special knowledge beyond the language itself."

Even as the Viscount spoke, Carina realized how right he was about the written word. She remembered how she had been struck by the number of printbooks she discovered in the settlers' Library when she first arrived on Mars. In the present context, it made much more sense to her now than it had back then — printbooks were easy to transport and easy to read. Of course, the flip side of that same coin meant the Viscount's precious genealogy records would do her little or no good.

"So my trip to see you has been wasted," she sighed, crestfallen.

"No, not at all," he said, rising to his feet and crossing to a filing cabinet on the far side of the room. "In a year's time, maybe two, we should be able to extract the information that you want." Glancing at a file, he said, "In fact, my people are working on the 2250s even as we speak."

"I don't have that kind of time."

"Shame," he said, sliding the file back into its proper slot. "But there may be another way."

"Yes?" Her voice was suddenly hopeful.

"Go to America."

"America? There is no America."

"No, Froken, not in the way that there used to be. But yes, there is still an America. People have been going there for years."

Carina turned up her nose. "But those people are nothing but criminals and slugs; losers in every way."

"Yes, I'm told it is quite dangerous," the Viscount admitted. "And you mustn't go there alone. But I do know of a place where many of the records you seek have been maintained in a written form. With my introductions, they should allow you to see them."

"And where is this place?" she asked skeptically.

An impish grin crossed Viscount Nordman's face. "At its height, back in the days when America was young and free, this place went by the name of Saint Louis. Named for a French king, I believe. Now it goes by Sane Lou. But I'm warning you, Froken. Do not be fooled by the name. This place is anything but sane. I really don't know my geography well, but it's inland somewhere. Along a great river."

"Sounds easy enough to find," she said, rising to her feet as if she meant to leave.

"Not so fast," he intoned, slamming his harmless little fist down on the desktop for emphasis. "You must not journey there alone! It is dangerous."

"I can take care of myself."

"No doubt. But I'm telling you, Froken. Sane Lou is no place for an attractive woman. You must have protection."

"I appreciate the warning, I really do. But you, of all people, shouldn't worry about me. I'll be fine."

And with that, Carina let herself out the way she had come in.

Dangerous adventure indeed!

TWENTY-ONE

Saron's Place

With each passing decade the pace of technology ebbed and flowed. The fortunes of civilization rose and fell. The prospects for prosperity grew and withered. But, throughout it all, certain things never changed.

Sex, for one. Regardless of whether he was on top or she was, it was always a gratifying experience.

A home-cooked meal, for another. No bistro could match the delights that popped out of your mama's oven with seemingly no effort at all.

Simple pleasures, for a third. Games of chance, a brisk fall walk, a day at the beach. A good smoke, a good meal, a good woman.

Nothing much had changed since the dawn of mankind. And so it was tonight at Saron's Place.

A thin film of smoke hung in the air of the Commons. Winter was already in full swing, and a cold wind could be heard howling like mad outside. Logs of dried and pressed lichen were burning — smoldering, actually — in the fireplace. In the far corner of the room, a disconcerting racket blared from a sort of antediluvian jukebox. It wasn't music, not really, for it had no regular beat. To one old man just coming into the place, a man who slowly took off his coat and got himself comfortable at a table, the strident screeches coming from that jukebox were reminiscent of an artillery barrage, perhaps a train wreck. A sober man couldn't stand to listen to the noise for long. But once he was thoroughly drunk, the music took on an endearing quality all its own.

A thick, alcohol-laden odor permeated the air. From across the room, Saron looked ravishing. Her cheeks were glowing red and, as Sam sat down to unbundle his game board and pieces, he nearly forgot what had drawn him here tonight in the first place. Sam had come to this, his home away from home, to partake in one of the simplest pleasures of all — a game of chess.

Despite a thousand years of history, the board was still the same, eight by eight square. And the pieces too. Oh, their shapes had changed with the times, and even their names on occasion. But the pieces remained unaltered. Eight pawns. Two each of the rooks, knights, and bishops. A Queen. And a King. And the moves were the same: diagonal for the bishops; rows and columns for the castles; straight ahead for the pawns; every which way for the Queen and King. The objective? Checkmate. It was still the quintessential game of strategy and tactics.

Sam sat across the table from Fornax. Gunter would join them shortly. There had been trouble again at the motor factory, and he had to first secure the place for the night.

"It's good to see you up and about again, old-timer," Fornax said. "Are you finally feeling a little better?"

"Oh, leave me alone, I'm doing fine. Any word from Carina? It's been nearly two weeks." As Sam spoke, he tenderly unwrapped the black and white onyx pieces from the felt bag he always carried them in.

"You know I would have told you if I'd heard from her."

Sam could tell from the tone in his friend's voice that Fornax was perturbed. They all were. With construction on the factory nearly complete, rising tensions between Newton and Colony One had everyone on edge.

"Perhaps a drink will settle your nerves," Sam suggested, signaling to Saron at the bar to send over one of her girls. So far, only Saron had perfected the correct formula for brewing Martian grains into a palatable, nonlethal potion suitable for the pleasure of inebriation. Her brew had become such a mainstay of colony life, she was compelled to keep the recipe a well-guarded secret, one which would someday make her eldest grandson a very wealthy man.

"Two Saronales, please," Sam said when the pretty young thing arrived at the table. Then, as she scurried away with their order, Sam produced a coin. It was one of those old Earth coins, from Zealand or perhaps the Euro block. "Shall we flip for who plays white?"

"I thought we were playing best three out of five? Sam, you of all people should know the rules. — Loser always goes first."

"That would be me then," Sam grunted, taking the white pieces to his side of the table.

"Where did you get this set?" Fornax asked, admiring one of the dark onyx playing pieces.

"Cancun, Mexico. Carina and I wintered there once about ten years back. The locals are very adept at making things with their hands, you know. I bought this set from a street vendor. I remember it plainly. The man refused to take pesos but was delighted with Zealand dollars."

"It's strange, but chess is known the world over. I wonder where it all began?" Even before the words were out of his mouth, Fornax knew he had made a mistake. His question was just the sort of opening Sam would be looking for to tell him another one of his stories.

"It's interesting you should ask that," the old fellow began, warming to the subject. "Essentially every ancient civilization has laid claim to the invention of the game — the Egyptians, the Greeks, the Hindus, the Babylonians — all of them. But, like most things in life, the truth is simpler — and more complex. The oldest name for the game of chess is *chatauranga*, a Hindu word referring to the four branches of the Indian army — elephants, horses, chariots, and foot soldiers. Though its exact age cannot be determined with any degree of accuracy, the game itself is at least three thousand, if not as much as five thousand years old. The Hindus played both a two-handed and a four-handed version, both with dice and without."

"Chess with dice? What a novel idea!" Fornax exclaimed, adding fuel to the fire.

"As the game spread eastward from Indiastan, its rules were altered to suit local tastes. The Burmese opened the game with the Kingside pawns on the third rank and the Queenside pawns on the fourth. The Chinese placed their pieces on the intersections of the lines rather than on the squares and added a 'celestial river' — rather akin to a no-man's land — between the two halves of the board. Their version had only five pawns to a side, but they added two 'cannons' ahead of the knights, plus a 'counselor' on either side of the King. And, in deference to their emperor, the King wasn't called a king at all, but rather a general. The Persians learned chatauranga from the Indians, shortening the name to *chatrang* and codifying its rules."

"Shall we begin?" Fornax broke in, putting the last of his pieces in place. By this time, their tankards of ale had arrived, and they each sipped a frothy head off their brew.

"By all means, let's begin," Sam said, sliding his White King's Pawn up to King 4.

The first moves were rapid, and Fornax met the charge head-on, advancing his own King's Pawn to King 4.

Sam answered with King's Knight to Bishop 3.

Black Queen's Knight to Bishop 3.

White Bishop to Queen's Knight 5.

Queen's Rook's Pawn ahead one square.

Stymied, White Bishop pulled back to Rook 4.

Black King's Knight advanced to Bishop 3.

"Chess spread very rapidly in the Persian Empire," Sam said, plotting out his next move. "And even more rapidly once the Empire fell to the Moslems in the seventh century. Like so many other skills, the Euros learned chess — and chess lingo — from the Moslems. The English word 'chess' is the vernacular corruption of 'scac', the ninth century Latin rendering of the Persian 'shah' or king. The pawn is the equivalent of the Arabic 'baidaq' or foot soldier. Rook is a direct corruption of 'rukh' or chariot. Interestingly enough, our castle-shaped pieces come, not from medievalistic ramparts, as most people suppose, but from Farsi Indian pieces which represented the tower carried on an elephant's back."

Even as Sam continued with his explanation, he fingered his White Queen's Knight, contemplating his next move.

"The knight was originally 'faras' in Arabic, meaning horse, which is of course the usual shape of the piece. The bishop evolved from the Arabic 'al-fil' or elephant. In England, the split at the top of the piece, intended to represent an elephant's tusks, was probably mistaken for a bishop's miter. The French took the same split as a fool's hat, so in France, the piece is a 'fou' or jester."

Suddenly, without warning, play resumed. Bounding, White Queen's Knight jumped to Bishop 3.

Without delay, Black responded with Queen's Knight's Pawn to Knight 4.

Stymied again, White King's Bishop retreated to Knight 3.

Licking his wounds, Sam went on. "The present-day Queen, as it is called in English-speaking lands, began life as the 'counselor' or 'farz' or perhaps 'firz'. The Italians made it into 'farzia' or 'fercia'. The French adopted it as 'fierge' and later 'vierge', meaning virgin. This is how the gender shift got started. The male counselor of the Chinese game had undergone a sex-change operation. Now, as to the rules . . . "

"Enough already!" Fornax bellowed, unable to concentrate on his next move. Looking up, he spied a new face in the crowd. Gunter had finally arrived. Fornax waved for him to come over. A troubled look crinkled his forehead as he sat down on the bench beside Sam. Facing Fornax from across the table, Gunter told them both what he had learned.

Before they knew it, the chess game was forgotten.

TWENTY-TWO

Treachery

Samuel Matthews, Fornax Nehrengel, and the man from ASARCO were huddled around a heavy oak table in the corner of the Commons farthest from the jukebox. The chess pieces hadn't been touched since Gunter first sat down to join the other two. Serious looks clouded their faces even if they had managed to get themselves more than a little intoxicated guzzling tankards of Saronale.

The threesome was trying to have a conversation over the din, but were meeting with limited success. What presently held their attention was the small collection of men grouped around a table in the opposite corner of the room. Rumor had it this bunch was out to destroy Colony One any way they could.

Ever since the asteroid-movers began moving in in great numbers, bringing with them their crude prosperity and their vulgar boisterisms, the most determined of the Newtons had resented their presence. The resentment threatened to now boil over into sabotage, or worse — whatever it would take to drive the interlopers away. Gunter suspected that arms were being smuggled into the colony, though he didn't yet know how or by whom. Ten days ago, when Saron came to check Sam out of the hospital, she had alerted him to the fact that such plotting was underway. He, in turn, had informed Gunter. Hunched over the table, now, Sam's face darkened as he strained to eavesdrop on what the foursome across the way was saying.

The biggest one, Lotha, was insistent about whatever point he was making. Sam recognized Lotha as being from the first group of settlers, the group that, two years ago, had blasted their way out of an Afghan prison, then accompanied him and Fornax to Mars. Lotha had impressed Sam as a Neanderthal back then. Nothing in the man's demeanor served to change that impression now. If anything, his large, bony skull seemed more misshapen than ever.

"I don't see any way for us to peacefully coexist with these people!" Lotha bellowed, rapping his big, hairy fist down on the table for emphasis. The tankard of ale before him jumped at his exclamation point.

"But rather than blowing up the motor factory or killing innocent people simply to make a point, wouldn't it be smarter to try negotiating with them first?"

The speaker was Nehru, a small timid man who was nervous about the repercussions their actions might visit upon them. While intellectually bright, Nehru was a coward by nature. It bothered him that Inda Desai might just be crazy enough to have a crate filled with explosives stashed somewhere in the village. Such a development could only lead to further trouble.

"Negotiate?!" Lotha exploded, his dark eyes drilling into Nehru like a jackhammer. "What's to negotiate? If you wanted to negotiate with the bastards, why did you even bother showing up for this meeting? We're here to discuss a plan of attack, you fool, not a plan of retreat!"

Lotha's younger brother Nandu, the fourth member of the party, nodded his head in agreement. He said nothing, however.

"I know all that," Nehru granted. "I only thought . . . "

"You *thought*?" Inda exclaimed. "Now there's a contradiction in terms. Since when was the last time you . . . "

"There's no reason to get personal about this," Nehru said, shrinking from the other fellow's assault.

"To the contrary," Inda said, brushing the long hair back from his eyes. "Everything about this is personal. We came here to start a new society. Now we find that it is to be just as polluted, just as congested, just as crowded, as the one we left behind."

It was hard to deny Inda's sincerity. — Or his physical presence. Inda was a tall, thin man; not nearly as muscular or robust as Lotha, yet a formidable figure nonetheless.

"I'm just not that sure about all this newhuman stuff," Nehru admitted, crossing his scrawny arms and scrunching up his thick eyebrows in doubt.

"Me neither," Lotha revealed. "But that's besides the point, isn't it?"

Again Nandu nodded his head in agreement with his older brother, but said nothing.

"If you're not even sure about being a newhuman, then why the hell do you want to blow the Colony One'ers off the face of the planet?" Nehru queried in an exasperated tone. It irritated him no end how slow-witted Lotha could actually be. Nehru found it difficult to hide his contempt for the other man.

"Because that's my way," Lotha said, proud of his pedestrian, narrow-minded approach to life.

"Well, that's not my way," Nehru exclaimed, rising to his feet and edging backwards toward the door.

"Where are you going?" Inda asked in a derisive tone. He made no attempt to camouflage his dislike for his fellow Newton.

"Home," Nehru answered, tipping his hat in their direction. "To my wife and kids."

"You're a worthless slug!" Inda said, the derogatory words rolling easily off his tongue. "A pansy. A velcroid."

"Call me what you will," Nehru answered. "But until you and King Kong here have thought this whole thing all the way through, count me out!"

With that, he flung open the heavy wooden door to Saron's Place. This allowed a blast of cold air to filter into the long house as he stepped out. Still weak from his illness, Sam shivered at the frigid gust of wind.

"Maybe Nehru's right," Inda conceded now that his rival was gone. "We don't want to be too hasty about this, do we?"

Motioning now to the far side of the room, Inda said, "I see where Councilman Matthews is here tonight — I wouldn't mind hearing his opinion on the subject."

"That old fossil?" Lotha said, critical of Inda's sudden willingness to listen to the old fellow. "What could he possibly have to offer the discussion?"

"Well, let's go ask him," Inda said, rising to his feet.

As he turned towards the table at the opposite end of the room, Inda focused his eyes on the three men sitting there. Each, in their own way, stood between him and a life of happiness with Carina.

She was obviously infatuated with one of them, Gunter, the big Euro. It was an infatuation Inda couldn't quite understand.

Then there was Fornax, yet another obstacle preventing him from claiming Carina as his bride. Fornax had taken the girl to Earth, though for what reason, Inda did not know.

Truth be known, Inda was still deeply embittered by the fact that his liaison with Carina had turned out to be nothing more than a one-night stand. Then again, on the off chance he might still have a chance with Carina, he had to mend fences with the girl's father. Who knows? — he might yet be faced with having to ask Councilman Matthews for the girl's hand in marriage. The old man had money, plenty of it as far as Inda had been able to learn. That was a big plus. *No sense passing up an opportunity to try and get back on the old fellow's good side.* Inda said as much to his friends as he eased his way across the bar in Sam's direction.

"Come on, you two — what possible harm could come from spending a minute or two to hear what the old fart has to say?"

Silent until now, Nandu suddenly decided he had something to contribute. "I agree with Inda," he mumbled, knowing full well his older brother would be irritated.

"Oh, shut up!" Lotha boomed as he and Nandu tailed behind Inda towards the opposite side of the room.

From her post at one end of the bar, Saron followed the progress of the three troublemakers with her eyes. She expected fireworks at any minute.

"Shush, here they come," Fornax whispered as the three men approached their table. His voice was just barely audible above the sound of clanging music.

"Hell's bells," Gunter said, adopting the singsong intonation of a man who'd had too much to drink.

"Land's sakes!" Sam said, taking Gunter's cue and putting on an show of being equally polluted.

Fornax joined in, raising his lager of ale and displaying all the outward trappings of being totally inebriated.

"May we?" Inda asked, grabbing hold of an empty chair.

"By all means," Fornax swaggered, motioning for him to take a seat. Following Inda's lead, the other two men pulled up chairs as well.

Fornax barreled drunkenly on. "What's on yer mind there, Inda? It isn't very damn often you condescend to sit and have a drink with the likes of me. But then that's not why yer here, is it? You and yours don't approve much of all the newcomers Sam and I've been bringing here to Mars, do you?"

Fornax couldn't have hit the nail more squarely on the head if he tried. Immediately, Inda's face went red with anger. Most of the settlers Sam and he had brought here to Mars were just unimportant no-names wanting a chance at a new life. Few were of the pedigree that devoted Newtons like Inda Desai believed were so critical to their hoped-for utopia.

"As a matter of fact, I do not approve!" Inda roared, reaching in his pocket and lighting up one of his harsh Martian cigarettes. "In fact, that's why I'm here: to talk to Sam about that very subject."

"That's Councilman Matthews to you," Sam replied, eyes narrowing.

"My apologies, Councilman. The point is this: Everyone in the settlement respects you — me included. We're all interested in knowing what you think can be done to better segregate the two colonies. Our newhuman experiment is never going to succeed unless a way can be found to insulate the Newtons from all the rest."

"Your newhuman experiment is never going to succeed no matter what I do."

"You don't really believe that, do you?"

Sam stared quizzically at Inda. He didn't know where to begin. There was just too damn much intellectual ground to cover, and it was just too damn painful for him to try and cover it all again just now. Still, the man had asked him a fair question and he deserved a fair answer. Of all the Newtons, perhaps only this one was influential enough to make a difference.

The old man took a deep breath, blew the smoke from Inda's cigarette out of his face. Then he cleared his throat to speak. In his hand was the White King from the chessboard. He stared at it thoughtfully.

"I find it peculiar that — to a man — every single one of you left the land of your birth for one reason and one reason only — to escape persecution back home. Now, here you are, in a new land, a land of opportunity, a land without kings, without tyrants, without preexisting or established elites — and the first thing you do — the very first thing — is to set yourself apart as if you were better than the rest."

"Well, it's not as if we were persecuting anyone," Inda countered. "All we want is to be left alone. Where's the harm in that?"

"Everywhere!" Sam answered tersely. "The harm is everywhere! Bigotry is never a one-way street, don't you know that? Hatred breeds hatred. And that is the least dreadful part of it. Like all common beliefs, no matter how superstitious or perverted, there's always a speck of truth lurking somewhere near the bottom. This experiment of yours can only end in one of two ways. Either your colony will succeed, or else it will fail. If it succeeds, and Newton becomes rich and powerful, the citizens of Newton will dictate the affairs of the planet in whatever way happens to further their ends — up to and including killing or expelling those who don't fit their newhuman recipe. On the other hand, if the experiment fails and the Newtons become outcasts or refugees, the residents of Colony One will not extend them a helping hand. To the contrary. After having been told over and over again by the newhumans how they are nothing but genetic relics, the Colony One'ers will no doubt slap the arrogant Newtons down. You'll be lucky if they let you get away with your lives. More than likely, you'll be dispatched in short order, and Newton will become nothing more than a footnote in Martian history, much as the Oneida Community was in early American history."

Even as Sam spoke, Saron wandered over to the crowded table, handed him an ale and kissed him on the forehead. Much to everyone's surprise and amazement, he patted her lovingly on the behind as she walked away.

"Guerilla warfare always defeats Army regulars," Lotha interjected, the sweat on his sloping forehead making him look even cruder than he actually was.

"That's right," Inda said, thinking of the cache of explosives Oskar Schaeffer had given him. Now that he had been taught how to properly wire the explosives and set them off, he could level any building on the planet he wanted. "Think of the examples — the American colonists versus the British, the Viet Cong versus the Americans, the Afghans versus the Russians, the Amerinds versus the . . . "

"All true. But the analogy you are making is totally wrong. In the first place, God always fights on the side with the artillery. Plus, in each of the cases you mentioned, the organized armies were the *invaders*, not the defenders. In none of those instances were the Army regulars defending their own homelands. The Colony One'ers will be. The Newtons will lose."

"Well, aren't you the arrogant one!" Inda said angrily. "There's no way Colony One can hope to defend itself against a determined band of terrorists!"

Suddenly Fornax was on his feet. From seemingly out of nowhere, a blaster appeared in his hand. He called it "Jenny." She was durbinium-powered, just like the *Tikkidiw*, and capable of vaporizing an entire platoon in an instant. He pointed her in Inda's direction.

"Should Colony One come under attack, pray that you're not in the line of fire of my Jenny. No terran weapon can match this baby's firepower on an ounce-for-ounce basis. Believe me when I tell you, Inda — nothing can stop her. Nothing."

Shocked by his fellow countryman's defiance, Inda let his jaw fall open. "Am I to understand, then, that you — a newhuman, no less — will stand against us?"

Fornax's reply was unequivocal. "I stand neither for you, nor against you. But be clear on this, my friend — I stand against anarchy and in favor of freedom. I stand against terrorism and in favor of a person's right to choose. I stand in favor of capitalism and free trade and against communalism. If that puts us on opposite sides of this dispute, so be it."

"I couldn't have put it better myself if I tried," Sam echoed, as he got to his feet and stood next to Fornax. Gunter did the same. Anyone could see the time for talking had come to an end.

"So the lines are drawn then?" Inda said, uncomfortable with the outcome.

"So they are," Fornax confirmed, sliding the blaster back into its holster. "So they are."

TWENTY-THREE

London

The boat moved upstream from the ocean. The Thames narrowed and the city came into view. Londinos to the old Celts and Druids; Londinium to the Romans; Lundenwic to the Anglo-Saxons — remarkably little had changed in three thousand years. The River was still there, the wide boulevards, the Globe Theatre, the Clink Dungeon, Parliament, and, of course, the Queen. Remembering her father's sage advice that she should go see J, Carina's next destination after SKANDIA was the City of London.

Much to the woman's amazement, getting an appointment to see this high-ranking official proved surprisingly easy. When she arrived at the offices of Commonwealth Intelligence in the center of the financial district, she was greeted by a pleasant woman who handed her an official-looking form. Her request was to be put in writing and she would be notified within a week whether the Commissioner would take the meeting. All Carina wrote on the form was her name, and that she needed to locate BC. The next day a driver asked for her at her hotel.

The driver took her deep into the center of the City, down a ramp and into a darkened garage. From there she was escorted to an elevator and whisked upstairs. J's office was buried deep within the bowels of a giant complex of governmental buildings, each one meticulously framed in red brick. The stern-looking man commanded chambers protected by the highest level of security Her Majesty could muster. When Carina entered his office through a heavy wooden door the man sat hunkered behind an enormous wooden desk. A stylish Victorian lamp hung over his head. His hefty, gray-haired bulk dominated the room. Bulletproof glass lined the windows that admitted light into his utilitarian, yet elegant surroundings.

The man the intelligence world knew only as "J" stared out at her now from across the top of his swimmingly huge desk. His husky hands were folded together in front of him. He was the first to speak.

"Tell me, child," he said, his arrogant tone sickening her. "Tell me why I should lift so much as a finger to help you find BC. You and your father have been nothing but a thorn in my side ever since the day I first laid eyes on you. Come to think of it, you both still owe me for the favor I did you two years ago."

"Oh, what favor is that?"

"Saving your lives, for starters."

Carina nodded her head. It was hard to deny the debt she and her father owed this man. J was responsible — at least in part — for them having survived a close brush with death when Whitey attacked them without warning on the Moon that day two years ago.

Yet, it was equally true that J was the one most responsible for getting them into that jam to begin with. Like so many men of his ilk, J shamelessly massaged the truth to fit his audience. While most Euros would undoubtedly have considered him one of the "good guys," the head of Commonwealth Intelligence was just as lawless, just as ruthless, just as power-hungry as any despot who had ever walked the face of God's Green Earth. The man ruled his fiefdom through intimidation and bullying, and he had not even the slightest remorse for the welfare of the people he puppeted.

He continued, now, in his heavy British accent. "All I ever wanted from you people was the secret of the Fornax Drive. Deliver me that and I'll deliver you BC. Is that so much to ask?"

"Go to Hades, Sir."

"I probably shall," the man growled ominously.

Carina tried to stare the man down. J was a stout man, with a grizzled face like an ex-Marine. A dense mat of curly, black hair gripped his arms, the back of his thick neck, even the skin of his swollen knuckles. Beneath the man's shirt, his chest was like a gray forest. The hair on his stubby legs, an untended lawn.

"Listen, you," she said, digging in her heels. "If I go to America unescorted and wind up dead, you will never get your hands on Fornax's precious Drive. If, on the other hand, BC goes along with me and I live, then at least there is a *chance* for you to get what you want. I can't trade you something I don't have — the Fornax Drive — for something *you* don't have — knowledge of my family's gene-map."

"Touché, young lady. Well done. You might make a good secret agent yet. Only problem is, it's not up to me. It's up to him."

"You mean to tell me you can't order BC to protect me? Who the hell is in charge around here anyway?"

"What I mean is, I won't."

J's tone was firm, and his intransigence infuriated her. Carina began to wonder whether the initial he went by was short for a proper name like John or James, or whether it was just short for something simpler like jackass. She was just about to ask the question, when she changed her mind.

"You're a son of a bitch," she said.

"If you think flattery will help change my mind, you are sorely mistaken."

"Bastard!" she swore, springing to her feet with tears in her eyes. "Dirty bastard!"

*   *   *

BC watched her go. Sitting on the other side of the one-way glass, staring into J's office, BC watched her go. Just as she had once watched him leave, now he watched her leave.

His steel-blue eyes were cold. Dispassionate. He and J had agreed beforehand that if at any time during the meeting BC changed his mind, all he had to do was lift the receiver on the extension in the darkened room. That would illuminate the third button on J's comm as a signal, a signal that BC was going to accompany her after all. The light had remained unlit throughout.

How long had it been? he asked himself as the outer door slammed shut, punctuating her exit. *How long?*

BC let his thoughts drift back in time. He remembered their last moments together, how badly it had all ended.

He cracked his knuckles nervously. The pops echoed off the walls of the tiny chamber. How long *had* it been? Six weeks? Six months? BC didn't know anymore. After he returned to the Agency, he had tried to blot out the whole sordid affair from his mind.

She looked well, there was no question about it. Almost too well. Like she had been working out.

But the one thing BC found strange was that she hadn't asked J about their son, not even once. That bothered him. Maybe she just flat out didn't care. If so, he'd made the right decision with the boy after all.

BC had had his doubts. After he left Mars, what was the right thing to do? He thought about it for several days. In the end, he took the boy to the same orphanage where he himself had been raised. It was in the hedgerow country south of London.

The visit had been a bittersweet experience. Sister Theresa was still alive, and still as stern as ever. After depositing the boy into her custody — BC was calling him Sam Jr. by now — she gave BC the battle-scarred pine cane that had arrived with him on their doorstep that day many years ago when *he* was first abandoned by his father.

It was a curious cane, one which — on closer examination — proved to be a rather nasty weapon. Somewhere along the line, some enterprising young fellow had hollowed out the insides and inserted a large-bore rifle barrel in its place. Hidden in the crook was a hair-action trigger. Anyone could see that the staff had enjoyed a colorful history. Two sets of initials had been carved in the handle by two different owners — F.W. and N.M. But Sister Theresa didn't have a clue whose initials they were, nor did BC. When he returned to the office that day after leaving Sam Jr. with her at the orphanage, he tossed the useless relic into J's umbrella stand.

Now, as BC entered J's office through the side door from the room with the one-way glass, he passed it, still in the umbrella stand where he'd left it only a month ago. Not paying the ancient cane a second thought, he said, "I'm going to follow her, sir."

"I wondered how long it would take for you to come to that decision," J murmured with disapproval.

"I don't see as if I have any choice." BC's gaze was unflinching.

"Quite. Which leaves me no alternative either." J returned BC's unflinching look with one of granite.

"Sir?"

"You're a good man, BC. But, if you go in after her, you go in DK."

BC nodded. In intelligence lingo, DK translated as "Don't Know." If he got arrested or was compromised in any way, he couldn't count on J or anyone else from Commonwealth Intelligence to bail him out. Even if his life hung in the balance, he would receive no help or support whatsoever from the Agency. To anyone who asked, the Agency would claim they *Didn't Know* him, had never heard of him, couldn't care less. In other words, BC would be totally on his own. Come to think of it, that didn't bother him. He preferred it that way actually, always had.

"DK it is," he said, gathering his things.

*   *   *

As Carina endured the ten-hour-long trip from London to Reykjavik and then on into Toronto, she reflected back on what her father had once tried to tell her of their family's long history in North America. Though she'd always made a point of pretending she wasn't listening — an irritating habit, which infuriated Sam no end — she had in fact absorbed every detail.

The history of the white man in Illinois Country, where she was headed, dated back to the late 1600s with the arrival of Marquette and Joliet. Following close upon their heels, French fur traders came to the area, establishing Fort Pimiteoui as the southernmost point of Canadian jurisdiction. The fort took shape at approximately the location where the modern city of Peoria would eventually be built. In those days, except for the occasional Jesuit mission, the fort was occupied almost exclusively by Amerinds until the Illinois Country was surrendered to the English in the mid-1700s. In fact, the earliest mention of the Matthews clan could be traced back to this era, though in those days the family went by the somewhat longer name they had brought with them from Scotland — Matthewson.

Because of repeated Amerind attacks during the American Revolution, Fort Pimiteoui ultimately had to be abandoned. The French traders didn't leave the area, however, and soon founded a new village downstream from the fort at the foot of the lake in the river. This new site — Au Pied du Lac, in French — later anglicized to Old Peoria — featured a fort plus about fifty buildings strung out along the banks of the Illinois River. There, in Old Peoria, is where the first Matthewson, Ian, made his mark as a blacksmith.

From those humble beginnings, the Matthewsons dug their roots into the rich, fertile loam of the Illinois River valley. They were a proud and patriotic bunch, and from that day forward, every Matthewson served his country with distinction. Indeed, the name of a distant ancestor who died defending the Union — Private Byron Matthewson of the 11th Cavalry — was inscribed, along with the names of several hundred others who suffered a similar fate, at the base of a monument that stood in the Court House square in downtown Peoria. Byron had been the son of a pioneer who had settled in Illinois. Opposing slavery, he had fought with the North in the War Between the States. With each succeeding generation, there had been at least one Congressman, or Captain of Industry, or War Hero to bear the name of Matthewson, later shortened to Matthews when the family moved their thriving business downstream to be closer to St. Louis.

Sam's great-grandfather, Nathanial "Tiger" Matthews had been the Governor of Missouri. His son, Nate Matthews — Sam's grandfather — had been that state's ranking U.S. Senator and Chairman of the powerful Military Oversight Committee.

But there the scion ended. Sam's father had been a slacker, and Sam himself had been sent to Canada for safekeeping before he ever had a chance to make a name for himself in America. After the Great War, all that remained of the Matthews' fortune, the Matthews' name and power, were some long forgotten records in the bombed-out catacombs of a half-dead city now called Sane Lou.

It was this place, Sane Lou, that was her ultimate destination.

TWENTY-FOUR

Of High Priests & Fools

Sam sat alone in Saron's Place. Everyone else had gone home for the night. He stared through bloodshot eyes at the White Rook in his hand. In the end, it had given its life to save his Queen. The Rook had died an honorable death and, by making that sacrifice, he had allowed Sam to win this latest round. For the moment, the series between him and Fornax was even. Now, as he sat there in the pub thinking, he couldn't help but compare their present situation with that of the Israelites following their escape from bondage in Egypt.

Moses had come down from on high with a concise list of Do's and Don't's for his ignorant followers to observe. In his day, several thousand years before Christ, with superstitions running rampant and with memories of the Pharaohs' mysticism still fresh in their collective consciousness, the minds of those poor, wandering souls were ripe for a strict set of rules prescribing correct behavior. Sensing this, Moses spake to the People about theft, about adultery, about slander, murder, and greed. And, despite some reversals, the People listened. And they obeyed.

Yet, if Moses had crossed the Reed Sea to Mars instead of to Canaan, if he had led a bunch of Newtons out of Egypt instead of a tribe of ignorant Jews, if Moses had stood in the shadow of Omen instead of Mount Sinai, he would have faced a whole new galaxy of problems.

For one thing, after generations in bondage, the Jews were conditioned to taking orders. The people who came to Mars were quite different. They were too well-informed, too nonconformist, too contrary, to be very accepting of a set of rules. Not God's rules, and certainly not the rules of any self-anointed high priest. No, if Moses had climbed the Martian equivalent of Mount Sinai, he would have returned with his precious tablets only to discover that everyone had gone home early to throw another dried llama spoor on the fire and take a nap.

For the most part, the settlers would have agreed that how an adult conducted himself was not a community concern. But, as more and more people poured into Mars, the potential for trouble multiplied.

To begin with, there was the question of property rights. With millions upon millions of hectares of untamed land yet to be conquered, and with each square meter of land yielding to the spade only after untold hours of work had been expended to remove boulders and rocks, should a quarrel erupt between two neighbors and no amicable solution be quickly reached, the two might literally fight to the death to get their way. Early on, Sam realized that this would just not do. If Mars was to ever have a commercial future, a small body of law had to be established to deal with such problems. Otherwise, a simple dispute had the potential of spinning hopelessly out of control, drowning the entire colony in a sea of acrimony and anger. It was with this mind that he and Fornax and a few other far-sighted souls founded the Council of Arbitration back when the colony was still young.

Two years had passed, now, and Sam was tired and ready to step down from his post. He had headed the Council since its inception, and had run it as a sort of unelected benevolent judge. Being the planet's elder statesman, he was well-regarded by both colonies for his keen intellect and uncanny sense of history. His practical philosophy on how things ought to be done was widely accepted, and his counsel often sought on matters of importance, just as Inda had done the previous night. To make the Council workable, Sam had patterned its structure after what he knew of two venerable institutions that had governed simple peoples thousands of years ago on Earth — the Icelandic Thingvellir and the Iroquois Great Law of Peace.

Almost to the day, fifteen centuries ago, the Vikings discovered — and began to settle — a large, fjord-creased island rimmed by volcanoes and glistening glaciers, yet blessed with broad green valleys as well. This place was called Iceland, and the first wave of colonists arrived there in the year 870. The place proved to be such a cornucopia, within a mere sixty years all the usable land had been taken up by newcomers.

Unlike the thin and sleek raiding ships the Vikings used to plunder Europe with, the Icelandic settlers arrived in *knorr*, ships heavy enough to negotiate the North Atlantic and large enough to convey the settlers along with all their household goods plus their livestock. As they had done back in their native land, the early Viking settlers favored sites amenable to seafaring, fishing and farming. What they looked for in the ideal homestead was two things — enough level, well-drained ground to build a farmstead and plant a few crops, plus a location near the shore with easy access to a sheltered spot where a boat could be safely beached. The competition for such spots quickly became intense.

In many ways, Iceland was like an arctic Eden, with abundant fauna like salmon, seal, and great auk, plus enormous stands of willow and birch. At least in the early years, before population pressures threatened to destroy the ecosystem, land was for the taking. A man could claim as his own all the territory he could cover on foot in a single day carrying a lighted torch. A woman was entitled to as much land as she could travel while leading a two-year-old heifer in good condition on a spring day between the rising and the setting of one sun.

As the fledgling Icelandic colony grew, the need for a ruling body became apparent. But, after what they had seen in the Old World, the colonists resolved to be free of Kings. They set out to govern themselves through regional assemblies led by local chieftains. In the year 930, the most powerful chieftains on the island united to establish the Althing, Europe's first parliament. It constituted the closest approximation to a self-governing republic since the days of ancient Rome. At the outset, the Althing consisted of a council of 36 chieftains called *godar*, literally "godly ones." They maintained their positions by protecting and representing their regional subjects in exchange for their fealty.

The Althing met once each year in June at a place called Thingvellir, an open field located on the southern plateau. Delegates from all over the island met there to discuss the laws of the land, as well as the future course of the country. They brought with them their entire entourage and erected temporary living quarters in what amounted to a massive VIP campground. Inbetween sessions of the gathering at a cliff called the Law Rock, the delegates socialized and transacted business.

But the Law Rock was the focal point of their proceedings. There, they listened to the reading of the Icelandic legal code (one-third was read aloud each year), heard lawsuits, considered new laws as well as amendments to old ones, and elected a president to serve a renewable three-year term. Their elaborate legal code established regional Things and courts, set forth penalties that miscreants would have to pay, and prescribed terms of settlement for the feuds that constantly erupted among high-status Icelanders.

Five hundred years later and two thousand miles to the west, the Amerinds of eastern North America also managed to organize themselves in a fashion that Councilman Samuel Matthews believed worth emulating. This particular detail of history was a lesson Sam had learned as a boy from a man he revered very much — his grandfather. Nate had taught him about the Iroquois Great Law of Peace and how their form of participatory government influenced the Founding Fathers in framing the U.S. Constitution.

The Iroquois governed through an elected Council of Elders. They perfected an arrangement responsible for promoting long-term peace and prosperity among their peoples. As Sam's grandfather explained it, the history of democracy and of freedom had always been one of crafting systems of law to prevent the ruling elites from stomping down upon and enslaving their subjects. The Founders drew not only on the lessons of the Magna Carta and the prototype democracies of ancient Greece, but also on something closer to home — the Iroquois Great Law.

While historians have long attributed the central tenets of the Constitution to the likes of Thomas Jefferson and Benjamin Franklin, few people realize that the League of the Iroquois greatly influenced the colonial Founders as well. The Great Law of the Iroquois embraced not only the basic ideas of democracy and federalism, it also gave each of the tribes comprising the League an equal voice. The Great law included several things later adopted by the Founders — a guarantee of religious expression, a mechanism for impeaching poor leaders, and a formula for amending the centuries' old constitution. Benjamin Franklin in particular saw the Iroquois system as a model on which to base the American Union, and this was on Sam's mind as he contemplated how Mars itself should be governed. It seemed to him that each time humanity had another go at reinventing democracy, it owed it to those who had come before to build in a new layer of protections for its citizens.

*   *   *

One of the first acts of Sam's Council of Arbitration was to develop a practical calendar for the local population. Keeping track of time was a matter of no small consequence, and Sam saw no compelling reason why it should be measured according to the days and months of Earth's calendar. In fact, the terran system was becoming more and more absurd with each passing week. Already the seasons were out of sync. It was early winter here on Mars, but only September back home.

With the number of hours that elapsed between sunrises very nearly the same on both planets, the calendar dilemma they faced didn't center on the length of their respective days — it centered on the length of their respective *years*.

At 687 earth-days, the Martian year was nearly twice that of the Home Planet. Therefore, the timing of the seasons, as measured by Earth's calendar, held little meaning for the homesteaders here on Mars. With farming the principal occupation, settlers needed to know with some precision when planting should begin and when harvest time had arrived. Thus, the issue of seasonality became an early concern taken up by the Council. Sam was the first to propose a workable solution.

Dividing the Martian year into 17 months of 40 days each, and setting eight days as the length of a Martian week, Sam neatly cleaved each month into precisely five weeks, a symmetry sorely lacking from the Gregorian calendar still in use back home. This arrangement left seven days unaccounted for, seven days that Sam recommended be stuck in as a celebration period following BeHolden Day. As it was back on Earth, BeHolden Day would be recognized at the close of the fourth week in the tenth month.

What to call these days and months was at once a lively issue. Here too, Sam had a modest proposal to make, one which retained vestiges of the terran system, yet still offered some incremental improvements.

In Sam's scheme, the eight-day-long week would open with Onesday, a variation on the old Monday. Like the names for all the days of the week — and the *length* of the week, for that matter — terrans had the Babylonians to thank. They were the first ancient civilization to award a day of the week to each of the seven heavenly bodies known by them to move through the sky — the Sun, the Moon, Mars, Mercury, Jupiter, Venus, and Saturn. Of course, when the Romans adopted the Babylonian seven-day week, they renamed the planets — along with each one's corresponding day — for their own stable of gods. Later still, the Germanic peoples on whose language much of English was based, substituted the names of *their* gods for Roman gods having similar qualities or characteristics. Tuesday, for instance — the day Romans set aside for their god of war — was Mars's day in Latin, Tyr's day in German, and Tiw's day in Old English. On Sam's calendar, it would be renamed Twosday.

And so it went. Wednesday became Threesday. Thursday, Foursday. Friday, Fivesday. And so on. Nobody liked the names Sevensday or Eightsday, so Saturday and Sunday were retained. Apparently, in matters where the Sabbath was concerned, tradition ran deep.

In a sense, leaving the names of the two weekend days unchanged was appropriate to secure two other objectives, both worthy. To begin with, after a six-day-long workweek, the meaning of a weekend was just that much more profound. Since Roman times already, Saturday had been a diminutive form of its namesake, the Saturnalia, an orgiastic revelry held each December to reward, in a sense, the previous year's hard work. In modern times, Saturday served this function in similar fashion. Which left Sunday as a quiet, even muted day of recovery before the next six-day stretch began.

There were other considerations besides naming days of the week. Switching over to a new calendar required setting a "start" date, a date after which all records would be kept according to the new system. Sam's recommendation was that the Council arbitrarily assign January 1, 2431

Gregorian — approximately the date on which the first settlers arrived on Mars — as Primus 01, 00 A.L., the A.L. designation referring to "After Landing." Today's date, September 25, 2433, would therefore be twenty-five Martian months later, or Octium 31, 01 A.L.

The Council of Arbitration did more than just keep track of the date. But, at this early junction, it had no regular, official business to conduct and met only as needed, about once a month. On Mars, there were no taxes to collect, no armies to conscript, no welfare to be paid, no bread, and no circuses.

In an agrarian barter-economy, which this still was, money had little role to play. What money that did circulate was earth-money, like the Johannesburg dollar or the Japanese yen. Collecting taxes on these currencies would be difficult if not impossible.

Similarly, armies could not exist without soldiers, and conscription would be doomed to failure when you had nothing to pay them with and draft evaders could simply disappear over the next hill.

As for welfare, with resources stretched thin at every turn, each had to take care of his own.

In fact, the Council's first law of consequence took aim at a resource that was in particularly short supply — trees. The point of this directive was to give Mars's fledgling forests a chance to develop undisturbed long enough that there might be an adequate supply of lumber at some point in the future.

The history of mankind versus the tree has always been a tug-of-war, with the tree the clear loser in places as diverse as the Brazilian Outback, Iceland, Madagascar, and Indonesia. This, the first law of the land, stipulated that upon penalty of expulsion from the planet, no tree could be girdled or cut down, nor any live limbs sheared, prior to Primus 01, 25, and then only if five new saplings rated of equal or greater hardness were planted to replace the downed tree.

Defending the forests against poachers proved to be a relatively simple matter compared with the problem the Council wrestled with next — how to define who owned what land and which livestock belonged to whom.

It was the sort of universal question that had plagued mankind since the dawn of time. If the land you lived on was unoccupied prior to your arrival, on what basis could you claim it for yourself now? And, if you did claim it, how *much* of it could you rightly call your own?

Similarly, if an unmarked herd of animals was found wandering on this same open prairie, on what basis could you claim that any of the herd belonged to you?

Did they belong to you simply because they happened to be munching grass on the land you laid claim to? Or, did proof of ownership require something more, like a brand? Then, to be sure it was genuine, did brands have to be registered? Or, was simply tying a bell around their neck enough? And so on.

Homesteaders on every continent have had to work out the messy details, and the people of Mars were no exception. After much debate, the Council decided to grant a homesteader title to however much land he could enclose with a fence of his own making. By extension, any unbranded livestock grazing on the land he had fenced also belonged to him. And, yes, brands would have to be registered.

Though this seemingly simple and innocuous statute was the Council's first attempt to deal with the question of what belonged to whom, it precipitated a crisis of the first degree, spawning the need for a dozen other laws. As always, the devil was in the details.

For instance, how should one properly define a "fence"? Of what material should it be built? How tall must it be? Should the fencing law apply equally well to llamas as it did to cows? What if there were a break in an existing fence, did that negate the settler's claim? How long would the break be allowed to remain before it had to be fixed? And so on, and so forth.

On one side of the controversy stood the idealists, who argued that since many of the animals were a gift from the past — descendants of the ones Carina cooked up that night in the gene-store — they belonged to no one single man, but rightly belonged to *every* man. On the other side of the line stood the realists who, with fists clenched, agreed that the animals belonged to no one single man — they belonged to them!

The inherent conflict between socialism and capitalism was a paradox as old as man himself. It predated the rise of the first civilizations. Here on Mars, the tug-of-war between the two 'isms was muddied further by the settlers' own heritage, a heritage where memories of Afghanistan died hard. In their native country, the wealthiest families were those who owned the most livestock. Since the law prescribed that only animals grazing on land you had fenced were considered yours, there were an ambitious few with notions of fencing hundreds of hectares and branding every four-legged beast in sight. The fencing law, by disrupting the previously communal nature of the animals' ownership, had the unintended effect of stirring up a witch's brew of trouble between the ranchers.

The chasm between socialism and capitalism revealed itself in a myriad of ways, some which Sam found downright bewildering. Humans were basically territorial creatures, after all, and so to him it seemed intuitive that every society would inevitably discover that capitalism was their only salvation. How, then, to understand the perennial appeal of socialism, especially among the young? And why the aversion among these people to money as a medium of exchange?

Ever the economist, Sam found it curious that the Afghan settlers preferred to trade their wares with one another barter-style, rather than to purchase or sell them on an open market employing an intermediary like cash. One night he discussed this practice with Saron at great length. She gave him a new way of looking at this phenomenon, one that hadn't occurred to him before:

Her point was that for almost the entirety of its history, the human race had subsisted in simple hunter/gatherer bands, where money had no meaning. Thus, maybe what Sam was observing here on Mars made sense in light of Newton's frontier mentality.

Sam couldn't help but agree. And yet, Saron had other points to make:

In other such pre-modern societies, all economic transactions were conducted face-to-face. As a result, barter became as much a part of our humanity as practically any other distinctly human trait. While money was without a doubt a much more efficient way to organize a society, and no industrialized civilization could manage without it, the subsequent few thousand years of development were but a fleeting moment from an evolutionary point of view, not nearly long enough to accustom all of humanity to faceless relationships like the pricing system which is so central to modern capitalism.

As a consequence, people have occasionally responded to capitalism's impersonal nature with an expression of their animal emotions. And when these sorts of primordial feelings have surfaced, people have gone out and bashed their "greedy" landlords, for instance, or resorted to rent controls, or looted their neighborhood grocery stores, all in spite of the intellectual and empirical case that proves they were actually impoverishing themselves by these actions.

While socialism has repeatedly shown itself to be unworkable, people have found it to be emotionally satisfying if for no other reason than it fulfills an immature nostalgia for a simpler world in which the high priests and tribal chieftains made all the important choices for their subjects and people didn't have to think.

The only reason capitalism survived the demise of the tribal chieftains was because of the material success it bestowed on the masses. Where poverty and turmoil accompanied the decline of the chieftains, capitalism didn't stand a chance. It was unfortunate. But this was a lesson mankind had had to learn over and over again.

What Saron said made sense, and it was Sam's fervent hope that as long as his health held out he could help guide the budding nation in the right direction. He felt a strong responsibility to press the Council into adopting rules that might lead the society away from collectivism and towards private ownership, even at the risk of disrupting the communal traditions many of the settlers had brought with them from home.

Getting up from the table, now, with the White Rook still clenched in his hand, Sam edged towards the door of the Commons. Saron was standing there waiting for him. To an extent he could never have anticipated, she had come to assume a central place in his life. When it was time for him to finally go home and die, he only hoped she would agree to make the journey with him.

TWENTY-FIVE

Sane Lou

With a letter of introduction from Viscount Nordman in her pocket, Carina Matthews descended into a world unlike any she could ever have conjured up in a nightmare. Though her father had warned her what a hellhole a big city in pre-Great War America could be like — the stifling pollution, the insane crowding, the crime, the street people, the bimbookers, the slugs — nothing in her experience could prepare her for Sane Lou. Conditions here were so forbidding, she found the weight of the blaster in her handbag to be of small comfort.

After the long drive south, she was sore and dirty — sore, because the only road from Chica to Sane Lou was broken and rutted; dirty, because in this heat she had had to travel the entire distance with the windows down and the conditioner off. By the time she arrived at the outskirts of the city, her face and hair were gritty with road dirt and pieces of flying insects. All she wanted now was a hot bath and a good night's sleep. *But where?* In the aftermath of the Great War, with so much of the country destroyed and so little of it having been rebuilt, her choices were limited.

The battle for North America had been a ferocious affair. China had met the U.S. threat in the Pacific. Mexico and her allies had swept up into Texas and California from the south. Canada into the heartland from the north. Brazil and Colombia up the eastern seaboard. What wasn't destroyed in the invasion, was demolished in the ensuing civil war.

Not everyone died, of course, nor was everything leveled. But the collapse of the infrastructure, coupled with the poisoning of the land, had proved a deadly combination.

It had been more than thirty years, now, since the end of the war, and there had been a trickle of people back onto the continent. Even so, precious little had been done to repair the physical damage. Burned-out buildings stood everywhere. Potholes the size of gtrucks reflected bomb damage in the road. Craters dotted what once were cornfields. No matter which way you looked, there were constant reminders of who had won and who had lost. Steel rails twisted beyond recognition. Hulks of sunken boats still floated in the river, half-buried in mud.

The vestiges of some towns remained. But they were few and far between. Joliet. Bloomington. Springfield. Collinsville. All little villages now, with a tenth the population they had at their peak, a hundred years ago.

When Carina arrived in Sane Lou, her selection of places to spend the night numbered only two. At her last stop for food and water, she learned of an inn down by the river, a place called The Last Resort.

In the twilight of a desperately long day, the heart of Sane Lou's river district shone red. This blighted area was a congested, confusing realm where winding, unpaved streets converged at the waters' edge. One street led to the broken-down remains of the Gateway Arch, another to the splintered doors of The Last Resort, her destination for the night. It was not what she expected.

When Carina stepped from the gcar, she still felt heavy and bloated, almost lethargic, from the dilatory effects of earth-normal gravity. She would have thought by now that she would have adjusted. But it was taking time.

As she paused on the steps of the rundown hotel to catch her breath, a foul-smelling man and two of his colleagues emerged from a cramped, subterranean bar. The drunken man had rancid breath and a beer gut that hung down over his belt. Carina could smell the alcohol from five meters away.

Teetering back and forth halfway up the concrete stairway, this disgusting specimen of humanity groaned then threw up on his pants and shoes. He sank briefly to his knees in agony. His friends reached out to him, but he shook off their help. He continued his wobbly ascent on his own, finally succeeding in reaching the top of the staircase. Arm in arm, the drunken threesome jostled one another through the open door and up to the front desk ahead of Carina. She followed them in, keeping her distance.

Though Carina had lost track of what day it was, she knew for certain it was late September. After the cool, crisp air of SKANDIA and then London, the night air here was surprisingly muggy. There were bugs everywhere, and in the still, stale air of the narrow hotel lobby, she felt a bead of sweat work its way out from under her armpit and roll agonizingly slowly down her side. Another accumulated in the crotch of her panties.

Overhead, a feeble excuse for a ceiling fan struggled to push the thick air aside. But it was making little headway.

Two men sat off in one corner, their bloodshot eyes fixed on a visicast screen exhibiting an explicit pornovideo featuring a Negroid woman coupling with a Euro man. The two men looked up at Carina with a longing gaze when she entered the room, a gaze that told her in no uncertain terms that as far as they were concerned, she was nothing more than a set of hips and a nicely-matched pair of tits. Ahead of her was the registration desk. She wasted no time joining the others in line.

The desk clerk noticed her immediately. He called to the back room for the night manager to come forward. This change in protocol alarmed her at first. But when the second man emerged from behind a curtain, he opened up a new check-in line just for her. He seemed unnerved by Carina's presence and wanted to make sure she was in the right place. Twice he pointed to the nameplate above the desk and asked, "Last Resort?" Each time, Carina nodded her reply.

Through a toothy grin, the man said, "You lady. You not interested in checking-in."

"Yes," Carina murmured, suddenly aware that every eye in the place was upon her. Then it dawned on her why — *hers was the only female face she'd seen since first entering the premises.*

The manager sucked his blackened teeth for a few seconds while the clerk glanced at him sideways. In desperation, he spoke again. "Understand? . . . Unusual hotel. . . Capsule hotel . . . "

Carina didn't have a clue what "capsule hotel" meant. All she knew was that she was dog-tired. She had to have some sleep. "I understand . . . capsule hotel."

Though Carina didn't know it at the time, beyond the lobby were hundreds of tiny fabricated units, each roughly one meter wide, one meter tall, and two-plus meters deep. They were piled four-high like Pullman berths, or — as she would come to think of them later — like a stack of coffins. The sleeping cubicles were all pointed feet-first towards the aisle and arranged in long, ghastly rows around the perimeter of the room.

The manager asked for forty credits, which she paid, and for her shoes, which she reluctantly surrendered. Then he pointed her in the direction of a unisex locker room. In this small corner of the world, gender was apparently of little consequence. He strapped a locker key to her wrist with a Velcro band, handed her a towel, and pointed her to an empty stall located midway between two half-naked men. She avoided making eye contact.

Over the public-comm came a woman's soft voice. The instructions were repeated every few minutes in several languages — Shower. Change into the clean underpants and happicoat provided by the hotel. Lock everything else up.

Looking around her, Carina could see the two men changing at their lockers in awkward slow motion. They were drunk enough to require the support of the walls, plus the guidance of the sweet-sounding voice. From opposite ends of the locker room they kept up a slow, friendly banter — not the common talk of friends, but more like off-duty soldiers. Comrades perhaps, safe at last among allies. Unabashedly nude, they paused for a long stretch to study her nubile, young body before putting on fresh boxer shorts and a skimpy, white happicoat. The garment resembled a terry-cloth hospital gown.

Carina warily eyed the two rogues as they went slowly through their motions. She went to the sink to scrub her hands, face, and hair. Though she desperately needed a shower, she didn't dare disrobe in front of these two miscreants. Having consensual sex was one thing, being forcibly raped was something else again.

Barefoot, she tiptoed into the lavatory, clutch in hand. The ceramic floor was cold and wet. She placed her handbag on the edge of the sink within easy reach. When Inda gave her a blaster to protect herself with after BC took the boy and left, he promised her it was unstoppable. Now, of all times, she wasn't about to let the weapon out of her sight.

Much to her surprise, a receptacle on the wall of the washroom dispensed free disposable toothbrushes. Not only that, paste had already been applied, presumably to assist the unsteady guest who couldn't get it together. By the time Carina was done cleaning up, the two men had disappeared.

The number on the key velcroed to her wrist told her which locker was hers. It also told her which sleep-capsule. But before settling down for the night, Carina first needed to find something to eat. She hadn't had a decent meal since early yesterday morning.

Moving beyond the locker room, Carina returned to the front desk. There, the manager directed her towards the rest of the hotel.

At close quarters was a common-room where the lowlifes she met earlier on the stairs outside the hotel were now bivouacked watching the second half of the same pornographic video that had been running in the lobby. Glancing briefly at the screen, she saw a large Negroid woman performing fellatio on some man with stupendous proportions.

Gasping audibly, Carina retraced her steps backwards toward the door, bumped into a lounge chair and nearly fell to the floor. As she scrambled back to her feet, suddenly afraid, the three cretins laughed at her antics. One of them offered her a hand in exchange for a blowjob.

All of a sudden, she felt hemmed in, encircled by chairs and walls and scores of vending machines selling pep drinks and tortan and contraceptives and dried squid and seaweed and Deludes and dog-penis aphrodisiacs. Though her stomach was empty, she was sure she was going to retch.

Covering her mouth with her hands, Carina made for the door. The taste of phlegm was on her tongue. The three ruffians laughed again — cruelly, this time. She stumbled towards the stairwell.

Two floors above the common-room, Carina found a half-dozen men floating on their backs, their thick arms propped up on the edges of one of several blue-tiled hot tubs. Each tub was a meter or so in depth and a little wider than a king-size bed. A weight machine and an exercise bike occupied two niches along one side of the room. A tanning booth, the blue glow of its hot lamps chilling the white ceiling overhead, was in a small room across from them. Lined up on the opposite wall were four open stalls, each outfitted with a gurney, each occupied by a prone man and two young women. Except for what was partly covered by a towel, each man was naked. The women were bare-chested but wore white slacks. In each stall the scene was the same — the women were bent over the man providing a full-body massage. Their foreheads bristled with sweat from the effort. For an extra fee, when they were done, one of the women would mount the man then move dispassionately along to the next client on the waiting list.

Continuing her tour of the hotel, Carina descended a flight of stairs to the restaurant. The restaurant was very simple, serving mostly noodles. Its decor included a fake fireplace, plus six small round tables spread out over a large carpeted dining area. On each table, free cigs were stuffed into a beer glass. Dispensers for toothpicks stood nearby. The tables formed a semicircle around a visicast set suspended from the ceiling on steel tethers. It was broadcasting the same sick pornovideo she had twice caught a glimpse of earlier. The patrons — all male — were laughing, joshing each other, smoking, and slurping noodles. They eyed her lasciviously as she entered, one in particular. He was a big, burly fellow who hadn't shaved in a week. His breath reeked of tortan-ale.

The menu was written in some sort of pidgin English she couldn't decipher, so she ordered *ramen*, a noodle dish, for five credits. The waiter, a diminutive Oriental, jotted down her wristband number on the bill. She would have to pay for the meal in the morning when she checked out, in exchange for her shoes.

The waiter scurried away like a rat with a tasty chunk of cheese. At the next table, a lout fell asleep, his forehead descending slowly into the soup bowl sitting empty before him. Two tables further over, the other men were hooting their approval as the big black woman on the screen fixed her gelatinous hips down on the pelvis of partner number three this hour. Across the room, the man who had eyed her so closely when she first came in, licked his lips with a tongue made red from some pep drink as he looked her over yet one more time. Carina shivered and turned away before he could finish his appraisal.

The food came quickly and she ate just as fast. Then, Carina withdrew to her sleep-capsule.

The hotel's stacks of square, plastic capsules were located within an angular labyrinth, eerily reminiscent of a morgue. Each was beige and covered with some sort of a plastic shade. Glancing at the number on her wristband and comparing it to the numbers on the four-high stacks of capsules, she found she was assigned to row 188, level 3.

For Carina to enter an upper capsule, she first had to climb six steps up a narrow ladder that was attached to one side of the stack of capsules. Then she had to twist sideways to sit on the ledge of opening number three. Leaning back, she launched herself into the square capsule headfirst and horizontally. Presumably, the less athletically inclined guests — not to mention the drunken ones — were assigned to bottom-level berths for reasons of triage.

The smell inside the capsule was appalling — a mixture of chlorine vapors descending from the bath area, dirty dishwater rising from the kitchen, plus urine and vomit from who knows where. A one-inch-thick futon lay on the floor of the capsule, slightly cushioning her bottom. After scooting backward inside, she leaned forward, now, to pull down the translucent plastic shade which covered the opening.

It was a shade in name only. Not only did it not lock shut in any meaningful way — clipping loosely over an eyehook instead — it did nothing to shut out the presence of live bodies surrounding her on every side. Like a low-tech pup tent, the capsule walls blotted out nothing but the view. For a voluptuous, unattended woman, it was unnerving. Carina placed the blaster within easy reach of her hand.

At the foot of the smooth plastic capsule, a white bedsheet and beige blanket lay folded together like old sheets of computer paper. At the opposite end of the capsule, the end farthest from the opening, there was a tiny visicast screen, a radio, a mirror, a reading lamp, and a digiclock. The speaker for the visicast was positioned right next to her ear so that the sound wouldn't annoy others, except that it did.

She turned it on and adjusted the volume. Among the offerings was the same pornovideo being shown throughout the entire establishment. She turned it off and turned on the radio instead. All she got was static. She turned it off as well. Spreading the bedsheet out over the futon, Carina laid down. A sigh of exhaustion issued from her lips.

From the very start, it was apparent sleep wouldn't come easily. The blanket was too short to cover both her chest and her toes at the same time. And when she did pull it up to warm her neck, her feet caught a breeze from the aisle just outside. All around her was snoring. The vibrations felt as though the fellow on her left were shoveling a pint of phlegm back and forth inside his nasal cavity. On the exhale, the mucous would flap out to the edge of his nostrils before he caught it and breathed the sticky mass back in again, nearly swallowing it whole, but not quite. The noise he made was deafening.

From nearby capsules came other sounds. A cellophane wrapper being torn and wadded. A helping of squid being chewed for a very long time by someone who didn't shut his mouth. Teeth being brushed by someone who had returned from the washroom with the toothbrush still stuck in his cheek. Heavy staccato breathing as someone close by masturbated himself to sleep. One noise after another, these activities generated an uninterrupted dull growl which kept her continuously on edge.

Carina felt the press of bodies around her — five human beings within one radial meter. Each stranger had a force that extended one meter around and pressed against *her* force, *her* personal space, *her* privacy, trying to invade it, extinguish it, violate it. The woman felt uncomfortable, hemmed in. A pool of sweat formed in the pocket behind her knees, another in the small of her back. The partially digested noodles in her gut began to do barrel rolls.

The person below her, the one who had been masturbating himself to sleep, shifted violently, slamming against the side of his capsule, shaking hers. Something that could only have been his face smacked against the plastic wall like a slab of meat. She felt him drag his beefy arm along the capsule's smooth wall, his watchband or wedding ring scraping the interior.

Two rows over, someone struggled to draw closed the shade at the foot of his capsule. Hooking the latch at the bottom was a complicated operation, yet one which she had mastered easily enough. Then again, she had been sober. This fellow obviously was not. Each failed attempt sent the spring-loaded shade chattering up like a machine gun. It took him eight tries before he was successful.

From another capsule, the sound of dry retching. From another, a cough. From another, a sneeze, then a fart. Carina hated these men around her, these sick broken specimens of manhood. And yet, their incessant noisemaking is what saved her life.

Her first hint of trouble came when she sensed a presence on the ladder that ran vertically alongside the entrance to her cubicle. She hadn't heard a nearby shade being unhooked, so it couldn't have been anyone leaving his capsule. Besides, by taking inventory of the noises around her, Carina could tell that all the neighboring capsules were still occupied. That could mean only one thing — *someone was coming up the ladder*, someone whose destination was a berth that was already in use. Her berth!

Suddenly terrified, Carina grabbed for the blaster and held it flat against her tummy below her breasts. Her breathing was shallow.

The intruder fumbled with the hook on her shade, trying to unclasp it quietly, but clumsily botching the job.

"Who's there?" she said, her voice barely a whisper.

Her answer came in the form of an angry grunt. The intruder, deciding there was no longer any need for silence, tore the shade from its moorings and commenced his assault.

At first he tried to climb in on top of her, thinking that perhaps there was enough room inside the capsule to rape her right there.

But Carina wasn't going to go down easily. With a vicious snap of the leg, she kicked the man in the face as hard as she could. There was a cracking sound and a gush of blood from his broken nose.

Falling backwards to the floor, the man came at her, now, with fury in his eyes, clamping his muscular hands around her ankles.

Carina put up a terrific fight. But, without anything solid to brace herself against, it was impossible for her to stop him from pulling her out of the capsule.

Tightening his grip, the man tugged at her writhing body with all his might. Then, with one final jerk, she flew out of the smooth plastic capsule, futon, blaster, and all. Crashing to the concrete floor, she landed on her back, the wind knocked out of her.

Before she knew it, he was on her, spreading her legs apart with his knees and tearing at her nightclothes.

Carina fought like a wildcat, gasping for air, clawing at his face with her fingernails, screaming at the top of her lungs for help. But no one came to her aid.

He ripped off her panties. Then, stroking himself twice, he began moving in on her, his manhood extended like a cannon at her genitals.

She scooted backwards as far as she could, but her head banged against the bottom rung of the ladder.

Then her hand was on the blaster. She pulled it up in front of her. She aimed at his chest. He was at point-blank range. She pressed the contact. There was a flash of light and then the air was filled with a pink mist.

Blood gushed from the man's open wound like a fountain, but the man himself was gone.

The stench of seared flesh filled her nostrils, and she gagged.

What was left of the carcass fell against her like so many pounds of rancid meat.

The adrenaline was pumping through her system, now, like a juggernaut, and despite the harsh tug of Earth's gravity, Carina had a moment of superhuman strength. She screamed and tossed the dead man off her like a rag doll.

From the nearest capsule came an explosion of laughter. The occupant peering out at her from behind the shade of his sleep-capsule found her predicament amusing. She leveled her blaster in his direction and squeezed off a round, shattering the capsule into a thousand pieces and causing the four-high stack of cubicles to come tumbling down. Angry shouts ensued as bodies, many of them naked, were scrambled out onto the floor.

Carina snatched up her belongings from around her and bolted for the lobby and the front door. The look on her face was stone. If she remembered that her street shoes were still in the custody of the night manager, it didn't seem to faze her. That her half-naked body was covered only in torn shreds of cloth, didn't seem to faze her either. She paused only long enough to retch again at the top of the stairs, and then she was in the street, barefoot and running.

Her father wouldn't have recognized her. Carina's chest was soaked in blood. A trickle of pee ran down the inside of her leg. Her hair and face were a mess. The woman hadn't slept in twenty hours. Whatever little she had eaten in the past day, she had now thrown up. Her head was pounding. Under the pressure of three times the gravity her body was accustomed to, her legs were like pillars of concrete.

Pushing her muscles to the limit, Carina crossed the street at a trot. The sun was at a low angle, just above the horizon. It was early morning. Rounding the corner, she suddenly found herself bathed by a blinding flash of sunlight.

Carina threw up her arms to shield her eyes. But she never saw the delivery gtruck that struck her from the side as it darted out of a blind alley.

There was a crunch of skin and bones as the fender shoved her tender body roughly aside like so much street litter, the crinkle of metal and glass as rubber tires flattened her blaster against the pavement.

There was a moaning and a cry of anguish as consciousness faded away.

And then all was quiet.

TWENTY-SIX

Ruffians

An Icelandic saga tells of a Viking who had unusual, almost menacing features, including a skull that could resist a blow from an axe. Indeed, Egil, son of Skalla-Grim, was the most memorable Viking to appear in the Old Norse sagas. Born in Iceland in the early tenth century, Egil Skalla-Grimsson participated in Viking raids and wild adventures all throughout SKANDIA, the east Baltic lands, England, Saxony, and northern Germany. Fierce, self-willed and violent, Egil Skalla-Grimsson was also a fine poet and a man with a sense of ethics. He epitomized the Viking urge to travel into an unknown world seeking action and fortune. From Athelstan, King of the Anglo-Saxons, Egil received valuable gifts and pledges of friendship. But, from Erik Blood-Axe, the Viking ruler of Norway, he heard nothing but death threats. Combining courage and brawn with high intelligence, Egil survived war and treachery to live to the ripe old age of eighty. He died among his kinsmen in Iceland around the year 990, apparently from natural causes stemming from longevity.

For all of Egil's heroic stature, there was something deeply troubling about his character. Despite his prowess and secure social status, his temperament as well as his physical appearance caused great alarm to nearly everyone he met. Egil was portrayed as an ugly, irritable, brooding individual. In this respect, Egil resembled his father and his grandfather, men both described as being physically menacing. The saga clearly distinguished these men as physiologically different from their kinsmen, who were otherwise described as being fair and handsome.

What set Egil Skalla-Grimsson apart from others of his kind was more than simply a small, personal peculiarity. Through prose and verse, the saga reported that Egil became deaf, often lost his balance, went blind, suffered from chronically cold feet, endured headaches, and experienced bouts of lethargy.

Furthermore, the saga described him as having unusual disfigurements of the skull marked by prominent facial features. He had a broad forehead and large eyes; a nose which, though not long, was enormously thick; and lips which, when seen through his beard, were both long and wide. His head hung forward, an unnatural posture. He had a remarkably broad chin, and this largeness continued throughout the length of his jawbone. He was thick-necked and broad-shouldered, and more so than other men, hard-looking and fierce when angry.

Though they had no name for it in his time, Egil suffered from an affliction called Paget's disease, a genetic syndrome that resulted from a quickening of normal bone replacement.

Tonight, as Samuel Matthews looked across the smoke-filled room at the opposite table where Lotha sat, he couldn't help but reminded of the saga of Egil Skalla-Grimsson. Like Egil, the big Afghan also suffered from this condition in which one's bones grew drastically out of control. Lotha had that same broad forehead, that same fierce look. His facial bones were grossly thickened and asymmetrically deformed.

In a way, Sam felt sorry for the man. But then again he felt sorry for himself. Samuel Matthews was too young to die. And he certainly didn't want to die here on Mars, not now anyway. When the time came, he preferred to play out his last innings from the comfort of his estate back in Auckland.

The night was as hot and humid as any the Red Planet had yet to offer. Whereas staying warm was the usual battle Martians had to fight, people hadn't yet had time to adjust to the violent swings in temperature which the new climate had ushered in. Few buildings on the planet had fans, and fewer still, air conditioning.

The freighters which moved in and out of Colony One with some regularity now were loaded down with scores of rough-hewn characters. They were all looking for work, either in the motor manufacturing plant or else in the asteroid moving facility. The shifts normally ran 'round the clock — twelve hours on, twelve hours off — which left the workers with plenty of time for rabble-rousing in their off-hours. While Colony One sported its own brand of diversions, from saloons to virtual-reality bars, some of the off-duty drifters would inevitably find their way to Newton and to Saron's Place. Tonight was one of those nights. Around 10 p.m. on this muggy Martian evening, four asteroidors entered the premises.

At first, Sam didn't pay the newcomers close attention. All four men looked as if they had been cast from the same, extra-large mold. They were burly characters ranging in height up to about two meters, and in weight from 95 to 100 kilos. All four were big, muscular sorts with closely-cropped hair and thick necks, and each one of them had a colorful nickname. Tex, Nuke, Puck, and Jackhammer. The four were already liquored-up from an earlier stop they made in a pub at Colony One. By the time they reached the doorway to Saron's Place, they were farting and belching with some enthusiasm.

The place was crowded with Newtons and a thin film of smoke hung in the air. It gave the tavern a sweet, musty smell. Though no one was listening to it, the latest in cack music rumbled from a jukebox in the corner. Inda, Lotha, and his younger brother Nandu sat at a table warily eyeing the four strangers as they entered. Sam, Gunter, and Fornax sat at another table, watching both sets of men with growing interest. If things went according to pattern, it wouldn't be long, now, before the hulking Lotha confronted the outsiders and asked them to leave.

"Fetch me a tortan," Puck demanded even before his butt hit the seat of a chair. Though Puck was clearly the runt of the litter, he was at least as tall as Sam and half again as big around.

"Yeah, what kinda service ya got here in New-Scum Land?" Nuke boomed, deriding the colony's name in sarcastic fashion. He had broad shoulders and a large, sloping back that was accustomed to lugging around heavy loads.

Saron sent one of her prettier girls scampering over to the newcomers' table, her tray overflowing with tankards of ale. She wanted to head off any trouble before it could get out of hand.

"May I help you, boys?" the buxom waitress asked in the sweetest voice she could muster. Like all of Saron's girls, this one wore a low-cut blouse and a short, pleated skirt. Each article of clothing was designed to reveal one of her several, well-proportioned selling points. Known to the regular patrons only as Swivel Hips, this dark-haired beauty always had a legion of admirers following in her wake.

"Yeah, you kin help us," Puck leered, his eyes fixed on the woman's bosom. "Come here, ya little tart, and sit on me lap. Show ole Puck what ya got there under that dress." Even as he spoke, the repulsive scalawag gently massaged the girl's bottom with his callous-hardened hands.

Swivel Hips pulled away, not appreciating the man's demeanor. "I only serve drinks, sir," she said curtly. "If you need servicing, you'll have to see the boss." The girl motioned to where Saron was leaning against the bar, arms crossed in head-of-the-household fashion. "She sees to the men."

"Then tell yore friggin' boss to get her heinie over here!" Puck boomed, snatching a tankard of ale from off the girl's tray. As his voice reverberated across the room, every head in the place turned his way. He enjoyed the attention.

"And have her make it quick," Tex added drunkenly. "We all need servicing."

"Whatever you say," the bar hop replied, handing around the other three mugs. "I'll see that the boss comes right over."

Swivel Hips slung the empty tray under her arm, receded in Saron's direction as quickly as she could. A sullen expression clouded her pretty face. She could smell trouble brewing.

From their corner of the room, Lotha & Company had watched the proceedings with an ugly look of disapproval. Seeing the three Newtons shift nervously in their chairs, Sam knew for certain a fight was about to erupt. He dispatched Fornax to take up a position near the door and for Gunter to edge over in the vicinity of Lotha's table.

Saron smiled weakly in the direction of the asteroidors as the girl related to her what the men had said. Saron had stared down these sorts before and wasn't the least bit afraid to wander over to their table, now, and see if she couldn't defuse the situation. From where Sam sat, on the other side of the room, he watched her closely.

It was at times like these that Sam wished he were young and virile again, young enough and strong enough to protect his favorite woman without another man's help.

Sadly, those days were gone forever. *Curse old age!* Curse whatever was killing him! Curse the loss of innocence and beauty! It would all be over soon enough!

"My girl tells me you boys need servicing," Saron said in a provocative tone as she drew closer to the unruly bunch. Out of the corner of one eye she had seen Sam dispatch Fornax and Gunter to their respective posts. She was glad for it. Up close, these four men looked mean. "It'll be a hundred credits for a full job; fifty for an oral."

"That's outrageous!" Puck exploded, jumping to his feet. "We ain't payin' no hundred for the likes of you!" he exclaimed, grabbing hold of Saron's arm and tossing her roughly onto the table. "You'll do us all — And you'll do us all for free!"

Before anyone else knew what was happening, Puck had begun ripping Saron's blouse off her chest. He groped for the fiery-red nipples of her breasts with his hands. Tex and Nuke helped their buddy out by pinning her arms flat to the table. The more Saron struggled, the more the men laughed.

Still glued to his chair, Sam cringed at his own inability to protect the woman he loved from these heathens.

Something about the way the four men worked together suggested this wasn't the first time these four had joined forces to assault a helpless woman.

Following a well-rehearsed routine, Jackhammer pulled a mean-looking blaster from his belt even as Puck hiked Saron's skirt up over her hips. Waving the blaster in the air to get everyone's attention, Jackhammer shouted out a warning to the stunned patrons:

"This don't concern you other folks none," he said. "If you wanna stay alive, you'll let us do our business. Then we'll be on our way."

For a long, terrifying moment, the crowd froze as if everyone in attendance meant to blindly obey Jackhammer's instructions. Then all hell broke loose.

As Puck unzipped his trousers to do the dirty deed, Lotha, Inda, and Nandu sprang to their feet. With no thought for themselves, the three charged the four would-be rapists from across the room. Gunter circled around behind the four, a broken chair-leg clenched in his fist. Even Sam rose from his chair, readied himself to take Fornax's place at the door.

"Stop or I'll shoot!" Jackhammer yelled, hoping to head off the approaching Afghans.

But, when the warning went unheeded, Jackhammer leveled his piece at Nandu and fired, blowing a gaping hole clean through the man's chest and the wall behind him. Entrails and bits of ribcage flew everywhere. Though not hit herself, Swivel Hips was suddenly soaked in Nandu's blood. She began screaming like Holy Hell.

By this time, Gunter had climbed up on a chair and launched himself against the man who called himself Nuke. Gunter rapped the ruffian in the head with the chair-leg he had been brandishing, knocking the big man away from Saron and freeing one of her arms. She lunged outward, now, with all her might, tore at Puck's grimy face, drawing blood with her fingernails.

Fornax joined the fray from the other side. He yanked Tex off her and sent him crashing to the floor with a single well-placed jab to the kidneys.

Swinging around to help his friends, Jackhammer fired another volley from his blaster, narrowly missing Swivel Hips, but sending an oil lantern flying across the room. The burning oil ignited a tablecloth. The flames quickly spread to the table and chairs next to it.

Approaching Jackhammer at a run, Lotha and Inda tackled him, forcing the gun from his hand and pummeling the shootist into submission.

By this time, Saron had kneed Puck in the groin and was busy ordering patrons to dump their tankards of ale on the fire to douse the flames. It was quickly extinguished.

"Let's kill the sons of bitches!" Lotha clamored, wanting blood. He was sitting atop Jackhammer's limp body now, his massive fist cocked as if he were ready to administer the coup de grace. The blood vessels in his face and neck looked as if they might burst under the pressure. The outlines of his giant, misshapen skull were more hideous than ever. "The bastards murdered my little brother," he roared, signaling to where Nandu lay in a pool of crimson.

"Yeah, let's kill 'em all!" Inda echoed. Any hesitation he might once have harbored about striking back at Colony One had now evaporated.

"There'll be no lynching," Sam said calmly, from his side of the room. Despite the rabble, his firm voice commanded respect.

"Says who?" Lotha taunted, dragging Jackhammer to his feet and shoving him like a rag doll against the bar.

"Says me," Sam replied coolly, drawing nearer to the big Afghan. "The Council will handle this matter. That's what we're here for. You cannot take the law into your own hands."

"Oh no? Just watch me!" Lotha exclaimed, bloodying Puck with his fist while brandishing Jackhammer's blaster before him. There was mean resolve in his dark eyes.

"Sam's right, laddie," Gunter said, the chair-leg still cocked in his hand like a baseball bat. "The Council should handle this one."

"This is none of your concern," Inda shouted. "These people wouldn't even *be* here if it weren't for you and your damn mining company. Anyway, I thought you were on our side. I thought you were one of us."

"Hell's bells, I'm not one of anybody," Gunter said. "I go my own way as always. But deciding the fate of these ruffians should be left up to the Council. On this one, I have to stand with Sam."

"Me too," Fornax said, still lording over Tex. In his outstretched hand was his own formidable blaster.

Inda was defiant. "Do you intend to blast us all?"

"Listen, you stupid son of a bitch — we want a land ruled by laws, not one ruled by outlaws. Tie up these bums and I'll see to it they stand trial before the Council. Refuse, and you'll stand trial right alongside them."

"Inda, the boys are right." This was Saron speaking. She had hastily pushed her torn clothes back into place and come out onto the floor of the pub to reassert her prerogative as its proprietor. "As you can plainly see, I'm okay. So is Swivel Hips. No permanent harm has been done here today. So let's clean up this mess and get on with our lives."

"One calls me a stupid son of a bitch, and the other tells me I'm wrong? This from a woman, no less? What's the world coming to?"

Inda could see that he wasn't about to get his way. It infuriated him. He stomped toward the exit of the Commons with a determined air and signaled Lotha to do the same. The big Afghan let go of Puck, and the smaller man dropped to the floor. Lotha put Jackhammer's blaster in his belt and followed Inda to the door.

"You haven't heard the last of this," Inda said as they left. "Not by a long shot." His mind was already made up. — It was time to put an end to Colony

One's arrogance once and for all. *Oskar Schaeffer's weapons would sit idle no longer!*

As he passed Gunter on the way out, Inda said, so only he could hear, "You're a dead man."

When Gunter didn't respond, Inda drew nearer. "Carina belongs to me. You never should have gotten in the way. If I can't have her, no man will. After tonight, you had better watch your back. I'll be gunning for you."

And then he and Lotha disappeared into the night.

TWENTY-SEVEN

Siona

"So far, anyway, we have 'er tagged as a Jane Doe," the orderly sniveled, leaning over to talk to the Mother Elder. The patient he was referring to lay motionless in the makeshift hospital ward. The ward was located about four city-blocks from where the accident occurred. It was run by an order of nuns. Only these weren't your ordinary nuns. These gals had sex, got married, drank like fish, and swore like kickboxing champs.

"Goddamnit!" the Mother Elder swore. "Who the hell brought her in?"

"That fella over yonder," the orderly said, pointing to a good-looking man. The man was pacing nervously back and forth just down the hall. He had fair skin and a mop of blond hair. "The fella' won't give us his name. But he's no Yank, I kin tell you that much fur sure. An' he's got medic training. You wanna know how I know? 'Cause he'd already set 'er leg before he drug 'er in here. Says he just happened across 'er in the street. But I don't believe 'im — and neither should you. I kin tell he's lyin'. Kin see it in 'is eyes, I can. He knows 'er and I think he's soft on 'er. I kin tell..."

"Okay, goddamnit! I get the picture already!" the Mother Elder bellowed, clearly flustered by the orderly's unending explanation. The lines in her face made her look much older than she actually was. But then, she hadn't had an easy life. "Let me talk to him," she said, quickening her step in that direction.

In three strides she was there. The Mother Elder wasted no time getting to the point. "Who the hell are you?" she asked gruffly.

"Who wants to know?" he replied, not easily intimidated.

"I ask the questions here — I run this place."

"Is Car — I mean, is the girl I brought in okay? She was sideswiped by a gtruck down there at the corner." He pointed in that direction.

"I thought you told the orderly you didn't see the bloody accident?" the Mother Elder challenged, her eyes narrowing.

"Well . . . " he stammered, boxed in by a slip of his own tongue.

"Look here, my son. Is the truth so horrible you can't tell a sister of the cloth what really happened?" Her vernacular had abruptly swung from gutter-language to Sunday best.

"I was following her," he answered, caught off guard by the sudden change in tone.

"With mal-intent?"

"Not at all. I was supposed to protect her. Only . . . "

"Only what?"

"Only she didn't *know* I was following her. And if she had known, she probably wouldn't have wanted me to."

"I see," the Mother Elder replied, getting lost in his cold, blue eyes. Though she was easily old enough to be this man's mother, she couldn't help but notice his splendid build. She felt a warm, twitching sensation between the legs. Nice looking men were few and far between in these parts. Suddenly embarrassed, she turned away. "You're in love with this girl, aren't you?"

"Once maybe. But no longer."

"Who the hell is she?" Her tone became rough again. "And where is she from? And while we're at it, bub. Who the hell are *you*?"

"Her name is Carina. She's from Zealand."

"Zealand? Why in the name of God's Green Earth would a good-looking single woman leave a beautiful place like that to come here?" There was a disbelieving quality to the Mother Elder's voice, as if she knew everything there was to know about emigrating from one land to another.

"It's a long story."

"As you can see, I'm not going anywhere." Even as the Mother Elder spoke, the orderly hurried by gripping an f-photon scan of some patient's abdomen in his hand. From the look on his face, the prognosis was poor.

"Carina's father was an American. Lived somewhere around these parts before the War. Now he's dying."

"We all have to die sometime." It was a surprisingly cold answer for someone in her profession.

"Yes, of course. But it's some sort of genetic thing. She came down here to research her family's gene-map hoping for an answer."

"That would be the Genealogical Institute outside of town on Budweiser Boulevard, I believe."

"That sounds about right," the good-looking man said. "But what concerns me most right now is the girl. Do you think she's going to be okay?"

The Mother Elder was frank. "I'm afraid we don't have the sort of medic facilities one might find in a first-world country like Zealand. This is Sane Lou, for Chrissake!"

"Can I move her?" he asked, easing his way up the hall toward Carina's room.

"At your risk, not ours. I wouldn't advise it." At this point the Mother Elder took hold of the clipboard hanging just outside Carina's door, made some notes on her chart. "Does this Carina have a last name? Do you have a first?"

"Matthews. Carina Matthews."

His reply was answered with a stunned look. It was the first time since they began talking that the Mother Elder seemed to be caught off balance.

The man was confused. It seemed inconceivable that the mere mention of a person's name could have such a devastating effect. The Mother Elder staggered backwards as if she had been shot.

"You look as if you have seen a ghost," he said, bewildered by her reaction.

"Perhaps I have," she answered, her eyes misting. "What did you say her father's name was?"

"I didn't."

"Please. I must know." Her voice was choked with emotion.

"Samuel. Samuel Matthews."

The blood drained from the woman's face.

"Are you okay?" he asked, touching her arm. She shivered involuntarily.

"No, I'm not," she said, inching towards a nearby bench. From the next room came a moan as another patient of twenty-fifth-century Sane Lou suffered at the hands of nineteenth-century medicine.

"Sit down then," he suggested, letting her lean against his shoulder as they walked.

"Yes. I must sit."

"Tell me what's wrong. Did you know Sam from somewhere?"

"God, yes," she declared.

Her answer was followed by an explosion of tears.

"Were you two lovers?" he asked, jumping to the only logical conclusion for her tears.

"God, no," she sobbed in big cathartic gulps.

"What then?" The crinkle in his brow spoke of confusion.

Her river of tears turned into a flood.

"Tell me," he pleaded, drawing up close to her. "I insist."

She spoke between tears. "After the Great War . . . Carina was maybe two . . . I had moved south, out of Canada . . . the genetic cleansers took Nasha away . . . Sam and the baby left for the Hawaii Free State . . . I never saw either one of them again."

"That was what, thirty years ago?"

"Give or take a little."

"So, why the tears? He's alive, and so are you."

"So is *she*!" the Mother Elder revealed, meeting his steely gaze.

"She who?"

"Nasha, you dolt! Carina's mother. Sam's wife. *The woman is still alive!*"

"Oh, my God!" the young man exclaimed, color draining from his face. "And all this time Sam thought his wife was dead? How is that possible? How do you know this anyway?" Then, before she could answer, he said, "Criminy, what if Carina were to now all of a sudden die? What if she were to die before being even reunited with her mother? That musn't be allowed to happen!"

The Mother Elder brushed back the tears from her eyes, tried to compose herself. "Maybe you should return to Zealand straightaway. Get Sam up here before it's too late."

"He's not there."

"What do you mean, he's not there? I thought you just said she was from Zealand? Where the hell does her father live?"

"On Mars," the young, clean-cut man replied.

"Mars? You expect me to believe that crap? Are you out of your head?"

"I wish I were. But I'm telling you the truth."

"So, he's the one."

"Yes, he's the one."

"I had heard stories of a man named Sam, a man who helped people escape. But I'd never put much salt in them. I figured the stories were like a fairy tale people kept telling themselves to keep each other going, to keep from losing hope. It never occurred to me the fairy tale might be true."

"Mark my words, Sister. This is no fairy tale. Now tell me, how did you come to know Sam?"

"We met in Canada, Sam and I. My fiancé and he were fraternity brothers. They hung around together all the time."

Again it looked as if dredging up distant memories was going to lead to a torrent of tears. This time, though, her eyes remained dry. It was obvious that she had made up her mind about something. When she turned to him once again, it was as if they were meeting for the very first time.

The Mother Elder extended her hand. "Hello, my name is Siona. Sister Siona. What's yours?"

"BC."

"Well, Mister BC. If you will follow me, I will take you to a man I know who might be able to help save your friend. You first-worlders might call him a witch doctor or a medicine man. But down here, we call men like him healers."

BC rolled his eyes. There was a hint of contempt as he spoke. "Are we talking about home remedies here?"

"Sometimes," Sister Siona said, taking note of his severe look.

"Placebos? Hallucinogens?"

"Yes, sometimes. But he's also our only legitimate source of pure, undiluted Acceleron." Even as Sister Siona spoke, she started down the three flights of stairs to street level. BC had to hurry to keep up with her.

"That's expensive stuff — even in civilized countries. I'm nearly out of cash," he explained as they exited the building.

"You looking for sympathy?"

"Not at all. But, I wasn't sure what I'd be getting myself into down here when I arrived on the continent. What's this doctor friend of yours charge for a recovery dose of Acceleron? I have essentially no credits on me."

"Don't worry," Sister Siona said, "I've got plenty of money on me."

"Well, then how do I repay *you*?"

"Simple. My price for helping you is that you help me escape. I buy enough Acceleron to save Carina's life. You help me get out of this hell-hole. I want the fairy tale, a free ticket to Mars."

"And give up all this?" BC asked, encompassing with one wide sweep of the hand the squalor that was Sane Lou.

She nodded.

"Fair enough," he grinned. "I think that can be arranged."

TWENTY-EIGHT

Tovex

Gunter was flat on his belly following closely along behind the man from Bosq. They were working their way beneath the giant cooling pipes at the depths of the lowest sub-basement beneath the motor factory. That's where, less than a quarter of an hour ago, the night watchman had spied an eerie green light while he and Max were making their rounds. The man had promptly called it in, as instructed, and now it was a race against time. Only problem was, neither Gunter nor Lieutenant McPherson knew exactly how much time remained before the bomb blew.

The terran headquarters of the South African Police **Bomb Squad**, or Bosq for short, were located on an upper floor of a precinct house in the West Village of Johannesburg, a neighborhood known for its unconventional lifestyles. This brown, flagstone building had been Gunter's first stop when Oskar Schaeffer ordered him home ten days ago to recruit McPherson. ASARCO sorely needed help dealing with the sabotage-minded Newtons, and McPherson had a reputation as a hardnosed bomb-defuser.

Finding the squad room where Lieutenant McPherson worked hadn't been difficult. Up a staircase and around a corner. There, in the middle of a nondescript hallway hung a bright-red aerial-bomb-casing suspended from the ceiling. It pointed like an arrow to the squad room door. Inside the doorway, mementos of previous jobs were interspersed throughout three large rooms. Mortar rounds doubled as bookends. Artillery shells leaned in a corner like a collection of rolled-up maps. Manual firebombs sat scattered haphazardly on the floor. Contact grenades littered a desk. Booby traps of all sorts clogged a closet. Land mines served as doorstops as well as paperweights. Without exception, every single piece of ordnance had been confiscated somewhere in the province of Johannesburg within the past year.

Lieutenant Cragit McPherson, the commander-in-chief of Bosq, had a glass display case in his office. It was crammed full with military ordnance and homemade bombs that had been rendered safe, including a white polyvinyl-chloride pipe-bomb (the latest fashion on the street), plus an ordinary-looking lunch box packed with a thermos and two sticks of TNT. Hanging on his wall was a small, tattered Commonwealth flag recovered from the rubble on level minus-four of the Ministry Center, a site bombed by Neo-Rontanians just two years back. In a far corner of his office stood two big filing cabinets devoted to terrorist groups threatening one corner of the globe or another. That day, after introducing himself, Gunter had handed McPherson a dossier to add to his collection, a dossier he had compiled on mankind's newest fringe element, the Newton Liberation Party of Mars. Gunter had already connected all the dots and everything he learned so far pointed to Inda Desai as the ringleader, though how the man had gotten his hands on explosives was anybody's guess. Gunter's only clues led him in a direction he didn't want to go.

The Johannesburg Bomb Squad was the oldest and largest entity of its kind in the world. Over the many years of its existence, it had dealt with numerous insidious plots to destroy tunnels, factories, and schools all over the sprawling city-state. They had confronted a host of twenty-fifth-century extremists, both religious and political, including many who took Rontana's manifesto — *Deicide, Infanticide & Ecocide* — as gospel. In addition, the squad had routinely dealt with the misguided schemes of more prosaic lawbreakers — spurned lovers seeking revenge, rival gangsters, disgruntled employees, deranged lunatics, thrill seekers, extortionists, even teenagers playing with forbidden or dangerous chemicals. The list was endless. Each year, anywhere between ten and twelve thousand bomb threats were made in the city-state of Johannesburg. Each year, anywhere between fifty and eighty explosive devices actually blew up — or would have — if they hadn't been defused first. In almost every instance, Cragit McPherson himself had been on the scene to do the defusing firsthand.

Gray-haired, in his early fifties, and dressed in a conservative blue suit, Lieutenant Cragit McPherson looked like a partner in a downtown law firm. But he talked like a tough beat cop. A thirty-year veteran of the Johannesburg Police Department who planned to retire soon, McPherson came to the squad with ample experience investigating arson, a crime in which the motive was normally money. His current job carried some heavy responsibilities, some with political overtones. Bosq conducted security searches for visiting dignitaries. They dismantled, transported and disposed of bombs, fireworks, explosives, and dangerous chemicals. They even investigated bomb explosions after the fact. His jurisdiction extended from the Cape of Good Hope north to the equator. He was growing tired of the responsibility.

Gunter introduced himself that day and they got down to cases. Yes, McPherson wanted to retire soon, but, no, Mars didn't interest him. On the other hand, as a public servant he wasn't looking forward to a very generous pension. How much was ASARCO offering?

Gunter had been given carte blanche from Oskar Schaeffer, and McPherson liked the sound of the number he heard. But if he took the job as Head of Martian security, there were a few rules he refused to bend. For openers: No matter how important the Colony One motor factory was to ASARCO, McPherson wasn't about to jeopardize lives — including his own — just to protect private property.

On this they agreed. Buildings could be repaired in a way human beings could not. In every situation, McPherson's overriding concern would be the safety of civilians — and the members of his bomb squad.

He explained Bosq's procedures. They had been devised to minimize the risk of injury and to always use state-of-the-art equipment.

But, as bombs grew ever more sophisticated and terrorists ever more evil, the nature of the threat changed constantly. Even so, in the seven years that McPherson was commander of the squad, not a single member of his team had been killed or maimed by an explosive device.

That was an impressive statistic, especially considering that in the three years before he took over the squad, seven men had died. Still, it was the sort of statistic that could be rendered obsolete in a flash by one false move. This was the reason why, despite his administrative duties, it had always been McPherson's practice to join his officers on the scene whenever his instincts told him a real bomb was involved. Now, tonight, as he and Gunter worked their way beneath the giant cooling pipes at the depths of the lowest sub-basement, his presence soothed — to a degree — Gunter's fear.

McPherson's voice was raspy as he spoke. "The vast majority of suspicious packages yield contents that are harmless."

"What do you mean harmless?"

"Oh, I don't know, a variety of crap. Oil-soaked newspapers, dirty diapers, boom boxes, sexual aids, dead animals, that kind of stuff. Hell, once we even found the skeletal remains of a human hand."

"How do you tell the lives ones from the dummies?" Gunter asked as they cleared the last pipe. They were deep underground, several stories beneath the factory floor. Drawing up to a standing position, now, they could see the eerie green light that had started it all. The light was on the wall twenty meters ahead of them. Max was curled up on the floor in front of the thing. When he saw the two men approach and recognized McPherson, the bio-canine came to attention just as he had been trained to do.

"How do you tell the live ones from the dummies?" Cragit echoed. "Instinct. Instinct and practice. We train constantly. To ward off complacency. To help prevent stupid mistakes. To keep our minds focused on the task at hand. The squad practices incessantly. We use both dummy bombs and live explosives. Our motto is quite simple: It's a bomb until it's not a bomb."

Gunter was apprehensive. Somehow, talking relieved the tension. "What's the worst?" he asked.

"Do you mean the biggest — or the hardest to handle?"

"I don't know what I mean. What is this one?" he asked, jerking his head in the direction of the green light.

"I would say chemical. And they're the worst."

"Hardest to handle?"

"By far."

McPherson undid the heavy leather satchel he had been toting along with him. If not for the planet's one-third gravity, the man might not even have been able to carry the heavy satchel this far without help. As he opened it, he continued with his explanation.

"Chemical explosives are unstable substances that can be rapidly converted into gases of much greater volume. The process by which they detonate is similar to the burning of a log in a fireplace, only with one big difference. Unlike a log, which burns slowly and steadily, the combustion of an explosive is nearly instantaneous and is accompanied by a shock wave. With high explosives, it is the blast which produces the most devastating effects."

"Explain that, would you?"

McPherson continued to unpack his bag. "At the point of detonation, hot expanding gases exert pressure on the surrounding atmosphere with a force on the order of 1.4 million pounds per square inch. This huge mass of compressed air rushes outward from the source of the explosion at speeds up to six thousand meters per second. It weighs tons, and it rolls outward in a spherical pattern like a giant tsunami. The shock wave smashes or shatters anything which happens to lie in its path."

"Six thousand meters per second? That's like what — twenty-two thousand *kloms* an hour! That's almost as fast as a spaceship at escape velocity."

"Yeah, something like that."

"Wow!" was about the only word that popped into Gunter's head, though he kept it to himself.

But rather than dwell on the level of destruction that would accompany a blast of that size down here, three stories below the factory floor, Gunter thought instead about what McPherson had told him earlier, on the way over here from his temporary headquarters where he'd been sleeping. After the night watchman notified the company that his bio-canine had turned up something suspicious in the sub-basement, Gunter had gone to the barracks to wake McPherson. That's when the tutorial began. It proved to be quite enlightening:

The idea of killing someone with a package full of explosives dated back at least nine hundred years to the middle of the sixteenth century. In those days, "infernal machines," as they were called, were sometimes disguised as jewelry boxes or casks of wine. But gradually, bomb-makers got smarter. Soon, they were hiding them in everything from shortwave transmitters to garage door openers to handheld comm-units. Unlike rounds of ammunition, which had been standardized and mass-produced for centuries, every improvised explosive bore the "signature" of its maker, subtle wrinkles and idiosyncrasies only an expert like Cragit McPherson could notice or detect. As a rule, each device employed a simple, yet wickedly ingenious method for completing an electrical circuit — a mousetrap striking a swatch of tinfoil, a set of wire loops sliding along a smooth dowel rod and impacting a metal plate, a coiled spring, a mercury switch, a tiny ball rolling down a track. For obvious reasons, McPherson preferred defusing a bomb that had been assembled with competence. It was the amateurish jobs, with their loose wiring and their faulty connections, that made him nervous. Fortunately, most of these devices killed their bomb-makers well before Bosq ever got called in.

Normally, McPherson would send in a robot to scoop up the suspected bomb and place it in a TCV — a Total Containment Vessel. But not tonight. The space down here in the catacombs below the factory floor was too cramped for a robot to maneuver. Not only that, the radio signal would be lost among the thousands of feet of metal pipe.

So, instead of handling this one remotely, as he would have preferred, the two of them had to go "on target." Among other things, this meant protecting themselves with a bombsuit. There were two of these suits stuffed inside the heavy leather satchel McPherson had been lugging with him since they first left the elevator. He pulled them both out, now, and handed one to Gunter to put on.

A bombsuit weighed in excess of twenty-five kilos and covered the front of the body only, from chin to toe, in thick kevlar armor. There was no armor on the back — hence the adage: *Never turn your back on a bomb* — nor the hands, which remained wholly unprotected.

The round helmet had a blower attached to it. It was supposed to keep the visor from fogging up. But the contraption was so loud, they could hardly hear one another when it was on. Visibility was extremely limited, and the suit itself was stiff, clumsy, and uncomfortable. Though it afforded excellent protection against shrapnel, it could do little to shield them from the worse effects of a strong blast wave. Almost nothing in the bomb squad's arsenal could prevent them from being injured by the overpressure that ruptured soft tissue and vital organs. Indeed, beyond a certain point, a bombsuit was more of a hindrance than a help.

Following McPherson's lead, Gunter slipped one of the bulky body-armor-suits on, thinking how the dee-dee he had worn to the top of Olympus Mons felt roomy and comfortable by comparison. Tugging at each other's straps to draw them tight, McPherson and Gunter stared at one another with mild amusement. They each had the appearance of a olive-green astronaut.

Max yawned a big bored dog-yawn as he waited patiently for the two men to finish getting ready. This was the difference between a sentient animal and one that was not — fear. Fear came from understanding what *might* go wrong. Dogs didn't worry about losing a leg or a hand or even an eye — people did.

As in this case, most bombs were discovered by bio-canines. Since every form of explosive exudes some sort of trace chemical, expensive mechanical "sniffers" had been invented that were capable of detecting a few parts per billion in a sample of air.

But none had proved more efficient than the nose of a good old-fashioned dog. Actually, they weren't that old-fashioned; they were genetically modified. Even so, Bosq's Labrador retrievers were familiar with the scent of every common explosive known to man. They were trained never to touch a bomb when they came upon one, but to sit nearby and wait for a trained technician to arrive. This, Max had done. The sweet-faced Lab was still there when Gunter and McPherson arrived on the scene.

No amount of affection could satisfy the pooch, and it was hard to believe that his little nostrils could mean the difference between life and death for Colony One. McPherson knew, however, that Max was dependable. On one occasion, he had hid a mere 75 grams of dynamite in a large squad room. With tail wagging, Max had required just eighteen seconds to find it. But Max's job was done for today, and McPherson sent him to wait a safe distance away.

"If something goes wrong now," he explained, "there's got to be someone left alive to pick up the pieces." It was no joke. Things were about to get dicey.

McPherson pulled a tiny, scanning device from the pocket of his coveralls, a portable x-ray machine the size of a handheld calculator. It gave him a thirty second peek into the suspicious-looking package strapped with duct tape to the side of a standpipe. Then it recorded the image digitally for later study at a safer distance.

Even before McPherson was done with his scan, the man began cursing. "Damn!" and "Tovex!" were the only two words Gunter could clearly make out.

"What is it?" Gunter cringed, thinking his partner's outburst meant it was going to blow at any second.

"Here, take a look at this."

McPherson lumbered over to where Gunter stood hypnotized by the ghostly glow of the green light. Though the bomb specialist moved with some dispatch, he never turned his back on the potentially lethal gizmo. He drew close to Gunter, then illuminated the miniscule high-resolution screen on the underside of the scanner. "Tovex. In the right hands, it's real nasty stuff."

On playback, the machine was capable of projecting a 3-D image of any one of the fifty most recently scanned items, positioning them for easy view from any angle and providing detailed cutaway cross-sections for easier analysis of the wiring and triggering mechanisms.

Deftly manipulating a few knobs and dials, McPherson highlighted the cylinder of explosive chemicals. The Tovex was wrapped in a pink casing, like a sausage. With the right label, it might even have passed for a kosher salami. As the 3-D image hung in the air before them, McPherson talked:

"With this nasty stuff, the blast wave is not like getting hit by a brick wall. It's more like having one pass right through you. Believe me, I've seen every sort of combustion known to man — a piece of Detasheet, identical in shape and size to a twenty-page manuscript, can tear a steel-belted radial tire into a thousand pieces. Half a stick of dynamite placed on the firewall of a gcar can hurl the hood seventy-five meters into the air, embed the steering column into the driver's seat, and blow the speedometer into the trunk. This is half a stick, mind you. A chunk of C-4 plastique the size of a baseball can reduce that same gcar to scrap, and turn *you* into a pink mist. But Tovex is worse, much worse."

"So how do we disarm the damn thing?"

"With precision," McPherson replied, carefully scrutinizing the 3-D hologram. Every bomb had its weaknesses, and he was trying to ascertain this one's.

"Is it ticking?" Gunter asked breathlessly. The fog was building up on his visor, making it impossible for him to see.

"No, it's not on a timer. See here," he said, pointing to a stiff, thin filament running along one side of the image. "This honey's got an antenna. She's set to go off remotely."

"But if we couldn't use the robot down here, on account of all the interference from the pipes and such, how can . . . "

"Maybe they're not smart enough to realize that. If so, that's in our favor. Or maybe they're using some sort of ultra-low frequency or relay we haven't discovered yet. Either way, we have no choice but to disarm this bastard. A bomb is a bomb, until it's not." McPherson's voice was resolute.

"Not to sound like a broken record, but how do you plan on disarming the thing?"

From another pocket McPherson produced a long cylindrical object shaped roughly like a phallus. It was, in fact, a narrow steel tube capped at one end with its own explosive charge and filled inside with three ounces of water. The other end was sealed with an ordinary condom. McPherson explained its use:

"Sometimes, a bomb can be disarmed with a water disrupter," he said, rolling the cylinder slowly around in his palm for Gunter to see. "This baby fires a burst of water with enough force to punch through a block of wood three centimeters thick. An electric circuit takes approximately three milliseconds to complete. Water from the disrupter strikes the target in under one, stopping the firing train before the bomb can explode."

"Hell's bells, what if it's not an *electrical* circuit? What if the damn thing's a biologic?"

"Well, then it's been nice knowing you," McPherson quipped. "Now roll that TCV over here. If this thing doesn't blow when I try to disarm it, in the tank she goes."

Whenever an explosive device had to be transported for disposal, it was placed in a Total Containment Vessel, a bright-yellow globe that looked like a diving bell. Made of HY80, the same resilient alloy used in the hulls of suborbital transports, a TCV could contain a very big explosion. That day, when Gunter was at Bosq Headquarters in Johannesburg trying to convince McPherson to take this job, he had witnessed a demonstration. The team was out in the yard behind the building. While he watched, they detonated ten pounds of dynamite inside a TCV. It was amazing! The big yellow thing leaped about a foot into the air, then hissed like a kettle as black smoke poured out of its innards. Other than that, the detonation was a nonevent.

Gunter looked, now, at Lieutenant Cragit McPherson. Here was a man who was not easily unnerved. The man had stood alone once, inside a cramped, hot storage room littered with fuses, blasting caps and other explosives, and opened a suitcase with a Mickey Mouse face painted on it, only to discover seventy-eight sticks of dynamite inside. He had calmly chatted once with a woman who was wearing a necklace of kitchen matches. She held a lighter in each hand and was threatening to ignite a gtruck-load of gasoline bombs on the steps of Parliament. He had even wrestled a human bomb to the ground, struggling to defuse a powerful explosive device strapped to the man's chest while two other officers pinned down the madman's arms to prevent the metal bands on his wrists from touching and completing a circuit. These things he had done and more.

And yet, even through the cloudy plastic of Gunter's visor, he could see a bead of sweat forming on the other man's forehead. McPherson was clearly worried, despite his calm exterior. The furrow in his brow deepened as he rolled the TCV into place beneath the Tovex bomb and carefully positioned the armor-plated robotic arm that would clamp onto the explosive package then automatically retract into the containment vessel on his command.

"Disarming this thing is only half the job," McPherson explained, as he mounted his water disrupter on a tripod just level with the circuit he wanted to neutralize. Then, running his fingers across the keypad mounted on the side of the TCV, he punched in the grid-coordinates he had taken off the 3-D scan of the bomb's interior. The machine gently whirred and lined up the target in its sights. As it did, McPherson backed slowly and silently away.

Gunter stopped breathing, afraid that the pressure of his own sound waves might set the infernal thing off.

"We still have to identify the bastards who did this," McPherson said, tracing his steps backward. "And punish them."

Then, before Gunter could say he had a pretty good idea who was behind this thing, McPherson acted, depressing a button on the palm-sized shortwave radio in his hand.

In the next instant, the disrupter flooded the firing mechanism with water and the robotic arm jerked the bomb from its moorings on the standpipe, thrusting it into the TCV, and slamming the thick metal lid shut with a thump.

The sound of the lid hissing closed must have been a signal of sorts to Max, because he came forward, now, from where he had been hiding, tail wagging and tongue hanging lazily out of his mouth. He waited at attention alongside his master.

Hot, flushed, and smiling, McPherson motioned to Gunter that it was okay to unstrap his bombsuit. The two men shared a subdued, giddy feeling of relief. Had anyone else been there to watch this drama unfold, they would have agreed that personal courage of this calibre was a rare, almost archaic quality these days. But then again, no one else was there, just Cragit, Max, and Gunter.

TWENTY-NINE

Killjoy

BC was out of his element here. Indeed, he felt rather silly. *But then who could blame him?* The woman he was following through the littered streets of Sane Lou was old, old enough to be his mother.

Still, he had no choice in the matter. He neither knew where they were going, nor exactly who it was they were about to see. All he knew was that this man had Acceleron, something Carina needed desperately if she was to stay alive.

A few minutes ago, on the steps of the hospital, Sister Siona had mumbled something about Dr. Jekyll and Mr. Hyde, then instructed him to stay close behind her, something which he obediently did. They hadn't gone more than a couple of blocks before they were in the squalor of Snake Alley.

"Why do they call it Snake Alley?" he asked, glancing nervously over his shoulder at each passerby. Never, in all his many travels, had BC seen more downtrodden people than the ones he saw stumbling along the dirty streets here in Sane Lou.

"Newcomer men drink snake blood for a sexual boost," she answered. "Physicians call it mimetic consumption. You know, like the old Chinese notion of *chin pu*. Eat a tiger's eyes and you gain its visual acuity. Eat the penis of a tiger or drink the blood of a snake or a tiger, and you gain sexual power."

Even as Sister Siona described the unusual fetish, BC nodded as if he needed no further explanation. He had learned long ago that whenever science had no ready answer, superstition often did. In many cases, whatever practices shamans instituted years ago, were still being blindly followed today — even if, in the interim, science had proved them lacking. From his medic training, BC knew that since ancient times physicians had been prescribing the ingestion of human or animal heart tissue to produce courage. Brain matter to cure idiocy.

An unappetizing array of other body parts and secretions to ameliorate various ailments, including bile, blood, bone, feces, horns, intestines, placenta, and teeth.

But it was the sexual organs, along with their various secretions, that held the most prominent place in this bizarre therapeutic gallery.

The ancient Egyptians were perhaps among the first to accord medicinal powers to the testicles. But there were others. The Roman scholar, Pliny the Elder, reported that the penis of a donkey — when soaked in oil — and the penis of a hyena — when covered with honey — served contemporary women as sexual fetishes. The Āyurveda of Susruta (circa 1000 BC) recommended the ingestion of testicular tissue as a treatment for impotence. The *Pharmacopoea Wirtenbergica*, an eighteenth-century German compendium of remedies, mentioned horse testicles and the phalluses of marine animals as aphrodisiacs. Even Rontana himself, in his manifesto *Deicide, Infanticide & Ecocide* (circa 2230), recommended ingesting children's genitals as a part of his recipe for staying young. Near as BC could tell, for ancients and moderns alike, it seemed impossible to separate sexual myth from sexual biology.

He looked at Sister Siona, now, and said, "Mimetic consumption, eh? Seems they're still searching for Love Potion Number Nine."

"Yeah, something like that," she answered, though her mind was clearly somewhere else.

"What's the local poison?"

"Down here, snake blood is the cheapest aphrodisiac hit available," she said, stopping to ask directions from a bearded street vendor.

BC's eyes wandered. In the next booth over, a hawker was pitching a tonic containing an extract of tiger and seal penis for 8 credits a shot or 40 per bottle. A small group of onlookers had assembled to hear his spiel, and the man was busy demonstrating the efficacy of his love-tonic with the help of two scantily-clad bimbookers. As BC watched, one of the prostitutes stepped behind a gauze screen. Then, on a signal from the hawker at the climax of his pitch, one of his male assistants mounted the woman. Applause erupted from the audience, and immediately, money and tonic began feverishly changing hands.

Somewhat amused by the hawker's success, BC edged further in that direction to see what two young girls were excitedly pointing at. Laid out before them on a table in front of the establishment, on folds of yellow velvet, were a tiger penis and a set of testicles. Curious, BC edged closer. As he scrutinized the appendage, the girls looked him over, giggling their approval. He blushed.

The testicles on display were vaguely anthropoid. But the penis was completely alien. It was an odd, slender organ jointed at the midpoint and all insect-hairy at the tip. Had BC been forced to guess, he might have taken the thing for some giant, specialized appendage belonging to a mosquito the size of a gtruck. Had his eyes the magnification power of a zoom camera, what looked like insect hairs would have resolved themselves into hundreds of backward-pointing barbs.

BC tried to imagine these pointed spikes in action. Suddenly, it all made sense. More than once in his life he had been launched out of bed by cat-screams in the middle of the night. Domestic felines, skewered by the barbs on a smaller version of this same wicked piece of equipment, could set off a caterwauling that had the power to wake an entire city block.

But, of course, that was small potatoes compared to this thing. Talk about your *tiger*wauling! Any forest folk within earshot of *that* noise would no doubt have pulled their blankets a bit tighter about them and moved just a bit closer to the fire.

Seeing the quizzical look on BC's face, the two young girls inspected the hairy thing for themselves, then moved away to rejoin their boyfriends. Each was now proudly holding a 40-credit bottle of love-tonic in his hands. It was clear how the boys intended to spend the rest of *their* day!

By this time, Sister Siona had obtained the information she was looking for and signaled BC that it was time for them to be moving on. With each passing minute, the streets were becoming more and more alive with people, and BC felt increasingly ill at ease as he and Sister Siona were hemmed in by the crowds. He kept quiet about what he had seen laid out on the yellow velvet. But she had no problem reading his mind.

"Tiger-penis soup is eaten here in Sane Lou, mostly by men. It is thought by many to aid male sexual performance. That man back there has a restaurant, the *Pu Chin Pu*. He prepares dishes using recipes which supposedly originated in the Imperial kitchens of the Ching dynasty. That tiger penis he had laid out there will make soup for eight, and it will cost about 300 credits per serving."

"Lord . . . " BC gasped, overwhelmed as much by the price as by the idea.

"If that seems a bit pricey to you, deer penises are always available as a cheap substitute," she said, sporting a wicked smile.

"But these people. They have so little. Why waste it on medieval remedies?"

"The brain, not the cock or the cunt, is man's primary sex organ," she said indelicately. "It's what you think you're capable of that makes you successful. Plus, there's an element of intrigue here, of forbidden fruit. A lot of the stuff you'll see here has been imported at some risk — and at great expense — from Indiastan or perhaps China. As a matter of fact, tigers from northeast China are much preferred. Cold climates are thought to produce the most potent penises for soup making."

"I admit I've heard of such practices. But it still stuns me how, in this day and age, people would actually kill such a rare and beautiful animal just to harvest a single organ."

"Oh, don't be silly. There's more to this practice than just a single organ. People have found uses for practically the entire carcass! The fur, as you can well imagine, plus the heart, the paws, the tail, even the skeleton. Tiger-bone is believed to be good for removing all kinds of evil influences, and for calming fright. Depending on which healer you talk to, it also cures ulcers, dysentery, rat bite, abdominal pain, typhoid fever, malaria, and hydrophobia. Powdered tiger-bone is just the thing for eruptions under the toenail. In infants, it's said to prevent Devil possession, convulsions, scabies, even boils. If placed on the roof of one's house, powdered tiger-bone will keep the Devil away, not to mention curing nightmares."

Suddenly, Sister Siona's pace slackened mid-sentence. BC sensed that they were getting close to their destination. She banked hard to the left and entered what appeared to be a dark and abandoned storefront.

But instead of it being a room filled with shelving units and display cases, the "storefront" actually turned out to be a narrow corridor. It opened into a courtyard ripe with the smells of a poorly-maintained indoor zoo. The stench of uncollected dung and mildewing hay and animal urine hung heavy in the air.

When, after a few moments, his eyes adjusted to the murky light, BC realized that it wasn't a zoo at all, but rather a sort of pet store filled with odd-sized cages and animals of every sort, all exotic. The collection included Bengal tigers, clouded leopards, rattlesnakes, giant sea turtles, and several rare primates.

Directly in front of him, filling his view, was a tangerine-colored ape. Their eyes briefly met. The orangutan's look was calm, though mournfully resigned. His wise old eyes gazed out at BC through the heavy-gauge mesh of his enclosure. BC decided it was a strange looking animal, homely yet Buddha-like.

Their eyes met again, then the orang's eyes shifted quickly away. To many primates, a direct gaze was rude, a challenge. In Malay, orangutan meant "Man of the Forest," and this particular one sat close to the mesh of his cage pretending not to be interested in either BC or Sister Siona. It would have been a quiet, even serene encounter if not for what happened next.

A heavily-bearded man entered the courtyard from an opening on the far wall that BC hadn't noticed until now. The man had on a pair of soiled coveralls and a worn pair of hip boots. A deadly, electronic whip was clutched in his right hand. BC recognized the evil instrument for what it was. He had seen pictures of prisoners in the South African gulag. One flick of an electronic whip could maim a man. A second flick would surely kill him.

BC eased backwards, thinking that the man dressed in coveralls was about to attack him and Sister Siona. He reached for his blaster with one hand even as he shoved Siona behind him with the other.

But, no sooner had BC grabbed hold of his weapon, than he realized the rough-looking man wasn't interested in the two of them at all. The man in coveralls was heading for the orang's cage instead. That's when it hit BC — *orangutan skulls were prized by some as mantle ornaments.*

In the time it took for BC to decide whether or not to interfere, the man acted, flicking the lethal whip at the animal through the bars of his cage.

BC gasped. Like a surgical scalpel of unestimable sharpness, the electronic whip cut deeply into the primate's flesh.

But instead of it being a clean incision like one might get from a laser knife, the whip left behind a jagged, gaping wound that was many times more painful and all that much harder to heal.

The orang screamed out in pain. It was a guttural, primeval scream.

At the knowing look of disbelief in the animal's eyes, BC was shocked to a new reality. Until this very moment, it had never occurred to him. — Only a handful of genetic differences separated him from this gentle beast of the forest. The great ape before him was a sentient beast — and it knew it was going to die. This made BC angry.

Bright red blood began to spurt from the animal's torn flesh, and as it did, BC felt his own blood come to a boil. *He couldn't control himself.*

Seconds seemed like minutes, and everything went into slow motion. The bearded assailant recoiled his electronic whip for another attack. But before he could manage it, the orangutan collapsed to the floor in a writhing mass of yellow fur. After several involuntary jerks, the giant ape let out a sorrowful whimper. Then all motion inside the cage ceased.

At the sight of such inhumanity, such utter cruelty and needless slaughter, Sister Siona turned her head and gagged. She had spent the better part of her adult life helping others, and this made her sick to her stomach. BC was less forgiving.

"You bastard!" he yelled, hatred burning from his eyes as he lunged forward.

The man with the electronic whip had no time to react before BC was upon him, pummeling his face and chest with his bare fists.

"Not so fast!" came a new voice from the shadows. "Lucifer works for me. If you have something worth saying, I suggest you say it to me."

At first, BC didn't hear the man. He had the ape-killer in a chokehold and was about to break his neck, when the call came again.

"I say there. Lucifer works for me. If you don't like what he did, you had best take it up with me."

Sensing that this was the man Sister Siona had brought him to see, BC loosened his grip a notch on the throat of the man who killed the orang. The whip was still curled up on the floor where Lucifer had dropped it during the attack. BC kicked it away, now, and let Lucifer out of the chokehold. The scoundrel quickly backed away, trying to get out of BC's reach.

White-faced and trembling, Sister Siona trotted over to speak with the man in the shadows, Lucifer's boss. Her hand was outstretched, as if they had met before and were perhaps friends. For a moment, the two talked in whispers, then BC was invited to join them.

"Doctor, I want you to meet my friend BC. BC, this is Doctor Killjoy."

With a pug nose, jutting jaw, and penchant for slang, Doctor Killjoy exuded a kind of blue-collar integrity. He struck BC as a man who, while doggedly courting the truth, often said to hell with the consequences. Even so, BC was not quick to extend the old man his hand. In fact, his face was still crimson with anger over what he had just witnessed.

"Sister tells me you're from Mars," Doctor Killjoy said, smiling widely. By now, Lucifer had regained enough courage to enter the orangutan's cage toting the electronic whip. While BC watched, the man fixed a harness onto the beast in order to lift it. Once the animal was transferred to an operating table in the next room, Lucifer and an associate would disassemble the saleable parts of the carcass — the head, hands, feet, and penis — then grind up the rest and pass the powder off as either tiger-bone or deer meat.

"Well, I'm not actually *from* Mars. I live in London. That's not quite true either — I lived on Mars for two years. But now I've returned home for personal reasons."

"Is it true then, what they say, Pilgrim? I mean, are people actually *living* there?" The many finely-etched furrows in Doctor Killjoy's eighty-year-old brow crinkled tightly in a hopeful, yet skeptical manner. In a place as far removed from civilization as Sane Lou, there existed a fine line between myth and reality.

"Yes, people are actually living there. A great many, in fact. And more each day."

"Have they found any locals yet?" the Doctor asked eagerly.

"Locals?" BC replied, not quite understanding the question.

"You know, Pilgrim — local life-forms. Surely the colonists must have discovered something by now, some domestic plant or horrible microbe."

"None that I'm aware of, Doc. Carina — that's the girl who needs the Acceleron — has always thought like you do. She believed that Mars was once alive — and might still be. But so far as I know, she never found a shred of

proof to support her claim. Now, are you going to help me save her life or not?"
There was an undeniable urgency in BC's voice.

"Not so fast, my Limey friend. You'll get your Acceleron in due course.
But how many times do you suppose I get the chance to meet someone who's
been to Ares?"

"Ares?"

"Yes, you know — the Greek god of war, the son of Zeus and Hera, the
lover of Aphrodite. The Greeks called the Red Planet Ares. The Romans,
Mars. What I am interested in is the perennial puzzle of the young and the
intoxicated — How did we come to be?"

"Honestly, I haven't a clue," BC said, looking to Sister Siona for help.

"Nor does anyone else," Doctor Killjoy replied, his jaw jutting as he spoke.
"As hard as it is to believe, Pilgrim, most of the DNA in living creatures is
exactly the same from one to the next. This is curious, wouldn't you say?
Wouldn't you think that given the great variety of life-forms we see all around
us, there would be more differentiation?"

The question was rhetorical; it required no answer. Doctor Killjoy
continued:

"Remember, DNA is an incredibly ancient substance. Most human beings
walking the streets of the world today, bouncing their pink new babies on their
knee, hardly stop to think about the chemical that makes it all possible. This
chemical, the one which began the dance of life, is incredibly old stuff, nearly
as old as the Earth itself. In fact, the DNA molecule is so old, its evolution was
essentially complete more than two billion years ago. Since that time, there has
been remarkably little in the way of anything new added — just a few relatively
recent recombinations of old genes, and not even much of that. If you were to
compare the DNA of a human being with the DNA of a bacterium, you would
find that only about ten percent of the strands are different."

"We're all cousins under the skin, is that it?"

"That's not the half of it, Pilgrim. We are all made, literally, of *stardust* —
elements forged in the cores of stars and flung out into space by supernovae.
But the question is: How did we get here?"

BC shook his head. His emotions were oscillating somewhere in the
nether world between disbelief and incredulity, between doubt and suspicion.

"Come on, Pilgrim, the seeds of life must have come from somewhere, why
not space?"

"Well . . . I don't know . . . "

Doctor Killjoy continued, blind to the look of skepticism on BC's face.
"Listen, Pilgrim, if you were to think of the entire four-and-a-half billion
year history of our planet as being a single twenty-four hour day, and if you
were to realize that repeated asteroid impacts would have rendered the Earth

uninhabitable for the first four hours or so, then life appeared in the next thirty minutes. It's amazing if you think about it.

"You've got to discover DNA. You've got to make thousands of enzymes — chlorophyll, hemoglobin, adrenaline, testosterone. You've got to do it all in a very hostile environment. And you've got only thirty minutes in which to do it. So you see, Pilgrim, whenever I sit down to put it all together, it just doesn't add up. The spontaneous generation of life on Earth is about as likely as the assemblage of a ground car by a tornado passing through a junkyard in Sane Lou."

Though the whole scenario was completely absurd, BC found himself nodding in agreement as Killjoy spoke. *Yes, of course* — life must have originated elsewhere. *What could be more obvious?* But then again, Carina would have disagreed. Had she been in attendance, she would have relished the opportunity to debate this man. What questions would she have asked him?

"So tell me Doctor — if there wasn't enough time, as you suggest, how did life get here? Where did it come from?"

"Space."

"Space?! You're out of your bloody head, old man!"

"You dare speak to me that way? If a chap lives to the ripe old age of eighty, he deserves more respect. When I was young, your age perhaps, the old-timers regarded me as an outrageous young rebel," he boasted with a rakish grin. "But now that I'm old, youngsters like you regard me as an outrageous *old* rebel. But make no mistake about it, Pilgrim, I'm not looney. In all probability, life here on Earth had its start out there." Killjoy pointed to the heavens. "Organic chemistry has run rampant through our solar system, and beyond. Indeed, there is a vast population of small worlds covered with organic matter."

"Such as?"

"Well, to name a few — the C-type asteroids in the main Belt. The nuclei of comets, including our friend Halley's. The newly-discovered class of asteroids circling out at the edge of the solar system. Even many of the moons circling Saturn and Jupiter. From the primordial days of the solar system, asteroidal and cometary fragments have been plunging into the Earth's atmosphere, carrying with them vast stores of organic molecules. Some of these molecules survived the intense atmospheric heating upon entry, and, over time, made a significant contribution to the biotic soup that led to the origin of life on our planet. Similar impacts would have delivered similar supplies of organic materials — along with water — to other worlds besides just the Earth. On Titan, for instance, a giant moon of Saturn's which is every bit as large as the planet Mercury, we see the synthesis of complex organic molecules happening right before our eyes. In fact, the planetoid is thick with a dark, organic goo we scientists call Titan *tholin*, from the Greek word for muddy. New tholins form continuously in the upper atmosphere and percolate out like an unending dirty rain."

"Okay, so you've impressed me with your extensive knowledge on the subject, but what the hell are you really trying to tell me?"

"Space is literally *teeming* with microbes, Pilgrim. Bacteria. Viruses. Other organisms. You name it."

"And what, these little buggers arrived here on Earth hitching a ride aboard some asteroid or passing comet?" At this point, BC made no attempt to hide the sarcasm in his voice.

"Let there be absolutely no question in your mind. These little buggers, as you call them, arrived here hidden in the bellies of our galaxy's trojan horses — the comets, asteroids and vast unseen clouds of dark matter. These space-faring microbes were not only responsible for spawning the start of life here on Earth, they also helped spur evolution on afterwards."

"Now I've heard it all."

"Have you really? I ask you, Pilgrim: Was it the impact of an asteroid colliding with Earth sixty-five million years ago that wiped out the dinosaurs, or was it perhaps something else?"

"That's been proven — it was the collision which made Earth temporarily uninhabitable."

"It hasn't been proven at all. Did anyone ever stop to consider the possibility that some lethal disease might have arrived here on Earth *onboard* that killer asteroid? That it was a virus which did 'em in, and not the explosion? Think about it, Pilgrim! Has scientific thought become so rigid, so fixedly correct, that there is no longer any room for revision?"

When BC had no reply for the man's rhetorical questions, Doctor Killjoy barreled on:

"And, if an unexpected epidemic wiped out the dinosaurs, where does that leave *us*? Consider this possibility: whenever the Earth passes through one of these pathogen-filled clouds, it rains terror down upon us, triggering epidemics of influenza, Niles Disease, bubonic plague, whooping cough, or other contagions. Don't forget, Pilgrim — Halley's comet arrives again in just nine years!"

At this proposition, BC objected. "That's crazy talk! I suppose you'll tell me next that some galactic supernatural intelligence must be directing the evolutionary pathway of life."

"You may be on to something there, Pilgrim. You have to admit, there are too many things that look too perfect for all of them to be pure accident. Can natural selection alone account for the rapid evolution of life on Earth, for there being just the right amount of oxygen in the atmosphere, for there being just the right temperature, just the right distance from the sun?"

A shiver ran down BC's spine. *Talk about shades of Carina Matthews!* What if Killjoy were right? Then astronomy was a sham, biology a house of cards, and modern medicine an illusion.

"I don't know, Doc — what you're describing to me sounds awfully close to the theory of Explosive Diversity."

"You've heard of it?" Killjoy intoned, genuinely impressed for the first time by what BC had to say.

"Of course, I've heard of it. The girl I came to see you about, the one lying in a hospital bed in Sister Siona's ward, the one who desperately needs a shot of Acceleron, that girl wrote the *book* on Explosive Diversity — the actual book."

"Oh, my God, why didn't you say so?" Killjoy exclaimed, his eyes brightening. "On second thought, I guess you *did* say. Only I was too dense to make the connection. Your Carina is Carina Matthews, isn't she?"

"That's what I have been trying to tell you, Doc."

"Well, that makes all the difference in the world, doesn't it? Precious few women are as smart as that one. A woman possessing a mind as keen as hers musn't be allowed to die. Brilliant intellects are a damn precious commodity in this world; and good writers, few and far between. Carina Matthews happens to be both. Words are like harpoons, Pilgrim — once they go in, they're very nearly impossible to pull out."

BC didn't know what to say, and for a very long moment he just stood there mouth agape.

"Well, Pilgrim, what are you standing around here for, let's get going!"

THIRTY

The Cane

Sam was having serious misgivings about even being here. All he knew for certain was that after Carina paid a visit to Viscount Nordman in SKANDIA, she came here, to London, to see J. After that, no one had seen or heard from her since. Which left Sam no other choice. If he were ever to have any hope of meeting his grandson before he met his maker, he too would have to see J. Then, with that business out of the way, he could go home to Zealand and die in peace. Saron — bless her heart — had agreed to accompany him on this, his final up at bat, then stay with him until the bitter end.

Sam and Saron were about a week behind Carina when they finally made their way to London. Though Sam wasn't depressed about dying, he knew his time was running out. Each day he found himself fumbling with a sense of his own mortality. So perhaps his present impatience was warranted.

Sam was pacing nervously back and forth, now, across the carpeted floor of J's outer office. This, despite Saron's repeated exhortations for him to sit down and be quiet. His mind was not only on his grandson, but also on the powder keg he had left behind on Mars.

Sam's last act before leaving for home had been to sit down with the other six Councilman and deliberate the fate of the four asteroidors who had caused so much trouble that night in the Commons. Saron had been assaulted and Nandu murdered. It was up to the seven of them to mete out the proper justice.

Tex and Nuke were ordered to pay a fine for their part in the attempted rape. Puck was ordered to pay a larger fine for instigating the attack, plus wash dishes and bus tables in the Commons every night for the next three months. Jackhammer was expelled from the colony for killing Lotha's brother, and handed over to terran authorities in Johannesburg for prosecution.

It was this last decision, the decision regarding Jackhammer, that had infuriated Inda and his cohorts. Their anger was understandable. But, in all honesty, the Council's hands were tied in the matter. Thanks to a quirk in the law, Jackhammer would in all probability escape incarceration, and there wasn't a damn thing Sam or anyone else could do about it. Just like every other factory worker on the planet, Jackhammer was bound by South African law. It was, after all, a condition of his employment. The city-state of Johannesburg claimed jurisdiction over all legal matters to which the African Smelting and Refining Company (ASARCO) was a party. That included operations at the motor plant on Mars. Under South African law, the murder of a non-citizen by a citizen was considered a misdemeanor punishable by no more than thirty days in jail. Therein lay the problem.

Jackhammer was a citizen; Nandu was not. To Inda Desai and many of his followers, the Council's handling of this incident amounted to little more than a slap on the hand. By the time Sam left Mars to come here to London, the entire colony was up in arms. Fortunately, the first act of sabotage was defused; Gunter and McPherson had seen to that. But, the next incident might not end so agreeably.

At long last, J's receptionist announced their presence. "There's a Samuel Matthews to see you, Sir," she mouthed over the intercomm. "And a lady."

"Show them in," came the gruff reply.

Sam had been in J's office on one previous occasion — after he was wounded in that fiasco with Whitey on the moon. Now, when the door to the man's inner sanctum swung open today, Sam could see that nothing much about J or his surroundings had changed since his last visit. The man was still as stern-looking as ever, the room just as utilitarian. Sam wasted no time coming to the point.

"Where is my daughter?"

J acted as if he hadn't heard the question. "Samuel Matthews, is it? I never expected to see you here again," he hissed from behind the giant desk.

"Nor I, you," Sam snarled right back, pulling up a chair close to J's desk. Saron did likewise.

J's tone was brusque, and he didn't stop what he was doing to extend a welcoming hand. "If memory serves, you still owe me a favor. The last time we sat across from one another we entered into an agreement, an oral contract. And, if memory serves, I held up my half of the bargain. You, however, have yet to deliver on yours. I find your presence here today somewhat curious, even disconcerting. Have you finally come, after more than two years, to discharge your debt?"

Sam turned to Saron in the next chair to explain "There was a battle on the moon. Carina, myself, my brother, Fornax, and BC were on one side, and a nasty fellow named Whitey — plus a half-dozen of his thugs — were on the other. At the time, BC worked for this . . . this . . . man."

"And does again," J broke in, blind to the disdain in Sam's voice.

"And apparently, does again," Sam echoed. "I got hurt in the confrontation, and J here was charitable enough to put me up in one of his hospitals until I mended. In exchange for saving my life, this man made me promise to help him steal the secret of Fornax's Drive."

"But you never did," Saron observed.

"No, I never did."

"Had you done so, Mars might never have been colonized, and we two might never have met."

"I'm not unaware of the irony."

"Well, then, Sam did the right thing," Saron said, looking J directly in the eye.

"He may have at that," J granted. "But that doesn't change a thing. I took the man at his word."

Saron wasn't done with him. "You're the Head of Commonwealth Intelligence. You're paid to be smart. You're paid to guess what the other fellow is gonna do before he does it. You must have anticipated ahead of time that Sam wasn't going to do your bidding, or why else would you have let him go? So let's have no more crap about promises broken, shall we?"

"Smart girl you've got there, Matthews. Now why are you here really? As if I couldn't guess."

"Carina has been to see you?"

"You know that she has."

"Yes, of course. And where did she go after leaving you?"

"America," J replied, meeting Sam's uncertain gaze. "I don't believe she told me exactly where she was going. I'm not even sure she knew herself. But from what I could gather, it was inland somewhere."

Saron gasped. "But why, in God's name? From what I understand, America is now like what much of Africa used to be — a dark and forbidding continent."

"For the most part that is true," J said. "After the War, with most of the infrastructure destroyed, America itself has become a dark and dangerous place. But Carina is trying to hunt down some long lost genealogical records. Someone put it in her head that her only chance for finding them was across the pond, there in America."

"Yes, I almost forgot," Sam murmured, his voice barely a whisper. "She had it in her head to try and solve the mystery of what has been killing me — Matthews Disease." His voice faded off. "And my grandson? Did she inquire about him?"

"The subject never came up."

"I see." Sam was obviously disappointed, though not entirely surprised. "And BC? Is he still here, or did he journey to America with her?"

J leaned back in his chair, folded his arms across the narrowest portion of his barrel-shaped chest. The starched sleeves of his shirt rode up his arms, revealing more of his hairy, ape-like wrists. He made no move to answer Sam's question.

"Land's sakes, man! How can BC's whereabouts possibly be considered a State secret? Did the boy go with my daughter or not?"

"In a manner of speaking," J answered.

It was unfortunate. But the Chief of Commonwealth Intelligence was so accustomed to dodging questions, he couldn't even give a straight answer when there was no reason to be evasive.

"Of all the silly games, why do you feel the need to play one with me?"

"Because I can," J said, unfolding his arms and leaning forward across the desk. He seemed quite proud of himself.

"Well, thanks for nothing," Sam said, getting to his feet. "Let's go, Saron."

"Not so fast, you two. If you really must know, BC went in there incognito. He's tailing her, but he's certainly not *with* her."

Sam sat back down. "Why isn't he with her? And where is my grandson?"

"I have no idea where your grandson is," J answered without flinching. It was a bald-faced lie, but a passable one. J knew, of course, which orphanage BC's son had been placed in, but that didn't make the boy Sam's grandson. In any event, giving out such information would be in contravention of Agency policy.

"Well, if you don't know where my daughter is, and if you don't know where my grandson is, then I'll be on my way."

For a second time, Sam rose to leave. He edged towards the door with Saron's support. "I think everything you have told me is a lie. I find it difficult to believe that you don't know where my grandson is. Surely, BC wouldn't have gone off on some long, overseas assignment without first attending to his son. A neighbor, a friend, a parent, a lover — Land's sakes, man, *someone* must be looking after the boy!"

By this time, Sam was within feet of the door and just inches from the umbrella stand next to it.

J spoke. "Certainly you can see my dilemma. Even if I wanted to help, I couldn't. My hands are tied. I don't know for a fact who the boy's mother is, though I certainly can speculate. I have no proof that BC's son is also your grandson. He never told me either way. But, if it's any consolation, I can assure you the boy is being well cared for."

"So you do know where the boy is!" Saron cried out, stopping beside the umbrella stand to glare at J.

"Oh, my God!" Sam exclaimed, forgetting about his grandson and pointing excitedly. "Where the hell did *that* come from?"

Sam broke free of Saron's hold and reached for the knobby pine cane jammed in among the various umbrellas in the stand. Lifting it free of the stand and twirling it around in his fingers like a magic wand, Sam suddenly found his breath coming in short gulps.

His heart began to race as his mind was overwhelmed by the myriad of possibilities.

Now his skin turned cold and clammy, and he started to hyperventilate. His legs began to buckle beneath him.

Then, before anyone knew what was afoot, Sam had slumped to the floor unconscious!

*   *   *

When the medic brought him around minutes later, Sam was still confused. He dragged himself up into the nearest chair. "The cane. Where is the goddamned cane?"

Saron handed it to him. While he was out, she had given the thing the once-over. What she found surprised her. Saron knew a little something about weapons, from her days as an Afghan freedom fighter. The walking stick was in fact a nasty rifle. The insides had been hollowed out to make room for a gunbarrel. The trigger was hidden inside the crook.

"Do you know whose cane this is?" Sam croaked, on the verge of tears.

Both Saron and J shook their heads. "Haven't the slightest."

"See this initial here?" Sam asked, pointing to the FW burned into the handle. "That stands for Felix Wenger. General Felix 'Flix' Wenger. And how do I know this? Flix was my grandfather's personal adviser when my grandfather first became a United States Senator. This was before the Great War. Flix was one of the great men of his time. Along with my *great*-grandfather, 'Tiger' Matthews, Flix was part of the commando team that assassinated Rontana, bringing an end to that scourge of mankind."

"You know, now that you mention it, I remember that episode quite well from your file. I had my people research it when we were building our dossier on you. Nasty affair, as I remember."

"You have a dossier on me?" Sam sputtered. "I should have known as much. Anyhow, when General Wenger died, he willed this cane to my grandfather, along with a place he owned up in Maine. You see the other set of initials here?

NM. Nate Matthews. That's my grandfather. But what I don't understand is, how did the damn thing get *here*?"

"I may be able to fill in a couple of the missing pieces," J offered in uncharacteristically helpful fashion. "BC was an orphan — all my top agents are — it's a lot cleaner that way — no family members to kidnap or be held hostage. Anyway, when he was given over to the orphanage as a baby, that cane arrived there with him."

"That's impossible!" Sam exclaimed, not believing a word J said. "Where is this orphanage?"

"It's south of London. But back in those days, it was situated in the Hawaii Free State. Just before the Great War an American philanthropist relocated the facility to an estate he owned here in the Isles east of Guildford. He left enough money in trust to run the place in perpetuity."

"BC's my son." The way Sam said it, it was a fact, not a supposition.

"That's preposterous, Matthews! You must have hit your head when you went down. The boy's an orphan. His parents didn't want him. Can't you understand that?" J scowled.

"Oh, I understand what you're saying well enough. But you're wrong. And I'm not delirious from my fall. It all makes perfect sense to me now. Before the Great War, I had a lover, a wonderful girl named Sara. She escaped to the Hawaii Free State. My grandfather had me wire money to a numbered account for her there. I never knew it at the time, but I must have gotten Sara pregnant. BC's my son."

By now the color had come back into Sam's face. But he was still unsteady on his feet.

"And the cane? How did *it* get here?" J asked, not convinced.

"I really haven't a clue. My grandfather was dead. His son — my father — was a vagrant. By then I was living in Canada. Perhaps Nate left instructions for Sara to get some of his personal belongings after he died. She would have known how to use it."

"Use it?" Now it was J's turn to be confused. Unlike Saron, he had never taken the time to examine the antiquated walking stick closely.

"Yes, use it," Sam said, pointing out the trigger housing hidden in the crook. "It's a gun, you see."

"No . . . I didn't see," J stammered, stealing an angry glance at Saron. "Is the bloody thing loaded?"

"There's only one sure way to find out," Sam smiled, raising the cane until it was level with J's head. "Now tell me, you son of a bitch . . . where is my grandson?"

"Are you mad?" J asked, staring down the long, rifled gunbarrel at the loaded chamber. A bead of sweat had formed on his brow.

"Angry, yes. Mad, no. But then, how would you expect me to feel? Inside of five minutes I find out I have a son I never knew I had. I discover that my only grandson has been given over to an orphanage without my knowledge or permission. I learn that my newly found son and my only daughter have been unwitting lovers for two years now, and that the both of them are currently lost somewhere in the middle of the most uncivilized continent known to man. And you . . . you wonder whether or not I'm angry?"

Sam laughed a wicked laugh. Still holding the gun, he approached to within one meter of where J stood there fidgeting. Sam was calm, his aim steady. His eyes were cold and devoid of humor. He kept the business end of the cane centered on J's forehead as he spoke:

"Now, smart guy, don't give me any crap about how I'll never get out of this place alive if I blow your brains out. I'm short for this world anyway, or don't you have that in your dossier? No matter. Listen, and listen closely, because I'm only going to say this one last time. After that you're a dead man. Have I made myself clear?"

J nodded.

"So tell me, you son of a bitch . . . where is my grandson?"

THIRTY-ONE

Saboteurs

"Any chance you have this one wired correctly?"

The two men sat crouched in the shadows waiting for the night watchman and his bio-canine to move past. It was a muggy night. Beads of sweat gripped Lotha's forehead where the band of his hat met the skin of his misshapen skull. Kneeling beside him on the ground was his good friend and comrade-in-arms, Inda Desai. Inda was a man of medium build and mediocre looks, although next to a robust man of Lotha's dimensions, he was at once both scrawny and handsome.

Inda spoke as he worked. A pair of metric pliers was in his palm.

"Listen, you big oaf, I had the last one wired correctly. I don't understand why you won't believe me. It's that South African that Gunter brought here with him, who messed things up for us. McPherson found the bomb and disarmed the damn thing before I could set it off."

With a grunt, Inda tightened the last tiny hex-bolt into place.

"What were you waiting for anyway?" Lotha boomed, receiving a warning to whisper in return. "Why didn't you just blow the place as soon as you were a safe distance away?"

"I've already explained that. I wanted to detonate the bomb during the day shift, when there would be more people around. Only I never got the chance. And it's a damn shame too, because that would have gotten everyone's attention back home."

With each passing month, Earth found itself more and more dependent on the relatively cheap source of ore the asteroids and their movers now provided. It was a simple question of supply and demand. With the inexpensive and easily accessible veins of Earth mined out long ago, even the comparatively complex matter of swinging an asteroid out from the Belt and into Earth orbit was cheaper than drilling a hole dozens of kloms deep into the bedrock or else recycling the materials bound up in other products.

In fact, the deluge of new mineral supplies from the Belt was causing a bit of a renaissance back on Earth, a rebirth that promised to raise living standards across the entire face of the planet. In much the same way that harvesting the moon for precious metals had altered life on Earth in the twenty-first century, mining the asteroid belt was destined to do so in the twenty-fifth. These planetoids were a treasure-trove of nickel and iron ore, plus lesser amounts of manganese and bauxite. And, with the newly-terraformed Mars serving as a convenient and stable base of operations, the booty was all now within man's easy reach.

To serve Earth's insatiable appetite for raw materials, ASARCO had established a colossal motor factory on Mars almost immediately after assaying the core samples Gunter collected on his expedition with Fornax and the others to the Belt. Here in the motor factory, workers now assembled gigantic EMD's — electromagnetic mass drivers — which made the whole thing possible. Hitched first to a railgun, then fired into orbit, these massive, fully-automated motors would literally fly themselves out to the Belt, attach themselves to a predesignated asteroid using tungsten-steel-hardened pitons equipped with explosive tips, and then, without further need for human intervention, start the rocky mass on its month-long journey back towards Earth.

Along the way, the EMD would use the asteroid itself for fuel, expelling slivers of rock outward at high velocity so as to slow the asteroid's orbital velocity and propel the remainder of the planetoid forward along its intended trajectory. It was Newtonian physics at its simplest. Once the asteroid was within reach of any of a dozen earth-orbiting smelters, the robot engine would brake the asteroid's fall and insert the valuable chunk of rock into a geosynchronous orbit, where it could be easily mined. The finished ingots could then be dropped to the surface below.

At the outset, with memories of the silver cannonball incident still fresh in people's minds and with a snootful of alarmists on every side to remind those who had forgotten, citizens objected to ASARCO's asteroid moving operation on environmental grounds.

But, as the influx of new raw materials helped lower prices and curb inflation, and as safeguards such as an EMD-tracking station on Earth were set up and manned, public support for the project grew. In less than six months' time, there was no turning back.

But on Mars the situation was different. People were still angry over the Jackhammer Incident, and some of those people were looking for ways to get back at the company. The search had begun for a weakness they could exploit to put a stop to the whole operation. Although no one at the company liked to talk about it, a glaring one existed.

From the moment an EMD left the Colony One factory floor until the asteroid itself arrived in orbit high above the Earth, the entire process was mostly out of man's direct control and governed either by physics or the onboard computer. There were, of course, fine adjustments to be made in its flight path as the asteroid drew closer to Earth. But other than these several midcourse corrections sent remotely by radio from the EMD-tracking station, the asteroid was essentially a "free bird." Therein lay the problem.

With so much of the EMD's key functions fully automated, the operation practically begged for an unscrupulous pair of someones to come along and sabotage it. Inda and Lotha were the perfect stooges for the job, egged on as they had been by the likes of Oskar Schaeffer. Already incensed by the Council's handling of what had now become known as the "Jackhammer Incident," these two miscreants were about to commit a desperate act of terrorism so extreme, it had the potential to end for all time mankind's brief tenure as custodians of planet Earth.

The sequence of events leading up to this moment began shortly after that night in Saron's Place. Although penalties were imposed by the Council on the four Colony One'ers for their roles in the disturbance, the penalty of expulsion leveled against Jackhammer for the murder of Nandu hardly seemed sufficient for the crime.

And, if that weren't heat enough to bring the witch's brew of revolution to a boil, the Johannesburg court system proved to be little more than a puppet for Oskar Schaeffer and his cowardly board of directors. Not wanting to endure the publicity of a messy, high profile trial, the big mining company saw to it that Jackhammer was acquitted without delay and set free. This miscarriage of justice only served to make Inda and the several members of the Newton Liberation Party that much more determined. Now, nothing short of shutting down the motor factory for good would do.

Thus, it was with this singular objective in mind that the two Afghans had hatched a simple, yet devastating plan. Disguised as unemployed immigrant laborers, the co-conspirators applied for jobs as micro-seam welders at the motor works, positions which would afford them numerous opportunities to tamper with a motor as it moved slowly down the assembly line towards completion. It was at the end of that line, as the giant motor was being readied for service, that Inda Desai would do his dirty work.

Each EMD manufactured at the motor works was more or less identical. The differences lay in their programming — The coordinates, velocity and spin of the target asteroid. The acceleration coefficients necessary to boost the mass Earthward. The physical location of the Earth itself. And, finally, the calculation of the exact moment for reversing the particle flow from the electromagnetic mass driver so as to slow the asteroid's fall and avoid a horrendous collision with the Home Planet.

Unfortunately, despite the massive computational power of the most modern of modern computers, programming a precise trajectory ahead of time through the maze of planets, moons, and bits of rock that the solar system was, was out of the question. There were just too many variables, even for the most advanced computer. Gravity was, after all, a force that worked its magic at immense distances. With hundreds of thousands of asteroids, nearly a dozen planets, and upwards of fifty moons all interacting with one another, each hurtling through space on a slightly different flight path, the task of plotting a fixed course through the solar system in advance was all but impossible.

Therefore, since midcourse corrections would be frequent and necessary, the progress of each EMD-guided planetoid was closely monitored by space-traffic controllers back on Earth. Whenever one seemed to be drifting from its intended glidepath, a radio signal was sent aloft to trim its EMD thrusters accordingly.

The weak link in the chain-of-control, the link that could easily be sabotaged, was the radio receiver hardwired onto the superstructure of each EMD. If the unit could be damaged or otherwise put out of commission, space-traffic control would no longer be able to radio up the necessary midcourse corrections. The results could range from the benign to the disastrous.

On the one hand, the errand chunk of rock might spin harmlessly off into space, reaching the inner stretches of the solar system and eventually falling like a briquette into the sun.

On the other hand, it might lurch awkwardly into orbit about the Earth much like our own moon did eons ago. Or, calamity of calamities, it might slam into the Home Planet killing hundreds of millions.

No matter how it turned out, the loss would be an immense embarrassment to ASARCO. A setback of this magnitude — especially given the political clout of the Green Party — had the potential to shutter the entire asteroid-harvesting venture. At an absolute minimum, an investigation would be launched and a hearing held in World Court to air all manner of concerns, from lax plant-safety to charges of extensive environmental degradation. In that forum, the pleas of the Newton Liberation Party would be heard. And this was, after all, why Inda and Lotha were here in the first place, crouching in the shadows just outside the factory gates. As soon as they could enter the plant unobserved, they would move swiftly across the broken ground with the homemade bomb clutched in their hands.

Inda made a sign, now, to his buddy, that the coast was clear.

"You absolutely sure you got this one wired right?"

Lotha whispered the question in an accusing tone as the pair of saboteurs slipped past the night watchman's unattended desk and moved silently out onto the factory floor.

"Give it a rest, will you? I know what I'm doing. Let's get this thing over and done with, then get the hell out of here before we're caught."

Even as Inda spoke, he slid the explosive device into a hidden pocket on the inside of his coat. The tiny device was coated with a polymer that made it invisible to the metal detectors at the factory gate.

The two men made their way to the far end of the assembly line. There, with micro-seam welders in hand, they joined up with two others already hard at work on the final systems check of newly-build motor. This was the last production step before the EMD was to be mounted on a railgun and catapulted into space for its intended rendezvous with an M-class asteroid.

"Where the hell have the two of you been?" one of the workers asked. "Not hitting the Saronale again, I hope. Boss don't want no one in here who's drunk, you know. Are you two sober?"

With jaw jutting and forehead protruding, Lotha dared the other man. "Ya wanna smell my breath?" he barked, approaching to within several inches of the man's face and expelling a big gulp of foul-smelling air.

"Oh, leave him alone, ya big ape," the second, overall-clad man said. "He meant nothing by it. We just don't want to lose our jobs, that's all. Now, let's get back to work or else the boss'll dock us *all* a half-day's pay. This baby here's due for delivery to the big gun in under three hours."

Lotha nodded his assent and backed off. Together, the four of them moved over towards the electromagnetic inducer coils. These were the guts of the motor. The rest was just so many gears and magnets.

While Lotha and the other two were hunched over the control box busily checking relays and logic circuits, Inda removed the magnetized detonator from his coat pocket and planted it on a steel girder next to the main antenna housing. Security inside the factory was light, and he was confident no one saw him do it.

The chemical grenade measured barely five centimeters in length, and only three in width. This made it all but impossible to notice against the gray steel of the hundred-meter-long mass driver.

But small or not, the bomb's puny dimensions revealed nothing of its potential to do harm. By placing it in such close proximity to the EMD's main antenna, it wouldn't take much of an explosion to knock the whole unit off-line.

The bomb itself was equipped with its own mini-receiving-dish and tiny onboard computer. Inda had programmed the computer to respond only to a pair of signals transmitted simultaneously along two preset frequencies. As a precaution against someone else tampering with his transmitter and accidentally setting off the explosion prematurely, Inda had scrambled the bomb's activation code mathematically. His plan was relatively simple:

Once the EMD reached the Belt and made contact with its intended M-class target, it would attach itself to the asteroid's leading edge. Then, after testing each of its twenty piton anchors to be certain they were securely fastened, the mass driver would kick in to begin propelling the big chunk of rock along the first leg of its journey Earthward.

Some three-and-a-half weeks later, when the asteroid made its closest approach to Mars, it would have also reached its maximum velocity. Normally, this would be the point in the trip when the first major midcourse correction would take place. Space-traffic controllers on the ground would apply their most advanced computational skills to recalibrate the asteroid's trajectory and keep the stony missile on track for a rendezvous with Earth a month hence.

It would only be then, after the midcourse correction had been made and the asteroid had achieved its top speed, that Inda would act, sending the radio signal that would detonate the small explosive device, thereby knocking out the EMD's antenna. In doing so, he would be forever foreclosing the possibility of further altering its course. From that moment forward, the tiny moon would be on automatic pilot, a "free bird," its actual destination unknown.

By then, the most anyone would be able to say with certainty was that directly after making its first midcourse adjustment, an asteroid larger than the one reputed to have wiped out the dinosaurs was on a collision course with planet Earth.

THIRTY-TWO

Brigham Smith

Flesh didn't take lightly to metal, and a dose of Acceleron couldn't change the fact that her body had been crumpled under the fender of a gtruck. It couldn't change the fact that there had been trauma and great pain, severe bruising and widespread internal damage.

But what it *could* do was greatly speed the healing. What would have taken six weeks to heal otherwise, now would take just one. This was day five.

Carina dragged herself into a sitting position in bed. With great effort she swung her legs out over the side of the bed and leaned against the mattress as she tried valiantly to stand up. Her bruised ribs were still quite tender, and every breath hurt like the Devil.

Still, after spending what seemed like an eternity flat on her back, the woman was eager to be up and about. Today — in a short while, in fact — she was finally going to get out of this dreary place. Too much time had been lost already. She had to get on with the project that had brought her here in the first place — learning all there was to know about the genetic history of the Matthews family.

The last five days were a blur. The cretins in The Last Resort. The attack inside the sleep-capsule. The blaster scattering blood and guts everywhere. The barefoot run into the alley. The squealing of tires. The pain of impact. Even when she regained consciousness, it was still all a dream. BC had been there, but somehow he had seemed ambivalent about saving her life, as if his heart wasn't in it or he'd had other things on his mind. Like Carina, he was eager to get this over and done with, impatient to return to his old, new life.

Carina placed her feet on the floor and took a tentative step. Her legs were shaky. But she made it across the room to a nearby chair.

Plagued by pain and the delirium of a drug-hastened recovery, she hadn't felt like saying anything to BC about the baby until now. For his part, the man hadn't broached the subject yet either. So far, whenever she would grab for his hand or try to cuddle up against his chest, he would pull away. She put it down to a reflex action. The man was still hurting, even after a year and a half.

But Carina didn't need proof that he cared. He had, after all, followed her to this godforsaken continent. It didn't seem possible. But mankind had once called this America the land of milk and honey. It certainly wasn't so now.

Sister Siona's hospital ward was a strange and eerie place. Part medic facility, part community center, it was a magnet for all manner of people, an oasis in a desert of suffering. Parked in the hallway, just outside Carina's door, were several oldsters and their kin. She listened intently to what they were saying:

The elderly man, flushed with pride, was recounting in voluble fashion his experiences and impressions. His aged wife joined in periodically with meticulous corrections involving completely unimportant points, these being given and taken in the best of humor. To all this, the young ones listened with the greatest attention.

To Carina it seemed as if these scruffy, street people outside her door were as warm and human as any she ever had the pleasure to meet. It was at times like these, especially, that she wondered whether or not there really was such a thing as a newhuman, or whether it was all a very big mistake. It was at times like these, especially, that she missed her mother so much that it hurt. Had Nasha only lived long enough for Carina to have known her, maybe she wouldn't always have been so lonely, so aloof, so desperate for affection.

Carina put her hands to her face and cried. It was the drugs, yes, but also deep emotional scars. In time she drifted off to sleep. But it was a fractured, insecure sleep.

Suddenly something popped her awake. A door slamming. A gruff voice. Doctor Killjoy had arrived in the foyer downstairs. They were about to pack up and leave.

BC came to her room and helped her down the stairs. In a day, maybe two, she would be better, but for now she was still too weak to make it down the stairs on her own.

Doctor Killjoy was waiting impatiently for them by the front door. Carina took an immediate dislike to the man. Even the usually affable BC didn't seem to care for him much. Sister Siona was there as well, and of the three, she didn't appear to notice the man's peculiarities or his flamboyance.

As Carina quickly learned, Sister Siona had a much more pressing agenda on her mind. The woman intended to join them for the ride out to the Genealogical Institute. And, judging by the personal effects she hauled down to the gcar with her, and the way she acted and spoke to the orderlies they passed in the corridor on the way out the door, it was obvious she wasn't ever coming back. When Carina asked why, BC explained the deal he had made to get her a dose of Acceleron. When this was over, Sister Siona was going with BC back to Mars. He left out the part about Carina's mother maybe still being alive.

As Doctor Killjoy pulled away from the curb, he explained that the trip out to the Institute would take about forty minutes by gcar. Carina was happy for the rest and settled into her seat to stare out the window.

The city was ugly — ugly in a way she couldn't describe. Dirty, noisy, crowded, smelly, nothing like Auckland at all.

But once they escaped the confines of the downtown, the scenery became hauntingly beautiful. After the terrible nightmare of nearly being raped on the filth-covered floor of The Last Resort, after the terrible nightmare of being run down by a gtruck and then being hospitalized in a medieval medic ward — after all that, she found being out here in the open air, in the rolling hills and green pastures, was a refreshing change of the first order.

Although she really had no clue exactly where Doctor Killjoy was taking her, Carina knew they were traveling crosscountry somewhere in the vicinity of her family's ancestral home — Farmington, Missouri. Staring out, now, at the landscape as the man drove, Carina wondered about her father.

As a boy, had he ever called these rolling hills and wooded glens home? Would he have recognized any of these landmarks still today?

Out here, west of Sane Lou, at a place the locals called Cease Flags, was the Genealogical Institute she had come from the other side of the solar system to see. Supposedly, the flags had something or other to do with the number of colonial overseers who had at one time or another claimed this territory as their own. According to Killjoy, these included the French, the English, and the Spanish, though the names of any others escaped him for the present.

The road followed a winding course. As they approached the Genealogical Institute from the east, Carina could see how the facility was actually a series of low-slung brick buildings set in a valley between two heavily-wooded hills. There was also an underground bunker not unlike the one she had visited in SKANDIA. This depository was even more extensive than the first. It was filled with documents collected over the course of six centuries of American history — birth certificates, baptismal records, marriage licenses, divorce decrees, death certificates, gene prints, even adoption proceedings.

Unlike the jovial and impish Viscount Nordman, this place was run by a thin, severe-looking man who might have been happier as a Bible-throwing preacher back in the wild days of the Old West. Carina took an immediate dislike to the man, and he was more than happy to reciprocate. It was evident from the man's demeanor that he didn't care much for visitors, and certainly not for women, at least not the nosy type armed with all manner of pesky questions.

As Doctor Killjoy explained on the ride out, the head of the Institute, one Brigham Smith, was a most curious fellow. Named for two of Mormonism's most prominent founders, Brigham Smith was the last of a breed that should have died out long ago. As rich as the history of the Matthews family was here in eastern Missouri, richer still was the story of the Church of Jesus Christ of Latter-day Saints.

Joseph Smith founded the Church in New York in the early to mid 1800s, after having had visions of God in which he was told he would be the instrument to restore Christianity. Because of religious persecution, the Church was forced to move first to northern Missouri and later to Nauvoo, Illinois. In keeping with Smith's philosophy of securing a Kingdom of God here on Earth, missionaries were soon sent to England and to SKANDIA, with most of the converts eventually emigrating to the United States.

Although the Church prospered in Nauvoo, neighbors resented the Mormons because they voted as a bloc and were constantly proselytizing. When rumors began to spread that Smith had secretly introduced polygamy into Mormonism, the townspeople became irate. Feelings peaked while Smith was being held in a Carthage, Illinois jailhouse. Before it was all over, an armed mob had shot him dead.

The head of the Church's Council of Apostles, Brigham Young, was voted leader to replace Smith. He organized and directed an epic march from Nauvoo, across the Great Plains, over the Rocky Mountains, and on into the Great Salt Lake Basin. It was an exodus in every sense of the word.

In Utah the Church continued to grow, although not before a full-scale war nearly erupted over the acknowledgement of polygamy as a Mormon tenet. Eventually, the matter was settled when the U.S. Supreme Court denied that religious freedom could be claimed as grounds for a plural marriage. By the end of the nineteenth century, Mormons had officially ended the practice altogether. Yet, in spite of the controversy, more than 50,000 new settlers from the Midwest and Europe soon joined up with them.

Brigham Young helped found more than 350 new cities and towns as he sent colonizing parties scurrying out across the West. The Mormons built canals to irrigate the soil, and engaged in farming and home industry in an effort to become economically self-sufficient. They believed strongly in community self-reliance, and members abstained from the use of alcohol or tobacco.

As for the importance of genealogy to the Church, this went straight to the heart of their beliefs. Faith was based on four books: the Bible, the Book of Mormon, the Doctrine and Covenants, and the Pearl of Great Price, all of which were (and still are) considered scripture. Latter-day Saints believed in the eternal progress of humans from a spiritual state to mortality, and then on to an afterlife where resurrected individuals would receive their reward. Vicarious baptism for those who had died before them was a distinctive Mormon practice. Because of it, the Church laid great emphasis on genealogical research so that its members might undergo baptismal rites on behalf of their ancestors.

To this day, half a millennium later, descendants of Brigham Young and Joseph Smith maintained that tradition, carefully collecting and preserving genealogical records, not just on behalf of the Church, but, at one time, on behalf of the United States government itself. Even after the calamity of the Great War befell the nation, the effort continued. Brigham Smith, of the Genealogical Institute west of Sane Lou, was the current custodian of that treasure. He viewed this wealth of information as his heritage, and the bunker it was stored in as his personal fiefdom. The contempt he felt for everything and everyone non-Mormon was evident in his voice when he spoke.

Instead of something cordial like *Hi, how are you?* he began with, "Why are you here, woman?" His tone was indignation personified, and, despite everything Doctor Killjoy had done to prepare Carina for this meeting, she was startled by the chilly reception.

Suppressing her disappointment, Carina came straight to the point. "I am here in search of information."

Even as she spoke, Carina advanced ahead of Brigham Smith and the others. She crossed the tiny parking lot, where Doctor Killjoy had stopped the gcar and headed towards a concrete bench she spied sitting beneath an oak tree outside the front door of the Institute. Despite her best efforts to hide it, Carina was still nursing a broken leg that hadn't yet fully mended. She moved, now, with a limp.

Chasing after her, Brigham Smith continued to object to her very presence. "My good woman, even before you arrived, Doctor Killjoy briefed me on why you have come and on what it is you are after. You must understand that this isn't a public Library. What gives you the right?"

"The right?" she said, more perplexed than before. "I honestly don't understand. Is there a moral issue here I'm unaware of?"

Carina glanced first at BC, then at Sister Siona for help. They answered with a shrug of the shoulders. Even Doctor Killjoy's eyes told her she was on her own.

When Brigham Smith spoke, his mouth was a thin, vehement slice. "Woman, these are religious artifacts. They don't belong to you. They belong to us. To *me*."

"But I was told you were merely the *custodian* of these records, not their owner."

"Woman, you were told wrong."

Even in her present weakened condition, Carina was still a formidable woman, not at all the sort to back away from a fight.

Springing to her feet, now, Carina vaulted the short distance that lay between him and her, coming to within inches of Brigham Smith's face. Her face was burning red with anger. Her eyes seethed with contempt for this petty, little man.

"Now listen to me, you son-of-a-bitch. In the first place, you will address me as Carina or Carina Matthews or even as Doctor Matthews. But under no circumstances will you call me 'woman'. Is that clear? Just nod if you understand. Furthermore, given what I've already been through, there's no way I'm going to stand here and put up with your stinking arrogance. Since I arrived on this lousy continent, I have been beaten up, ridiculed, assaulted, and put in the fucking hospital by a goddamned gtruck. Believe me when I tell you, I have traveled thousands of kloms at great risk to stand before you here today, and I'll not be spoken to in the tone you have taken with me. Not by you, not by my father, not by any other man. Now, you either start dealing with me straight, or I'll scratch your eyes out and eat them along with your gonads for lunch! Are we clear?"

By this time the color had completely drained from Brigham Smith's face. Never in his life had he ever been confronted by a woman such as this one. And now that it looked as if she might actually do what she threatened, his demeanor softened appreciably.

"Let's try to reach an understanding here, shall we? As the Chief Apostle of the Church's Council, I can do whatever I please here at the Genealogical Institute. Which is not to say that we cannot do business together, only that it will cost you. What have you to offer?" Smith asked, caressing her shoulder in a much too familiar fashion.

"Don't touch me, you bastard!" she shrieked, slapping him hard enough across the face to leave a mark.

"Yeah, hands off," BC barked, shoving Smith aside. "I've had just about enough of your mouth. Now, are you willing to help out Carina or not?"

"Okay, already," Smith capitulated. He touched his palm to his cheek to see whether she had drawn blood. "What can I do for you, young lady?"

"Carina," she corrected him.

"What can I do for you, Dr. Matthews?" This time, as Smith spoke, he motioned his four guests toward the front door of the Institute. A rush of cool air escaped the building as the automatic door opened wide.

"Chief Apostle Smith, I would like to have a gene-map printout on all my lineal ancestors going as far back as you have records."

"But that would take hundreds of manhours," he objected. "I can't spare that kind of time. Anyway, why do you need them? What is the point?"

Carina explained. "My father is ill. If there's any possible way, I would like to identify a close living relative, one that I can extract a donor gene from. With a complete template to work from, perhaps I can devise a cure."

"What you suggest is simply not possible," Smith harrumphed as the five of them pressed ever deeper into the caverns of the Genealogical Institute. "It is true, of course, that genetic markers for every common genetic disease were discovered long ago, along with the appropriate treatments. But no work has been done in a hundred years, and certainly not on defects narrow enough to affect only one family. Plus, as someone with your experience surely must know, the vast majority of genetic flaws are not the result of a single glitch in a person's DNA. The human genome is literally riddled with flaws. Yet, because there are so many built-in redundancies and duplications and subsystems designed to correct errors and fix oversights, it usually takes multiple failings before something really serious goes haywire. A gene is only a *piece* of DNA — it rarely represents a one-to-one link with a specific disease. Chances are, the defect you are looking for is the result of two or more *linked* genes, and they may not even be located on the same chromosome. This is not Mendelian genetics, for goodness sake — one gene, one trait — it's rather more complicated than that."

In her heart, Carina knew Smith was probably right. Even so, she couldn't help but feel as disappointed with his reply as she had been with Viscount Nordman's.

"But I've come all this way," she moaned, on the verge of tears. "How could I have reached such an impasse?"

For the first time, Chief Apostle Brigham Smith seemed to care. Seeing how dejected she had become, he offered her an alternative.

"Perhaps, instead of working backwards from the present, what we need is the name of an ancient ancestor of yours, along with an approximate date when he lived and died. Then, maybe we can work *forward* from there to the first Matthews with a gene-map on file."

Suddenly, Carina's eyes lit up with newfound hope — *Indeed, she knew of just such a person!*

THIRTY-THREE

Byron

By this time, the five of them had reached the Institute's meeting room deep inside the mountain. The room was modestly furnished, with a large board-of-directors-style wooden table, plus a dozen or more Shaker-style, straight-backed chairs. Tasteful music played in the background.

Chief Apostle Brigham Smith took a seat at one end of the long, rectangular-shaped table. Carina sat down across from him. Within easy reach of Smith was an info-terminal and keypad. He switched the unit on. The screen flickered briefly, then shone a pale green as it awaited his commands. As was his custom, Smith recorded the entire proceedings on a microdiskette with autotranscribe capability.

Carina placed her hands flat on the smooth tabletop. The polished wood felt cold to the touch, and she shivered involuntarily. The three others found a seat, and Carina began:

"As luck would have it, I happen to know the name of an ancient ancestor of mine. As a matter of fact, he was originally from somewhere around here. Private Byron Matthewson, of the 11th Cavalry. Died in the War Between the States."

"That's wonderful!" Smith exclaimed, his suddenly eyes lighting up. "Not that he died, of course. But that he was in the military. Even in those days, the militia kept fairly good records."

Smith's fingers glided swiftly over the keys as he began to enter search parameters into the computer. Somewhere down the hall, hidden from view, eighteen pairs of magnetic tape drives began to whir as the machine canvassed millions of entries for a match.

"How did you come to learn of this fellow?" Smith asked, his eyes fixed on the screen. Next to him, the microdiskette recorded everything the two of them said.

"My father. The man's like a walking history book."

"Lucky for you," Smith murmured approvingly. "Men like your father are rare. You did say Matthew*son*, didn't you?" he asked, confirming her earlier input. "Not Matthews."

Carina nodded.

"Now, if I recall my U.S. history correctly, the War Between the States dates to the early or mid 1800s." His fingers were paused on the cusp of depressing the ENTER key.

"1860s, to be precise," Sister Siona spoke up unexpectedly.

When everyone looked up in surprise, she explained. "I was a history major back in college. And yes, before you ask, that *was* before the Great War."

Tabbing backwards, Smith corrected his entry. "All our data is stored by decades. I'll set the range as being between 1860 and 1870 and see what we get."

The machine responded almost instantly to his inquiry. Brigham Smith skimmed nearly as fast down through the biographical information, summarizing outloud what appeared before him on the screen.

"According to the *Adjutant General's Report/Illinois*, Volume 8, covering the five-year period from 1861 to 1866, a Byron Matthewson is listed on page 290 as having enlisted in the 11th Cavalry, Company B, January 8, 1862. He died at Vicksburg, Mississippi, May 1862. His residence prior to enlistment is shown as Trivoli, Illinois."

"That's it?" Carina exclaimed, disappointed. "That's all you can tell me?"

"My dear woman, that was nearly six hundred years ago. I've already told you a great deal."

"There must be more," she said insistently. "What was his father's name? His mother's name? Did Byron have any children? Was he even married? Where in the world is Trivoli, Illinois, anyway? For that matter, where in the world is *Illinois*?"

"Patience, my dear. There is more. Like I said, the Army kept good records. And keeping track of family trees has been a project of the Church since the days of Joseph Smith. Don't forget, Mormonism got its start just down the road from here, in Nauvoo, Illinois. One branch of the Church was even headquartered in northeastern Missouri for the next three hundred and fifty years. Illinois, by the way, lies on the other side of the big river you crossed coming into Sane Lou. You drove across it when you came down from Chica."

"God, what a dismal place, this Illinois. All fields and flat land. Not like Zealand at all. What else can your machine tell me about Private Byron Matthewson?"

Though her tone was impatient, Chief Apostle Smith didn't seem to notice. He resumed reading from the screen:

"The *Adjutant General's Report* includes a <u>History of the Eleventh Cavalry</u>. Let's see whether it sheds any light on our Byron, shall we?

"Yes, here it is. In October of 1861, Robert G. Ingersoll of Peoria and Basil D. Meeks of Woodford County obtained permission to raise a Regiment of Cavalry and commenced recruiting at Peoria that very month. Twelve full companies were raised, and this Regiment of Illinois volunteers went into Camp Lyon at Peoria about November 1, 1861. They were mustered into the service of the United States on December 20 of that same year. The Eleventh Cavalry — that would be Byron's unit — was under the command of a Major James Johnson. The Regiment remained at Camp Lyon until February 22, 1862, when they broke camp and marched to Benton Barracks, Missouri, arriving there March third. Shortly thereafter, the recruits were armed with revolvers and sabres. One battalion was issued carbines."

"Now we're getting somewhere!" Carina exclaimed, taking notes as he talked. After so many setbacks, she found it hard to believe that she was finally getting some pertinent information. "Do go on."

"On March 25, the Regiment proceeded to the Tennessee River where, on April 1, the First Battalion landed at Crump's Landing. The balance of the Regiment landed the same day at Pittsburg Landing on the west bank of the Tennessee River about ten miles above Savannah. They camped about two miles from where they put in."

Even as Smith spoke, a computer-generated map popped up on the screen, each location he mentioned being illuminated in turn. By keeping an eye on the vid screen, it was easy to trace the Regiment's movements across Illinois, down the Mississippi, up the Ohio, and down the Tennessee.

His reading of the salient facts continued. "The Third Battalion, which included the Eleventh Cavalry, encamped on the north side of Snake Creek. On the sixth and again on the seventh of April, the Regiment was engaged in the great Battle of Shiloh, a bloody contest between the forces of General Ulysses S. Grant and General Albert Sydney Johnston . . ."

"Wow!" Sister Siona interjected. "It's all coming back to me now. Your man Byron was in the bloodiest land battle of all time. No way he could have come out of that thing alive."

Brigham Smith glared at her. "Keep quiet, woman, and let me finish. Where was I? Oh, yes. Following the death of Major James Johnson in battle on May 22, 1862, there were mass defections from the ranks of the volunteers.

In the months ahead, what was left of the Regiment participated in operations throughout southwestern Tennessee and northern Mississippi."

"Wait a second!" Carina interrupted, glancing at her notes. "Something doesn't add up here. Play back your recording. I thought you said Byron died at Vicksburg in May of 1862? Well, Vickburg's way down here," she said, pointing to the computer-generated map. "Now you're telling me his unit was engaged in the Battle of Shiloh in *April* of that same year. That's way up here," she said, pointing again. "There's an inconsistency here. According to this map, Vicksburg, Mississippi, was deep in Confederate territory at the time. How in the world did they fight their way all that distance in just a little over a month? And didn't I see on an earlier screen a list of all the pivotal battles of the war? I could've sworn it said the big fight at Vicksburg was in 1864, not 1862."

Flipping back to the previous window, Smith exclaimed, "By George, you're right! The Battle at Vicksburg *was* in 1864! It says right here in the commentary on the Eleventh Cavalry that one company of this Regiment, and one company alone — Company G — was detached from the rest of the unit in the fall of 1862, and that this was the only company from that Regiment to serve in the Vicksburg campaign of 1864. That's curious, because Byron was in Company B not G. I have to admit, this is all a bit confusing."

For a moment, no one said a thing. Then, like a flash of light, it hit her. "Maybe Byron didn't die at Vicksburg after all. Maybe he died at *Pitts*burg!"

"As in, Pittsburg Landing?"

"Precisely."

"Or maybe he was captured," Smith suggested, offering up a more plausible alternative. "It says here that all prisoners of war were taken to Vicksburg for recording, then held there indefinitely. Maybe he died in a POW camp."

Carina scratched her head. "Were there any other volunteers from his hometown? It had a funny name, as I recall."

"Trivoli."

"Yes, that's the one. It seems to me, the younger the man, the less inclined he would be to volunteer alone. He'd join up with friends."

"Makes sense," Smith agreed, flipping down through the computer-generated pages of the *Adjutant's Report*. He quickly fell upon an interesting entry.

"Yes, here's a Frank Hitchcock. Residence — Trivoli, Illinois. Enlisted — September 3, 1861. That's four months before Byron, by the way. Well, I'll be! It says here that he deserted in May of 1862."

"May 1862, eh?" Carina remarked. "Byron dies, so his buddy Frank deserts?"

"Looks that way."

"Or maybe they *both* deserted, only Byron gets listed as a casualty because some buffoon misidentifies the body. Sister Siona said it was a huge battle; there must have been bodies everywhere."

"So, if they deserted, where did the two of them go?" Smith asked, thinking her interpretation of events farfetched.

"Home," she answered in that petulant it-ought-to-be-obvious voice of hers. "It's May. Springtime in North America. No doubt these people were farmers. There were crops to put in."

Smith nodded as if it all made perfect sense.

"What information do you have on Byron's family?" Carina was in her element here; she reveled in the challenge of unraveling yet another mystery.

"Well, let's see. By all rights, Byron would still have been living at home in Trivoli during the time of the 1860 census. So, let's find out what the computer has to say about our friends the Matthewsons."

Punching a few buttons and manipulating a couple of dials, Brigham Smith set the machine to work scanning through the voluminous decennial census records. At light-speed it flew backwards, first to the exact decade, then on to the right state, then to the correct county, and finally, to the proper township. The screen flickered once, and he began to read:

"Here we go — On the rolls of August 1, 1860, a Matthewson family is listed with a rural address. Two parents plus seven children. Father — Benjamin Matthewson, age 48. Mother — Elizabeth (Betsy) Matthewson, age 39, born New York."

"That's quite a difference in age, wouldn't you say?"

"No, not really, not for those days anyway. Elizabeth may have been a second wife, for all we know. We'll check for that possibility in a minute. But one thing's for sure — the Matthewsons were pretty well off. The census lists their real estate holdings — probably farm ground — as being worth $6000. Their personal effects are valued at $1500."

"That doesn't sound like much. What's a dollar worth anyway?"

"Silly girl, it's all out of context. Not only do these figures probably underestimate the true extent of their wealth — after all, some taxing body probably based their levies on these highly-subjective self-appraisals — but there's been nearly six hundred years of inflation in the interim."

"What difference should that make?"

It was one of those typical Carina-type questions. It only served to point up her naiveté regarding all things financial.

Smith shook his head. "In the genealogy business, one can never lose sight of the old maxim that time is money. Compound interest, my dear — it's powerful stuff."

"How so?"

"I take it you are unfamiliar with the Rule of 72?"

"Never heard of it."

"Why doesn't that surprise me? Well, no matter. The Rule of 72. You divide a given rate of interest into the number 72, and that tells you how long it takes for a sum of money to double. At four percent, for instance, money doubles in eighteen years. Eighteen times four makes 72. At four percent, then, how many doublings per century?"

Carina quickly did the math. "Eighteen goes into a hundred, five times. With ten left over."

"And don't forget those leftovers, because they add up fast, especially at four percent. Okay, five doublings per century, but over how many centuries?"

"Six."

"So that's thirty doublings."

"Plus the ten years remaining from each century, makes sixty more, or three more doublings. Thirty-three in all."

"Precisely!" he exclaimed, his fingers flying over the keypad. "Now, if we take $7500 — which is the six thousand in real estate plus the fifteen hundred in personal effects — and double it thirty-three times, we get . . . wait a moment . . . wait a moment." He let out a low whistle. "Six point five times ten to the thirteenth."

"Wow."

"Wow indeed. Assuming, of course, that I entered the figures correctly, that would be a six followed by thirteen zeroes."

"That's an impossibly large number."

"Yes, it is. But don't necessarily assume that just because these people had a little bit of money they were living on easy street. In those days, the agrarian way of life was brutally hard and completely unmechanized. A little bit like today, I guess. And prosperity is never straightline — the Matthewsons had their setbacks along the way, just like everyone else. Plus, having enough hands to help with the chores was always a challenge. In fact, the August 1860 rolls show this couple as having seven children: Byron, age 20; Nancy, 16; Charles, 12; Mary, 7; John, 5; Sarah, 3; and Elli, 8 months."

"Sounds as if Lady Matthewson couldn't keep her knees together," Carina quipped immodestly, wondering whether all the women in her line had been equally lusty.

"It's a woman's duty to bear children," Chief Apostle Smith said, deadly serious. "And to do so without complaint. Now, can we please concentrate on the matter at hand?"

"By all means," she answered gravely.

"If Byron were 20 when this census was taken, that would have made him perhaps twenty-two when he died . . ."

"You mean when he deserted, don't you?" Carina interrupted, continuing to amend history as she saw fit. As was so often her way, the woman wasn't about to be swayed from her version of events. "What else can you tell me about Byron's parents? When were they married, for instance?"

"Give me a minute to switch reels," Smith said, his fingers clicking away at the keyboard. "Once the switchover is complete, it'll be a snap for us to check the marriage records. Let's see now — if Benjamin was 48 years old in 1860, he couldn't have been married before, let's say, 1827. And if Byron was age 20 in 1860 like the census says, he would have to have been born by 1840 or so. Assuming he was born in wedlock — which is a big 'if' for those days — we can safely use 1840 and 1827 as the upper and lower limits for our search. Benjamin was almost certainly married between those two dates."

It took a moment for the computer to complete its trace. "Here we go . . . Illinois . . . Peoria County . . . it's arranged alphabetically by last name. Here!" he exclaimed, slowing the scrolling screen down to a crawl. "Benjamin Mathewson — spelled here with one 't' — married Dorothy Thompson on November 4, 1838. The marriage was certified by a James Hitchcock."

"That would fit in nicely with Byron's date of birth as having been sometime in 1840," Carina remarked, "but let me check my notes — I could've sworn you said earlier that the mother's name was Elizabeth, not Dorothy."

"Yes, you're right. Here it is in the 1860 census — Elizabeth (Betsy)."

"Maybe Dorothy died."

"Then there would have been a second marriage," Smith replied enthusiastically. With each layer of the Matthews mystery they peeled back, his opinion of Carina rose. Smith was unaccustomed to working in tandem with a woman of such keen intellect. "Listen, Doctor Matthews, if you could stay with me awhile here in my world, we could do great things together. I sure could use a tenacious researcher like yourself."

Carina narrowed her eyes and gave Smith a queer look. She didn't have to put words to the unspoken answer, her eyes said it all — *You have got to be kidding.* Instead, what came out of her mouth was, "How do we find out whether or not there *was* a second marriage?"

Obviously peeved by the rebuff, Smith said, "Let me check. Nancy — child number two — was age 16 in 1860, so let's run a scan of the marriage records from 1840, the year of Byron's birth, to 1844, the year of Nancy's birth. Wait a minute . . . wait a minute . . . Here it is!" he said, pointing excitedly to the screen. "Benjamin Matthewson to Betsy Holcom. February 9, 1842. Witnessed by N.P. Cunningham, Minister of M.E. Church. Here Matthewson is spelled again with two t's."

"So Dorothy must have died giving birth to Byron . . . or else shortly thereafter."

"It would appear that way."

"Which means, of all the Matthewsons, only Byron had Dorothy's genes. All the rest of us — me included — carry Betsy's."

"How can you be so sure?"

"It only makes good sense," Carina answered. "Was Byron married? Did he have any children?"

"Not as far as I can see," Smith said, shaking his head as he checked his datafiles.

"So Byron might very well have been the last Matthewson not to be sickened by the damaged gene."

"If that were the case, that would make Betsy the carrier. But honestly . . ."

"And it would also mean that I'm out of luck. Now, if only I could go back in time and find out for sure," she mused before abruptly changing gears. "Did I hear you say that James Hitchcock performed Benjamin's first wedding?"

"I believe it said 'certified' but, yes, a James Hitchcock is listed as the witness of record."

"And didn't you say that a *Frank* Hitchcock, also of Trivoli, deserted the very *month* Byron was supposedly killed?" Carina cross-examined, eagerly playing the part of the detective.

"What are you getting at?"

Carina practically bubbled with enthusiasm. "What are the odds? Don't you see? *These families knew each other.* Frank deserted; so did Byron. It has to be." Her mind was made up.

Smith chuckled. "Let it never be said that you don't have a rich imagination, little one. I'm going to print this out for you," Smith said, touching a key. "And you may also have this microdiskette to listen to later on."

A few feet away a nearly silent printer spat out a page with several dozen lines of closely-spaced type. Smith took the sheet and handed it to Carina along with the microdiskette.

"Now, if only I could go back in time and find out for sure," she said again, accepting the printout from him. On it were all the details about Private Matthewson's life — his father's name, his mother's name, their rural address, the date of his supposed death, and his place of burial. She carefully folded the sheet Brigham Smith had given her and slid it into her pocket along with her own notes. When they were done talking, she would give BC the microdiskette for safekeeping. Later, once they began the long trip home, she would have to have it transcribed and put with her diary and e-pad.

"Well you can't physically go back in time," Smith harrumphed. "But there may be a way to do something almost as good — find out where Byron's buried, dig up his bones, and try to harvest his DNA that way."

"Honestly, after all this time, what are the chances of finding and positively identifying his remains?"

"Slim," Smith admitted, getting up from his chair and wandering down towards the opposite end of the room. For a while now, Sister Siona and BC had sat quietly at the other end of the long table, arguing about something or other. Though they had been doing their best not to raise their voices or attract attention, the two were clearly on opposite sides of whatever issue was being discussed. Doctor Killjoy wasn't taking sides.

"If not that, then what?" Carina asked, obviously at wit's end.

"There is another way," Smith said as he moved. "While it's not foolproof, it could narrow the field a bit."

"Tell me," Carina insisted, following him down to where the other three sat huddled. As she approached, a strange thing happened. No sooner had she come within earshot, then the three of them grew quiet. It was as if they were trying to hide some deep, dark secret from her.

Brigham Smith explained his plan. "If I had a fresh sample of your father's blood, I could run a cross-sectional analysis against the standard model and print out all the anomalies. We could see whether or not any of them matched up with our database of known cures."

"Why can't we just use a sample of my blood? Getting a sample from my father could prove to be rather difficult — that's assuming he would even agree to it in the first place."

"I'm afraid your blood won't be of much help," Smith replied. "For all we know, you may not even have inherited the defect. Anyway, why should drawing a sample of your father's blood be so darn difficult?"

"Trust me," Carina said. "He's not from around here."

"She's right," Killjoy suddenly spoke up. "The old man's not from around these parts. Isn't there another way?"

Smith thought for a moment. "It's a little more complicated and it would take several hours of computer time, but there is one last possibility. With a sample of Carina's blood, plus one from her mother, I could perform a backtrack analysis."

Killjoy shook his head. "What the hell's a backtrack analysis? I've never heard of such a thing."

"Don't imagine you would have," Smith acknowledged. "It's a technique we worked out here at the Institute. Think of it this way: Just as adding the number two to six gives you eight, subtracting the number six *from* eight gets you two. We've found that the same principle holds true in genetics. If I subtract your mother's genome from your own, whatever is leftover is your father's."

"That's amazing!" Killjoy exclaimed. "Simply amazing! You say your people developed this process?"

"It won't work," Carina said flatly. "I don't believe it'll work at all, and it certainly won't work in my case. My mother has been dead for thirty years."

Silence fell over the group, and in the stillness of that moment Carina's gaze shifted from BC to Doctor Killjoy to Sister Siona and back again. She saw anger in Sister Siona's eyes — and reluctance in BC's.

"What?" Carina asked, confused.

"Are you going to tell her?" This from Sister Siona to BC.

"Tell me what?"

BC turned away, unable to face either woman.

"Tell me what? Damnit to hell, what is going on?"

"Your mother may still be alive."

THIRTY-FOUR

Flames Of Desire

Saron bathed slowly, the warm water dancing against her nipples. Earth wasn't like Mars in this respect. Here, on the Home Planet, bathing was at once more pleasurable, more sensuous. Here, the water dripped from your body when you stepped from the tub. On Mars, with its lesser gravity, you had to literally *push* it away.

Even the water itself was different. On Mars, it was hard. Harder than what dribbled from a rusted spigot in a flea-bitten, dust-blown town out of the American West. Harder than what flowed from a shallow well in a dry gulch on the steppes of her native Afghanistan.

On the Red Planet, the water was too new, too laden with iron and sulphur and a dozen other minerals to make for first-rate bathing.

But here, in Sam's house in Zealand, the water was splendid! It was as if it had been percolating down through the soil to the bedrock-aquifers for a hundred million years — aging to perfection each inch of the way.

Back on Mars no one ever felt clean, not really. There, no matter how hard you scrubbed, no matter how much soap you employed, no matter how much time you took, there was always that inextinguishable film.

But here on Earth, oh Lord, a bath felt good. Only here, on Earth, with its soothing water and its blessed gravity, could a woman really get herself clean, squeaky clean the way a man wanted her to be. Only here on Earth, where the water was soft and sweet, could a woman experience the real pleasure of bathing. That's why, for Saron, this bath was an orgasmic journey.

Before entering the tub, Saron had turned off the harsh lights over the vanity and lit a pair of candles instead. To a woman like her, there was still something fiercely erotic about bathing by candlelight. And yet, there was more than mere eroticism at work here.

In all the many hours that she and Sam had spent together over the course of the past two years, never once had he let on about his great wealth. Oh, as proprietor of the Commons she had heard stories, plenty of them, especially from newcomers who had gathered here on the grounds of his estate in Auckland, waiting to be taken aboard the *Tikkidiw* for their flight to Mars.

But she never lent them much credence. Most of the settlers, especially the Newtons, were poor, after all, and desperate. Any house might have looked big to them, any direction might have appeared up. Who could blame them, really? To make a new friend, why not tell a stranger an exaggerated tale, why not boast about something even if it wasn't true? *But the strange thing was, it was all true — and then some!*

To begin with, the grounds outside Sam's home were exquisite and well-kept. And, once the windows were opened up to air-out the place, what lay inside seemed like something out of a fairy tale to her. For starters, just consider the bathroom she was presently in. Saron had never seen anything like it in her life!

It was one of those self-cleaning lavatories only the superrich could afford. Sam had talked her through its operation only the night before. When she was done bathing, all she need do was seal the bathroom door shut and manipulate a few knobs and dials. That would engage the auto-clean cycle. Recessed nozzles in the ceiling and each of the walls would open wide, and high-powered jets of soapy water would let loose, hosing the room down in its entirety. Tiny scrub brushes would follow a few moments later, working their magic on the porcelain walls, the toilet, the countertops and the vanity. Finally, when everything was clean, all the water would be flushed out through a drain in the floor. Blasts of hot air would bake the ceramic surfaces to a shine. Nothing could be simpler. Or more amazing.

As if the bathroom weren't enough to give Saron pause, the foyer and grand sitting room were crammed full with a wonderful collection of paintings, statues, and archeological finds. Every piece was of museum quality. On a small endtable next to his favorite chair was Sam's most prized possession — a portrait of his daughter taken perhaps five years ago.

But aside from that, the rest was an eclectic mixture of antiquities and objets d'art, including an Egyptian mummy case, a thousand-year-old suit of English jousting armor, a Scottish targe complete with steel pike, a mace, several shields, and an erotic bronze statue of a naked woman perched on her knees, head thrown back in a spasm of ecstasy, lithe body consumed with passion.

Saron splashed the water around her hips and assumed a like position in the bathtub. In her mind she pictured that naked wench wrapped in the throes of orgasm. The hot water pulsated against her body, against her tummy, against her breasts. She couldn't help but be aroused herself.

She took her hands and inspected her own, rather attractive frame. A smile came to her lips. Saron was a muscular and well-proportioned woman, not hard like an athlete, but soft like a woman ought to be. Her breasts were full and round. They rode high upon her chest, proudly surveying the fertile landscape beneath. These wonderful orbs had satisfied the cravings of many a man. Yet, they were little worse for the wear. Her buttocks were firm and tight, the center of her love as elastic as the day she first lost her flower.

Saron shifted her wet and glistening body in the sumptuous, oversized tub. She posed for the candle and the mirror, just as the naked model must have done for her artist, arching her head back and imagining herself joined at the hips to a man.

Suddenly, Saron was hot and burning with desire. The fire within her was ignited, and she moaned audibly. It was time, she thought, time to make Sam come upstairs and do his duty.

She bathed more quickly now, letting the hot water pour over her body until her fingertips were wrinkled and her nipples erect. The candlelight made the bathroom look orange and her skin copper. She washed her private parts carefully to make sure no smell remained. Then she grabbed a towel and rubbed herself dry, becoming further aroused in the process. Outside the house, a raindrop fell. Then another. And another.

Saron wore a white silk blouse with no bra so her nipples would show, plus a pair of sheer panties which barely covered her crotch. Sam was downstairs in the darkened kitchen, staring out over the back porch at the gathering storm. The window was open. Electricity filled the air. A flash of lightning briefly illuminated his face.

An unlit candle stood on the refrigerator. She took a match, lit the wick, then came and stood beside him, her arm brushing against his sleeve.

Sam was glad for the company and said so. The wind coursed along the floor, upsetting a stack of old newspapers, and climbing the walls to swing on the curtains. She leaned forward over the sink to pull the window shut, and as she did so, her sleek silk blouse rode higher, exposing the small of her back to his bright and hungry eyes.

Animated, Sam pressed himself flat against her from behind, tugging at her earlobe with his mouth and cupping her breast with his hand. The other hand probed further below, triggering a shock wave of desire to sweep through her loins. Saron shivered with delight.

Struggling not to lose control, Saron moved through the house shutting windows ahead of the storm. Sam followed playfully along close behind, squeezing her buttocks, rubbing her tummy and caressing her neck. When the last of the windows downstairs were closed, she paused before turning to face him. But when she did, he pulled her close, gripping her bottom with both of his hands and anchoring himself firmly against her pelvis.

The pace of their lovemaking was unhurried, even leisurely. She took his tongue in her mouth, and they kissed like this for a long time. Outside, the pace of the rain quickened. A roar of thunder rolled in from across the bay. Lost within themselves, the two lovers wandered slowly upstairs to the bedroom, kissing all the while. The candles in the bathroom were still burning, making their shadows dance against the wall.

He entered her with a sigh, moving back and forth and from side to side. She felt herself growing loose and warm as he sucked upon her nipples. Then she came in waves, waves so strong she felt herself vanishing beneath him. It took Sam an instant longer, but finally, he too erupted in a quivering climax of hot flesh.

Spent, he sank down on top of her. Outside, the rain came in sheets, and the thunder was like explosions inside a tunnel. A breath of wind leaked in through the open window and the candles were out.

Then they were too.

*   *   *

It was not the thunder that woke him, but the sound of a baby crying. Mother Nature had done a splendid job developing an alarm system guaranteed to roust a sleeping parent from even the deepest of sleeps. Along with the howl of a beagle, the rat-a-tat of a woodpecker, and the scrape of a fingernail against a chalkboard, few sounds were as grating, as distressing to a parent's ears, as the wail of a baby, especially the pangs of a little one bedeviled by colic. *That's why parents had to be young*, Sam thought as he dragged himself out of a warm bed half-asleep.

He trundled down the hallway, the one that connected the master bedroom to the rest of the upstairs. *I'm too old to be getting up in the middle of the night*, he told himself. Behind him, still half-naked, was Saron. She caught up with him, squeezed his hand, and smiled.

The touch of her hand changed everything for him. He relaxed, and his pace slowed. It was curious, but somehow, despite his age and deteriorating health, he had never felt quite so young and vital as he did right at that moment.

Saron meant everything to him. She was his fountain of youth, his elixir against growing old. Between the physical attention she constantly paid him and the mental stimulation of seeing his grandson maneuver through the first steps of the long labyrinth of life, Sam found his spirits lifted.

Sam had had his doubts at first. But pulling the boy out of the orphanage had been the right thing to do. Sam harbored no ill will against BC for placing him there; Sam might have done the same thing himself, given the cards he'd been dealt.

What else could BC have been expected to do? Raise the boy as a single father? Take care of the boy himself?

If there was anyone Sam should be angry with, that would be his daughter. But he buried that emotion down deep as he and Saron entered the boy's room. The nanny they hired back in England was already on the scene.

The boy was standing in his crib, bouncing up and down with delight. He had only recently found his legs, and was now babbling up a storm. The boy wasn't sick with colic at all. He just wanted attention. Too bad Mother Nature hadn't done an equally good job setting circadian rhythms as She had done perfecting the evolution of a child's wail.

Sam couldn't help but smile. The resemblance was uncanny. He had seen pictures of himself as a boy, and he looked just like him. Now, here he was, his grandson, standing up in bed and bouncing higher with each thrust of his legs. Sam couldn't help but think how much he and Sam, Jr. looked alike. Of course, a chasm of years separated the two, but the boy was unquestionably a Matthews.

It almost brought a tear to his eye to think how strangely these events had played themselves out. After J told him where to look, Sam had rushed to the orphanage with Saron. All he had when he arrived were questions. An hour later, most of them were still unanswered.

It had been a strangely detached conversation, with a woman as ancient and weather-beaten as the hills. The prehistoric old bird did her best to recollect events that had taken place thirty years earlier. But her mind was in a fog, and the details were sketchy.

Yes, a young woman *had* arrived on the front porch of the orphanage with a newborn in her arms one night long ago. Sorry, but the girl's name was not particularly memorable, nor was Mother Theresa's memory what it used to be. Yes, her name might have been Sara. But no, she couldn't be certain. Yes, she had been young and beautiful. But then, weren't they all? It was just something about new mothers. No, she didn't have any records dating back that far. Only the essentials had traveled with them when they made the move from the Hawaii Free State to the south of London. But yes, she was quite certain the cane had come to the orphanage at the same time as the baby.

As for the much more recent arrival of Sam, Jr., Mother Theresa was not likely to forget that day anytime soon. *This* infant had arrived along with a very nice honorarium drawn on the Exchequer of the Currency. Even so, the Mother Superior was delighted to find a permanent home for the lad, especially if a generous donation were to be offered as an inducement to rush the paperwork.

Sam didn't hesitate in the slightest. Not a poor man to begin with, the asteroid mining venture he and Fornax had cobbled together with ASARCO had made him wealthy beyond any one man's needs. He handed Mother Theresa a huge check on the spot. All he asked in return was the name of a reliable nanny he could hire to help look after the boy. This, she gladly gave him.

Nanna Purdy took to the boy immediately. More importantly, Sam, Jr. took to her. Even now, in the dead of the night, the smiling, red-faced matron was a passable surrogate-mother, cradling the little cherub in her thick, Lithuanian arms and doing her best to coax him back to sleep.

Sam was grateful for Nanna's attentiveness. After playing pattycake with the little guy for a few minutes, he and Saron drifted downstairs to let Nanna do her job. They had slept too long already and couldn't possibly go right back to sleep so soon. It was still raining outside, so they sat in the front room, poured themselves a glass of wine, and listened to the pitter-patter of drops against the porch roof.

"To the next generation of Matthews," Sam said, raising his glass in honor of his grandson.

"To the *current* generation of Matthews," Saron replied, clinking her goblet against his.

"To you, sweet child. Close friend. Intimate companion. May you live forever."

"So tell me, oh wise one," she teased, looking at him over the top of the glass. "Why do we make a toast whenever we salute someone's health or good fortune? I mean, what does *toast* have to do with it anyway?"

"Aah, it's no wonder I adore you so much, my dear. You always ask the best questions. Breaking bread with friends is one of the most ancient of traditions. In the early days, it was common practice to float a piece of toast in a glass of liquor. Some say this was to sop up the impurities in the alcohol. Others contend that it was to ensure that no one was forced to drink on an empty stomach. But, for whatever reason it got started, the bread floated on top until, fully sodden, it sank to the bottom of the glass. Voilà, the toast was born!"

"Unlike so many of your other tales, this one sounds totally made-up to me," she scolded playfully.

"Tsk, tsk, ye of little faith," Sam retorted. "I'll have you know, I never make up such things. And yet, I am reminded of another tale. A group of young men had just gathered to admire a famous beauty enjoying the mineral waters at Bath in Shakespeare's England. In an attempt to win her favor, one of the men dipped his glass into her bath water and drank to her health. Not to be outdone, another eager suitor leapt into the water alongside her and claimed the lady herself. As the story goes, he announced to his compatriots that, although he liked the liquor well enough, he would much rather eat the toast."

"Cheeky rascal, I take it you are still hungry?" There was a devilish twinkle in her eye as she spoke.

"You bet," he said, reaching out to her. "I won't have had my fill for a good long time yet."

THIRTY-FIVE

In Absentia

Roughly translated, an old Chinese proverb holds that every man has his price. Which is to say, so long as the prospective buyer hits upon the proper sum and the right form of payment, a person can be persuaded to do almost anything, even sell out his own mother.

For some, the ticket is sex. For others, cash. For still others, revenge or power. In each particular instance, it is simply a matter of identifying that particular person's need — and negotiating the proper price.

In Nehru Sher'if's case, there was a principle involved. And, like all good starry-eyed idealists, anything that furthered the cause had to be worth the risk. It didn't take much, therefore, to convince the man to betray a couple of his fellow Newtons.

To begin with, Nehru and Inda had been at odds for months already. And, to top it all off, Nehru thought of Lotha as nothing but a big dope. Thus, when Gunter and Cragit McPherson stopped by Nehru's hut for a chat one night not long after the Tovex bomb was discovered and defused, Nehru had plenty to say. The only problem was, he didn't have a stitch of proof to back up his suspicions.

Even on Mars, with its Icelandic-style government, a charge of sedition couldn't be taken lightly. Before any arrests could be made, tangible evidence had to be gathered and weighed. The question posed that day to Nehru Sher'if by Cragit McPherson, newly-installed Chief of Martian Security for ASARCO, was simple and direct.

Would Nehru be willing to help put a stop to all the rabble-rousing that was going on?

Nehru's answer had been equally simple and direct. *Yes, of course!*

And what, McPherson asked, *would be the price for Nehru's cooperation?*

A permanent seat on the Council, was Nehru's answer. *One with veto power. Plus, a company-built home for him and his family.*

Done! McPherson readily agreed, promising him whatever in the way of listening and recording devices he might need.

Shaking hands, Nehru set right to work learning what he could. An opportunity presented itself not long afterwards.

The two men Nehru was now spying on had spent the better part of the evening down at the Commons drinking. The place was a little rowdier now that Saron was gone with Sam on Earth, and the two men — Lotha and Inda — had taunted Nehru several times from across the room looking for a fight.

But when, after a couple of tries, he didn't oblige them, they gave up their efforts and settled into their chairs, a distant glazed look plastered across their grimy faces. Eventually, one of Saron's girls came over and told the two they had had enough to drink for one night and should go home. Surprisingly, though both men were roaring drunk, they didn't put up much of a fuss. After settling their bar bill, the pair left. Nehru followed at a safe interval, holding tight to the listening device McPherson had given him. It was good up to at least a couple hundred meters.

The more sober of the two was speaking. His voice was loud, making it easy for Nehru to hear what was being said:

"It began raining like hell one afternoon," Inda recounted, slurring every third or fourth word. "The little sheila was outside lookin' for her damn dog or somethin'. Well, anyways, the storm was like a monsoon and she gets all cold and wet and turned around. Then, all of a sudden, she gives up and sets down on the ground like she's gonna die. So I sees all this from my hut, and I go out to save the little wench. The next thing I know, she's ballin' me like there's no tomorrow."

"No shit?" Lotha barked, scarcely able to believe his ears.

Inda stopped, unzipped his pants and began to relieve himself against a big red boulder. Steam rose from the spot where his hot urine hit the cold ground.

"Oh, if only I could make up a story that good. On my mother's eyes, I swear it is the truth. But you wanna know what the irritating part is? The next thing I know, the little sheila's tearing at the pants of that Gunter fellow. Only, he's a homo or something, 'cause after their climb to the top of Omen, I learned from one of his Sherpas that he never even laid a finger on 'er."

By this time Lotha also had his pants open. He was too soused to realize he was dribbling on his own shoe. "No shit?" It was the same words spoken in the same drunken voice as before.

"I swear it's all true," Inda insisted. "Perhaps now you can understand why I hate her so much. She never shoulda parted her legs for me if she didn't mean to be my woman."

"So that's why you been secretly using her place to store weapons all this time? To get back at her?"

"Sure," Inda said, putting it back into his pants. "She'll be gone for who knows how long. If anyone should accidentally stumble across the stuff I've hidden in her hut, how're they gonna trace it back to me? To us?"

That's all Nehru was able to overhear. But it was enough. Small-minded man that he was, he had already indicted and convicted these two characters for treason. They were obviously using Carina's empty hut to conduct some sort of nefarious undertaking, and McPherson would almost certainly pay dearly for what Nehru had just learned. All he need do to clinch the deal was set up a listening device inside her hut, then record the two men's conversations for the next several days. And so it began.

Although it might be argued that in his own, woefully naive way, Nehru's intentions were perfectly honorable, the man was totally blind to the repercussions his actions would set in motion. The response to his initial report was swifter, and of a higher order of magnitude, than Nehru had been led to expect. Indeed, it smacked of overkill. Instead of just simply knocking down Carina's door to see what Inda and Lotha were up to inside, McPherson promptly notified Oskar Schaeffer of his findings. Less than twenty-four hours later, Schaeffer ordered a company of private troops brought in from Earth. Because the only ship capable of moving that many men that fast was the *Tikkidiw*, the job of transporting these mercenaries fell to Fornax.

Let it only be said ahead of time that Fornax was not a willing participant in this "police action." From the outset, he balked at the idea of bringing in troops to quell this so-called uprising. As far as he was concerned, Schaeffer's policy of containment was shortsighted, overly harsh, and would eventually blow up in his face.

But Schaeffer held all the cards. In an emergency meeting of the ASARCO Board of Directors, Fornax was reminded that the company had already made a huge capital investment in this asteroid harvesting project, and that he, too, had a personal stake in its outcome. The issue was not whether or not he agreed with their methods, but whether or not they would even choose to continue doing business with him if he didn't cooperate. The smelters belonged to the company, after all, not to Fornax, and if he didn't comply fully with their demands, they would simply cut him and Sam out of any future profits from the deal.

Without Sam at his side to help bolster his position, Fornax found it impossible to resist the company's demands. The Board of Directors was not about to risk having the company's motor plant blown to bits by a handful of disgruntled settlers — and there was nothing Fornax could do or say to stop them from taking this step to protect their investment. His instructions were to pick up a contingent of men from the spaceport and transport them in the *Tikkidiw* to Mars. After that it would be out of his hands and up to them.

On the day of the raid, a heavy fog hung over the colony. It was as if Ares himself were doing what he could to hide the painful truth from the rest of the galaxy. All Fornax really knew in advance was that the security teams he had flown in with him from Johannesburg were going to hold Inda and Lotha for questioning, then establish a round-the-clock presence outside on the grounds of the motor facility plus inside on the factory floor itself.

Had Fornax known what was *really* going to happen, he never would have permitted himself to be talked into this course of action in the first place.

But then again, Fornax was in the dark about a great many things, least of which was that Oskar Schaeffer himself had been the one who had originally armed Inda Desai and the rest of the Newtons to begin with.

Had Fornax known *that* truth, he probably would have shot the man on the spot. Even so, with all the preparations going on around him on the day of the raid, Fornax should have caught on. Had he been paying closer attention to the details, maybe the end result wouldn't have come as such a surprise.

For starters, Fornax should have been alerted to the double cross on the basis of sheer numbers alone. When it came time to make the pick-up, in excess of a hundred fully-equipped men boarded the *Tikkidiw* for the trip to Mars. When Fornax questioned McPherson on this point, the man justified it by explaining that a contingent of a hundred men amounted to only thirty-five per eight-hour shift. *Now, thirty-five's not so many, is it?*

Once again, Fornax was put on the spot and had to reluctantly give in. Who, after all, was going to argue with a hundred armed men? These weren't ordinary men, mind you — anyone could see that. They were a crack unit of the White Brigade — mercenaries feared in their own country for their extremely cruel and unusual methods. Now they were on his planet, rounding people up. Much of what happened next was beyond his control.

On the ground, the "peacekeepers" moved with dispatch. After dividing up into two heavily-armed garrisons, the expeditionary force fanned out, with one garrison arresting everyone who had gathered at Saron's Place, while the other made a hut-to-hut canvass of the entire colony.

Then, as the Newtons were rounded up in groups of two or three, they were cuffed, thrown into a landrover, and transported to the motor factory where a temporary holding pen had been set up outside. The guards kept control of the pen with electronic whips. Inside an hour, they were holding more than two hundred men, women and children as prisoners. Lotha and

Inda were among the last to be brought in. They had already been badly beaten by the time Fornax arrived on the scene. He couldn't believe his eyes.

"What in the *hell* are you two doing?" he demanded of McPherson and Gunter as the two bloodied prisoners were dragged from the landrover and shoved roughly to the ground.

"Cleaning house," McPherson answered. His voice was calm and unhurried as if he had done this sort of thing before. "It's actually much like dealing with the bubonic plague — first you exterminate the rats, then you burn the village down."

"You must be mad!" Fornax exclaimed. "Have you gone and lost your head? Who in the world do you think you are anyway? You don't have that kind of authority here."

"Don't be an idiot," McPherson answered. "ASARCO has a fortune sunk into this place. Did you think they were just gonna let a pack of lowlifes wreck it all for them? Hell, you and Matthews ought to be thanking these soldiers, not castigating them. They're here to protect your investment, you unappreciative fool!"

"You know damn well that Sam would never have agreed to this!"

"Hah! That old fossil? He doesn't care. He's too busy boinking that bim Saron to care. Hell, if he objects, he can file a complaint with the magistrate in Johannesburg."

"A lotta good that'll do him — you've got every judge on the bench in your pocket."

"That does make life somewhat easier, I'll grant you," McPherson said with mock pride. "Now step aside and let me do my job," he said, stealing a satisfied look at the silent Gunter standing next to him.

"And if I don't?" Fornax roared.

"You'll be detained as well."

Discomforted by McPherson's reply, Fornax's head drooped. He had hoped that Gunter would at least speak up in his defense. But when he didn't, a look of resignation spread across his face.

"Gunter, you of all people should understand the social dynamics of the situation here on Mars. Incarcerating these people isn't going to change a thing. Anyway, what's to become of them?" Fornax asked, motioning with a single sweep of the hand to the hundreds of Newtons being held prisoner against their will. Many were shivering in the cold night air, still dressed only in the bedclothes they were wearing when the White Brigade struck. All wore faces of fear.

For a second, it looked as if Gunter might agree with Fornax. But before he could say anything, McPherson jumped in.

"I'm touched you should even care what happens to these heathens," McPherson said, his answer laced with contempt. "But to answer your question, after we're done interrogating the ringleaders, we're gonna load every last one of them aboard your ship and take the whole bunch back to Earth to stand trial. The courts will dispose of them in their own time."

"You bastard!" Fornax reacted, tightening his fist. But before he could act, Lotha and Inda were thrust between them by a guard. Though bruised and bloody, the two were still putting up quite a fight as they struggled to get free of their restraints.

"You're too late," Inda spat, blood oozing from a gash on his cheek and another on his bare left arm. He met McPherson's gaze without flinching. "It's already done."

"What's already done?" McPherson asked, the color draining from his face. His first thought was that this cretin had set another Tovex bomb to go off inside the factory.

"Newton's First Law," Inda said, perfectly aware that his words held a double meaning. "An object in motion tends to stay in motion unless an outside force acts upon it."

"What is this, a physics lesson?" McPherson scowled, glaring first at Fornax then at Gunter. "Do you understand what this velcroid is saying?"

"I haven't a clue," Fornax advised darkly. "Why don't you ask him yourself?"

"Splendid idea," McPherson said, turning to address the guard standing beside him. "You heard the man. Ask our guest to explain himself. But by all means, ask him politely," he said, motioning with his chin to the electronic whip in the mercenary's hand.

At McPherson's suggestion, the man from the White Brigade permitted a tiny smirk to escape his lips. It was only too obvious from the sick and twisted look on his face that this man enjoyed his work. He moved so fast, Fornax didn't even see the man flick his wrist.

The snap of the whip was followed by a spray of blood. Inda didn't even have time to cry out before he crumpled to the ground with a spasmodic lurch.

Now, with the pagan display of the e-whip's awesome power complete, McPherson turned to address Lotha. "Now tell me, you big ape, what exactly have you two done?"

"Go fuck yourself!" Lotha bellowed fearlessly, moving suddenly to body-tackle the man holding the whip.

Though his hands were shackled, his feet were not. Lotha jammed his foot into the man's groin with every ounce of his considerable strength, breaking the guard's pelvis with a single Herculean blow. Swinging around, now, he turned to go after McPherson. But before he could act, three others brought him to the ground. As Lotha lay there panting, McPherson drew his sidearm.

"Now, I'm going to ask you one last time. What is all this doubletalk about Newton's First Law? And what did Inda mean when he said it had already been done?"

Lotha looked at Fornax with accusing eyes. *This is your fault*, he said without words. For the first time, Fornax saw that Lotha was right. In the short run, though, there wasn't a damn thing he could do about it. The best thing he could do for the moment was help Lotha avoid Inda's fate. For Lotha, the only way out of this was to give McPherson what he wanted.

"For your own sake, Lotha — tell the man what he wants to hear. Tell him what Inda meant by that remark."

By every human standard, Lotha was an ugly man. To say that he looked truly fearsome when he spoke, now, would be an understatement.

"If there is a God, you three had better pray he is forgiving. Inda Desai, proud member of the Newton Liberation Party, has closed down your damn mining company. Only, you're not smart enough to know it yet."

By this time, two grim-faced medics had arrived on the scene. They began attending to the man whose pelvis had been crushed. As they bent over the man, preparing to administer a shot of morphine, another team of uniformed men arrived, their arms laden with explosives and bomb-making materials. The team leader, dressed in full kevlar gear, spoke:

"We searched the girl's cabin like you said. The Afghan snitch was right. That's where they've been making the bombs alright."

"What girl's cabin?" Fornax asked, staring in confusion at the quantity of timers, fusers, and empty vials of Tovex.

"Bag it for transport," McPherson said, ignoring Fornax. "Bag it all. We'll need it for the hearing. Then start loading these people onboard the *Tikkidiw*. We'll be leaving for home soon."

"What girl?" Fornax repeated sternly. "What hearing?"

"Your old girlfriend," McPherson said smiling. "She's the one who's behind all this. She's the ringleader."

"Carina? You must be nuts! She couldn't organize a shopping trip, must less an insurrection. She isn't even *here* for Christ sake!"

"It doesn't matter where she is. The bomb that nearly blew up the motor factory was assembled in her hut, as was whatever else these two kooks cooked up. My boss knows all about this one. She's been preaching weird stuff for a long, long time. Put her away and we quell the whole thing."

"I must protest." This time it was Gunter who spoke up. He had been uncommonly quiet since this whole episode began. "Listen, Cragit, I know this woman very well, and I certainly don't subscribe to your interpretation of these events. Carina Matthews is many things, but a terrorist is not one of them. Leave the woman out of this."

McPherson's tone was downright mean. "The evidence is irrefutable. Anyway, you're just soft on her because she probably fucked your brains out on the side of that big mountain. You. Fornax. Every man she meets. There's not a one of you who hasn't fucked that slut."

In the next moment, it was a fair question whether Fornax or Gunter would be the first to reach Lieutenant Cragit McPherson's throat. But at the crack of an electronic whip, both men held their ground.

"Do you want these two men punished?" the senior guard asked, hoping the answer would be yes.

"Naw. But I do want a warrant *in absentia* issued for the arrest of Carina Matthews. Be certain a copy is sent to all agencies, including every port authority, every station, every municipality and jurisdiction. Don't miss a one. The woman's to be considered armed and dangerous."

"Yes, sir, whatever you say," the head guard declared, clicking his heels Johannesburg-style and goose-stepping away.

Turning to Gunter, now, McPherson smiled. "It would appear that your girlfriend is headed for the gulag."

THIRTY-SIX

Nasha

Finding their way back from the New World to the Old proved to be a more formidable challenge than Carina first supposed.

After saying goodbye to Chief Apostle Brigham Smith and the Genealogical Institute, Doctor Killjoy returned the three of them to Sane Lou. Carina's gcar was not where she remembered leaving it. BC never even had a gcar to begin with. He had hitched a ride into town aboard a coal-burner. Thus, they were left without transportation back to Chica.

Sister Siona suggested they take a paddlewheeler downstream into N'Orleans instead. Though this rowdy river town was filled with drunks and bimbookers, it was one of the few places in the heartland with suborb service across the Atlantic. The group came to a decision quickly, and headed for the docks.

It was a trip of several days' duration, and an uncomfortable one at that. All three of them had to share a tiny, unkempt cabin outfitted with just a single bed and one rickety chair.

Still, Carina was happy to be away from Sane Lou and everything it represented. Being out on the big, muddy river was a novel experience for her, one that she found deliciously refreshing despite the lousy food and inadequate accommodations. BC, too, seemed at ease. To hear him talk, she began to think this was the sort of life he had always dreamed of having for himself.

They stood on the promenade deck and leaned out over the rail. He stood next to her, as close as he had been in days. Carina let the man talk, and for the first time since they met, she saw his inner self. BC was a man after all, with feelings and hopes and dreams. He could be philosophical too, in a way she never recognized before.

There are two types of boys, BC said, the astronaut and the astronomer. The astronomer wants to see it all, but from the comfort and safety of his chair. The astronaut wants to *do* it all, no matter what the risk. BC saw himself as the latter.

But there was more to it than that. How one traveled went a long ways towards defining the man. Riding high in the saddle on horseback across the open prairie defined the cowboy. Flying in tight formation, strapped into the cockpit of a high-tech fighter, defined the pilot. Rolling along in an expensive, foreign-built roadster oblivious of the speed limit defined the successful upstart. Standing alone at the helm of a smoke-belching sternwheeler defined the riverboat captain. Though their best days were past, there was a time when a riverboat captain outearned a United States president. Even now, these rough-hewn men still plied their trade along the dirty, blue highways of North America.

Carina had never been aboard a riverboat before, nor seen a flowing body of water this large. And yet somehow, she felt at home here. Of course, the glamour which existed in the days of Mark Twain had long since evaporated. But the fact that her father was named for Samuel Clemens, the legendary riverboat captain turned author, made the whole experience that much more authentic. In each cabin, courtesy of the management, was a copy of Twain's *Life on the Mississippi*. It told of a time she could only imagine, a time when people lived on grand plantations, when big shoofly fans were manned by black slaves and homes were a marvel of splendid architecture. Like a veiled beauty, the Mississippi River was choosy about whom she revealed herself to. Her currents were swift and cold, her muddy water deep. For endless kloms, levees on both banks of the river blocked Carina's view inland, and the farther south they went, the more time warped backward with remnants of the Civil War visible everywhere.

Chugging their way downstream, the threesome had plenty of time on their hands, with nothing to do but read and talk. This was good in a way, because Carina had not yet gotten over the shock of learning that her mother might still be alive.

Had Carina been left to her own devices, she might very well have dropped everything and set off in search of her. But BC wouldn't hear of it.

First of all, there was no easy way for a woman to go west across America from Sane Lou, something she would have had to do to reach Edmonton, Canada, where Sister Siona had last known Nasha to have lived.

But there were other reasons. BC was due back in London, and Sister Siona herself wasn't about to let the man out of her sight until he had fulfilled his promise to her of getting her onboard a spaceship headed for Mars.

Thus, Carina had no choice in the matter — she had to resign herself to first going east. From N'Orleans she could reach London, and from London she could board a second suborb for Toronto via Reykjavik. She could then fly on to Calgary and later Edmonton. It was curious. But sometimes the shortest distance between two points was not a straight line at all.

Up on deck, now, with plenty of idle time to fill, Carina's questions were always the same: What could Sister Siona tell her about her mother? About her life? About her "death"?

About her life: Nasha was a sweet, intelligent woman of Amerind descent. She lived only to make those around her proud, finding no greater joy than having a husband who loved her, a father who cherished her, a brother who respected her, and a daughter who would follow faithfully in her footsteps.

As they stood on the deck, now, Sister Siona related a story which revealed something of Nasha's view on life. When asked by a status-conscious female classmate why she didn't aspire to a high-powered career like the one she had chosen for herself, Nasha gave an answer which Siona would never forget as long as she lived. It encompassed everything there was to say about men, about women, and about marriage:

Women want security, Nasha said, and men want attention. When a woman establishes herself in a career, she jeopardizes her marriage twice over. By finding her own security, she proves to her man that he is not as necessary as he once was. And, by busying herself with her job, she gives her man less of the only thing he wants from her to begin with, and that is attention. It is a fact of life that a woman is asked about her husband, whereas a man is asked about his rank. Nasha found nothing wrong with that, and the female classmate in question never spoke to her again.

About her death: This Sister Siona had pieced together only years later, after the fact, when she and Nasha met again by chance. Some of it came secondhand from Nasha's brother, Dark Eagle. Sam and Nasha hadn't been married long and she — Carina — was perhaps two years old at the time. The country was going berserk right before their eyes, and Amerinds like Nasha were the scapegoats.

The horrible nightmare that led to Nasha's "death" began early in the morning of a searing hot summer's day. It was the seventh consecutive day with a predicted high exceeding thirty-two degrees centigrade, a rare circumstance for a city as far north as Calgary.

But, in keeping with their daily routine, Sam, Nasha, and their baby girl departed just after sun-up from their musty, overheated flat at the edge of the sprawling metropolis, and headed downtown. Though the two of them didn't earn much, between Nasha's job at the driver's license bureau and Sam's summer teaching position, they were able to keep themselves in groceries.

Sam's rattletrap of a gcar groaned and creaked as it protested yet another trip into the city. Newer vehicles could ride the automated rail, which made commuting easy, but these two young people were oblivious to their poverty. Each was happy, and life was good.

Between talking to the baby and to each other, they listened off and on to the radio for the early morning news as they headed downtown. According to the broadcast, last night in the Amerind ghetto-district — a war zone sandwiched between the buildings of the gleaming downtown and the fashionable homes of the unending suburban ring — there had once again been sporadic gang-related trouble.

Sam was eager to learn the details of what had happened overnight. But he was distracted by the rush hour traffic as well as the commotion of watching Nasha feed Carina breakfast next to him on the front seat. Not until after he had deposited Carina with her grandmother for the day and dropped Nasha at the provincial offices where she clerked, did he have a chance to turn up the radio and give the newscast his full attention. What he heard made his eyes wide with disbelief.

According to the commentator, there had been a severe bout of street fighting during the night, plus several reported instances of vandalism on the fringe separating the Amerind ghetto from the innermost ring of suburbia. Apparently, a gang of drunken Amerind teenagers had hit the streets enraged over an incident the *previous* night, one in which a Mountie had purportedly shot and killed one of their peers over a trifling.

Clearly, the extremely hot and humid weather was getting to everyone, Sam included. Though he was still blocks away from the college, his body was already drenched in a pool of sweat as yet another unbearable day of blazing heat took hold. The angry young men prowling the streets of the city were like loose molecules in a very unstable social fluid, a highly-flammable fluid now on the verge of igniting. This was the meltdown phase of Chaos in action, the phase where tiny perturbations exploded into devastating consequences, the phase where recursive, interlocking events fed upon themselves until calamity resulted.

As Sam approached the grounds of the university, he realized that roadblocks had been established at two major intersections. There were swarms of police sporting riot gear with military-style helmets and brandishing automatic weapons. Some held force guns out in front of them like cattle-prods, others were sitting astride massive bio-stallions.

Sam was astounded. Never before had he seen so many Mounties together at one time. But he didn't make the connection between the newscast and the police presence. Perhaps he missed it on the news and an important foreign dignitary was expected soon on campus, or the provincial mayor. In any event, it was none of Sam's concern and he went straightaway to his tiny office, where he began reviewing the thick pad of notes he had made for his upcoming morning lecture.

Sam's first class was abuzz with news of a confrontation that had occurred on the lawn of the university within the hour. His students related how a mob of hoodlum prairie-niggers had stormed a police barricade, killing two officers and injuring a dozen more in the attack. The troopers had responded by cracking a few skulls with their billy clubs and arresting scores of protestors. There were even unconfirmed reports of deaths among the demonstrators. One piece of gossip had it that a rowdy bunch of Euros dragged an Amerind girl down into an underground satrap where she had been raped and murdered.

Sam settled the students down as best he could. But by lunchtime, the university was in pandemonium. There were stories of bloody face-offs throughout the city, plus rumors of riots and looting in the financial district where Nasha worked.

Alarmed by these developments, Sam tried to call Nasha's office from the public comm. But the line was dead and he couldn't get through. Apparently, the violence had already spread to the Underneath, where the trunk lines were buried. All the comm-links had been cut.

Distraught over not being able to reach his wife, Sam did what he could to quell his mounting fears. He dutifully went across campus to teach his afternoon class. From a roster of seventy-five, only three students showed up for class. What they had to report made him gasp for air.

The Prime Minister had been shot. The assassin was alleged to have been an Amerind. Fearing an uprising, the Deputy Minister had declared an immediate state of emergency. He ordered the arrest of all Amerinds in the district, especially those holding government posts. The miscreants were to be held without bail, at least through the weekend or until the full extent of the conspiracy could be uncovered.

Sam was stunned by the news and immediately cancelled class. As he left the room, his only hope was that Nasha's job at the provincial offices where she worked was too inconsequential to merit arrest, that Nasha herself was too unimportant for the authorities to bother with.

Even so, Sam wasn't taking any chances. Determined, now, to rescue his woman from the holocaust before it was too late, he raced down the corridor at top speed.

Outside the lecture hall, Sam was engulfed by a mob of frantic students. His breath came in labored gulps. The air was heavy and humid, with an acrid smell to it, like sulphur. It made him nauseous.

Sam twisted his head in desperation, lost as to what to do. He had been unable to raise Nasha on the comm. The exits from the parking deck were blocked, so he couldn't get to his gcar. There was no way to flag a taxi or board a bus. That left him only one option — to make his way on foot the twenty plus blocks to the driver's license bureau, where the two of them first met.

The going was slow. The streets and sidewalks were filled with people, many running but in no particular direction.

Sam grew more and more panicked with each block. Sirens constantly wailed in the distance. The sounds grew nearer, and more urgent. The closer he drew to the marble-columned edifice where she worked, the more often he was passed by paddy wagons filled with bloodied prisoners. Nervous tears ran down his face.

The granite steps leading up to the palatial building were thick with uniformed guards. It was obvious from the commotion outside that no one was being permitted to enter or leave the premises without prior clearance. Then, just as he was about to cross the street to inquire as to the whereabouts of his wife, Sam was suddenly approached from behind by a Mountie perched atop a sleek-coated bio-stallion. The big man held a force gun out in front of him like a medieval pike.

The two exchanged words and then the Mountie signaled Sam to move on. This Sam did with dispatch.

Guided now only by instinct, Sam melted into the crowd. He had but a single goal in mind — to reach his baby daughter before the lunacy unfolding around him could spread further, before the police could fan out and arrest every Amerind in the land.

Sam loosened his tie and dropped his satchel of books to the ground. He accelerated his stride, first to a trot, then to a run, sprinting one city block after the next, oblivious to the mind-crushing heat that rose up from the concrete to meet him.

Sweat poured off his body like a waterfall. But he didn't dare stop to rest or replenish his fluids. His head began to pound and his sides began to spasm. But still he pressed on. It was imperative he get to Carina, get her to safety before the tidal wave of hysteria flooding the country drowned her along with everyone else.

Somehow Sam made it, and he and the child managed to escape. But so far as Sister Siona knew, he never saw or heard from his wife again. Thousands of her kind perished that day or in the days ahead, so it was a fair assumption for him to have made that he had lost her forever. Plus, there was no way for him to find out for certain, at least not without endangering himself and the baby.

The irony was, Nasha survived! Somehow, despite the odds, she managed to hang on, though what happened next scarred her for life.

Those that survived the initial purge were exiled to an Alaskan gene-extinction camp. It was a nightmare unlike any Nasha could ever have dreamed possible.

Auschwitz was a Disneyland by comparison, and *it* had been the first thoroughly modern death camp put into service, a place where factory-efficient methods for butchering people were tested and honed to criminal perfection.

Godzded, Rontana's death city nestled in the mountains of Persia, was a quiet weekend retreat compared with this, and *it* had been the site of unspeakable horrors, including the dismembering and consumption of young children.

Yet, what Nasha faced on the tundra of the North Slope was worse. Without exception, each day of the brief summer brought air heavy with humidity and thick with mosquitoes. The blanket of bugs was so thick, Nasha got them stuck in her teeth whenever she parted her lips to eat or drink, so thick she had to spit them out if she didn't want to gag.

During the long, dark winter, it was cold and desolate, so desolate the guards stayed indoors and drank tortan-ale all day long. No one cared if a prisoner wandered off. It was a thousand kloms to the nearest village, and no man alive could survive that kind of exposure to the elements.

Had the prisoners been able to air their grievances, they would have had plenty. The conditions were intolerable, the place itself inhuman.

Nasha's tormentors were monsters. Without end, they constantly touched her private parts with their grimy hands, constantly made her do unspeakable things for a mere morsel of food.

All around her, prisoners were constantly being beaten with clubs, constantly being battered, pounded, and smashed until they were taught the first lesson of a concentration camp — *To be alive was punishable by death.*

For Nasha, surviving the brutalistic torture was a quest, not a goal.

But how many times can you be raped before being reduced to tears? How many times can you be beaten before agreeing to say whatever they wanted to hear? How many times can you be whipped before giving up and dying?

The answer depends on what you expect from life, on what you expect to come after. If there is a light at the end of the tunnel, no matter how dim, you press on. But if that light is extinguished, if all you see ahead of you is kloms and kloms of darkness, then why bother? You just curl up and die.

Giving up would have been easy. Giving in, easier still. Nasha did neither. Though scarred and brutalized beyond words, the woman clung to life, never yielding, never losing faith, never surrendering.

And then one day it happened — the Liberators marched into camp and set them all free!

It was a momentous occasion. But when the Liberators saw and heard how the Amerind prisoners had been treated, how not even the slightest tinge of compassion had ever been paid them, no guard's life was spared.

In a savage frenzy of retribution, those prisoners who still had the strength, fell upon their captors. They cut off their fingers, their toes, their arms, their heads, their penises. *Who could say what was right and what was wrong?*

*   *   *

Sister Siona finished her story. But not without regret. Carina stood next to her white-faced. She was stunned by what Sister Siona had told her. The tears, once started, would not stop. For hours they flowed, until Carina could cry no more.

How could she have been so stupid? No wonder her father had tried all these good many years to make Carina understand, to make her understand the evils of persecution. No wonder it had upset him so, that she had turned a deaf ear to his admonitions.

Now here she was, on the deck of a ship in the middle of nowhere, faced with a new reality. If nothing else, Siona's explanation had shed new light on her father's view of the world.

The volume of tears slowly decreased and Carina began to compose herself. In bits and pieces she found herself coming more and more around to her father's perspective.

She finally understood, at last, why he thought so little of her reckless push to set up a separate colony on Mars, a colony reserved solely for newhumans. He was afraid some sort of purge would erupt, sweeping her and the rest of the Newtons away, like the storm that took her mother. And though she had no way of knowing it, *that was exactly what was happening in her absence!*

*   *   *

When at long last, the circuitous trip via N'Orleans was over and the suborb set down in London, it should have been a simple matter of BC and Sister Siona saying goodbye to Carina and she going on her way. It turned out to be rather more complicated than that.

No sooner had they stepped off the suborbital transport in Heathrow and passed through immigration control than a pair of bobbies approached, one holding tight to an official-looking form, the other to an enforcer bar.

"Carina Matthews?" the man with the form asked, comparing her face to the picture at the top of the sheet.

Without thinking, she nodded in the affirmative.

"I have a warrant for your arrest."

"On what charge?" BC intervened, reaching for his blaster.

"Don't be foolish, sir," the bigger man warned, jabbing the enforcer bar against BC's ribs. "Our orders are quite specific."

"What is the charge?" BC repeated, looking anxiously over at Sister Siona for support.

"Sedition," came the curt reply.

"What are you talking about?" This time, it was Carina who was asking the questions. "I've done nothing wrong."

"We have our orders, ma'am. Now, if you'll just come along quietly. We don't want any trouble."

"Where are you taking her?" Siona asked, looking desperately back at BC to do something.

"The gulag," the officer answered, handing BC a certified copy of the warrant.

"BC?" Carina cried, her eyes filling with tears.

"Be strong, girl," he answered. "I'll get to the bottom of this."

And then, she was gone.

THIRTY-SEVEN

Dante's Inferno

East of Johannesburg

Carina stood outside the gates of hell and looked in. What she saw made her skin crawl.

What had her father always said? *The status quo hates to be upset.* Well, after spending the better part of her adult life doing everything she could to upset the status quo, now it seemed as if she were about to be made an example for her indiscretions.

The status quo in the science of evolution had always been Darwin. Carina took him down with her treatise on Explosive Diversity.

The status quo in the philosophy of religion had always been an innate belief in a single, immutable God. Carina upset things not by declaring that God was dead, but that He didn't exist at all, never had.

The status quo forming the foundation for humanity's egocentric smugness was the body of man himself. Carina knocked those supports away by declaring *Homo sapiens* obsolete, then posited herself as the heir apparent. Oh, the arrogance of it all!

*　　*　　*

Carina stood at the very gates of hell. She looked in. What she saw made her stomach turn.

Galileo had gone to prison for declaring that the Sun, not the Earth, was the center of the universe. Durbin had been incarcerated for suggesting that General Relativity was all wrong, that objects *could* move faster than the speed of light. Therefore, time-travel *should* be possible. Krakow for proving there *was* more than enough dark matter in the cosmos to halt the universe's expansion, thus dooming it to collapse into a lifeless singularity.

But what was *her* crime, and how would *she* be made to pay?

Smashing ideological pedestals had been a favorite pastime of her idol, the twentieth-century geologist Stephen Jay Gould. In fact, her research into biogenetics had been in Gould's tradition, only difference being, she had taken his thinking to its logical conclusion.

If, as Gould postulated, the progress of life on Earth was not survival of the fittest but rather survival of the *luckiest*, then the rise of man was the most unlikely result of all. And, if that were the case, *H. sapiens* was not a permanent fixture on the planet, but instead a poorly-designed intermediary waiting impatiently for a newer model to arrive. Newhumans — of which she was the first — were but an incremental improvement on that original sentient design. It was *this* revelation which gave weight to the cross she would now have to bear.

*   *   *

Carina stood at the very turnstiles of hell. Unable to look away, she was sickened by what she saw.

For the last thousand years, every gulag had been the same, no matter what its name. The same drawn faces. The same haunting, vacant stares. The same cold-blooded guards using the same tools to inflict the same pain. It was in this godless place called a gulag that the line between humanity and inhumanity blurred, that the basest of animal instincts revealed themselves, that people learned how much agony they could endure before they folded.

*   *   *

Now it was over. Carina no longer stood at the gates of hell. She was shoved, kicking and screaming through the doorway.

*   *   *

The voice that issued from her lips was not hers. Oh, it was she who spoke all right. But the voice did not seem to belong to her. Between lips that were cracked and a tongue that was swollen, Carina didn't sound like herself.

Her shoulder was bruised, where she had been punched. One eye was blackened, her cheeks bruised. These were all rewards for not permitting a husky, Alsatian guard of the White Brigade feel her up with his thick and muscular fingers.

Her nipples were sore from when another had grabbed at her from behind and yanked off her top. She kneed that one in the groin. He backhanded her with his fist. — And it was only day three.

Carina thought back over the past seventy-two hours. Before the first day was out, she had sat in the processing center beneath a lampshade pieced together from human skin. She had been examined by a medic who wore carpet slippers woven from human hair. She had viewed a piece of modern art so disgusting, she vomited. In a proud, father-like voice, the Commandant told her it was a mosaic of human corneas lined up on canvas one by one. That was her first day.

All around her were horrors. Blood. Pieces of flesh. More blood. Fingers chopped off at the knuckle. Little by little, as prisoners of the concentration camp up north succumbed to the rigors of gulag life, their body parts were being recycled, and in the most hideous of fashions. Lampshades. Slippers. Art work. Just a few of the sick and twisted ways her captors made use of the arms and legs and body parts that were discarded one slice at a time by their owners. The realization of how it would end for her made Carina physically ill.

On the morning of the second day, after a short night without sleep, Carina was taken in shackles from the filthy, rat-infested barracks she and the others had been forced to sleep in. They were led like animals along a narrow, winding trail down a steep hill to a rail line. On the tracks sat a train. From what she could see, the train consisted of an engine, a coal car, plus a dozen or so boxcars. The cars were in poor condition, with rust and peeling paint. Three of the cars were already filled to overflowing with prisoners. Their journey to hell had begun earlier, at some other collection center.

Carina recognized several of the detainees in line with her as fellow Newtons. But she spoke to no one. Thus far, she hadn't even been told the reason for her arrest, though she was getting the idea that in her absence something had gone terribly wrong on Mars.

The path she and the others were led along was littered with personal effects. It was as if the hostages that had come before her had been made to leave everything of value behind. There were shoes and e-pads, combs and wallets. Here and there, a handbag or set of eyeglasses. Plus other things she didn't recognize.

Not all the prisoners in line with her were Newtons. The procession included criminals and malcontents rounded up from a hundred jurisdictions for a dozen different crimes. Rape. Murder. Jaywalking. Speaking back to the wrong magistrate.

Like most of the others, Carina was barefoot. The underside of her heel had been bloodied by a sharp stone or piece of broken glass she accidentally stepped on back in the compound. At this point, it no longer mattered whether or not she was careful where she stepped. The entire length of the trail down to the rail line was one big razor-sharp hazard.

In any case, it was hard to concentrate on the ground beneath her feet when all she passed along the way were trenches filled with rotting corpses and guards holding tight to hardwood clubs. Using these clubs to batter human flesh must have been fun for these men, for they did it so often.

But what were they made from, these fierce-looking clubs? Birch? Ash? Too soft, no doubt. Walnut, probably. Or oak. Something hard. Something that could break bones, shatter fingers, knock out teeth.

And who were these terrible men? Misfits? Rejects from society? Or were they just bored? Bored men, with limited imagination? The sort who would find someone else's pain amusing.

Ahead of her, in the long procession of prisoners, was an old man. What happened to him made Carina recoil in horror. He was disciplined by a guard wielding one of those wooden clubs. The man had stepped on a sharp rock and cried out in pain. He had stopped to pull the jagged bit of stone from the thick pad of skin behind his toes. The prisoners were under strict orders not to speak or get out of line. This poor chap had done both.

The guard took his club in hand and struck the man. It was a single, well-placed blow across the back of the head.

The old man's skull cracked like a length of kiln-dried wood. Blood flew everywhere. A drop of it smacked Carina's cheek. She cringed, started to pee her pants. The man crumpled to the ground in a pool of crimson.

The next prisoner in line stepped over the damaged, inert body, as did the next and the next. When it was Carina's turn, she did the same. Somehow, she managed to shut her mind to the horror she had just witnessed.

One by one, the procession moved on, granite-faced, as if nothing unusual had happened. Carina didn't even feel the pain of the next stone when it gouged a hole out of the bottom of her foot.

The graveled path led them down a steep grade to a rail line. Nearly a dozen boxcars were lined up on the track. A guard with a snarling bio-canine directed Carina towards a car at the front of the train, just behind the engine.

Carina did as she was told. She entered the car. Once inside, the prisoners were free to mingle and talk, though few actually did. Indeed, barely a word was exchanged until after the coal-burner had fired up its steam engine and they began the long journey north.

The entire process, from camp to trail to boxcar, reeked of evil. Carina knew a little something of history. This was Dachau or Auschwitz, and the officers of the White Brigade were Nazis without the brown shirts.

The exterior walls of the boxcar were a latticework of vertical wood slats. Here and there, the sunlight streamed in through the open space separating the slats. When it did, the hostages looked like misshapen zebras trapped inside a wooden trellis. It would have all been quite amusing if it hadn't all been quite so terrible.

Once her eyes adjusted to the disparate lighting, it took Carina no time at all to discover a face she knew. Even in the shadows, Lotha had such a distinctively shaped skull, there was no mistaking him for someone else. But not until she had drawn very close did she recognize the man whose head he held cradled in his lap. Then she gasped. Inda's face was so badly broken, she had to turn away. He was half-dead, if not a little more so.

Carina wanted to speak. But the words would not come. She wanted to shout, to beat Lotha upside the head, to fall to the floor of the boxcar and cry until she could cry no more. *Why had this happened?* she wondered silently. *Had it really all come down to this, a concentration camp in the middle of nowhere?*

Finally she got up the nerve to speak.

"What has happened to us?" she asked, avoiding Lotha's eyes.

"It's all your fault, you know," he said without looking up.

Carina thought back to her first days on Mars. *Oh, Lord, was it true. Was she really to blame?* If only she had it to do all over again!

"Something must have happened while I was gone. Tell me the truth, Lotha — what have you two done?"

Lotha nodded his responsibility with resignation and began to explain. They talked in quiet whispers for a long time, the big man filling her in on everything that had happened since that day long ago when Inda took delivery on his first cache of weapons. The only part he left out was to explain where Inda had gotten the weapons in the first place. Carina didn't care enough to ask.

"You fools!" she finally said, raising her voice to a loud crescendo. "Who in the hell gave you the idea that blowing up the motor factory would solve things for us? Don't you realize what you have done? Now they blame *me!* "

"It's worse," Lotha grunted.

"How could it possibly be worse, you big ape? Tell me . . . how?"

Beneath him, Inda stirred. Lotha patted him on the head like an obedient dog, took a deep breath, and began to explain about the asteroid, the asteroid that was now headed like an unguided missile directly for Earth. Inda had had just enough time to remotely detonate the bomb onboard the EMD before the White Brigade took him into custody.

Carina gasped at the news. "Who . . . who knows about this?"

"Just him and me," Lotha answered, gesturing to his friend. "And now you."

"We must tell someone," she insisted frantically. "We can't let this happen. Life on Earth will be destroyed, and we'll be to blame."

Lotha shook his head. There was a practical tone to his voice when he spoke. "Now who's being the fool? If you start telling these cretins a story like that, all they're gonna do is cut out your tongue and use it as a doorstop. Look at what they've done to Inda, for God's sake."

"Then we're all dead. All of us. You, me, them, everyone."

"Better by an asteroid than by these bastards."

"Dead is still dead," Carina said grimly. "And I don't want to die."

THIRTY-EIGHT

Discovery

The mammoth room had all the trappings of an ordinary control tower located at any of a dozen suborb-ports around the world — only with two important differences.

This tower was much taller, for one — over a hundred meters taller than the one which stood outside Hilo, and that tower serviced all the air traffic over the Pacific.

Aside from that, there was something unusual about this tower, an anomaly made unusual by what was *not* present. For, next to this control tower, there was no suborbport. No runways. No passenger terminal. No tube into the city. Nothing. Just a parking lot filled with gcars.

So what was it about this control tower that was so special? Answer: This control tower housed the space-traffic controllers who kept an eye, not on suborb traffic, but on asteroids.

Each time an electromagnetic mass driver was railgunned into space from the motor factory on Mars, where it had been assembled, the EMD was given a tracking number by ground control. And, along each step of its journey Earthward, entries were made in an electronic logbook as to its progress — time of launch from Mars, time of first contact with its target-asteroid, time when the EMD first initialized retro-thrust, moment when the assembly made its closest pass with Mars, time when each of the seven planned midcourse corrections took place, time when it began its deceleration, moment when it swung into Earth-stable orbit. List and checklists; procedures and rules; managers and supervisors; computers and monitors; all designed to keep Earth safe from harm.

It was in the wee hours, now, of a wet morning. A fourth-class assistant, new to the job, sat before a flickering screen, his eyes bloodshot from hours of concentrating. It was the second night that he had seen the same strange anomaly on EMD 14, and the man wasn't sure if he dare mention it to Master Dawson, his shift supervisor. If the young man was wrong about the anomaly, Master Dawson might very well dismiss him. Jobs were scarce and this one paid well, had room for advancement. In six months he might be promoted to assistant third-class. Then he and the little woman might be able to afford that new couch she wanted, the one with the brown leather. On the other hand, if he *didn't* point out the anomaly and it turned out to be something serious, that could be grounds for dismissal as well.

Trembling, the young man brushed back a lock of hair, took a deep gulp of air and spoke:

"Sir, I was wondering whether I might disturb you a moment? If you wouldn't mind, I would like to have you come over and take a look at this."

"What is it, Popovich?" the shift supervisor boomed, obviously put out by the interruption. Supervisor Dawson had just opened his newspaper and sunk down into the deep folds of his thick padded chair. Nothing irritated him more than being bothered in the middle of reading the sports pages.

Leif Popovich tried to be as conciliatory as possible. "Sir, perhaps when you have finished with that section of the *Herald*. Then, if you wouldn't mind, I would sure appreciate it if you would come over here and take a look at this."

"It's too late for that already!" Dawson thundered, slamming down the daily and rolling to his feet. "My train of thought has already been broken by your damnable insolence. What is it, Popovich? What is so damn important that you couldn't wait 'til I was done?"

The big man lumbered across the room to where Assistant Fourth-Class Leif Popovich sat trembling before his screen. Dawson was big and fat, and his belly jiggled with each step.

"Sir, please take a look at these 3-D holographs," Popovich urged, fumbling with the knobs until the image came into sharp focus. There were hundreds of blips on the screen, some large, some small. One was illuminated in bright red; all the rest in a pale yellow. Like beads on a tiny string, each blip was perforated by a gently curving line, not a circle, but an ellipse that carved out its path through space. Two arcing lines emanated out in front of the red blip — one red, the other green. The red one was flashing.

The big oaf stared blankly at the holo-screen, studying the 3-D image from several angles. "What is it I'm looking at here?" he asked finally.

Popovich bit his tongue. Life was strange that way, he thought. Supervisors the world-over were hardly ever trained to do the jobs the people they supervised were capable of. It was obvious that Master Dawson didn't have a clue what he was looking at, or the dangers it revealed. But rather than just owning up to his ignorance, the big man huffed, "I see nothing here. Are you on blue-devils, boy?"

The color ran from Leif Popovich's face. To be accused by a superior of taking a controlled substance while on the job meant almost certain dismissal. Suddenly, the young man was afraid.

"No, sir," Popovich stammered, "I am not on drugs of any kind. Perhaps you are not familiar with this particular screen. It is a rather new one, you know — release six point four, I believe."

By couching it in these terms, Fourth-Class Assistant Popovich hoped to avoid directly accusing his boss of being the fat, lazy slob that he actually was.

"Sir, if I may — this machine plots an asteroid's projected path against its actual path. We use it to . . . "

"I know what the fucker is used for!" Dawson exploded. "To program midcourse corrections! I can see your 'roid is off course. Just fix the damn thing at the next interrupt point. Is that so hard?"

"Of course not, sir, and I will fix it as you say. But what concerns me is this: Only three days ago, we signaled EMD 14 to make a major Z-axis turn. It shouldn't be off course this far, this fast."

"No, it shouldn't," Dawson admitted. "You musta screwed up the turn."

"With all due respect, I used the figures you gave me."

"That's not possible. Run a relay loop and see if the onboard antenna acknowledges the test signal."

"Already did that, sir, and . . . "

"You ran a relay loop without my permission?" Dawson barked, his voice reverberating throughout the control room. Every controller's head in the place turned to see what was afoot.

"You seemed preoccupied at the time, sir. In any event, I don't need your permission," Popovich said calmly, reaching for the operator's handbook in the second righthand drawer of his desk. "According to Regulation fourteen eighty-two slash fifty-three, in the event of an . . . "

"Okay, already, we both agree you did the right thing. Don't worry. I'm not going to write you up. But tell me what happened when you sent the test pattern message to the EMD."

"Nothing, sir. Not a darn thing. There was no response."

"And the backup antenna?"

"Sir, backups only became standard beginning with unit fifteen. This is EMD 14."

"So we have a free bird?"

"It would appear that way to me, sir."

"Lord, help us."

*   *   *

Forty minutes had passed and Leif Popovich was now in the base commander's outer office, sweating profusely. Supervisor Dawson had gone in first and had only just now exited. In a moment it would be Popovich's turn. While he waited, Assistant Fourth-Class Popovich made some notes on the e-pad he carried with him from the control tower.

Like all base commanders, Lieutenant Colonel Nicholson was too smart to be a mere major, but not well enough connected to be a full-fledged general. In fact, lieutenant colonel was what the army called a "shit-house rank." Each day brought nothing but shit from above and crap from below. To make matters worse, his was a quasi-civilian post, a post from which he didn't expect to be transferred or promoted. While the military had jurisdiction over all man-made objects moving through the space — including EMD's — ASARCO was a private company. Who, then, could blame him when he didn't seem especially happy to have this particular problem dumped on his desk at o'seven-hundred hours in the morning?

Lieutenant Colonel Nicholson was stern-faced and curt. With a grunt he nodded to Popovich to be seated. "Supervisor Dawson tells me there's a problem. But as far as I'm concerned, the man's a blithering idiot. So I want to hear it from you."

"Sir, it's our belief . . . "

"Cut the crap, boy. There's no *our* about it, is there? You were the one who discovered this anomaly, weren't you?"

"Why, yes, sir," Popovich answered, his pride growing. "It's *my* belief that EMD 14 did not respond to ground control's last midcourse correction."

"And why would that be, son?"

"I do not know, sir."

"Speculate."

"Well, sir, the most likely scenario would be that a small, companion-asteroid, swept along by its mother . . . "

"Its *mother* ?" Nicholson roared. "Are you daffy?"

"Well, sir, that's what we call them. Two asteroids, one big, one small, moving along in tandem. The big one's the mother, the little one's the daughter. When they're in a group, they move like a family of ducks out on a pond."

"I see," Nicholson said. "And this companion-asteroid of yours, what did it do? Hit the antenna? Smash it?"

"Yes, I'd rate that as a strong possibility. Then again, maybe a chunk of rock flew off the main body and wrecked it. Same outcome either way. Main problem is, asteroids aren't solid — pieces are flying loose all the time. That's why the Space-Traffic Board recommended ASARCO start putting redundant antenna units onboard the newer EMD's coming off the line."

"Could it have been sabotage?" Lieutenant Colonel Nicholson asked. He had already read Cragit McPherson's report concerning the plot they uncovered on Mars.

"I don't see how," Leif Popovich decided.

"What if way back in the factory, a bomb had been planted on the frame of the mass driver right alongside the receiving antenna?"

"Well, that would do it okay, sir. But I've never been to Mars. Surely, their security must be tighter than all that."

"Apparently not tight enough," Nicholson sighed. "So, tell me, young . . . ."

"Popovich, sir. Leif Popovich."

"So tell me, young Popovich, how do we get the bloody thing back on course?"

"We can't. Not without an antenna anyway."

"Where will the bloody thing go?" Nicholson asked, his starched collar feeling a bit snugger than before.

Popovich answered as honestly as he could. "We don't rightly know, sir. Not yet anyway. There are too many variables . . . But it'll be close."

"Close? Close to what?"

"Close to us. Close to Earth."

"How close?"

"Can't say for sure."

"Lord!" Lieutenant Colonel Nicholson exclaimed, slapping his hands together in dismay. "It's the silver cannonball incident all over again."

"Begging your pardon, sir. But there's one big difference between what you're talking about and our current situation."

"Oh, yeah, and what is that?"

There was a levelheaded precision, now, to Assistant Fourth-Class Leif Popovich's voice as he spoke:

"The silver cannonball that caused such a stir way back when, was only two meters in diameter, barely four cubic meters in volume. The asteroid headed our way, though not of uniform density, is fifty-five-*hundred* meters across on its narrowest axis, seventy-five-hundred on its widest. And, sir, it is traveling eight times as fast!"

Pulling out his e-pad, now, Leif Popovich spoke faster. "I've done some calculations, sir, and the kinetic energy of an object is equal to one-half m times v squared, where m is the mass of the object in question, and v is the bugger's velocity. Now, if we use joules as a measuring rod — a joule, by the way, is the work done when a force of one newton moves an object a distance of one meter in the direction of the force — this bugger is packing . . . "

"Forget all that!" Nicholson suddenly shouted. "I get the idea. Son, whatever the figure comes to, I believe you. What I want to know is this: How soon will you be able to pinpoint its actual glide path with total accuracy?"

Popovich was nothing if not truthful. "Total accuracy? I hesitate to answer a question that calls for total accuracy."

"Best guess then."

"We should have a pretty good fix on her within five days, sir."

"Okay, then. You and that e-pad of yours had better get some shut-eye the next few hours. One or both of you has a long night ahead of them. Plus, you look like hell."

"Sir?"

"Let me explain. Leif, is it? I want a report on this EMD 14 on my desk first thing tomorrow morning. I need to know what it is capable of. In the way of damage, I mean. I need to know where it is headed, and I need to know how we might put a stop to the bloody thing. Are we clear?"

"Crystal."

"Then you're dismissed."

Popovich got to his feet. Though the man was no soldier, he knew enough to return Lieutenant Colonel Nicholson's salute as he left.

Maybe, if he did a good job, he wouldn't be an assistant fourth-class forever!

THIRTY-NINE

The Son Of The Father

Fornax had stood at this very spot countless times before.

This was the gate that led up the lane to Sam's estate in Auckland. Thus, for Fornax, there was no sense of awe, no feeling of astonishment, no nagging pangs of envy to learn where and how Samuel Matthews actually lived. The same did not hold true, however, for the man who was with him. For that man, being in the presence of so much wealth gave him pause. Without meaning to, Gunter found himself ogling at the enormity of the place as the two of them started up the drive towards the front door.

"So this is what you aspire to, eh?" Gunter asked, wondering if he caught a glimpse of avarice gleaming in Fornax's eye.

"I guess," Fornax answered noncommittally, his mind elsewhere. "Listen, Gunter, before we ring the doorbell and wake up the house, there's something I simply have to know."

"Hell's bells, Nehrengel, what's eating at you?"

"Well," Fornax stammered, a sheepish look crowding out his face. "It's like this. You spent two weeks with her out on that mountain, and three weeks before that, training her. What I want to know is . . . "

"What you want to know is, did I ever sleep with her?" Gunter said, finishing the other man's sentence. "Well, the answer is no, and not for lack of trying — on her part, that is. The woman must have asked me at least once a day."

"So, then, what I guess I want to know is, why not?"

"Oh, I get it now," Gunter replied, obviously peeved. "What you're trying ever so hard not to ask me is whether I'm a 'mo. Or worse yet, whether I'm celibate. Does the big, strong mountain climber from downunder prefer boys, is that it?"

Gunter suddenly caressed Fornax's shoulder, like a male-lover might, then burst out laughing. "Rest easy, mate. She's not my type. Besides, I'm married."

Fornax was genuinely surprised. "There's a Mrs. Gunter then?"

"And five little Gunters."

A look of relief spread across Fornax's face. As it did, Gunter added, "Hell's bells, man, when we find the damn sheila, believe me, the woman's all yours."

"If she'll have me, that is. Don't forget, there's still BC."

"And don't forget Inda," Gunter chuckled, ringing the doorbell.

"Thanks ever so much for reminding me."

"You're welcome, I'm sure. What else are friends for?"

Fornax smiled and punched Gunter playfully in the arm. After what the two of them had witnessed back on Mars, after the two of them had both been used and doublecrossed by the company and by Cragit McPherson, a silent alliance had been forged between the two men.

Now they both found themselves standing on the same side of the same issue. They both agreed the entire colony shouldn't be made to suffer, regardless of what one or two hotheaded Newtons may have done to try and shut the motor factory down. They also both knew that Sam had come home to his beloved Auckland to die. So, after leaving the prisoners in McPherson's custody back in Johannesburg, they came here to Sam's place straightaway. They were armed with the terrible news that a warrant had been issued for Carina's arrest.

Saron answered the door. The look on her face was somewhere between joy and tears.

"May we come in?" Fornax asked, matching his tone to her somber face.

"Of course," she answered. "But if you've come to see Sam, you'll have to keep it short."

"Why else would we be here? Now, is he up and about or not?"

"Don't get snitty with me," she said. "The man's not well. In fact, I'm afraid he's sinking fast. Have you come to pay your final respects?"

Fornax and Gunter exchanged glances. "It's that bad?"

Saron nodded.

"Actually," Fornax confessed. "That's not why we came."

"What then?"

"May we see him or not?" Fornax asked, dodging her question.

"This way," came the perfunctory reply.

Saron led the two men through the foyer and into the grand sitting room at the back of the house. Sam was propped up on a couch with a pillow behind his head. His color was poor and his breathing shallow. An oxygen tank was beside him, with a hose that led to a loosely-fitting mask. His eyes drooped and his fingers trembled. A puddle of drool filled the corner of his mouth.

Fornax was slack-jawed when he saw his old mentor. He had no idea the disease had advanced this far, this fast.

Sam opened one eye. "Do I really look that bad?" he asked, removing the loosely-fitting mask over Saron's protests.

"Naw," Fornax lied. "I was just surprised to see you in bed, that's all."

"You didn't believe me when I said I was coming home to die, did you?"

Fornax stammered out a reply. "Honestly, Sam, I . . . "

Sam held the mask to his face for a second, then coughed several times in succession. "It's exponential, this fucking disease. You know — picking up speed. Only three days ago, I seemed to be getting better. Saron and I shared a . . . well, what I mean is, now it seems as if I've taken a turn for the worse. When I heard the doorbell, I had so hoped it would be Carina. Not that I'm not delighted to see both of you, of course. But I can't imagine why in the blazes you two are here. Land's sakes, Fornax, you have a business to run — *our* business — you can't be wasting time running around worrying about me!"

Fornax didn't know what to say. He looked across at Gunter to see who should go first and decided it should be up to him.

"Sam, the whole thing's my fault," Fornax said. "If you must blame anyone, blame me. I'm the one who's responsible."

Sam took a big tug on his oxygen. "Responsible? Responsible for what?"

"You had already left Mars to come home," Fornax said, taking a chair and sitting down. "You've got to believe me, Sam — I thought I was doing the right thing. Schaeffer lied to me, the bastard. He lied to all of us."

"I knew the man was nefarious, that he couldn't be trusted," Sam declared, gathering his strength. Though Sam was confused by what Fornax was trying to tell him, with each passing moment he seemed more alert, more animated and uplifted by his friend's presence. "What did Schaeffer do? Renege on a royalty payment? Skip town with the payroll?"

"Nothing like that. Much worse. He said the troops were being sent in to restore order. But it was all a lie. They rounded everybody up, Sam. They . . ."

"Who, everybody? What troops? What in the *hell* are you trying to tell me, boy?"

By now, Sam had sat up straight in his chair and thrown his pillow aside. There was color in his face, the color of anger.

"They put out a warrant for Carina's arrest. We came as soon as we could."

"I don't understand," Sam said, turning to Saron to see if it was true.

Gunter took over. "Look, Sam, some damn fool tried to blow up the motor works. I'm pretty sure Schaeffer was the one supplying them with weapons and explosives. But, wherever the arms came from, Inda and his buddies were using your daughter's hut to store the damn things. Makes her look guilty as sin. ASARCO decided to swoop in and put a stop to it all, before things could get further out of control. Every single Newton was placed under arrest. A warrant was issued for Carina's capture. According to McPherson, turncoat that he is, Carina's the brains behind the whole operation."

"That's absurd — and you know it! Why wasn't I told of this sooner?"

"No time for that," Gunter said, eyes drifting into the next room. "Where is she now? Upstairs? In town? Carina has to hide. She has to go underground, before it's too late."

"She's not here," Saron spoke up. "We haven't seen her since we arrived. All we know for certain is that she went to North America in search of answers, answers about this disease that's killing Sam."

"North America?!" Gunter clamored. "Damn fool woman! One of these days Carina and her damn fool ideas are gonna get us all killed."

"My son may be with her," Sam interjected, his voice weak.

"Gunter's right," Fornax said. "We have to find her before the authorities do, before it's too late."

Only then did Sam's last sentence finally sink in. "What was that you said?" Fornax stammered. "Who did you say was with her?"

"It may be too late already." This was a new voice, and every head in the place turned to view the speaker. It was BC. Sister Siona stood beside him in the doorway. They had just come from a meeting with J. It was their first stop following Carina's arrest at Heathrow. He had told them where Carina and the others were taken. He had also instructed BC, in no uncertain terms, to avoid getting involved. This was a matter that should be left to the South Africans to handle. No mention was made by J of the cane or of Sam's contention that BC was in fact his son, only that Sam had sprung BC's kid from the orphanage, and that he and the woman had taken the child with them to Sam's estate in Auckland.

"Just what do you mean by saying that it may already be too late?" Sam asked, surprised and gratified to see his son. "And didn't anyone ever teach you to knock?"

BC apologized for barging in uninvited, then proceeded to tell them everything that J had related to him and Sister Siona. First, about the place where Carina and the other captives had been sent, then, about how the gulag was almost certainly a death sentence.

"You've got to save her, son." This was Sam talking.

"I'll try, Sam — I promise. Now that I know where they've taken her, now that I know I have two more comrades to help spring her, I think we might actually have a fighting chance."

"Call me Dad," he said with a smile.

"Whatever you say, Sam," BC replied, thinking the old man had finally gone out of his head.

"No, I mean it," Sam insisted. "Call me Dad."

Using every bit of strength at his command, Sam slid forward to the edge of his couch. As he did so, he motioned for Saron to get the cane from the other room. When she returned with it, he took the cane from her and gripped the hilt with both hands. He used it to help support his weight as he lumbered to his feet.

"Do you know where this cane came from?" he asked.

"No, I'm not entirely sure."

"See these initials here?"

"Yes."

"Well, sonny, let me tell you a story."

And he did.

It was a long, convoluted tale. But, by the time Sam was done with his explanation, the color had run from BC's face and he had sat down trembling.

"You mean to tell me I slept with my *sister*?"

"Half-sister," Sam corrected, coming to stand next to his only son. "Half-sister."

"Even so."

"No one's blaming you, boy. Spilt milk and all that. What matters now is that you have to save her. You have to go wherever they are keeping her. You have to save her life. You have a son upstairs. He has a mother. You must go find the boy's mother and bring her safely back here. It's your duty as a Matthews."

"A Matthews, eh?" BC liked the sound of that and forced out a smile.

Sam suddenly grabbed BC's arm for emphasis, and began giving out orders, as if he were in charge.

"All three of you men must go. You must go together and save my daughter. You have no choice. This is a dying man's final request. The women will stay here and look after me and the boy until the three of you return with Carina."

"Heh, wait a minute, Sam," Saron objected. "I was a freedom fighter long before the two of us even crossed paths. I should go with the men, help even the odds. Sister Siona can take care of you and Sam, Jr. Plus, you've got Nanny Purdy to help you."

Sam looked hard at the young woman he had come to love and, for perhaps the first time in thirty years, tears came to his eyes. The man couldn't say what he felt, but she seemed to understand.

"Lord knows, I'm certainly in no condition to stop you, woman. But God help us both if you get yourself hurt."

"I'll see to it that doesn't happen," Gunter said, stepping forward.

"I have your word?"

"You have my word."

BC cleared his voice to speak. He was still not entirely over the shock of what Sam had just told him. "Sam ... I mean, Father ... there's something more you should know before we leave."

Sister Siona cut him off midsentence. "Leave it to me. I'll tell him, BC. You four should go now."

"Do I know you?" Sam asked, his tired old eyes turning in Sister Siona's direction. "Your voice sounds vaguely familiar."

"It ought to, you old fart. You and I go way back. And we have much to discuss."

"Well then, let's get to it," Sam said, taking her arm.

Had there been music, it might have come up now. Instead, an old friendship was rekindled, if only for a brief time.

FORTY

Acid Rain

Lieutenant Colonel Randall Nicholson sat at his desk reading the report prepared by Fourth-Class Assistant Leif Popovich. His eyes grew wider with each paragraph he read of the neatly typed report:

Sixty-five million years ago, a mass-extinction was triggered by an extraterrestrial object that struck the Earth. Perhaps by analyzing this cataclysmic event, we can better appreciate the risk that EMD 14 poses to us today.

In the aforementioned collision, nearly half of all species, including the last of the dinosaurs, vanished. Virtually every land animal too large to find shelter perished. While this is by far the most famous mass-extinction event — as it ended the age of dinosaurs and ultimately made the origin of our species possible — the massive dinosaur extinction sixty-five million years ago was only the most recent of no less than five similarly documented episodes. In fact, this episode was quite minor when compared to the Permian crash one hundred and seventy-five million years earlier. That episode extinguished an incredible eighty-five percent of all animal species! It took five million years for species diversity to recover in any meaningful way. Indeed, life on Earth had an extremely close call.

The course of events leading to the mass-extinction sixty-five million years ago began when an asteroid perhaps seven to ten kloms in diameter, plummeted through the atmosphere, setting off an incredible chain of events, a chain of events documented in geologic deposits around the world.

Beginning with the publication of the Alvarez data in the twentieth century, a pronounced layer of soot was shown to have been laid down at the time of the extinctions. Although some scientists still harbored lingering doubts regarding the likelihood of such a catastrophe well into the twenty-first century, when an impact-crater of the correct age and size was discovered in the Gulf of Mexico, those doubts were all but erased.

The collisions must have been a stupendous impact. No fantastic allegory of Hell concocted by some fiction writer could possibly have matched the reality of Earth following the asteroid collision. The kinetic energy released by the crash would have been of a magnitude equivalent to detonating 100 million one-megaton bombs. It would have generated enough power to ignite the very nitrogen in the atmosphere, a development which would have promptly led to the formation of a world-girdling cloud of toxic smog.

On top of that, the impact would have lifted huge quantities of dust into the upper atmosphere, along with hundreds of cubic miles of water. The toxic-acid-smog would have combined with the dust and water to shroud the Earth in a film of near-total darkness, a black and yellow cloud that would have lasted for at least several months before beginning to thin. Starved of sunlight, the globe would have been chilled and nearly every green plant snuffed out. Yet, as unbelievable as it might seem, the worst was still to come.

The water vapor in the atmosphere would have readily reacted with the nitrogen and other toxic chemicals present in the smog. These reactions would have produced lethal rainfalls, certainly as corrosive as battery acid, if not more so. The results would have been staggering. A single cloudburst of this toxic-rain would have been able to wipe out an entire forest. Over the ocean, this same rain would have been capable of dissolving the very shells and exo-skeletons of countless numbers of marine creatures.

And yet still it wasn't over. Earth's nightmare worsened even further as ordinary lightning kindled the dying forests, producing horrendous firestorms on an unprecedented scale. The fires would have blackened the skies for a second time. Once again, temperatures would have plunged.

When the skies finally cleared months later, any creature that managed to survive the chill and the fires and the corrosive rain, not to mention the extreme shortage of green, living plants for food, would then have faced another crisis.

The sharp rise in atmospheric carbon-dioxide that came from burning so much of the world's biomass, would have triggered a greenhouse effect so enormous, temperatures would then have soared perhaps twenty degrees centigrade and remained that way for the next 100,000 years.

Those animals capable of regulating their internal thermostats would have been the ones most likely to have survived in the aftermath of the asteroid strike. On the other hand, cold-blooded animals would most likely have succumbed. Scavengers, yes. Passive grazers, no. Little animals, yes. Larger ones, no. Egg-layers and live-bearers would have fared better. Those that burrowed, the best. Small furry animals, in. Big grazing or carnivorous dinosaurs, out.

Thus, what can we conclude from this analysis, especially as it pertains to the present scenario of an errand asteroid?

The EMD 14 asteroid is on the order of ten percent smaller than the one that wiped out the dinosaurs. Even so, it would be silly to debate the precise outcome such an impact might have on life as we know it today. The results would be devastating, even at half the size.

Therefore, rather than address that particular issue, the balance of this report deals only with options for *avoiding* such a calamity. Because the author of this report is not an expert in such matters, these considerations are tenuous at best. Still, all viable options would appear to fall into one of three categories:

(1) the application of nuclear or other means to destroy the killer-asteroid before it can approach close enough to the Earth to cause any serious harm, or,

(2) the rendezvousing with — and installation of — a new comm-unit to allow a series of midcourse adjustments which would bring the bird safely into Earth orbit, or,

(3) the application of a sufficiently large tangential force (i.e., from a conventional rocket or other projectile) to nudge the asteroid onto an alternate trajectory that would swing it safely away from the Earth/Moon system.

A more detailed explanation of each option follows in the attached appendix. But, considering the costs associated with the various alternatives (not the least of which would be the loss of the mass driver, plus the loss of the asteroid itself), Option Two would seem to hold itself out as having the most merit.

While there is some possibility the asteroid will miss Earth of its own accord, that possibility is low enough to demand some positive action be taken. Again, Option Two makes sense, if strictly on financial terms. The loss of such a large ore body — and its motor — would represent a staggering financial reversal to one of the world's largest employers. The financial losses might be on the order of three-quarters of a trillion credits, at today's prices. Though the author of this report is no expert on financial matters, it isn't hard to speculate how the entire world economy could take a hit from which it might not soon recover.

Lieutenant Colonel Randall Nicholson put down the report and reached for his comm. As he encoded the first number, it occurred to him that some staffing changes were needed in the tracking unit. Fourth-Class Assistant Leif

Popovich should be bumped up two grades and Master Dawson should be dismissed.

But those changes would have to wait until tomorrow. Right now he had two calls to make — one to Oskar Schaeffer, his civilian counterpart over at ASARCO, and a second, more important call to a brutish little man he knew over at Commonwealth Intelligence, a man the world knew only as J.

*   *   *

Indifference deadened her spirit. Here or there, what did it matter? Today or tomorrow or the day after, what did it matter? She was going to die, of that she was now certain. But when? And how? Her brain was a cesspool of violent memories.

For three days now the coal-burner had chug-a-lugged north, and with each hour it pressed forward, the heat of the continent's interior steadily rose. Night or day, the inside of the boxcar was like an oven. The glimmer of moonlight or sunlight that shone through the slats revealed a tangle of human shapes — heads sunk on shoulders, cheeks wet with tears, bodies piled one atop the other, limbs jutting out at weird angles, feces and urine everywhere.

Unable to sleep, Carina tried to distinguish between the living and the dead, between those who were still alive and those who had already left this world. But it was impossible. Even those who were still alive looked half-dead, lying with their eyes open, staring into the black void.

Just before dawn, the train stopped in the middle of the jungle. She stirred. Outside, there was an open field and what appeared to be a hut. *We're here at last!* she thought, anxious to finally escape the confines of this hellhole on wheels.

The guards of the White Brigade moved along the row of boxcars. Like dull-witted zookeepers, they banged on the slats with their wooden clubs. The noise woke everyone up. What they said made her skin crawl. But the way the prisoners reacted was even worse.

"Throw out the dead!" the guards ordered, sliding open the doors. "We have no time to waste! Do it now! Throw out the dead!"

People around her, living people, cheered the news. And so it was down the line — heartfelt cheers.

By God, they are happy! Carina thought. That's when she decided she had now run out of reasons to live.

All around her was mayhem, and yet she sat in her place unmoving. Volunteers on either side of her set to work tossing the dead out the open doorway. Their reasoning was simple. With the dead gone, there would be more room, more air, a place to lie down.

Carina didn't budge. She didn't want to be part of this despicable act. Then two men grabbed Inda by the ankles and moved to throw him from the boxcar.

"Don't!" she screamed at the top of her lungs. "He's still alive!"

The men looked at her, looked at him, then laughed. They tugged at his clothing, at his socks, his shirt, anything they could keep and use for themselves later on.

She threw herself across Inda's inert body, crying, "It can't be! It can't be!"

"It is," Lotha said, his voice flat. "Let him go. He's gone."

Lotha clutched her in his powerful arms, dragged her away in tears to let the other men finish their dirty work. It didn't take long, only minutes, and the train again lurched forward, resuming its journey north. Three dozen naked dead were left behind, deprived of burial, soon to be dinner for a pack of wild jackals.

They were given no food, only water, over the course of the next two days. The train made four more "dead" stops as it continued north on its route into the Great Rift Valley.

The guards took great joy in making the prisoners miserable, and once along the way, just to see what would happen, a guard threw half a slice of bread into their car, like a tourist might if he were feeding a bunch of geese.

Carina couldn't believe her eyes. There was an immediate stampede! Inside of no time at all, a dozen starving prisoners — some men, some women — were fighting one another to the death for a few crumbs. This spectacle amused the guard so much, he tossed in another.

Now all hell broke loose. Men threw themselves on top of each other. Men, who only days ago were friends, now stomped on each other like wild beasts. Animal hatred shone from their eyes.

Carina held Lotha back when he wanted to join in. Surely, with all his strength, the big man could have easily won. But somehow, for some reason, she wanted him to stay above the fray.

Together they sat on the feces-covered floor of the boxcar.

"When all around you have lost their heads, you cannot," she whispered. Her frail hands locked around his arm.

Two pieces of bread later, there were more corpses.

Carina stared out through the wooden slats at the guard who had started it all. The man was laughing and having a good time. She turned to Lotha and said, "When this is all over, if you're still alive, I want you to break that fucker's neck."

"My pleasure," he grunted, committing the evil man's face to memory.

Soon, the train moved on. Carina didn't see the evil guard again until late the next morning, when the train of death reached its final destination in the land once called Ethiopia, now the Blue Nile Kingdom.

At the camp, the very first order given was that the prisoners be separated. Men were to be sent one way, women another. The best-looking women were to become bims, treated well and fed regularly as long as they serviced the guards. The not-so-good-looking, field workers or worse. When Carina was put in line with the other consorts, she finally cracked. The woman dropped to her knees and wept like she never wept before.

The Great Rift Valley was where it all began, human history that is. And here is where it all would end, at least for her. Under no circumstances would she become the unwilling sex partner for some gestapo-slug. She would commit suicide before that. Slice open her wrists with a blade. Swallow a bottle of Deludes. Charge a guard holding an electronic whip.

Then it occurred to her — she had been here before, long ago, during those frightful nights on Mars. She had thought about killing herself, back then, when there was no hope.

But something had stopped her then, and something was stopping her now. She remembered what Sister Siona had told her, what she had told her about her very own mother. How Nasha had never given in. How she had never given up. How she had submitted and toughed it out to the end. Suicide wasn't the answer. There had to be another way!

Carina dragged herself to her feet. But as she did so, a guard in need of a consort approached. She had to think fast.

"I prefer a woman with big tits," he asserted, tearing open her blouse to take a peek.

"You don't want me," she said, wiping her eyes clean but not pushing him away.

"Oh, and why not?" he laughed, rubbing her breasts with his open palm.

"I have Matthews Disease."

Carina held her ground, even though it was killing her to let this filthy man fondle her breasts.

"You're lying," he said, straightening up after putting one of them in his mouth. "There is no such thing."

"Suit yourself. But you see that big man over there?"

The guard turned to see who she was pointing at. Her index finger was aimed at Lotha.

"Yeah, what about him? He's like a big, dumb Frankenstein. Quite repulsive. Why should he concern me?"

"Ever seen a head like that before? He caught it from me. It only affects men, you see. If you fuck me, you'll get it too. And you should see what it does to your prick."

"You're lying," the guard stammered, a note of uncertainty creeping into his voice.

"Well, if you're so sure of yourself, then I say we go for it right here and now. I can't wait to see what you'll look like in two weeks. That man fucked me only a month ago."

The guard looked at Carina through narrowed eyes then shunted her off to the other line.

She sighed a breath of relief and drew her blouse closed. *Perhaps she was tough enough to survive this place after all.*

Only time would tell for sure.

FORTY-ONE

Afar Triangle

From the Dead Sea in the north, to Olduvai Gorge at the south, the crust had gradually buckled. And, as the continent of Africa ripped itself apart in geologic time, the Great Rift had opened. Now, oceans lay to the east, mountains to the west, and nothing but valley inbetween. There was no access by air, only by land or by sea. And there were no roads from the north or from the south, where they could travel unobserved. Which meant taking a boat.

Arriving from the east across the Gulf of Aden, the three men and one woman met choppy water about six kloms out. For Fornax, it was an inauspicious start. Here was a man who was highly susceptible to bouts of motion sickness, even in calm seas. In fact, while BC was at the helm, Gunter at the nav-charts, and Saron down below changing, Fornax hung over the side of the vessel throwing up his life.

The foursome had timed their crossing of the strait so as to make landfall before dawn. They were now a few minutes ahead of schedule.

Gunter had been tracking their progress across the Gulf using the nav-codes BC had given him, plus the help of the global positioning satellite overhead. But now, when Gunter said they were close to their destination, BC seemed not to hear him.

"I say there, mate. — This is where we have to put in."

Still lost in thought, BC didn't react. He never had a family name before, nor the obligations that came with it. *Just what did being a Matthews mean?* BC wasn't sure. But he did see now that he had made a big mistake. He had been wrong to stick Sam, Jr. in that orphanage. He would have to apologize to the boy's grandfather for that, just as soon as this was all over.

"I say there, mate. — Cut the damn engines or someone is gonna hear us!" Gunter exclaimed, putting aside his charts and tapping BC on the shoulder.

BC snapped to and nudged the throttle back a notch. The leading edge of the launch settled lower in the water. He lessened their speed further, and the boat slowed to a crawl as the shore drew closer.

"Over there," Gunter pointed.

A low fog hung over the water. But, if a man strained his eyes, he could just make out the channel where a flat, muddy river junctioned with the sea.

Coming to port, BC kept the craft in the deepest portion of the narrow channel as they headed slowly upstream. The idea was to find a suitable spot a half-klom upriver to beach the boat and offload the electric dune buggy.

BC kept one eye on the river, the other on the depth-indicator. Only an amateur would ground the boat, not him. *But what were their chances, really?* BC wondered.

It was one thing to mount a raid on an enemy compound and slaughter everyone inside; quite another to do it without killing a soul. And yet, that is precisely what they intended.

In this incursion, the standard siege weapons would be useless. The force gun, with its ability to blow a fist-sized cavity clean through a man. The megaflare, with its ability to burn and maim an entire battalion as its glowing, airborne shards showered the battlefield. The manual firebomb, with its power to lift a fourteen-ton gtruck clear off the ground. — All useless.

No, the approach here had to be a bit more delicate, a bit more subtle. — And a helluva lot more quiet. *But how?* And with what?

Though this little group didn't have the numbers to pull off an Entebbe-style raid, they might just be able to duplicate a reasonable facsimile of the Krakow rescue.

Years ago, before the Great War, Walter Krakow proposed a solution to one of mankind's longstanding questions — whether or not there was enough dark matter in the universe to close it, which is to say, make it collapse back onto itself once again, thus spawning an infinitely heavy black hole. He said there was. The Big Crunch, as he called it, would be followed by yet another Big Bang in a long, never-ending series of echo-bounces.

Unfortunately, this line of thinking didn't set well with the Scientific Inquiries Board. For his heresy, Walter Krakow was packed off to a gulag not unlike the one Carina was being held in today. The Krakow rescue consisted of gassing everyone in the place, then carrying the unconscious Krakow out by hand and transporting him to a place of safety. A similar tactic might be made to work here as well, only with a couple differences, one of them critical.

The first and foremost difference was that Krakow's rescuers had access to a powerful anesthetic, something much more powerful than what BC had been able to lay his hands on in the few hours allotted to him. Which meant the inhalant wouldn't cover as wide an area or keep the people out as long. The bigger the man, the less he would be affected.

Plus, they would be operating in unfamiliar territory, with the wrong equipment and limited personnel. They would all be lucky to come out of this thing alive. If only they had someone on the inside they could count on for assistance, that would improve the odds markedly.

A lot depended on the itty-bitty. When fully charged, the electric dune buggy — or itty-bitty as Gunter liked to call it — had twelve hours of battery power. That gave them six to get in, and six more to get out. Plenty of time to spare, as it shouldn't take them more than two hours in either direction. Gunter had great confidence in this sort of contraption, as he had even used one on Mars to haul their gear to the start point before making his climb to the top of Olympus Mons. All the four had to do today was aim for the line of peaks that formed the western rim of the Rift Valley, and they should be there.

Gunter drove, mainly because he was the one most familiar with the vehicle. In the seat behind him, BC and Saron were working feverishly to prepare the megaflare launchers for the upcoming attack. Instead of hurling lyddite-gel-filled globes over the target area — globes that ordinarily would have incinerated the enemy in a firestorm as they descended — BC and Saron were using a vacuum pump to fill the globes with a powerful knockout gas.

If they were lucky and caught the wind just right, this concoction BC had cooked-up of sodium pentothal, chloral hydrate, and nitrous oxide, just might work. If not, there was always the conventional weapons to fall back on — plus Jenny, of course. Which is where Fornax came in.

Using the same wondrous material that made it possible for his ship, the *Tikkidiw*, to vault across the solar system in a matter of minutes, Fornax had developed a prototype of an extraordinary, new generation of blaster. Dubbed "Jenny," this awesome nuclear gun emitted a single beam of directed energy so powerful, it could take out a hundred men in a single, lethal blast.

The problem Fornax faced presently was a different one. He was afraid that Jenny's highly-effective beam was so diffuse, he might unintentionally vaporize the very people they were trying to save. What he was attempting to do now, as they drove along through the bush, was adjust the focusing element so as to make the neutron spray that much narrower and thus more precise. That way, it could be used more like a delicate laser scalpel intended for microsurgery, instead of a cut-down-everything-in-sight chainsaw for clearing a forest — precision versus bludgeoning.

But between the stomachache he brought along with him from the launch, and the bouncing of the itty-bitty as Gunter flew across the savanna, Fornax wasn't having much luck. He was just about to object, when all of a sudden the vehicle slowed to a crawl.

"We're here," Gunter said. "Or at least very close."

Within a matter of two hundred meters, they came to a fork in the road. Veering left, the itty-bitty descended through a series of sharp switchbacks that ended when they reached a bridge at the river. There, Gunter pulled off the road and hid the vehicle in a thick grove of trees.

"We walk from here," he said, as he reached for his weapon and rucksack.

Inside the pack were cutting tools for the inevitable fence, plus heavy-duty gloves for the barbed wire, a gas mask and six manual firebombs. BC had demonstrated their use last night before setting out on the water. Gunter paid close attention. He was an expert with climbing gear and the like. But working with explosives was certainly not part of his skill set.

As Gunter quickly learned, a firebomb was circular at the top like a conventional grenade. But that's where the similarity ended. Its hull was covered with a sheet of heavy plastic, and at its base was a handle that enabled the thrower to hurl the incendiary device with great accuracy. The trick was in the timing, for once the plastic shield was torn off, the thrower had only fifteen seconds to complete his throw before the firebomb exploded.

Gunter had tried it once, at BC's urging, and found the thing easy to throw. But now, as he swung the rucksack up and over his shoulders, he wished he had practiced his throwing a couple more times.

The four of them set off into the bush at a good clip. They traveled in almost total silence, something BC was glad for, as he had a lot on his mind. Since leaving Sam's place in Auckland, no one had said a word to him about Carina and him being brother and sister, or about him being Sam's son. They could see he was troubled by the news, but had kept their opinions to themselves. Only Saron had broached the subject and even then only to nudge him in the ribs and ask how he was doing. All BC had done was grunt and say how he just wanted to finish this job and get the hell out of here.

It didn't take long — under an hour from where Gunter ditched the itty-bitty — and they were there. They had agreed beforehand that only the men would venture into the compound. Saron was to hold back until she had her bearings, then launch the knockout grenades from a distance of some three hundred meters out. Of the four, she was the only one with any real experience handling a megaflare launcher. She had become somewhat of an expert during her stint as an Afghan freedom fighter. Plus, the three men were chauvinists at heart — *No way were they going to place a woman as fine as she was directly in harm's way.*

It took another half-hour after leaving Saron for the three men to get into position. But once they had donned their gas masks and scooted in close enough to the fence to hit the enemy with a volley of manual firebombs, the signal was given.

Saron performed her job like a pro, lobbing three of the chemically-filled globes over the target area and exploding them on schedule. One struck the barracks directly and the other two came close. The three men waited for the drugs to take effect, then dropped their masks to the ground and moved in towards the fence. This was either going to be the shortest rescue in history — or the most dangerous.

Inside the compound there was mass confusion. As soon as people started dropping like flies, Lotha knew that something was afoot, that this might be his only chance for escape.

The big man moved without hesitation. He seemed unaffected by the gas. The first guard he reached, he pummeled into submission with his fists. When he headed for the door, two other prisoners followed close behind. As the effects of the anesthetic became more pronounced, they began propping each other up.

The layout of the camp dictated their escape strategy. The male prisoners were being held in six concrete bunkers arranged in a semi-circle at the north end of the camp. The females in three wooden buildings at the opposite end. Inbetween lay a messhall, a shower house, the guards' barracks, a maintenance shed and a utility shed. The entire complex was ringed by a double set of electrified, chain-link fences rigged with both motion and heat sensors.

Lotha was smart enough to know that if some sort of rescue attempt was actually underway, the power to the fences would have to be cut — and he would have to be the one doing the cutting.

Though the camp had obviously been gassed by some kind of airborne chemical agent, the gas itself was having an uneven effect. Some bigger men, like Lotha, though stumbling around a bit, could still function, while others were out cold on the ground. From what Lotha could tell, he was one of the few hostages that hadn't passed out from the gas.

Grabbing a force gun from the inert hands of a fallen guard, Lotha made a beeline for the utility shed. It seemed the only likely place from which to interrupt the power to the fences. The two men standing guard outside the cement-block building were crumpled in a heap on the ground.

Lotha approached the building with caution. He had already pulled all the way back on the knob to set the force gun to maximum. He checked once over his shoulders before taking aim, then blew the lock off the door, and the door off its hinges.

But one thing he didn't count on was the gun's tremendous recoil. An explosion of pain shot through his body as his shoulder separated beneath his shirt.

The pain was excruciating. Big man that he was, Lotha sank to his knees, faint.

If not for a cry of "Help!" somewhere in the yard, a cry that brought him back to his senses, Lotha would surely have passed out on the spot.

Instead, he struggled back to his feet using the barrel of the gun as a crutch. He was just about to start inside the shed to turn off the power to the fences, when he heard a sound behind him.

Lotha twisted clumsily around to face his attacker. He moved slowly, like a glacier, burdened by the biting pain that raced like a lightning bolt down his arm from his splintered shoulder.

Lotha was barely halfway through his turn, when the man behind him swung his quarterstaff, striking Lotha in the head. It was one of those hardwood clubs the gulag was so famous for.

The blow would have killed an ordinary man, cracking his skull like tinder, and laying open his brains.

But Lotha was no ordinary man. He suffered from Paget's disease, a disfiguring bone ailment that had left his braincase more than three inches thick in spots. Sure, the blow broke the skin, and sure, blood flowed from the torn epidermis, but no, it didn't come close to killing him. *All it did was make him angry!*

In an ordinary man, a surge of adrenaline could do wondrous things — make him forge a stream he couldn't possibly jump otherwise, allow him to lift a weight he normally couldn't budge, compel him to swing a fist with the power of a sledgehammer.

Only, Lotha was no ordinary man. Inside *his* body, a rush of adrenaline became a tool for killing. When he recognized the face of the man who stood over him clutching a hardwood club, Lotha went berserk, setting aside the force gun to seal this bastard's fate with his own two bare hands. For this was none other than that ugly specimen of humanity, the guard who had fed morsels of bread to the prisoners through the slats of the boxcar as if they were little more than pathetic house pets.

For a brief instant, Lotha just glared at his assailant. Then, in one swift stride, Lotha was there, standing beside the brute from the White Brigade.

He tore the club from the man's grip, broke the man's fingers with his own. Then he hauled back on the club and smacked the man once in the face with the gnarled, butt-end of the stick.

Teeth flew everywhere, and the man screamed out in pain. Blood gushed from his mouth. His eyes were white with horror and he tried to protect his face from another swing. The man was astonished Lotha could even move after the punishing way he had hit him, much less retaliate. Then the guard cringed, realizing the big Afghan wasn't done with him yet.

Taking a step backwards, Lotha wound up on the quarterstaff like a baseball player at the plate. Then he swung the club with all his might, striking the guard across both knees at once. There was a terrible cracking sound as the blow shattered the man's kneecaps. He buckled under the pain, writhing and groaning grotesquely before he fell to the dirt.

"That's for Inda," Lotha said as he drew closer. Blood still oozed from the side of his head where the guard had hit him. Now he raised his fist.

"You animal!" the prone man spat. "You'll rot in hell for this."

"One can only hope." Lotha grinned through crooked teeth.

Then he grabbed the crippled man by the collar and lifted him from the ground. Their eyes were now level. Behind them, near the men's barracks, shouts rang out, then gunfire.

"What are you going to do to me?" the panic-stricken man screamed. Tears rolled down his cheek.

"Break your neck," came the calm reply.

And then, with one vicious twist, he did.

The dirty deed done, Lotha tossed the dead man aside like he was nothing. He turned and stepped across the threshold into the utility shed, force gun at his side. Sparks flew as he blew out everything that looked important — comm lines, circuit boards, fuse boxes, everything. By the time he was back outside, prisoners and guards were locked in hand-to-hand contests all over the compound.

Lotha fought his way in the direction of the women's quarters, where Carina was being held. He took out as many of the guards as he could, even those who were still unconscious. *Why worry about fighting them later, if he could kill them easily now?*

Somehow, in the confusion, he spied Gunter crouching at the corner of a building thirty meters away. After what happened on Mars, Lotha had every reason to hate this man. As far as Lotha was concerned, Gunter was as responsible as anyone for the fate that befell every Newton on the planet.

Lotha raised his force gun to eye level, centering his quarry in his sights. Then, just as he was about to squeeze off a round, a familiar voice shouted, "Don't shoot! Gunter's on our side! He's one of the good guys!"

Lotha couldn't believe his ears — it was Fornax Nehrengel, of all people! But before he could utter a syllable in protest, BC yelled at him from the opposite direction. "Where in the hell are they keeping Carina?"

Lotha pointed to the closest of three buildings at the southern perimeter of the camp. BC nodded, broke cover, and began running in that direction. Just as he took off, Lotha saw Fornax take out two guards, plus part of a building, with a single shot from his blaster. They just disappeared in a puff of blue smoke.

BC covered the ground in no time at all, with Fornax providing cover. Gunter, then Lotha, followed in his footsteps.

Moving quickly now, BC burst through the doors of the women's barracks. Inside he found what amounted to a big dormitory filled with row upon row of bunk beds.

But the stench from inside was incredible. It knocked him back about ten feet. The whole place stank of excrement, like a plogged toilet that had run over but never been mopped up. Unconscious bodies lay everywhere — on the floor, on the bunks, on each other.

While Fornax covered the door, BC ran from bed to bed trying to find her. *But Carina was nowhere in sight!*

By this time, Gunter had joined Fornax at the door, and BC had swallowed his panic. He went back through the room for a second time, slowly turning over each inert body, carefully studying each face, repeatedly calling out her name. This time, he found her.

BC could scarcely believe his eyes. The once vibrant woman, the woman he had lived with for nearly a year, was now little more than skin and bones. When he found her, Carina was stark naked and out cold on the straw-covered floor of the barracks. Her hair had been chopped off. She was dirty and smelled of urine. Never a heavy woman to begin with, now she was thin to the point of gaunt.

BC reached down, wrapped his sister's emaciated body in a blanket, and slung her over his shoulder. Then he started for the door.

"We've got what we came for," Gunter said, still guarding the entrance with Fornax. "Let's get the hell out of here!"

BC nodded and girded himself to make the run across the compound with Carina balanced on his shoulders.

"Wait a minute," Lotha said, blocking their exit. "You bastards only came for her? What about me? What about all the rest of the Newtons?"

"Sorry, but we only came for her," Fornax said, sliding his blaster into his gunhand in case Lotha tried to stop them from leaving.

"So where does that leave the rest of us? Up shit-creek without a paddle? Don't we count for anything?"

"We have transportation out of here only for us. Everyone else will have to fend for themselves."

"Maybe we could arrange to come back later," Gunter offered unexpectedly

"Yeah, that might be possible," Fornax nodded.

"You wouldn't lie to me, now would you?" Lotha said, unsure whether or not the three of them could be trusted. "I have your word, right? You will come back for the rest of us later, won't you?"

"You have our word," Fornax said. "I'll bring the *Tikkidiw*. I can put her down in a clearing about a klom east of here. Just follow the road."

"Good. In that case, I'll stay here and finish off the rest of these bastards. How long until you return?"

"Give us half a day, maybe less."

And then they were off.

FORTY-TWO

Option Two

The three men were huddled around the nav-console onboard the *Tikkidiw*. They stared out the porthole with some apprehension at the giant spinning asteroid that filled their field of vision. It was an oddly-shaped monstrosity, with one side back-lit by the sun and the rest a mysterious place of unseen shadows, black and gray. Though the big planetoid lay off the starboard side some seventy-five kloms away, it was so large, it seemed as if they could just reach out and touch it.

Locating the rocky mass had been the easy part, and that was already behind them. Once they had established radio comm-link with newly-promoted Assistant Supervisor Leif Popovich back on the ground, he had simply read them the x, y, and z coordinates off his 3-D holo-screen. Then it had only been a matter of Fornax inputting the coordinates into the *Tikkidiw's* nav-computer and flying the three of them out here.

The trip itself had taken under ten minutes. But what was to come next was rather more difficult. They had to match the asteroid's rotational attitude — the "rotatt" as Popovich called it — spin to everyone else.

Though the asteroid was falling inward towards the center of the solar system along a regularly-shaped elliptical path, the rest of its motion was nothing if not bizarre. Instead of flying nose-first through space like a ballistic missile might, the big rock was in a multi-axis spin, tumbling end-over-end and from side to side like a poorly thrown football, only not so smooth.

In order to level out the spin and allow ground control to reestablish communications with the EMD, a replacement antenna-unit had to be hooked up next to the mass driver. This was no easy task. It meant someone had to approach to within two hundred meters of the planetoid, cross the remaining distance "on foot," as it were, then do the installation atop a spinning gerbil.

That someone was Fornax, plus his two buddies, BC and Gunter. No other ship but his could get there in time. Plus, Fornax had an LGLA onboard to assist the nav-computer in matching the asteroid's erratic rotatt.

In reality, the *Tikkidiw* was nothing more than a refurbished shuttle once used for hauling nuclear waste. But, Fornax had been making improvements ever since he got his hands on her. His latest was a laser-guided landing array. The LGLA sat on the outside of the ship's hull. It was designed to assure a smooth descent and a safe landing under the most difficult of circumstances and even in the most unfamiliar of terrains. Once the LGLA was given a landing site to lock onto, it repeatedly adjusted the angular thrusters until the ship had assumed the identical rotatt as the surface it was approaching. Setting a ship down on any surface couldn't be made simpler than that.

And yet, despite having this highly advanced piece of navigational equipment onboard, maneuvering in this close to a wildly spinning asteroid was a gut-wrenching experience for all three of them, but none worse than Fornax. Just imagine being trapped alone on the deck of a small sailing ship, one that was anchored far from shore in choppy seas. Now, imagine further that you have been strapped to a chair fitted with coasters at the bottom of each leg and forced to down several liters of ale on an otherwise empty stomach. With each roll of the ship, you are wheeling uncontrollably to-and-fro across the wave-splashed deck. Overhead, an airchop circles slowly. It is hauling beneath it a weighted rope that is pendulumming back and forth before your very eyes. It isn't long before nausea crowds out all other sensations.

The asteroid alongside them was in a similar three-axis roll. That meant it was tumbling not only end-over-end but also spinning clockwise on its long axis and counterclockwise along its short axis. The laser-guided thrusters onboard the *Tikkidiw* were operating as they should, methodically working to match the ship's rotatt to the big rock's rotatt. Nevertheless, the adjustment process wasn't instantaneous. It took time to make the corrections, and it proceeded in fits and starts.

Without a fixed reference point to focus their tired eyes on, watching the slow dance unfold out through the bulkhead window was a sure recipe for scrambling one's guts. Plus, it didn't help much *not* to watch, because once the brain caught a glimpse of what was happening outside, the stomach quickly followed suit. Suffice it to say, before it was over, all three of them — Gunter, Fornax, and BC — had thrown up.

Yet, despite everything they had already been through to this point, the hard part was still to come. If Popovich's people down on the ground were to ever regain control over this deadly unguided missile, it was up to these three to install a new comm-unit onboard the EMD, a unit which could take the place of the factory-installed unit Inda Desai had destroyed with his homemade bomb.

Fornax held the antenna-unit in his hand, now. It seemed rather small and unpretentious, especially considering how vitally important it was to controlling something the size of an asteroid. The unit had come direct from the manufacturer sealed in a durable polybag, and he felt its weight as he deposited the thing into Gunter's knapsack along with the electro-solder gun, a pair of pneumatic pliers, a spool of electrical tape, and a riveter. The shiny Bolt Gun hung from a metal clip on his webbed tool belt.

"I guess it's time," Gunter said, pulling the last of his shoulder straps snug.

Turning to BC, the big Aussie double-checked the bio-readouts on his wristband with the levels BC was showing on his onboard monitor. Oxygen, heart rate, pressure — all green line.

"Are you sure about this?" Fornax asked, still feeling woozy from the rotatt synchronization. "You've got family. So does BC. I should be the one going on the spacewalk."

"Hell's bells, man, you're in no condition. Besides, you're the only pilot we got. If something goes haywire, you're the only one who can get us the hell home in one piece."

His mind made up, Gunter fastened his helmet shut, then edged towards the airlock. He and BC traded jibes as he went, chatting with one another on the remote to be absolutely certain everything was in proper working order.

No matter what either of the other two said, Gunter knew he was the logical choice to carryout this mission. He was, after all, an experienced alpinist, and everything about this spacewalk had the qualities of scaling a steep mountain wall. Clearly, Gunter was the only one skilled enough with ropes and climbing techniques to have a chance at successfully pulling this off. Besides, if he lived out the day, Gunter had big plans. He still had a bit of a score to settle with a disagreeable fellow named Oskar Schaeffer. With J's help Gunter had been able to gather all the evidence he would need to put Schaeffer behind bars for supplying Inda and the Newton Liberation Party with arms. Only, Gunter had no intention of letting the man off that easy. There would be no Johannesburg magistrate for Herr Schaeffer — just a harpoon to the belly. But no time to think of that pleasure just now.

"Open the hatch," Gunter instructed, clipping himself to the safety tether. Several hundred meters of it sat neatly coiled on the deck behind him. If he got himself into a jam out there, the other two could haul him back in, in no time at all.

Fornax did as he was told, and — as the hatch swung free — Gunter floated out into empty space. It wasn't actually empty, of course — directly in front of him, some two hundred meters away, was an enormous rock, a rock that carried a frightful amount of kinetic energy, 40 trillion joules, or some such ridiculously large figure if Popovich had done the math right. It didn't matter anyway; even a fool could see this rock was of dinosaur-killer size.

Gunter looked at the asteroid, now, with amused eyes. It seemed so tranquil, even idyllic, not dangerous at all. But the serenity was an illusion. The enormous boulder was spinning madly, careening ever closer to Earth. But, since the asteroid's motion relative to Gunter's own was zero, it seemed to just hang there quietly, patiently waiting for him to do something brilliant.

Gunter swallowed his fear and began. His plan of attack was simple and straightforward. Using the Bolt Gun he had taken from his climbing pack, the same Bolt Gun that made it possible for him and his crew to scale Olympus Mons, Gunter would embed a secure tether in the rock adjacent to the repair site. Then, using his own, patented mechanical-ascender, he would cross the gap separating the *Tikkidiw* from the asteroid and rivet the new comm-unit into place. Strip and wrap a few wires, and voilà, EMD 14 would be back online!

Attached to the bolt he would be firing was a loop, and snaked through that loop was a cable. This was the cable he would be "hanging" from when all the connections were secure. Aiming and firing the bolt had to be executed with some precision — If he aimed too high, the bolt would go flying off into open space, cable attached, and him with it. If he aimed too low, he would punch a hole clean through the side of the EMD. Though Fornax had assured him the mass driver wouldn't blow up like a can of petrol might, he had also suggested the electromagnets wouldn't take too kindly to being punctured.

Thus, it was with this fear in mind, now, that Gunter directed his full attention to getting the bolt on target. He ignored any thought of what would come after, something that would shortly turn out to be a serious mistake. In all his preparations, Gunter had forgotten one very important thing — *a Bolt Gun packed quite a wallop!*

As soon as he pulled the trigger, Gunter knew he was in trouble. A Bolt Gun had been designed with climbers in mind, not spacemen. Indeed, it fired a diamond-tipped bolt with such force, the bolt was capable of penetrating nearly any type of rock. Out on the mountain, where there was plenty of gravity, not to mention air friction as well as restraining ropes, the recoil from firing a bolt into a rock face was of small consequence. Oh, there was the occasional bruised shoulder or even broken finger. But certainly nothing to compare with the devastating consequences of firing the Gun in open space.

It all happened so fast, Gunter never knew what hit him. In the space of a micro-second, everything was a blur.

One second he was floating a meter or so away from the *Tikkidiw*. The next, he was in excruciating pain.

Having been so close to the ship when he pulled the trigger was his big mistake of the evening. Immediately, the right-handed Gunter was hurled by the blast into a vicious, clockwise spin. Kicked backward by the force, he couldn't prevent his gunhand from being slammed against the hull of the ship with tragic results.

At the collision of flesh against metal, there was a terrible cracking sound, one which could be heard even inside the ship. The impact had been at such an angle, his wrist and hand were totally shattered by the blow.

Gunter screamed out in pain. Acting, now, out of anguish, the injured man pulled his mangled appendage closer in to his body, thus adding even more inertia to his spin, much as an Olympic ice-skater might, to liven-up her act. After three or four dizzying turns, Gunter blacked out.

Inside the ship, BC was the first to realize that something had gone terribly wrong. All the bio-readouts on his monitor spiked, then went to zero. Though BC didn't know it yet, along with Gunter's wrist and hand, his wristband had been smashed in the accident as well.

"Bloody hell, something's wrong," BC yelled. "Help me get him back in!"

Fornax immediately dropped what he was doing and sprang across the cabin to give BC a hand. The two men worked as fast as they could. Still, precious minutes slipped away. They not only had to haul their injured friend back inside, they had to pressurize the airlock, undo his suit, and try to figure out what the hell had gone wrong out there.

At first, none of it made any sense, and with Gunter still out cold, their answers were slow in coming.

While BC applied chem-ice to Gunter's wrist to slow the swelling, he and Fornax talked. One of the two of them had to go out there and finish the job.

When the two men got right down to it, it wasn't actually a question of drawing straws. BC was the only medic onboard. Even though Gunter was now beginning to stir, it only made good sense for BC to be the one to stay with him. Which meant Fornax had to be the one to go.

There was, however, one piece of good news. In spite of hurting himself, Gunter's aim had been superb. They could see through the viewfinder that the bolt was secure and precisely where they wanted it to be.

Now all that remained was for Fornax to swing across and save the world from the worst asteroid collision in more than sixty-five million years!

Unlike some men, Fornax wasn't the natural-born-hero type. Oh, he was brave enough when he had to be. Only, somewhere along the line he had decided that staying among the living was preferable to being revered as a fallen hero.

For some inexplicable reason this was on his mind as he anxiously clutched the handgrip at the doorway of the *Tikkidiw* before stepping out into open space.

Fornax drew a deep breath to flush the adrenaline from his system. Then he clicked on the mechanical-ascender and held tight. Ever so slowly it began to ferry him away from the ship.

It was peaceful out here, he thought. Peaceful and quiet. Quiet and cold. Like during the winter. After a snowstorm. Beneath a blanket of fresh snow, all sounds were muffled, even laughter.

Fornax hadn't gotten far, perhaps fifteen meters, when it happened.

It began much like a rainstorm. First one drop, then a second, then a third, then a torrent. Only, this was no rainstorm, not of the water variety anyway. This was a rainstorm of particles, big and small, a rainstorm of pebbles!

Like Leif Popovich had once tried to explain to Lieutenant Colonel Nicholson, asteroids were like ducks on a pond, little "chicks" trailing behind their mother. Only now, propelled by the asteroid's centripetal force, loose bits and pieces of rock were flying everywhere, some as large as three-quarters of a meter long and weighing up to . . .

Thunk!

When the boulder struck Fornax's helmet just behind the ear, it gave off a low, hollow sound, like a cinder block dropped into deep water from a boat dock, or the shoe of a horse against the wooden slats of a covered bridge. *Thunk.*

Instinct ruled response.

The reflex reaction to a blow on the head, one honed to perfection by a hundred thousand generations of hominid evolution, was to clasp one's fingers around the back of the skull and press one's arms flat against the temples to ward off any further blows. This, Fornax did instinctively. And without giving it a second thought.

In nearly every conceivable situation this built-in response to a threat made perfect sense. Except this one. Now, when Fornax swept his hands back to protect his head, he released his grip on the bars of the mechanical-ascender. This was a mistake he would not soon forget.

Caught in the wash of the continuing blizzard of particles, both big and small, Fornax was swept along by the current like a rafter thrown from his craft in a fast river. The glittering, whitewater carried him downstream, away from the ship. If not for the safety tether, he would most assuredly have been dragged away and lost forever.

In the moments before the accident, BC had been paying out the safety rope to Fornax in regular lengths. Now, suddenly, he was forced to reverse course. Gunter jumped in to help. But, with his broken hand, it was all but impossible for the two of them to tow poor Fornax back in again quickly.

They talked on the remote. "What's your status?"

"Actually, I'm fine," Fornax said. Though badly shaken, he didn't seem to be hurt.

BC's face was grim. They were running out of time. Before long, the asteroid would accelerate beyond the point of no return. They scarcely had enough time to get Fornax back in and BC into a suit and back out.

"Can you finish this?"

"Oh, yeah," Fornax said, raring to have another go at it.

"This time, feed the damn tether through the loop on the mech-asc," Gunter instructed sternly, still nursing his busted wrist. "That way it'll stay with you no matter what. And another thing — Don't forget to lock yourself down at the other end before you start popping rivets. We don't want a repeat of my numbskull move, now do we?"

Fornax nodded his understanding, and prepared for his next move. Like a well-trained puppy, the mechanical-ascender was still sitting out there on the line, waiting for him to climb back aboard. It had stopped moving the instant he let go of it. Now he had to find some way to get back out to it.

Plunging ahead, now, for a second time, Fornax covered the fifteen or so meters hand-over-hand, hanging like a trapeze artist from the line. Weightless, it was a piece of cake.

When he reached the mech-asc, he ran the safety tether through the loop as Gunter instructed. Then he continued his journey. A hundred and eighty-five meters of open space remained.

In some respects, Fornax didn't have a clue what to expect out here. Oh, he knew the technical details well enough — Ride the mechanical-ascender across the cable. Rivet the antenna box into place, one rivet in each corner. Hook red wire to red, white to white, and green to green. Hurry back to the ship.

But that simple list said nothing of the terror of hanging in open space 200 million kloms above nothing at all.

It said nothing of the dread of touching the wrong wire, of heating up the EMD, of being melted into a sticky blob of human flesh.

It said nothing of the fear of being held responsible for destroying an entire world if he fouled up.

His breath came in gulps now.

All Fornax could hear was the sound of metal scraping against metal as the mechanical-ascender ground its way across the two hundred meters from ship to rock.

A cable, a double-wheeled pulley, and a locking device were all that separated this scared young man from oblivion.

Fornax could feel the veins in his temple pop out. He could feel his heart pounding inside his chest. He could feel his breath coming faster. And faster.

All of a sudden, Fornax couldn't seem to get enough air!

Something was terribly wrong!

BC screamed at him through the comm. "Slow down your breathing or you'll pass out!" He had been monitoring Fornax's vitals on the bio-function terminal inside the ship. "I mean it! Slow down your breathing or you will hyperventilate!"

Fornax scolded himself for his stupidity — *Some hero you turned out to be,* he thought.

His breath came slower now. The big rock filled his field of view. Here, somewhere in the void between planets three and four, the future of mankind would be decided. *There was no tomorrow, only today.*

The nearer Fornax drew to the egg-shaped asteroid, the heavier he became. It wasn't that the asteroid was massive enough to produce measurable gravity, only that the comm-unit that needed replacing was out along one axis, rather than being located near the spinning planetoid's center of gravity. Thus, he was gaining centripetal force the closer he got to his quarry.

He could feel it building up on him with each step. Where before, he was weightless and giddy, now he was heavy and lethargic. Where before, the contents of his stomach had been floating free, ready to gurgle up at any moment, now everything had sunk like a rock to the pit of his abdomen. His arms felt heavy. Even the weight of his suit began to drag him down.

Sensing danger, Fornax slowed his approach. The g-forces were tugging at him with some conviction now. His legs began to drift up and out to his left, away from the center of gravity of the spinning rock. Except for the lumina-beam shining from the top of his helmet, everything was dark.

He tightened his grip on the crossbar of the mech-asc. The closer he drew to the big rock, the harder he was being pushed away from it.

Only ten meters to go!

Fornax was close enough, now, to see the results of Inda's handiwork. The bomb had torn away the entire antenna housing. It was a blackened mess. Had the saboteur used a couple more ounces of Tovex, the EMD itself would have been ruptured, making this whole exercise useless.

Fornax clawed his way the last few meters against the crushing centripetal force. Finally, with almost no strength left in his arms, he reached out with one hand and clipped himself directly to Gunter's diamond-tipped bolt. *It was time to get down to work!*

The rivet gun was in his hand. The spool of beryllium-copper alloy electrical tape was in his pocket. The knapsack was off his back, now, and in his hand.

He tore away the polybag protecting the comm-unit and tethered it to the velcro strip running down the length of his right leg. Propelled by the g-forces, the rucksack floated away from him, drifting off in the same general direction his legs were pointed. The polybag followed suit.

Fornax moved quickly. In went one rivet, then a second. But, just as he was about to punch in the third, he was suddenly blinded by the most intense light in the entire solar system.

Fornax reeled backwards. Up to now he had been working in the shadow of the asteroid, on the side opposite the sun.

But now, all of a sudden, he had ridden the beast through a revolution and been spun into the light. The timing couldn't have been worse.

As his gloved hands flew to his face to shield his eyes, the rivet gun fell from his grip. The glass on his visor darkened almost immediately. But, for an instant, he couldn't see. He reached blindly for the rivet gun. But already it was too late — the tool had been swallowed up by the darkness.

"Damn!" he swore, alarming BC in the cabin.

"What happened now?" came the reply over the mike.

"I lost the rivet gun."

"What do you mean, lost it? Can you get the bloody thing back? We don't have another one, you know. How can you attach the bloody antenna without rivets?"

"Don't have a cat, my friend. I got two rivets in before I dropped the gun. Upper left and lower right. It just might hold. Anyway, you might have warned me about the sun."

BC fumed. "This is *my* fault? Why you son of a . . . "

Gunter interrupted. "Two ought to hold her. Look, mate, you've got only about twenty more minutes of air left. Is that gonna be enough time to finish the job?"

Though Fornax answered, "Yes," he wasn't sure himself. There was still the small matter of reconnecting the loose wires. He silently prayed that like all the wiring onboard the *Tikkidiw*, these wires were magnetized, each color charged with a slightly different polarity so they would stick only to another wire of the identical color. Otherwise, as clumsy as he was working with these bulky gloves, reconnecting them could prove to be quite a chore — and a time-consuming one at that.

Fornax reached for the spool of insulating tape in his pocket. He popped the insulation back on the first wire and found all his prayers answered. *The wires were magnetized!*

He moved quickly now. Red to red, white to white, green to green. Then he was on his way back.

Thrown outward at first by the centripetal force that he had had gained, he slowed his descent with the brake on the mech-asc.

Weightlessness returned. His legs hung free once more. His breathing slowed. The *Tikkidiw* filled his field of vision. *It was over!*

All that remained now was to pull the ship a safe distance away from the big rock and radio Assistant Supervisor Leif Popovich that it was time to warm up the electromagnets.

BC pulled his friend into the airlock. Fornax collapsed onto the floor and pulled off his helmet. Saving the world had been a heady experience. But he still had to do the one and only thing that really mattered, and that was to figure out where he stood with the woman he loved.

By comparison, the job he just finished had been easy.

FORTY-THREE

Ad Astra

Carina Matthews, Ph.D. sat in the shadow of Omen, her sharply pointed tool in hand, and scratched at the sedimentary rocks at her feet.

Long ago, in an earlier age, these finely-etched layers of stone rested on the floor of an ancient sea. Theory had it, this vast body of water had once been alive with stromatolite-like organisms. Carina Matthews was determined to be the first scientist to uncover definitive fossil proof of their existence.

Thinking she might have found something, Carina held the fragment of rock up to the light. Behind her, eyeing her every move with suspicion, was a mountain of stupendous proportions. She had scaled its heights in a prior lifetime, yet the question still remained. *How many more mountains would she be expected to climb before she finally found an answer?*

Carina's back and shoulders still hurt, a constant reminder of what she had recently been through. Though the Acceleron, in concert with plenty of rest, had healed her wounds, Carina would never forget. Like her mother before her, Carina had somehow survived the rigors of the gulag. It had changed her life forever.

Humbled, now, by the terrifying experience, every question of substance she ever had to wrestle with, had a new and more frightening answer. Her father's perennial question. The one dealing with persecution.

Ever since she was a little girl he had always wanted to know why — Why were people so prejudiced? He would ask her — *What possible purpose can it serve? What was the driving force behind it? Tell me, Carina — certainly there has to be a reason!*

Now, when it was all said and done. Now, after all she had been through. Carina thought she had the answer. There *was* no reason, none whatsoever. Persecution was nothing more than hatred by another name. It was just that simple, though it tore her apart on the inside to admit it. To hate someone, all you needed was an excuse — and not even much of one at that.

Over the course of the past ten thousand years, the human race had experimented with a thousand different religions and another thousand different cultures. But still, nothing could change the fact that Man was little more than a brilliant, tool-using scavenger living out on the brink.

Back on the savanna, where *Homo sapiens* first evolved, each day meant finding a way to outsmart an unforgiving environment, finding a way to grab for yourself and for your kin whatever was needed from whomever currently had it.

And, with living conditions on the veldt being as marginal as they were, it only made good sense to have a healthy disregard — if not outright resentment — for your neighbor down the road, because whatever *he* ate, whatever resource *he* used, was one you could not. His survival might mean your demise. His success might spell your failure.

Driven by primordial forces as powerful as these, natural selection could only have taken one course, and that was to reinforce the already instinctive urge to beat the hell out of your neighbor and send him packing anytime you felt threatened.

Back in those early days, with most of the world uninhabited by human beings, if some bully chased you off your land, you simply pulled up stakes and moved on up the valley. Small wonder, the race spread across the face of the earth in nothing flat.

But, in more recent times, with the carrying capacity of the planet strained to the bursting, there were no longer any unoccupied valleys to move up. Now, instead of merely chasing his neighbors away, the bully began to strike them down. Only, somewhere between the savanna and the first pogrom, a complication arose.

As might be expected of a sentient being, we humans evolved a tad bit of guilt along the way. Now, all of a sudden, our oversized brains demanded a *reason* before it killed. And the reasons we came up with were no less amazing than our creativity in other areas.

They're fat, they're stupid, they're black, they're greedy, they're white, they don't believe in what I do, their eyes are slanted, they're clumsy, they eat strange foods. Oh, how dare you suggest they look the same as me! Oh, what do you mean when you claim we're all identical under the skin? Can't you see the differences? They speak strangely, their ideas are dangerous, they believe in one god, they believe in three gods, in no god, they worship the Devil.

It doesn't really matter so long as there is a reason.

All this and more burdened Carina's mind in the days following her arrest. At each step along the way, from Heathrow to Johannesburg to the confines of the boxcar to the compound in the Great Rift Valley, she had struggled to understand. Now, at long last, she thought she did.

Two weeks had passed since the day of the rescue, and they were now all back on Mars. Well, almost all. They had buried Sam six days ago. He had died young, though at least he'd died a happy man, with his son, daughter, and grandson all at his side at the end.

There hadn't been time to try and locate Nasha before the funeral. But even if there had been time, Sam wouldn't have wanted her there. *Why put the woman through all that just to stand there and watch him die?* Carina would have to track her mother down one day, but it was more than she could handle right now, so soon after her father's death.

At the end, it all happened so fast. Sam had simply run out of gas. He lacked even the energy or the inclination to amend his will before he passed. Thus, everything he owned — the land, the stake in ASARCO, his interest in the asteroid mining venture, the bonds, the house, everything — went to Carina.

Ever the gentleman, BC didn't object. But anyone could see that this outcome wasn't exactly fair. Nor was it fair to Nasha, should she still be alive.

In any event, Carina quickly remedied matters. She filed a disclaimer with the circuit judge and disavowed one-half of the inheritance, putting everything in trust for her and her brother. It only made good sense. She hardly had any interest in money and certainly knew nothing about investments. When she returned to Mars the next day onboard the *Tikkidiw*, BC stayed behind to settle their affairs and to arrange for a caretaker to keep watch over Sam's property in Auckland. It was agreed Nanna Purdy would stay on and help BC take care of Sam, Jr.

Gunter decided to return to Mars as well, especially now that Carina had dropped her demands that Newton be a sanctuary reserved for newhumans alone.

And Sister Siona too. BC had promised her a seat onboard the next shuttle headed for Mars, and he was good to his word. Together, all four of them returned — Gunter, Siona, Saron, and Lotha — each intent on doing what they could to rebuild the colony the White Brigade had destroyed.

As for Lotha, the bravery he displayed back in the gulag had earned him a certain notoriety. He had it in his head to run, now, for Sam's vacant Council seat at the upcoming biennial election.

In Carina's opinion, a better choice would have been Gunter. But then nobody listened to her anymore. *As if it really mattered!* All Carina really cared about these days was putting the shattered pieces of her life back together again. Which left only Fornax. Where exactly did *he* fit in?

Carina stared at the sliver of rock in her hands. Somehow, in her reverie, she had forgotten all about it. It was yellowish, with speckles of white. Granite, perhaps.

She pulled out her magnifying glass to study it closer. In the distance came the whine of a landrover. Someone was fast approaching. Hopefully it wasn't that pain in the ass Nehru again, or worse yet, his wife.

Ever since it was revealed in the days following the funeral that Nehru had been the one responsible for pointing the finger at Inda and Lotha to begin with, he and his family had been shunned by what remained of the community. In everyone's eyes, Nehru had violated the Afghan Code of Honor. By all rights, the man deserved to be put to death.

Instead, he kept showing up at Carina's doorstep with this or that complaint, as if she had the power to square things with the entire colony.

Quite frankly, Carina couldn't stand the man. Whether he meant to or not, Nehru was responsible for everything that had gone wrong in her life, including her own capture and arrest. She hated him for that. Of course, as Gunter pointed out to her the other day, if Nehru hadn't been the one to snitch, sooner or later, someone in their circle would have. It was only a matter of time. To coin one of her father's favorite sayings: *the status quo hates to be upset.*

The whine of the landrover drew closer. Much to Carina's relief, it wasn't Nehru's face that stared out at her through the windshield, but someone else's, someone just as difficult for her to face — Fornax Nehrengel.

Carina girded herself for the man's arrival. The encounter was bound to be a thorny one. Here was a man who had every reason to hate her. And yet, he kept on coming. Except for that one night 2 1/2 years ago, she had never given him the time of day. And yet, once again, he had saved her life. And not just *her* life, everyone's life, the whole world's.

Though Carina had been confined to a hospital bed in Auckland when it all happened, from what her brother told her, she managed to piece together a pretty good picture of how Fornax had saved humanity from a fate worse than death:

The news about the errant asteroid had gone swiftly up the chain of command from then fourth-class assistant Leif Popovich to his boss, Supervisor Dawson, to Lieutenant Colonel Nicholson to J, the head of Commonwealth Intelligence. J had, in turn, contacted BC in Auckland. He, Gunter, and Fornax had only recently returned to Sam's place in Auckland with the last of the Great Rift prisoners. By then it was a foregone conclusion that Popovich's Option Two was the only practical alternative open to them at this late date. The three men were given the proper coordinates, and then it was simply a matter of pulling the *Tikkidiw* up alongside the asteroid, matching its speed and heading, then sending a properly suited and tethered man across the few meters of open space to pop a couple rivets and twist a few bare wires. Voilà, antenna re-attached, crisis averted. When BC told her the story, he made it all sound so easy and simple. But judging by the enormous cast hanging from the end of Gunter's arm, Carina suspected it had been rather more complicated than that.

The door of the landrover opened, and Fornax stepped out. He came to her, hand extended in a gesture of goodwill. He did what he could to hide his apprehension. But he found it difficult not to reveal his true feelings.

Then again, why should a man who had stared death in the face just a week ago, be absolutely terrified of this woman now? It made no sense.

"How are you?" he began.

"Okay," she answered flatly.

For the next several minutes, they talked at length, like people do, about absolutely nothing. Finally, he got up the nerve.

"Is there a chance for us?" he asked, voice faltering.

As was her way, Carina's answer was veiled. "If the Old Testament is to be taken literally, after the Israelites escaped from bondage in Egypt, they were made to wander in the desert, lost for forty years. It was as if God Himself were trying to prepare them for a lifetime — a millennium, actually — of finding their own way."

"I thought you didn't believe in God?"

"I think that now perhaps I do."

"Why the change of heart?"

"Let me see if I can explain," she said, still fingering the small piece of rock. "Inscribed on the walls of certain burial chambers in the pyramids of the later Old Kingdom are Egypt's oldest religious literature — the Pyramid Texts. They describe a mythical figure, Atum, as being the creator of the world. I wonder, is this also the basis for Adam in the Old Testament? For Atlas in Greek mythology? For Astarte in the Phoenician? For Allah? For Atman? Don't you see, Fornax? Despite all their differences, there seems to be an uncanny continuity here, one that tends to bind the whole of western civilization together. It can't all be by chance!"

"I would agree. In fact, your father would have said the very same thing. But what does that mean for you and me? For us?"

For the first time in a long time, Carina smiled. She had her regrets, sure — like being unable to solve the mystery of Matthews Disease before her father died. But that was no reason to put Fornax off any longer. He deserved better than that.

"Maybe we were meant for one another," she said. "Maybe we were destined to wander among the stars together, like tigers stalking their prey. You'll have to admit one thing, Fornax — there's certainly a lot more for us oldhumans to do out here in space than just settling dusty, old Mars. We've barely scratched the surface."

The panorama of the Milky Way unfolded above their heads. A thousand million star systems, a hundred million viable planets, all sparkling in the night sky, all beckoning them forward.

Like Columbus staring westward across the Atlantic before setting sail, like Marco Polo looking eastward across the steppes before mounting up, like Alan Shepard gazing skyward into the clouds before that first crucial flight aboard Freedom 7, the adventure had only just begun.

Despite all its many frailties, all its shortcomings, all its faults, Mankind simply had no choice in the matter. He had to fan out across the heavens — It was his way, his destiny! Just like in the beginning, just like it had always been, if a man was chased off his land by the bully next door, he simply had to pick up stakes and move on.

It was time.

Fornax took her hand.

She didn't resist.

He touched her, but in a tentative way. To him, she was like a wild horse. If he moved too quickly, she would surely get spooked and bolt.

Impatient for the ride, Carina cantered gracefully before him. Her head was held high. "At the rate you're going, this is going to take all day. Hurry up already, we have so much to do!"

Other Books By Steven Burgauer:

THE NIGHT OF THE ELEVENTH SUN — Neanderthal meets human
A MORE PERFECT UNION — America's second civil war, a war fought over the Second Amendment
THE RAILGUNS OF LUNA —a murderous woman preying on the world
THE BRAZEN RULE — a killer virus on the loose
THE LAST AMERICAN — a country on the brink of disaster
TREACHERY ON THE DARK SIDE — sex, murder and intrigue at zero-g
THE GRANDFATHER PARADOX — an intense voyage through time
NAKED CAME THE FARMER — a round-robin murder mystery
THE LONG ROAD TO WAR — a true-life story of World War II
THE WEALTH BUILDER'S GUIDE — an investment primer

"Burgauer's *The Brazen Rule* is tightly plotted, has excellent characters, and shows basic human nature as it is, a thirst for power."

—— Philip Jose Farmer, three-time Hugo award winner

From the prestigious *Science Fiction Chronicle* (June 2001)
The Railguns Of Luna

Steven Burgauer writes old style science fiction in which heroes and villains are easily identified, the action is fast and furious, and the plot twists and turns uncontrollably. His newest is the story of a crack team of military specialists who discover that the brilliant but warped Cassandra Mubarak is planning to use advanced scientific devices to seize control of the world. To stop her, they must infiltrate her heavily guarded headquarters and rescue the fair maiden in distress. This is action adventure written straightforwardly and not meant to be heavily literary or provide pithy commentary on the state of humanity.

"A masterfully crafted story based on the universal human conflict between the desire for order and the desire for freedom. Burgauer gives us a heroine whose concern is for the future, and a hero who is keenly aware of his own mortality."

-- Loren Logsdon . . . Editor, <u>Eureka Literary Magazine</u>